DJINNI GOT THE JUICE!

One of the young men in black leather wiped his nose with the back of his hand. "I want power." He looked around quickly, as if daring someone to make fun of him.

"Yeah, " another youth laughed. "Show us, man. We see, we believe. Got that?"

Froister smiled at them. With the merest flick of will, Froister turned into a puff of smoke. As the astonished gang members watched, he turned from a formless cloud into a stream that poured itself into the lamp. After allowing the wonder time to sink in, Froister remanifested and solidified on the other side of the crowd.

"I want to do that, too!" one gangbanger exclaimed. "That's ba-ad!"

"Me, too!"

"Me, man, listen to me! Me first . . . "

Also by Jody Lynn Nye

Higher Mythology
Mythology 101

PUBLISHED BY
WARNER BOOKS

JODY LYNN NYE
THE MAGIC TOUCH

ASPECT®

WARNER BOOKS

A Time Warner Company

WARNER BOOKS EDITION

Aspect® is a registered trademark of Warner Books, Inc.

Cover design by Don Puckey
Cover illustration by Don Maitz

Warner Books, Inc.
1271 Avenue of the Americas
New York, NY 10020

Visit our web site at
http://pathfinder.com/twep

Ⓦ A Time Warner Company

Printed in the United States of America

First Printing: June, 1996

10 9 8 7 6 5 4 3 2 1

To the memory of my grandfather,
H. Leo Nye,
Recording Secretary of
the Chicago Federation of Musicians, local 10-208,
1958–1978

THE MAGIC TOUCH

Chapter 1

*T*he phone rang in an ordinary suburban household.

The woman looked from the sinkful of suds in which her hands were immersed to the phone and called up the stairs, "Honey, can you get that?"

"It's for you," her husband said a moment later, propping the phone on her shoulder.

The woman listened to the phone, all the time edging away to glance at her husband, looking uncomfortable because he was listening in so intently.

"Yes. Yes, all right. Are you sure it's got to be tonight?" she asked. "Yes, I know there have to be three of us or it won't work . . ." Another uneasy glance. "Yes, I've still got it. It's in . . . a safe place. All right. Pick me up at eight. I'll be ready."

She hung up the receiver and turned, a little breathlessly, to face her husband. "I have to go out tonight."

Looking terribly uncomfortable, the man gestured to her to sit down. His wife sank into a chair with wary, wide eyes.

"Sweetheart, I have to ask you this," he began cautiously. "I've been feeling funny about asking, but I have to know. The strange clothes, the basket, the notebooks you keep locked up. . . . I don't mean to pry. I know it sounds strange but . . . are you in some kind of cult?"

"No, honey," she said, taking his hand gently. "I'm a fairy godmother."

* * *

The fair-haired woman in the light blue suit leaned forward into the microphone on the lectern and smiled brightly at the huge crowd in the Assembly Hall. With a long stick tipped with a star she tapped on the wooden top for attention.

"Will everyone please rise, so we can sing the union song?"

Raymond E. Crandall, Jr., stood up with everyone else. He glanced around him out of the corners of his eyes at the people and wished the meeting was over so he could leave. He hated assemblies. Two weeks ago, when he graduated from high school, he thought he was through with sitting in huge rooms full of deranged people. These adults, ranging in age from his own eighteen years to what he thought of as near death, were all strangers, and they had dippy, intense smiles on their faces, as if they were brainwashed or something. The ones who noticed him looking offered him a friendly glance. Hurriedly, Raymond turned his stare away, feeling miserably uncomfortable and wishing he was anywhere else than wasting a Saturday night in an auditorium full of strangers. He was an adult now, in control of his life, right? Wrong. Here he was, following orders. His grandmother said he needed to expand his horizons. That was the last thing Ray was thinking of. He had one precious summer left before starting college. He didn't have a clue as to why Grandma Eustatia thought he ought to come. She didn't tell him a thing about the organization except to suggest strongly that it was in his best interest to join up.

He had a strenuous day job as a gardener's assistant for the city. In the evenings he ought to be out hanging around with his friends, or seeing his girlfriend, or something *fun*, not *significant*. At least there were other black people here.

At the back of the hall, an old organ stung a churchlike chord.

"When we listen to the dreams of children
"It's our task to make them come true."

What? Ray looked around at the people singing, and wondered if he could still get out before anyone jumped him and fed him whatever it was these folks were buzzed on.

"Joyful wonderworking is our forte
"Granting wishes is what we do."

A short, plump man with a round face standing next to him noticed that he wasn't singing. He obligingly extended toward Raymond the creased sheet of paper he was reading from, holding it between them so they could share. Ray tilted his head slightly for thanks. He still didn't sing, since he didn't know the tune, but he followed along.

"Fairy godmothers, use your magic wisely,
"Heart and head should have equal pull
"To keep them on the path to their future . . ."

Hokey as hell, he thought. *What am I doing here*? Well, he knew why he was sitting there in his best shirt, pants, and tie. It would take a stronger mind than his to go and tell his grandmother Eustatia Green he hadn't stayed where she'd told him to, so he'd stay. He wouldn't like it, though.

". . . Every child deserves one miracle!"

Buoyed by a hundred voices, the organ music rose to heaven, echoing off the tatty acoustic tile of the ceiling, then died away on a final chord. The members sat down. The woman at the podium picked up the stick with the cutout star on top, and waved it over the audience. Ray sighed. More hoke. Then, as he watched, a veil of silver light spread out from the arc of her arm over the heads of the crowd and settled down on them, sparkling as it fell. He started.

I'm out of here, he thought. *I am gone! I'm yesterday!* He braced his arms on the chair arms to push out, to get away from this weird place. A hand settled on his shoulder, shoved him down into his seat. It was the chubby guy.

"It's okay," the man said. "I wanted to do the same thing myself the first time, but it's kind of nice, really. You new to the FGU?"

"Hey, eff-gee-*you*, too, man," Ray said, defensively narrowing an eye. He might be interested in bettering himself, but he wasn't going to tolerate disrespect from anybody, especially not a stranger.

The plump man chuckled, and lowered his head a little closer to Ray's collarbone. "No, man, are you new in the FGU? Fairy Godmothers Union?"

"No, he's not a member yet, and if you don't stop talking, you'll distract everyone. Be quiet."

The woman behind them poked them both in the kidneys with a sharp forefinger. Ray turned around to glare at her, and she stared back, undaunted. Her big dark eyes were interested, harassed, and kindly all at the same time. She reminded Ray of his sixth grade teacher, Mrs. Howard. This woman's hair was a swirl of dark and light strands, all mixed together in an old-fashioned bun that covered the back of her head, and she had a broad, blunt nose and wide lips. She winked at him.

"Sit tight, honey," she said. "We'll talk later."

Fairy Godmothers Union? Ray thought. What had his grandmother gotten him into? Okay, so he'd seen some special effects, but that didn't mean that these people considered themselves anything but maybe public benefactors. Still, he spent the next few minutes trying to see where the projector that had made the silver veil was hidden.

The woman in blue raised her voice over the murmuring crowd. "Will you all make certain to sign the attendance sheet before you leave? Thank you. I declare this meeting of the Local Federation 3–26 open. Does anyone have any old business?" Her brows lifted as she looked around inquiringly at the audience. "Secretary Aldeanueva?"

A short, stocky, older man with wire-rimmed glasses and a mustache rose from his chair on the dais.

"I wish to register the minutes of the last meeting into the official records." He held up a few neat sheets of white typing paper.

The chairwoman nodded. "We'll waive the actual reading into the records. Any members opposed? So moved." The wand tapped down onto the lectern. "Anything else? Good. Then, on to new business." The secretary flipped through a notebook full of documents and handed one to the chairwoman.

She raised the sheet of paper to show everyone. "This is the preliminary draft agreement from the Central Union offices for a merger between the Fairy Godmothers Union and the Djinni, Demons, and Efreets Guild to form the Wish Granters Association." Immediately, protests erupted from all over the room. A middle-aged man with gray hair and a big nose sprang to his feet.

"I don't want to mix in with them!" he exclaimed. "I've said this before, and I'll keep saying it until someone hauls me out of here. They don't want the same things we do. It's a question of ethics!"

Ray rolled his eyes. *Politics*, he thought, piously. And over make-believe stuff, too!

"Mr. Garner, the draft agreement has yet to go to committee for discussion."

"I want us to merge with the DDEG," said a small, dark-skinned woman, standing up. She had a small hawk's beak for a nose, and black eyes set in wrinkled sockets. She fixed the angry man with a firm gaze. "My cousin Raj was in the DDEG in Delhi, and he is a good man! This will be a *good* thing for the FGU."

"Mrs. Durja, you are out of order, too," the chairwoman said, rapping. The chairwoman might look like a California Barbie, with her fluffy hair, blue eyes, and pert features, but she was all business.

"One good djin isn't going to help," Garner shouted. "You should hear about some of their practices."

"*Local*, only, perhaps," Mrs. Durja insisted. "Not internationally."

"You don't *know* that," Garner said, waving his arms.

The chairwoman rapped for order, and managed to make her voice heard over the hubbub. "Mr. Garner, Mrs. Durja, do you want to volunteer for the committee? You can argue these points in private. The Fairy Godmothers Union will be grateful for any clarifications that improve the agreement for both sides."

"You bet I do," the man said, pugnaciously. The short woman nodded, her eyes flashing. Raymond predicted that there'd be more shouting than clarifying done in those meetings. A few more hands went up, too.

"Mrs. Sayyid, Mrs. Lonescu, Mr. McConnell, Mr. Lincoln," the chairwoman said, and the bespectacled secretary wrote them all down. "Anybody else? All right, can we have a preliminary report for the next meeting?"

"I move we cancel the merger altogether," Mr. Garner said.

The chairwoman, whom Raymond was beginning to think of as the Blue Fairy, shook her head. "The majority of the FGU, local and national, have voted to go ahead with discussions, sir. We can—and should—cover our specific concerns in the agreement. The committee's suggestions will go to the national office. The only thing that can stop the merger now is if both sides refuse to accept the final agreement."

Mr. Garner led the dissatisfied muttering in his part of the hall. Raymond strained to listen, and heard intriguing fragments of sentences. ". . . Take advantage of young people . . . corrupt our mission . . . can't mix policies . . . mutually exclusive . . . no planning of their own . . . just want our pension plan." Ray's ears pricked up at the last. There was some kind of defined benefits plan going on around here. Well, a young man starting out couldn't begin to think about retirement too soon. Of course, a college education and a good job ought to come first.

"Ladies and gentlemen," the chairwoman said, rapping for attention. "We have to think of the future. It isn't our welfare that is important; it's that of the people we serve. The children."

"Hear, hear!" a thin woman called out. Some of the complaints died away into embarrassed silence.

Mrs. Sayyid stood up. "But won't that focus get lost if we merge with the DDEG? They're not strictly oriented toward young people."

"I agree!" Garner said, popping up and sitting down like a jack-in-the-box.

"Well," the chairwoman said brightly, "then they'll learn something, won't they? Don't think of it as the end of our organization. We will have as much effect on the DDEG as they will on us. Perhaps more. The FGU still has a most enviable and respected apprenticeship program. And with that in mind, I'd like to call upon our newest nominees for membership. As I read your names, will you stand up, please?" The chairwoman picked up a clipboard and read from the top page. "LaShawn Davis? David Silverman? Correct me if I get this wrong: Marisela da Souza? Raymond Crandall?"

Apprenticeship, huh? Ray thought. He stood up with his hands in his pockets and his chin down to his collarbone, to keep from looking at all the people staring his way. Maybe he might learn something here that could help him toward a successful future after all. He hoped it paid something, too. The chairwoman counted eight names in all, and stopped, then held her hands out to them with a big smile.

"On behalf of the International Council of the Fairy Godmothers Union and this federation, we want to welcome you to our organization." All the others started applauding. Ray bit his lip and studied his shoes, wishing it was all over so he could go home.

A sharp finger poked Ray in the kidneys. "Stand up straight, honey," the dark-haired woman said. "Your spine will grow in a curve."

Ray turned around to tell her to buzz off, when the chairwoman rapped on the podium once more.

"Ladies and gentlemen, we'll take a break now, while the apprentices meet with their assigned mentors."

She gestured the new members toward her, and herded them over to one side of the auditorium. Ray, who hated being shepherded, was amazed when he found himself meekly following her lead.

While most of the others went to take advantage of the coffee urns on a table under the window, a few of the senior members got up from all around the room and joined the group of apprentices. Ray noticed one nice black woman in a smoky green suit, and found himself gawking at her. She was a local celebrity. Ray had seen her on television a thousand times, and couldn't believe she was there in a meeting of maybe certifiable freaks. She caught his eye and smiled up at him. She had a sexy, curvy figure; surprising, light green-brown eyes; and a twenty-megawatt smile. Ray felt his heart pound hard enough to burst out of his chest. Whew! Maybe this down society had some ups after all.

The Blue Fairy paired off the new members one by one. Ray stood next to the foxy lady in hopes that he'd be assigned to her, and was disappointed when the Blue Fairy chose instead a very young white girl with long, light brown hair and worn jeans. He was even more disconcerted when the Blue Fairy gestured forward the plump woman with dark eyes who'd poked him in the back, and turned to him with a smile.

"Raymond Crandall, this is Rose Feinstein. She'll be your mentor during your probationary period. She's a wonderful person. You can feel free to ask her anything you want. I'm sure you'll be very happy together."

"How do you do?" he asked, not caring much what the answer was. He glanced around, feeling woebegone. The foxy lady was long out of sight.

"Very well, thank you," the woman said, briskly clasping his hand in a warm grip and pumping it up and down before he could pull it back. "We're going to get along fine, you and I, don't you think?"

"No," Ray said truculently, looking down at her. She must have been a good eight inches shorter than his six feet. "Why should I think that?"

"What's the matter?" Rose asked, wrinkling her brows. "Didn't your grandmother tell you about me?"

His grandmother? Raymond thought, all the starch knocked out of him. He immediately pictured Grandma Eustatia: a short woman, but broad and wide, with a hearty singing voice she occasionally used to raise the roof. In fact, Grandma didn't talk much to anyone. She was always singing, either out loud or to herself, around the house.

"That's right," Rose said, as if he'd said something. "I know your grandmother. Mrs. Green is a fine woman. She told me about you, and I thought you sounded perfect for us. She has all the qualities you'd ever want, and she thinks you have them, too, so here you are. I recommended you myself for membership."

"Want? Want in what?" Ray asked, annoyed by Rose's circumlocutious style of conversation.

Rose gazed at him as if he hadn't spoken. "So young. Maybe everybody looks so young when they first come in, eh? And such a chip on your shoulder, it's a wonder one side of your body isn't higher than the other. You're here because you're going to be a fairy godfather, sonny."

Ray stared at her goggle-eyed. Whatever he was expecting her to say, it wasn't anything like that. "No, I'm not. You must be out of your head. My grandmother sent me here to learn something, not to participate in some weird make-believe."

Rose tilted her head to one side to study him. Raymond was quite handsome. He had warm, deep brown eyes just two shades darker than his skin. His nose had character. His hair was cut in one of the modern styles that was becoming with his long oval face: very short on the sides and back, but a couple inches high on top of his head, and eschewing the idiosyncratic razor cuts that simulated plaid, sculpting, a side-parting, or other symbols. Though his shoulders were broad, his arms and legs seemed awkward and gangly, as if he hadn't finished growing into his body yet. This child was bursting with promise, so much it was squirting out of him in every direction but the right one. She took his arm and squeezed his hand lightly. To his credit, he didn't pull away.

"You want to help people?" Rose asked gently, trying not to frighten him. He looked ready to run away. "You want to do good?"

Raymond started, as if she'd been reading his thoughts. She'd only been reading his face.

"Uh, I guess so."

"Well, that's what we do," Rose said. To her it sounded self-evident.

"What do you mean by good?" Ray asked. "I mean, exactly."

A shrug. "Whatever really needs doing. You heard our motto: Every child is entitled to one miracle. We provide the miracle, one to a child."

Raymond gestured around him at the hall full of people. "But you're a union! That's no help to anyone I've ever heard. Not to children anyhow."

Rose sighed impatiently, and Ray wondered what he'd missed.

"Try to think of us as a guild, rather than a trade organization. We're a teaching society, a mutual assistance collective. We help each other to help others. Anyone can join who has the right attitude, the right *aptitude*. Honest, helpful, smart, *caring*, that's the important one. That's you."

Raymond felt his cheeks burning. "What about it?" he asked, defensively.

"*So*, you're going to make use of all those wonderful qualities. So you don't *waste* them." Rose put a fingertip almost to Ray's nose. He pulled back, but not too far. "Aha, that intrigues you, doesn't it?" The fingertip pointed up to the ceiling, then arrowed down toward the floor. "See here. As of right now, you're my apprentice. As your senior Fairy Godmother I'm supposed to teach you how to do good for children who need you. You're going to have to do what I tell you. Can you handle that, or not?"

She was throwing a challenge up to him. Would he let an old woman be his boss, a white woman, a Jewish woman at that? Raymond narrowed one eye at her, trying to stare her down. She glared back, as she had during the meeting. The old girl had guts, no question. She might well be a friend of Grandma Eustatia. And he liked the idea of helping out kids, whether or not he understood yet just exactly what was going on here.

"I can handle it," he said, in a flat voice.

"Good," she said, beaming, and clapping her hands together. "No time like now to get started, eh?"

"Started?" Raymond asked. He looked at his wristwatch, then at the clock on the wall. "But it's after eight o'clock!"

Rose patted his arm. "That's when our work really begins most of the time, young man." She turned to the Blue Fairy. "We're going, Alexandra. Where can I pick up his manual and wand?"

The chairwoman smiled and nodded toward the side of the room where there was a long table stacked with flyers and a pile of long, narrow boxes.

"Just take them, Rose. George will take care of administrative," the Blue Fairy said, checking off Ray's name on her roster. She smiled at him over her poised pencil. "Ray, welcome. I hope you'll be with us for a long time."

His face said "don't count on it, lady," but his mouth said, "Uh, thank you, ma'am." Rose smiled. The child had beautiful manners, and the curiosity had already gotten the better of him. He was hooked. He just didn't know it yet.

Chapter 2

"Order, blast it, order!" The thin, tall man in the expensive charcoal gray suit hammered on the glass-topped table. The sharp, thin sound rang throughout the showroom, and echoed off the shades and pendant crystals of dozens of lamps. He glared around. "Dammit, shut up!"

After a while, the thirty or so young men and boys crowded in amid the displays of lighting fixtures quieted down enough to stare at him. They looked decidedly out of place in the elegant shop. Of every skin color, height, and appearance of prosperity, they were dressed mainly in black. The only variation in the uniform was flashes of gang colors or patches depicting the logos of professional sports teams. Much of their clothing was deliberately torn, and in the current deplorable fashion, oversize to the point that another teenager could have shared the same pair of trousers with the wearer, without the two of them bumping cheeks. Froister caressed the stem of the brass Stiffel floor lamp that stood beside him, and wondered if it was not too late to truck in a supply of ordinary lightware, perhaps from, he shuddered, K mart, so as not to waste the good merchandise.

"My compliments, by the way," Froister said, turning his head slightly and speaking out of the corner of his mouth to the man at his shoulder. "When you said you'd be stepping up the membership drive, I should have taken you seriously."

"To hear is to obey," Gurgin replied, leaning forward with a grin on his swarthy face. He reached forward with one wrist out and clashed bracelets with Froister, a little too energetically, then crossed his arms over his chest. A formidable figure, he towered over the warehouse owner by almost a foot. He was an ancient type. The three-piece suit he wore only seemed a costume, as if he was used to appearing in more exotic clothing.

"Yes, well," Froister said, shooting his French cuffs down over the metal bands to conceal them. The other five old members, DeNovo, Timbulo, McClaherty, Bannion, and Carson, did the same. Froister clapped his hands.

"Let's get going. Welcome to Enlightenment, everybody. I am Albert Froister. The others and I are members of a . . . benevolent organization, the Djinni, Demons, and Efreets Guild, local chapter 19." A couple of the youths laughed at the name, and Froister stared them down, making certain they understood he was offended. "We offer opportunity to those we think worthy to receive it. You all know why you're here? Or what it is you came looking for?"

One of the young men in black leather shuffled uncomfortably and wiped his nose with the back of his hand. "The big dude said something about power. I want power." He looked around quickly, as if daring someone to make fun of him.

"Yeah," another youth laughed. "All of us want power. You'd have to be a dope to say no when somebody offers you something like that."

Froister smiled at them. "No one gives it to you. You have to earn it, but it's real, I promise you that."

The first young man used the side of his hand to wipe his nose again, then aimed the same forefinger at Froister. "Then show us, man. We see, we believe. Got that?"

"Of course."

With the merest flick of will, Froister turned into a puff of smoke.

The newcomers gasped. A couple of them broke for the door, but were easily restrained by Gurgin and the old members. Froister regarded them through the haze with pleasure, seeing them tremble but with fascination growing in their eyes. As the astonished youths watched, he turned from a formless cloud into a stream that poured itself into the decorative chimney at the top of the Stiffel lamp. Froister had a cloudy view through the translucent white shade as a few of the boldest rushed forward to paw the air where he had stood, and to examine the lamp itself. Gurgin kept all of them from handling the lamp too much. They exclaimed over it, jostling each other to get close, scared but more impressed by the moment. After allowing the wonder time to sink in, Froister remanifested the smoke and solidified on the other side of the crowd.

"Well?" he asked, hands out for applause as they spun to face him. There was a moment when the young men breathed in and out, then shouted all at once.

"I want to do that, too!" the shuffler exclaimed. "That's ba-ad!"

"Me, too!" "Way cool!" "Me, man, listen to me. Me first!"

Froister smiled. He nodded to Gurgin, who stepped forward with a box full of wristbands.

"Very well, then, if you want to join our little group, we would be delighted to welcome you," Froister said. "Here is the insignia of your membership, your union card, so to speak." Boys jostled each other to grab pairs of the steel blue wristlets out of the box. "In a moment, I'll ask you to put them on, and repeat after me the guild oath. 'I, your name, swear eternal fealty to the spirit of the lamp, and will obey the words of my master in exchange for eternal life and eternal power as a duly sworn member of the Djinni, Demons, and Efreets Guild.'"

"Master? I don't like this 'master' stuff," said one dark-skinned youth, edging back to the wall next to a verdigrised bronze sculpture of a cherub and dolphin on a seashell. The cherub looked up at him, blank-eyed. "I ain't *never* gonna call no one master."

"Well, it's part of the oath, young man. Who *will* you take orders from?" Froister asked. He took up a pair of bracelets and held them out temptingly, easing closer to the young man with the grace of a stalking panther. "You can't turn into smoke or do any other wonders without taking the oath of membership." He stopped at arm's length and jingled the steel rings in his hand. The young man stared at them, fascinated.

"I dunno, my parents, my teachers—sometimes," he admitted, with a sheepish turn of his head. "My mama, mostly."

"That's easy," Froister said understandingly. The bands clinked together sensuously. "Swear to obey the orders of the *mother* of your lamp. So long as it is an oath you will keep, the lamp will not care."

"I guess that's okay," the young man said. He snatched the bracelets off Froister's palm and weighed them in his hand. "I can really turn into smoke with these?"

"Every time."

The young man's face split in a brilliant white grin. "Cool."

The change of wording in the oath seemed to be acceptable to a lot of the newcomers. All of them had mothers. Froister and a couple of the old-timers exchanged meaningful glances. Things had changed a lot since the old days. There were improvements, like being able to choose any lamp as one's domicile. Froister vastly preferred a clean electric fixture instead of the traditional brass Persian slipper shape filled with rancid oil. But there were also departures, like having to change the ancient oaths to suit the new sensitivity. With the deepest misgivings in his heart, he continued.

"Choose a lamp that no one else is standing beside." He waited until the crowd sorted itself out. He thought there might be a violent argument over a handsome French table model, but DeNovo steered the second competitor toward an identical lamp in a corner. "Everyone ready? Put the bracelets on your wrists, and touch both of them to the lamp while reciting the pledge."

Froister listened as all of the young voices chanted haltingly in unison. As they spoke the last words, ". . . the Djinni, Demons, and Efreets Guild," there was a brilliant flash of light and a loud bang. Suddenly the huge room was empty of everyone except Froister, Gurgin, the other five members, and hundreds of lamps. The seven men smiled at each other.

"It is done," Gurgin said, folding his arms over his chest.

"Good," Froister said, rubbing his palms. "Now we have

the manpower to begin covert operations, just as we planned. Everybody!" He banged his wristbands together. "Out here, please, gentlemen! Just imagine yourselves standing on the floor again. Come on, now. I want to talk to you!"

One by one, the new recruits steamed out of the tops of Tiffanys, and Stiffels, and Beaux Arts reproductions, and stood beaming at each other. Even members of rival gangs gave each other high fives and complicated salutes.

"That is the *meanest* thing that has ever happened in my life!" one youth exclaimed, his eyes alight. "I'm a genie! I love it!"

"And you can do it every day, any time," Froister assured him smoothly, "during store opening hours, or whenever we have a guild meeting. We did things a little out of order tonight, by starting with new business. We'd like to go back and begin the meeting properly. May we?" He glanced around for approval, not much caring if any of the newcomers was paying attention. Many were smoking in and out of their lamps over and over, like children playing with a wonderful new toy.

"May we have the minutes of the last meeting?" Froister asked. Nick Timbulo stepped forward with a crumpled sheet of paper, probably disgorged from his toolbox. "We shall enter them into the records without reading, unless anyone objects?" Froister looked around at the young men, who paid him little heed. "Gentlemen, I'd like you to meet our recording secretary. Mr. Timbulo is worth your attention." Timbulo tipped them all a cocky bow. Except for the gray in his tightly curled brown hair, he looked younger than the fifty years he claimed. "He was once a lowly carpenter in my employ. But now, through the workings of the guild, he has his very own successful business. He should be an example to you all."

"How?" the shuffler asked.

"Your name?" Froister asked.

"Guthrie," the young man said, looking shamefaced. "My friends call me Speed."

"Well, then, Speed," Froister said, showing that he, too, could adapt, and that they were all mates here. "As members in the DDEG, we help one another. You can grant wishes now."

"We can?" This gave rise to another outburst, which Froister put down with difficulty. It took Gurgin's looming presence to quell the noise.

"Quiet! You can't grant wishes to yourself. You can use them for one another's good."

"I get it," said the young black man next to the cherub. "This is like those stories, where someone rubs on our lamp, and we have to do what they say."

"That's essentially it," Froister said. "That is why we have a guild to protect our interests—so not just everyone rubs your lamp and gets magical service out of you. We help one another."

The rival gang members began again to eye one another suspiciously.

"Then how come there's only seven of you?" asked a short, chunky youth with milk-chocolate skin and light brown curly hair.

"Do you really want to know?" Froister asked, showing his teeth ferally. He watched them shudder, then relented. "Too many of them decided that it wasn't worth it to have the magic under any circumstances. They couldn't abide by the rules. They gave up the bracelets—can you believe it? And without them, the magic is gone." He swept his hands in an arc. A few of them jumped, clutching their wristbands protectively. They were still enjoying their newfound ability, and couldn't imagine giving it up.

"I don't want to grant no wishes for no Backyard Wolves," said a thin-faced white boy wearing his sports team cap around backward.

"I ain't doing no deals for Riverside Jackals," said a Hispanic youth, glaring back at him.

"You are all bound in the Brotherhood of the Lamp now," Froister said, stepping between them. "You have to give aid and assistance to one another in need. Got that? Follow the rules, or you don't get any power. It'll disappear, like smoke!" He snapped his fingers, turning his hand into a cloud just for a second. The youths all gasped. The effect still wowed them, Froister reflected. And it was easy, the least difficult thing of which all of them were now capable.

"The chance to have *real* power, not Hizzoner the Mayor kind of power, but the thunder and lightning kind," said McClaherty, in a ringing voice that made them all pay attention, "has made friends out of the bitterest of enemies before this." The redheaded man gave the youths a moment to think it over. "You're not used to being allies, but I think you'll find it worth the trouble."

"We'll make it work," said the Riverside Jackal confidently.

"I don't want just anyone rubbing on my lamp," the young black man said. "How come we still using lamps nowadays? That's old. Why not something modern?"

"What about bottles?" another one asked. "They're more portable."

"Or rings?" chimed in a third.

"Tradition, my friends," Froister said, holding out his hands to them. "You'd be surprised how safe a lamp is. There's hardly any fear of discovery. If you were inside a VCR, you'd change hands six times a week in your neighborhood, wouldn't you? Yes, of course you would. A bottle? What if someone turns it in to a grocer for the deposit or, horror of horrors, sends it to the recycler to be melted down! Rings? How many people your own age do you know who have been gunned down for a piece of cheap jewelery? And don't you dare let me hear you suggest that you conceal the essence of your *souls* in something edible! Ah, but with *lamps*—lamps are *furniture*. People ignore them, knock them over, change the bulbs, push the switch, plug in, click, turn on, turn off, and even occasionally dust their lamps, but they hardly *ever* rub them. Our membership seems to appear accidentally these days only to Polish or Puerto Rican cleaning ladies, and though it takes a lot of . . . persuasion to run them through their three wishes and get our members out of their thrall," Froister sighed, "that's a minimal annoyance. Lamps are safe."

"Hey, do you hear something?" Guthrie asked. They all quieted down to listen. A rattle of keys against glass became audible, followed by the creak of door hinges and the slow pace of footsteps.

"Sst!" Froister said. "My night watchman! I didn't realize it was so late. Everybody into their lamps!"

In a moment, the room was empty. A man in an army green uniform shuffled through, looking around suspiciously. He shook his head and kept going out of the showroom toward the door that led into the warehouse. The footsteps diminished in volume.

Froister manifested himself immediately. "Let's wrap this up, gentlemen. He'll be back again."

"How come you don't want him to see us?" the Backyard Wolf asked suspiciously. Froister shook his head patiently.

"Do you want him telling anyone that the Backyard Wolves and the Riverside Jackals were having a secret meeting in a warehouse? What do you think would be the reaction if word got downtown to the Scarlet Dragons?" he asked reasonably, watching understanding dawn on their gape-mouthed faces. "They'd think you were forming a secret alliance, probably in preparation for a total turf war. They wouldn't believe the idea that you had been buying a lamp for your girlfriend."

"Hey, women! Yeah, women!" another youth asked. "How come there's no women in this club? Ain't they allowed?"

"Oh, certainly. They come and go," Froister said offhandedly. "It's rare that a woman of sufficient character appears and wants to join. It takes strength to handle power like ours. You're welcome to bring in anyone you think is . . . worthy." He accompanied this assurance with a feral grin. A few of the young men who thought they understood what he meant, grinned back.

"Naw, I don't want to share it with anybody," Speed, the nose-wiper, said. He clashed bracelets with the man next to him the way they'd seen Froister and Gurgin do. "You give everybody power, where's *your* edge? Come on, dudes, let's go out and score some booze."

"Hey, we can score anything!" the Backyard Wolf said. "We can slip under doors when we're made of smoke."

"Yeah," the Riverside Jackal said, the light of avarice dawning in his eyes.

The young black man paused. "We gotta be back in the lamps by sunrise, or something? I mean, do we melt or burn up if sunlight hits us?"

"Why, are you that sensitive to UVA?" Froister asked blandly, and the others laughed. "No. Live your lives as you always do. You'll come when called—I mean, needed."

"Cool, man," he said. He bent to unplug the cord of the lamp beside him. Bannion grabbed his arm.

"Hold it. You can't take that with you."

The young man shook loose and bent an uneasy eye toward Froister. "I thought you said these were our lamps."

"They are. But they stay here," Froister said in a tone that brooked no argument, then he softened his voice. "This is a lamp warehouse. Where could they be safer than among thousands?"

"Yeah, but what if someone tries to rub on us? Or buy them?"

"I will look after your lamps," Froister said smoothly, "as I look after my own. Lamps are my business. There's a top-grade security system here, and no one buys the floor displays without my specific permission. But any of you are welcome to arrange a rotation of standing guard on the lamps if you wish. That would be fine with me." He looked around amiably from face to face. As he had made no mention of compensation for the service, the initial enthusiasm was not sustained.

"We don't have to do that," the Riverside Jackal said, with a look at the Backyard Wolf to make sure there had better be no reason to have to stand guard. The Wolf nodded, arms folded.

"I don't like it, but I get it. The lamps are okay here."

"Fine, fine. Come back next week at this same time," Froister said. "Then, we'll begin to show you how to make use of your new power. In the meantime, enjoy."

The young members went out into the night air, talking in low voices, pushing each other, lighting cigarettes. One or another would occasionally turn into smoke, and resolidify on the other side of his group of fellows, cackling at his newfound ability. Froister locked the door behind them and set the alarm.

"Young hoodlums," he said. "But they'll be useful."

Gurgin smiled. "New blood," he said avidly. "Get them to swear allegiance before they start asking questions. By then, it's too late. We have them to do our bidding now."

"It's about time," DeNovo said. "The IRS is looking into my business again. I need a wish to get them off my back."

"You think small." Gurgin shook his head. "We have bigger plans. We're going to wish ourselves free. That's something I've been wanting for two hundred years."

"We need more kids," Bannion said. "Thirty is good, but it won't be enough."

"Patience!" Froister said. "It'll take some care to make use of their power. We have to go slowly so we don't frighten off the others while they're waiting their turns. I still think we should have gone for young schoolchildren, more easily controllable. Not these gangbangers."

Gurgin smiled again, showing the points of his teeth. "No one will come looking for these if they go missing."

Timbulo grinned. "That's true, Allie," he agreed, poking Froister in the ribs. "If they become inconvenient, you can ship them off to Taiwan in a container ship."

"Not right away," Froister reminded them. "We need them, and more like them."

DeNovo crossed his arms. "The system's worked just fine for hundreds of years. Why change things now?"

Froister banged his hand down on the glass-topped table. "That one boy brought up the same point that's always troubled me: security. I don't like my fate being so casually affected by others. I'm tired of having to safeguard my lamp day in and day out. I want to be free of the lamp, or any object, free to use our vast magical power for ourselves. To do that, we need power from another source, and we're moving in on it."

"How soon?" Timbulo asked.

"Soon enough," Froister said. "You and I just have to be

patient, but vigilant. We have to control our new recruits, and be ready to move as soon as I give the word."

"That was a smooth move of yours," Bannion said, "proposing an official merger with the upper-ups from both sides. It almost sounded legitimate."

"Well," Froister said, showing his teeth. "I want access one way or the other. If fair means don't work, we'll be ready with foul."

"I'm betting on foul," said Timbulo. He looked up. "Did you hear something?" The beam of the flashlight appeared near the open door to the warehouse.

"He's coming back," Froister said hastily. "Meeting adjourned." The six men vanished in their disparate puffs of smoke.

The night watchman hurried into the showroom, and looked around at the twinkling crystal and gold fixtures hanging or standing everywhere. He couldn't see a single living being.

He pulled the shortwave radio out of the loop on his hip, flicked it on, and spoke into it.

"Yeah, Charlie, it's Dave over at Enlightenment. I heard those voices again, men's voices. No, nothing's gone. No signs of a break-in. All the doors were locked. There's nobody here at all . . . I know, I know . . . I swear the place must be haunted. I'm quitting this danged job."

Chapter 3

"*I* mean, we're not really *fairy godmothers*," Ray said as he loped along beside Rose. They were walking down the busy street, and Rose seemed to be looking for something. "You know, not with magic or anything."

"What?" Rose asked, stopping short on a corner in the beam of a streetlamp. He all but ran up her heels, and cursed under his breath. She looked distracted, her gaze flicking over the buildings and bushes and lampposts, but not really seeming to see any of them.

Ray raised his voice over the sound of the traffic. "I mean, this is a benevolent organization or something, what you said. We raise money for needy kids, right?"

"No, we don't," Rose said, as if hearing him for the first time. She turned to meet his gaze, and the sharp, dark eyes looked straight into his. "Remember Cinderella? Remember her fairy godmother, the one who gave her clothes and transportation for the big night of her life? We get a child whatever he or she needs. By magic."

"But Cinderella was a kid's story," Ray protested.

"Not at all! Her fairy godmother was one of us, a member of Hochunit 23, in Bavaria, as a matter of fact. It's still in operation. A lot of the local federations have disbanded for lack of membership, but in many places we're still going strong. Like here."

"We buy clothes for kids?" Ray asked, struggling to hold

on to the part of her discourse that he thought he could understand. "Where do we get the money?"

"We help children more directly than that. Money doesn't solve every problem, Raymond, not the *really* important ones. The most important things in life can't be bought with money. You ought to know that by now."

Raymond thought about the car he'd been wanting ever since he got his first bike. That was *mondo importante*, but Rose's words brought back other memories, like his father's face beaming when Ray brought home a high school report card of straight A's. Never happened again, which made the memory all that more precious. He couldn't buy that moment back for a million dollars, and he could get fifty great cars for that kind of big bucks. Suddenly, he was back on the street on a hot, noisy night, and Rose was watching him.

"Yeah, I guess I know," he admitted, with an uncomfortable shrug. He was trying to keep his vulnerable side hidden from Rose, but it didn't seem to do any good. She read minds.

"You're thinking," Rose said, patting his arm and smiling up at him. "You're definitely Mrs. Green's grandson. *That's* where these children need our help, in the self-esteem department a lot of the time, but in other ways, too. Of course we really use magic. Otherwise we'd just be godparents, right? Not fairy godparents."

"Right." Ray still felt lost, but he was sure now it was Rose who was missing on half her cylinders, not him.

"Right," Rose said emphatically. A thought struck her, and she turned and pointed to the right, up a side street. "Yes! This way, Ray."

He hurried along beside her, the flap-flap of his sneakers hitting the pavement in andante accompaniment to the tick-tick-tick rhythm of her low-heeled shoes. Her legs were about half as long as his, but he had to scurry to keep up with her. "Ma'am, uh, Mrs. Feinstein . . ."

She reached out and grabbed his hand again. That seemed to be something she did. He'd just have to live with it, or quit and go tell his grandma he couldn't stand working with an old white lady. "Call me Rose, honey."

"Rose. Thank you, ma'am. Uh, where are we going?"

"First stop of the night."

"But where is it?" He looked up the street. Like miles and miles of other residential streets in Chicago, including the one he lived on, this one was full of brick or stucco houses, apartment blocks, and six-flats. Old-fashioned light poles topped by new, hot yellow sodium vapor lights shone at the corner and in the middle of every block, illuminating mail boxes, trees, little squares of grass surrounded by swinging chains, and bumper-to-bumper lines of parked cars on both sides of the street. The overhead El tracks cut through the neighborhood about three blocks away. "What's the address?"

"*I* don't know," Rose said, with a sharp look. She raised her hands to stave off another question. "All right. Lesson one. We go where we're needed, where a child needs us. How do we find the child?"

Raymond shrugged. More mysticism. She sounded like she was putting him on, but she was all business.

"I dunno."

"This is how you find out. Take out your wand."

"No!"

Rose looked impatient. "This is lesson one. You're my apprentice. Take out your wand."

Raymond looked around. There were people everywhere, some of them walking up the street between them right now. The wand was a puking, wimp thing, about eight inches long, painted baby blue. The little star on top had rounded points. He wanted to keep it right where it was, deep in his jacket pocket.

"No, ma'am."

Rose sighed. "All right, I'll do it." She reached into her handbag and drew forth a slender rod. Ray goggled, watching the thing getting longer and longer and longer. The bag was no more than seven inches deep, but the wand had to be a good foot and a half. In keeping with her name, it was rose-colored, and the star at the top gleamed and glistened silver, gold, and pink. Ray tried to study it, to find out how it made those moving rainbows even though the nearest light was a stationary streetlamp.

A man pushed by them, briefcase held out ahead of him to clear the way, too busy to say "Excuse me." Ray stepped in front of Rose to hide the wand.

"Hey, put that thing away," he murmured out of the side of his mouth. "People are going to think we're crazy."

"They can't see it, Ray," Rose said with a motherly smile, stepping out from behind him. "All they can see is our hands. Wands are invisible while we're on duty. They probably think I'm asking you for directions. Watch me." She took the end between her fingertips and extended the star in a broad arc. "When I hold the wand out like this, I can feel need strings. Each string is attached to a child who has a longing."

Ray put his hands in his pockets and bent down to see. He peered closer, expecting to see the same veil of light the Blue Fairy spread on them at the union meeting. "I don't see any strings."

"You can't see them unless you have your own wand out." Ray dug his hands deeper into his pockets. "Don't worry," Rose promised him. "Nothing bad will happen. That's just a training wand. It doesn't have enough *pfft*"—she blew through her lips—"to break a soap bubble, but it'll teach you every-thing you need to move on to the real thing."

"Yeah, right." Ray put all the skepticism he felt into two words. Rose smiled at him encouragingly. She must think the craziness was catching. At last, he reached into his pocket.

The baby wand had looked like a painted pencil when he got it in the guildhall, but when he took it out this time he felt a kind of electric shock. "Wow!"

Rose nodded, studying him critically. "You've got the apti-tude. No question about it."

Ray whisked the small stick through the air and felt texture there, as if he was running it over a ridged surface. Impossible. He tried it some more to make sure he wasn't simply imagining the sensation. It was *real*. Magic really existed? He goggled at Rose, but she just nodded encouragingly at him to try it again, so he continued to wave the stick around. After a few moments, he began to get a feel for the shape of the air. Some of the bumps were higher than others. The high ones were more intense-feeling than the low ones. He deliberately stopped with the wand resting on a high, and felt the thrill of tension.

"This is weird! How come I didn't feel this before, when I got it?"

"We suppress a lot in the hall," Rose said. "Otherwise the roof would blow off." Raymond let scorn and disbelief show on his face. She shrugged. "It happened once. Ask your grandmother. She was there."

He'd rather have dropped dead right there on the sidewalk than ask Grandma the kind of question she might answer with *that look*, so Raymond just returned his attention to the feeling he got holding the wand. A nice sensation. He should have been terrified of it, but the wand wouldn't let him. He couldn't fear it if he tried. He liked it. Rose was right, there was nothing bad in the wand. He didn't know how he knew that, but he just did. The feeling reached way down inside him and lit him up like springtime. He smiled and let out a deep breath.

"That's good," he said.

"That's exactly what it is." Rose nodded firmly. "It's good. You have a lot inside you, and it resonates."

"Aw, come on," Ray said, embarrassed. The sensation faded just a little, and he felt bereft at the loss. He clutched the little pencil-wand more tightly. Rose stared off into space, her eyes half-closed.

"There's that verse, by Tennyson I think, about Sir Galahad. Ever hear it? 'My strength is as the strength of ten, because my heart is pure.'"

Ray gawked at her. "Bullshit," he said.

Rose shrugged. "Not everything that's hackneyed is false, Ray. Keep your chin up," she admonished him, reaching up to chuck him in the jaw with her knuckles. "It comes and it goes. You enjoy the high points and wade through the lows. We all do. It's one of the balances of the job."

"About those rewards," Ray wanted to know, as Rose turned

to walk along the street again. "I heard something like a pension plan . . .?"

"Later," Rose said, with that exasperating smile of hers. "Wait until you do the job first, if you don't mind. There are children out there who need us. Follow me."

Half a block later, they stopped in front of a brick apartment building. Ray eyed it, wondering what was special about this one, out of half a dozen just like it to either side. The brick was the same yellow, the lintels and doorframes made of cast concrete just like the sidewalks. There was no neon in any of the windows saying "help me!" His fingers felt for the wand in his pocket.

As soon as he touched it, he felt those need strings again. Sure enough, there was one strong enough to pull him. They walked along the narrow sidewalk that led into the U-shaped building's courtyard, toward the entrance. Ray had all he could do to keep from veering off to the left where the sensation was emanating from. Somebody was hurting, hurting really bad. Ray wanted to make it better.

Rose reached the door and shook the black-painted doorknob.

"These security systems," she said, stepping back a pace to shake her head. "It seems like such a good idea, but it doesn't keep out a really determined burglar. The person who it makes the most trouble for is the person who lives there."

"For us, too," Ray said, looking over her shoulder. "So what do we do, ring all the bells and get somebody to buzz us in?"

Rose gave him an exasperated glance that approximated Grandma Green's *look* enough that he backed away from her.

"We have other means," she said. "Locked doors do not keep us from doing the job. Come on." She turned and trudged back toward the place that had been pulling Ray.

The wall rose steeply three stories out of a thick bank of juniper bushes like green steel wool. Rose looked up, and peered at the wall as if estimating a jump.

"Second floor," she said, pointing with the star of her wand. Ray saw, and felt, the need string going up to the window.

"Might as well be a hundred if we can't get in," Ray said.

"Oh, we can," Rose said. "Come on." Grabbing Ray's upper arm with one hand, and brandishing the wand with the other, she marched forward into the bushes.

"What are you doing?" he cried.

"We're going in," Rose said. Ray tried to yank back, but she had a good grip on him. He closed his eyes and covered his face with his free arm to protect it from the thorny evergreen. A dozen paces later Rose stopped short again, and Ray stumbled.

"Watch where you're going," she said. "You could hurt yourself."

Ray opened his eyes. The evergreens were gone. He couldn't see the stars, and the air was cool and musty instead of steamy. It took his brain a couple of minutes of terrified confusion until he realized he was actually inside the building. But how? He spun to look behind him. There was no door. A few feet away on one side was the outline of a boarded up window. They hadn't come from that direction anyhow. He wasn't *that* disoriented. There was only one conclusion he could reach, and he blurted it out before he could stop himself.

"We walked through a wall! We walked through a solid brick wall!"

"That's right," Rose's voice said. "You have to learn to trust me, you know. It's a terrible thing not to trust."

He couldn't see her clearly. She was a short silhouette in front of him. The only thing really visible, that he could hold on to for a reference point, was the star on the wand. It gleamed with a comforting light. Ray groped in his pocket for his own wand. The goodness made him feel a little better, but what he really wanted to do was sit down. He pushed away from Rose and felt around him for any kind of solid furniture, and finally sank to the dusty, coarse carpet. He wrapped his arms tightly around his knees.

"We went through a wall," he said to the pink star. "How?"

"We have special abilities when we're on the job," Rose said. "Do they help you when you've missed a bus? No. Do they help when you lock yourself out of the apartment? No. But *this* is so nothing can stand between you and a child who really needs you."

The children. Ray thought about them, and gradually the shock began to wear off. Magic was good, because it helped children. Rose acted like it was a normal, okay, everyday thing. Maybe this lady wasn't so crazy after all. He hadn't been seeing things in the Assembly Hall, and there were veils of light that came out of wands, and beams of light that led you to kids. He had a magic wand in his own pocket, and he was going to do stuff with it for children.

"Penny for your thoughts, honey," Rose said.

As his eyes grew accustomed to the gloom, he could see that he was in a big room. A hallway and the darker patches of two doors showed on the wall opposite the one they came in. Her short, plump figure became more visible.

"Rose?" he asked plaintively.

"Yes, honey?"

"What if I don't like being a fairy godfather? You didn't swear me to secrecy or nothing."

"Or *anything*," Rose's voice corrected him immediately. "If you find you don't like it, quit! Go home! You don't have to do this at all if you don't want to. It's entirely voluntary. We can't force service like this. No good would come of it."

"You gonna come after me and curse me if I do?" Ray asked. He was surprised how small his voice sounded in the empty room.

The shape that was Rose crouched beside him and drew him into the cosy pink light of her wand. Her face, in the unearthly glow, was very serious.

"There is and will never be any coercion on you from the FGU or from me, Raymond," she said, putting a gentle hand on his shoulder. "You can tell anyone you want to, about all of it. Who would you like to tell?"

Ray thought about telling his parents, or his little sister and brother, or his friends how he walked through a wall with a crazy lady, and how he was going to go grant wishes for unhappy kids. He thought of telling his girlfriend and watching her face go blank with horror and shock. In his vision the men in the white coats arrived in an ambulance and strapped him up in a straitjacket. He swallowed.

"I guess nobody now," Raymond said, looking up at her. "But I can if I want?"

"Anybody," Rose said, positively. "Come on. Our first customer is waiting." She waved an arm as he scrambled to his feet. "Help an old lady up, honey."

Rose led him out of the room by the light of her wand, opened a door, and let them out into a wider hallway that smelled of laundry starch, dust, garlic, and disinfectant. Along the hall to either side, Ray saw the outlines of two or three doors with a faint strip of light coming from underneath, and a split staircase leading down to the left and up to the right. He heard noises for the first time. Somewhere in the building were the sounds of conversation, a baby crying, a dog barking, and two or three televisions blaring. "Where do we go?"

"Shh," Rose hissed, holding her wand to her lips. "That's a deserted apartment we came out of." The star of the wand moved toward the stairs. "That way."

She stumped up the wide staircase. Ray trailed behind her, his rubber soles catching on the thin, Persian-style carpet on the broad treads. His heart pounded in time with his steps.

Chapter 4

"Pay attention, now," Rose said. "The wand can tell you more than just where you're going. It can give you some insight into your client."

The sound of a television came loudly from the apartment on the second floor where Rose stopped. Ray automatically headed for the door, but Rose pulled him back to a section of the corridor wall. A quick check of the magic-indicator in his jacket pocket assured him Rose was right. The need string led straight through the wall, right here. Purposefully, the little woman took his arm and started walking toward the worn, flowered wallpaper. Ray bravely kept his eyes open, determined that this time he would see how it was done.

He was so interested in watching Rose melt into the wall like rain soaking into earth that he almost missed it when his own arm began to disappear. It felt funny where it touched, as if something thick, heavy, and soft brushed over his fingers, then the back of his hand, his arm, his foot, and knee. He could only see the effect for a few seconds, because then the wall was in his face, brushing over it like a blanket, and then he was through it. All around him was darkness, but this time he trusted Rose and didn't pull back. It was no more difficult than passing into a shadow. Ray wondered excitedly if wall-walking was something he could try on his own with the little pencil wand, or if he had to wait for promotion to full status. Talk about benefits!

They emerged in a small bedroom crowded with furniture.

There were two pairs of bunk beds, two desks, four mis-matched chests of drawers, and one ancient armchair covered with dilapidated-looking flowered chintz that matched the blistering wallpaper on the upper half of the wall. Until his head was clear of the bunk bed frame (which tickled), he didn't notice the young black girl curled up in the old armchair. She looked to be about fourteen or fifteen, sitting clutching a blue stuffed plush toy so old and beaten up it was hard to tell what animal it represented. She started to scramble to her feet, gawking at them.

"Daddy!" the girl screamed. The television in the next room began to chatter loudly about indigestion, drowning her out even through the walls.

"Shh!" Rose said, brandishing her wand, holding the star out so it waved fascinatingly to and fro. "It's all right." The girl looked from the glistening star to the two faces, her large brown eyes torn between fear and wonder. "Please don't be afraid. I'm your fairy godmother. My name is Rose. What's yours?"

"Clarice," the girl said, relaxing a little, but still braced to jump up and run. The blue toy lay forgotten over one arm. "Who's he?" She pointed at Raymond.

"Raymond is my assistant," Rose said. She sat down on one arm of the chair and motioned for the girl to settle back on her cushion. Huge-eyed like a doe, the girl folded her legs to one side and sat on them. "A busy fairy godmother like me needs help sometimes. It sounded a little to me like you needed some help, too, Clarice. What a pretty name that is. What's bothering you?"

"I don't believe in fairy godmothers," Clarice said abruptly, her eyes still fearful. She glanced at Ray again.

Rose shrugged in a casual manner. She had this argument with half her clients these days. She blamed television for the hard skepticism she saw in almost every child.

"You just saw us walk through a wall, didn't you? How could we do that if we weren't actual fairy godparents?"

Clarice looked fourteen or fifteen, but she considered the

question with the solemnity of a much smaller child. "You could be ghosts," she said seriously.

Rose stuck out her arm. "Pinch me. Go on!" A little timidly, the girl did so. She grinned shyly. Rose grinned back. "There, I'm solid. I'm not a ghost. Is that all right now? Good. So, tell me a little about yourself. Who sleeps in all these beds?"

"My sisters," Clarice said. "Well, not just my sisters. My stepsisters, too. I got two of them. And four brothers, two steps and two halves. And there's another one on the way." She sighed and buried her face in the top of her toy's head. "My pop told me tonight."

"You've got a big family," Rose said. "So, what's the problem?"

Clarice sighed without looking up. "I'm just blue all the time. I miss my mama. She died when I was eight, then my pop married Janelle. Nobody cares about me. Everyone just looks out for the next one in line, and now there's another baby coming." She sighed, and her breath caught as if she was ready to cry. "One more to fit in somewhere. I've got to be the responsible one, my pop says. All the time, it's just me." Her voice rose to a tiny squeak. "Can you bring my mama back?"

Rose's heart twisted with sympathy. She put an arm around the girl's shoulders and hugged her tightly. "I'm sorry, honey. That's too big a job for just an old fairy godmother. You've got a nice family here. It looks like your daddy takes good care of you."

"Nobody cares about me," Clarice said, looking up at Rose and Ray with tears in her eyes. "Janelle takes everything for her kids, and leaves nothing for me. She even likes my sister! But not me."

Rose patted Clarice's back. "You're a good girl, and a beautiful one, did you know that? No? Well, you are. You have such a lovely line to your jaw, and your cheekbones are enviable. You should be a model. Your self-image could use a nice boost, that's all. Isn't anyone kind to you?" Clarice shook her head. "How about your favorite teachers? Friends?"

"Got no friends." Clarice looked down quickly, and

squeezed her toy. Rose nodded. She knew at once what the problem was. Clarice was shy, probably couldn't make friends easily. She glanced up at Raymond, who was watching with sympathy all over his sweet face.

"How 'bout a boyfriend?" Ray asked.

"Dyland dropped me for another chick," Clarice said bitterly. "He never notices me anymore."

Rose slapped her hands down on her thighs. "Then what you've got to do is make them notice you!"

"I tried that," Clarice cried, looking more woebegone than ever. "It backfired. I followed Dyland everywhere, trying to get him back. I . . . I offered him everything. Everything!" She stared down at her cuddle toy, ashamed to meet their eyes. "But he turned me down. I was so embarrassed, I never wanted to go to school again."

"You have to make them notice you in a good way," Rose explained. "Not with sex. Sex is too important to throw away on someone who doesn't love you. Right?" She glanced around the room, looking for clues to this shy child's personality. It was a pity the girl's own father didn't take a special interest in her. The demands of a big family had left nothing at all for this little Cinderella. Her eyes lit on a poster of teenagers playing on roller skates and skateboards on a sunny day. Those children were all smiling. "Honey, do you roller skate?"

"Sure do, but I've got no skates!" Clarice said. "My stepbrother stole them. I can't get 'em back. Janelle thinks he got them in a trade from someone in the neighborhood, not from *my* closet."

"Well, we'll see about that," Rose said. She stood up on her tiptoes and pulled Raymond's head down so she could whisper in his ear. "There's a grocery store on the corner. Get me a couple of cabbages."

"What?" Raymond squawked, pulling away. "They'll be closed by now!"

"Check out the garbage bin," Rose whispered urgently.

"You're kidding!"

"No, I'm not kidding," Rose said, exasperated. "Hustle!"

"Man, if anyone sees me . . ." Raymond said. He put his hand in his pocket and shot a wary glance at Clarice. With a big sigh, he drew his training wand. Clarice still stared at him in wonder. Reassured but still resentful, Ray walked away through the wall, muttering to himself. He shot a final, dirty look at Rose over his shoulder, and vanished. Rose smiled at Clarice.

"It'll be just a moment," Rose said, settling herself down on the chair arm with a bump. "You know us fairy godmothers. We need our special paraphernalia!"

Raymond was back in a couple of minutes with a plastic bag swinging gingerly from one thumb and forefinger. As soon as he saw Rose, he thrust it at her. Rose seized it with delight.

"Good!" she cried. She looked inside. The cabbages were only just barely intact. Ray must have dug through a heap of rancid vegetables and at least a couple of broken eggs to find these. He was certainly a willing young man, however he felt about the order. The sleeves of his jacket were stained at the end in six colors of goo. Rose promised herself she'd take care of that later. With a flourish, she presented one of the spoiling cabbages to Clarice. *"Voilà!"* she said. "Just what we need."

"Peeee-ew!" the girl protested, staring. "Need for what? Fumigation? That's gonna stink up the whole apartment!"

Rose rolled the second cabbage out and set both tattered green globes on top of the bag in the middle of the rug. She motioned to Ray and Clarice to stand back.

"Don't crowd," Rose said. "We've got a lot of magicking up to do. This is the first step to making Clarice bloom. Ready?" The two youngsters nodded back, uneasily.

With an eye, she measured Clarice's foot, and guessed a size nine extra narrow. No wonder the brother had found it easy to steal her shoes. Never mind; Clarice's foot suited her height, or at least the height the wand told Rose Clarice was going to be when she finished growing. If this pretty child found the confidence, she *ought* to go and be a fashion model.

Rose tilted her head, estimating all the things she needed to do. She choked up a little on the long wand so she wouldn't hit any of the furniture in this crowded little room. The wand tingled in her grasp, as if anticipating with pleasure the thought of making a child happy. Rose couldn't have agreed more herself. The power welled into her from her toes and fingertips and the top of her head, built for a moment into a tornado of warm joy, and flowed out of the star.

Clarice and Raymond both gasped as the soft pink veil of light spread out, then formed into a cone over the cabbages, concealing them, changing them. Strands of hot silver light arrowed in and out, in and out, while electric blue bursts popped off one after another in a line at the bottom of both blobs of pink, sparkling light.

The spell was complete. Rose lowered her wand. At first the youngsters looked disappointed as the light faded, then Clarice let out a whoop. She fell to her knees beside what had been a pair of rotting cabbages, and were now the sleekest in-line skates in the world. On a white background, fuchsia and purple were inlaid in a tiger-stripe pattern that cupped the back of each boot. The laces were purple, and the wheels were purple, too, with a sparkling pink star at the hub of each. Rose patted the wand in thanks for a job truly well done.

"These are fantastic!" Clarice said, her voice dropping to a reverent whisper. "Are they really for me?"

"Absolutely," Rose said. "And they won't fit your step-brother even if he tries to use a wedge to get his feet into them. They will fit you and only you."

Ray looked from the skates to Rose with awe. She winked at him, and he stiffened up at once. Poor Ray, trying so hard to keep that facade of toughness and control. Underneath it all was a good man. His insecurities made a hard barrier to cross. She guessed part of it was purely for survival purposes, but there were other things in life he needed to be open to. He'd learn. Only it took time.

Clarice yanked open the bottom drawer of one of the dressers and felt around in it. She came up with a pair of thick socks. Yanking off her thin sneakers, she tugged on the socks, and buckled the skates on over them. Rose nodded. Skating certainly was this girl's hobby. She knew better than to wear boots over bare skin. Clarice lurched to her feet, clutching an upper bed frame. Ray jumped forward to steady her. Clarice looked six inches taller, and not all of it could be attributed to the height of the wheels. Rose regarded her critically.

"Clothes," she said, forming an image in her mind's eye. Cute little skating skirts were thirty years out of date. What this girl needed was something showy, but modest, to suit her personality. Yes, carry the color scheme throughout. The pink star rose in her hand almost of its own volition.

Clarice watched, her mouth open, as the pink light appeared in a ring around her be-skated feet and swirled upward, over shin, knee, thigh, hip. The magical tornado surrounded her upper body, then sailed onward through the ceiling. Clarice's whole body quivered. She stared upward, watching the magic go, and Rose surveyed her handiwork. The girl's long legs were now clad in royal purple stirrup pants. On top she wore a thin fuchsia sweater with white and purple tiger stripes swooping down from one shoulder to the opposite hip. Clarice looked down at herself and squeaked with glee.

"This outfit is a one-night rental," Rose warned her. "Tomorrow, you're on your own for duds."

"Yes, ma'am!" Clarice exclaimed. She tottered to the mirror on top of the nearest dresser to look at herself, and her mouth dropped open. Rose had to admit the spell had been first-class.

A little magical hairdressing had combed the girl's hair, puffing here, braiding there, and tucked in a little pink star over one ear. Clarice looked radiantly happy, a transformation from the depressed, withdrawn child she'd been when Rose and Ray walked in on her just a short time ago. Rose nodded to herself. A little self-confidence. That's all it would take to bring out all Clarice's natural beauty. That Dyland would be sorry he walked away from such a treasure.

Clarice turned around, radiant with joy. "Now what do I do?" she asked.

"Now? You go skating." Rose felt in her purse. "Here's

five bucks," she said, extending a bill to the girl. "The local roller rink is only about six blocks from here, isn't it? You go down there and have yourself a wonderful time, all right? Those are magic skates. I promise you you won't fall on your can—not even *once*, and you'll be able to dance, or race, or whatever daredevil thing it is kids do." She raised a warning finger to still the girl's rising enthusiasm. "But be home by midnight, or these things turn right back into those old, moldering cabbages. Got me?" Clarice nodded, speechless. "Now, go get your daddy's permission to go, and you have a wonderful time, honey."

"Yes, ma'am! Thank you, ma'am," Clarice said, clutching the greenback like a lucky piece. Almost in a trance, she wandered out of the room.

"They won't really turn back into cabbages, will they?" Raymond asked, wrinkling his nose.

Rose smiled at him and patted his arm. "No, but I'm not going to tell her that. She'll need those skates. It'll take more than one successful night of people making a fuss over her before she comes out of her shell and sees the good things in her family situation. She needs to be home in bed long before midnight. Her father's a strong-minded churchgoer, and she'll have to be up with the family in time for service."

Raymond's brows went down. *He must think the old lady's trying to sell him a load of clams again*, Rose thought. *Ah, well*. And just when they were starting to make some progress in trust.

"How do you know this family goes to church?" he asked.

"I smell it," she said, tapping the side of her nose with her forefinger. "Duty, piety, and faith are strong in this house. You start to pick these things up after a while."

"What's he going to say about her new outfit? He gonna think she stole it?"

"Hah! It's just clothes. He won't notice." Of that Rose was certain.

Raymond had just one more question. "How do you know this will turn her around?"

"This is her miracle," Rose said. "You'll see."

* * *

Clarice flew past them on the long side of the big oval rink, her cheeks glowing. She glanced back over her shoulder, and let out a playful shriek as two tall teenage boys bore down on her. She tried to pick up speed by swinging her arms. The teenagers bent lower, pumping their powerful arms and thighs to catch up, then overtake her. Each of them grabbed one hand and pulled her out into the center of the floor, spinning her in circles, shouting to her all the while. Ray couldn't hear what they were saying over the loud music, but he could tell the girl was having a wonderful time. She pulled away from them, and skated a coy backward figure, leaning back and forth to propel herself in a serpentine line without moving her feet. The boys pushed off to follow, staying on either side of her. They made their way through the clusters of other skaters to the edge of the rink. One of the youths felt in his pocket for some money, and sent the other clomping up out of the rink toward the refreshment stand. Once his friend was out of the way, he moved to stand in front of Clarice, blocking her view of the rink, commanding her whole attention, talking animatedly and staring warmly into her eyes. Clarice was happy. Ray could feel her joy, like warm sunlight, lighting up the whole rink. He smiled, riding a kind of contact high of bliss.

"So she's no Kristi Yamaguchi. But what do you think?" Rose whispered up to him.

"All right, grandma," he said grudgingly, glancing down at her. "Not bad. But we could've bought her clothes and skates for the same reaction."

"Not at all," Rose said. "Part of it's the psychology. Magic breaks down barriers. If we'd just given her the goods without the spark, she'd have sat over there in the stands without once looking up. This way, she's the life of the party. They're coming to her."

Ray observed the second boy coming back with a tray of cups. The teenager noticed that his friend was monopolizing the pretty girl, and edged in front of him with the refreshments. A friendly scuffle ensued where each teen tried to put himself ahead of his friend to be the sole object of the girl's attention. Ray saw Clarice's eyes dancing. He felt himself grinning, sharing the girl's joy.

"I want to try it," he told Rose. "I want to make a child smile like that. Let me do the next one?"

"Whatever you say, honey," Rose said, patting his arm. "Let's see how you shape up on your own."

Chapter 5

"*I*'ve never heard of a fairy godfather."

The boy, an eight-year-old white kid with freckles and blue eyes, crossed his arms and stuck out his jaw stubbornly.

"Get used to it, kid," Ray said, a little annoyed. "Because that's who I am." This wasn't how he pictured things going. He was going to walk in, find out the kid's dearest wish, wave the wand, and make it all better. He felt plenty frustrated. Maybe it looked easy when Rose did it because she had so much experience. He'd felt pretty good when they picked up on the next need string, and he had even led the way through the wall. They'd popped in on Matthew here just as they had on Clarice. Ray had expected shock, disbelief, even fear, but not defiance.

"Do you believe in fairy god*mothers*?" Rose asked Matthew. She was standing back in the corner out of the way. She said she wanted to let Ray do as much as he could on his own, but he needed a start. He was stumped.

"Maybe," Matthew admitted.

"Do you believe in women's liberation?" Rose pressed. "Where a woman with the same ability can do any job a man can?"

"Yeah, of course." Matthew was scornful. "Anybody with a *brain* . . ." he began, then stopped when he realized he was sassing grown-up strangers who had just walked into his house without using a door. Ray had by now figured out where Rose was going, and hunkered down beside Matthew. He put a hand on the boy's arm.

"So why can't a guy do what women have done for centuries? Centuries—am I right, Mrs. Feinstein?" he asked Rose over his shoulder.

"You certainly are, Mr. Crandall," Rose said, a twinkle in her eyes.

"Oh," Matthew said, opening his eyes wide. He relaxed at once. Ray was going to have to remember that chain of logic for the next time somebody questioned one of his gender performing a traditionally female task. The boy didn't seem to have any trouble with his race, which meant he'd been raised right.

"So what can I do for you?" Ray asked. The boy's hurting was so tangible around him Ray ached, too.

"Nothing," Matthew said.

"I can do nothing really well," Ray said, "but that doesn't take magic. I wouldn't be here if you didn't need me. That's the way it works."

"Mr. Crandall," Matthew began.

"Ray," he corrected the boy quickly. "You don't need to be formal. Between you and me, it just makes me uncomfortable."

Matthew grinned, showing a half-grown bicuspid in the top of his mouth. "You're nice," he said.

I'm scared, Ray thought, but he replied, "I'm here to help. Why are you feeling so sad?"

"My dad went away." Matthew turned his head to look out the window. "He said he'd be back for my birthday. That's tomorrow. I'm gonna be eight."

"What's your dad do?"

"He's a salesman for Henkeltech. An international rep."

"The telephone people?" Rose asked, her eyebrows climbing up her forehead.

"Yeah," Matthew said. Ray looked around at the apartment. In comparison to Clarice's, or even his own family's place, it looked wealthy. The ambience was one of quiet well-to-do. The furniture wasn't flashy, but told you by the glow of the

wood and the warm depth of the color of the upholstery that
it cost money. Those three cabinets against the wall near the
door of the living room might have been antiques or copies
of antiques. The combination telephone/answering machine
on the bowlegged table was a top-of-the-line unit. Even though
it was cool in the room, no unit air conditioners were in the
windows. Dad had retrofitted central air into this big old
house.

"He must be very good at his job," Rose said, voicing Ray's
conclusion.

"I guess," Matthew said, his eyes big and sad. "But he's
never home. This time he promised. This time, he swore he'd
be here. I thought he meant it." The boy plumped himself
down on a raspberry red leather sofa that Ray had adored the
second he saw it. It must have cost six grand, but the little
boy in the middle of it was oblivious to its value or beauty.
Ray thought that it was less that Matthew took such nice
things for granted than he really thought having his father
around meant more. For a second he was glad his own father
had the kind of job that meant he came back every night.
This kid didn't have a home; he had a nice box to park in
until his parents had time for him. "He called to say he couldn't
come back in time. His boss wants him to stay another week!"

"Where'd he go this time?" Ray asked, sitting down beside
Matthew.

"Argentina. He's helping them set up their new digital
phone network."

"Very important work," Rose said, giving Ray an encouraging nod.

"He always sends me nice presents," Matthew said, hunch-
ing his shoulders. "That's okay. But I wish he was here
instead." Through the wand, Raymond felt the hurt pangs
start again. The father had broken his word too many times.
Matthew was about to give up on trusting his dad forever.
That would be wrong. It shouldn't happen. It wouldn't happen
if he could help it. He turned to look straight into Rose's eyes
and she nodded significantly. So this was it. He had to bring

Matthew's father home in time for his birthday, to keep that all-important promise. But how?

"Will you excuse me a second?" Ray asked, getting up. He took Rose by the arm, and led her across the room, out of earshot. Matthew looked at them curiously. Rose smiled and waggled her fingers at him.

"What do I do?" Ray muttered under his breath. "Do I beam the dad back, like on 'Star Trek,' or something?"

"No, of course not," Rose whispered back. "Free will is very important when you're dealing with people instead of things. If it was just another pair of roller skates, Matthew would have them this instant. But a human being must be given the opportunity. You have to form the wish so that it becomes possible for his father to come home. And he has to want to, too."

Ray whistled. "That's a tough one. What if he doesn't?"

"That's where we might fail," Rose said. "We don't want that, of course. Matthew?" she asked, raising her voice. "Where's your mother?"

"She's out with her friends," Matthew said, dejectedly. "I wish she'd've been here with me when Dad called."

"When's she coming home?"

"I dunno." Matthew looked at the clock. "Not until about ten, I guess."

"Good!"

"Why?" Ray asked.

"Because this could take some time," Rose said.

"What are we going to do?"

"No," Rose said, poking him in the chest with her forefinger. "What are *you* going to do." She pulled him over to Matthew. "Ray is going to grant your wish. He is going to make it possible for your father to be here tomorrow."

"He is?" Matthew's face lit up, and he sprang to his feet to give Ray a hug.

"I am?" Ray squawked, then repeated, in a confident tone that he hoped didn't sound forced, "I am."

"Yes," Rose said. "But Matthew, you have to understand there's one condition to this wish: your father has to want to come home. It's the only part we can't do by magic. Are you sure?"

"Oh, yes, he wants to," Matthew said, his eyes puppylike with hope. "Really! Please, Ray. Bring him home!"

"Okay," Ray said. "I'm going to do it." He held out the little training wand. He had no idea what he was supposed to do. How had Rose handled the process with Clarice? He'd been more intent on watching the girl's face than seeing how to make the magic. He looked at Rose helplessly. The senior godmother understood without having to have the problem spelled out to her. She took Matthew by the shoulders and sat him down on the couch with her.

"I'm going to tell you exactly what Raymond is doing while he's doing it," she said conversationally, to Ray's great relief. "This is the best part of being a fairy godmother, which is when we help you make your wish come true."

"Wow!" Matthew said, his eyes wide.

"You want to make certain everything is laid out correctly in your mind," Rose told them. Ray placed himself a few feet away, facing them. "Close your eyes and concentrate. *Think.* See the right thing happening, in as much detail as you possibly can." Ray obeyed, shutting his eyes and making the picture in his mind of Matthew sitting at a table with a big birthday cake and his mother and father on either side of him as he blew out the candles. "Remember, there's no good magic and no bad magic." Ray opened his eyes in surprise and stared at Rose. Matthew had turned his astonished gaze on her, too.

"What?" they asked in unison.

"Oh, well, there's no *smart* magic, either," Rose explained. "It's formless. You have to tell magic exactly what it is you want it to do. Ray will state the wish as if he was making it on a star." She pointed to the tip of the wand. "Here's the star. He thinks, then he speaks. He doesn't have to say it out loud, but Ray, wouldn't it be nice if we heard it, so Matthew knows what you're doing for him?"

"Yeah. Sure," Ray said uncertainly. "Uh, tell him how I keep a bad wish from coming true?"

"Intention is everything," Rose said, and turned to the boy.

"You see, Matthew, he doesn't wave the wand until he's sure he has it right. Got it?" She took a quick peek toward Ray, who nodded nervously. He felt sweat running down the back of his neck. "Good. Now, he'll do it."

Okay, Ray thought. *Dad, boss, make a change of plans, substitute, air ticket, taxi, on-time connections, arrival, birthday!* He pointed the wand straight at Matthew, then whirled it in a big circle as if stirring a huge pot.

"This wish is for Matthew," he said. His voice sounded small and uncertain. He cleared his throat. "I wish that Matthew's dad will be able to come home for Matthew's birthday tomorrow, with no bad things happening to anyone else. Just a change of plans, and he gets all the tickets he needs. Uh, if he wants to come of his own free will," he added at the last moment, "he'll be here on time." Matthew sat with a rigid spine, clutching Rose's hand, as Ray stirred the wand one more time.

He felt a force rushing through his whole body, speeding toward his right hand, gathering into a mass around the wand. Then pale blue light shot with silver flowed out of the tiny star, forming a cylinder on the floor of the apartment. Small images seemed to flash by, floating on the invisible surface, seen, and then unseen. He heard tiny voices, the far-off sounds of telephone connections, the roar of a jet engine, and little, bitty voices singing the last line of "Happy Birthday to You." When Ray was sure he'd shaken his whole string of instructions into the magic, he stilled his hand. The cylinder skittered away from him across the floor like a rampant tornado. Ray ran after it, wondering if he had done something wrong. The magic framework stopped only fifteen feet away, centering itself around a bowlegged telephone table near the living room door. Ray cartwheeled to a halt beside it, watching it spin more images and sounds, cotton candy–like, along its inner surface. The cylinder narrowed swiftly in diameter until it was the width of a drinking straw, then spiraled along down the phone cord, and sank straight into the wall. All the noises and sounds died away as if they had swirled into a magical drain. Ray stared at the place where the cord connected to the wall, almost expecting to see smoke rise from it. He felt exhausted and exhilarated.

"Very good, Ray!" Rose congratulated him. "Very nice."

"What happens now?" Matthew asked timidly. All the cynicism with which he had greeted them was gone. He was a humble, slightly scared little boy in the presence of a fabulous force he could not understand. Ray knew exactly how he felt. He was pretty well in awe of what had just happened, and *he* had done it.

"Now? We wait for a phone call. That seems to be the way that Ray made the spell work. Sit down, Ray," Rose said, patting the couch on her other side. "You look a little dazed. Magic can be a little hard on people, Matthew."

Ray tottered over and sank onto the spot she indicated. He rested his hands between his knees. His wand hand tingled. The sensation was like the goodness, but so much stronger. There must have been other forces in there, too: more direct, active forces that took his intentions and transformed them into energy that ought to be making reality happen. If he had done everything right.

"That was really cool. I bet you do this a lot," Matthew said to him. "You have a lot of . . . fairy godchildren, huh? Lots of kids you've helped."

Ray sat forward, his elbows on his knees, and looked him directly in the eye.

"To tell you the truth, I'm new at this," he said frankly. "This is my first day. And you're my first, uh, godchild."

Matthew's eyes widened. They studied Ray, then turned to follow the path of the magic tornado all the way to the telephone cord, trying to balance out superhero-power-movie-magic with the first try ever. Ray admitted it was hard for him to reconcile, too.

"Wow!" Matthew said at last.

"So that makes you special," Ray said.

"It was special. I'll never forget it," Matthew said solemnly. "That was the coolest thing I've ever seen in my life. Even if it doesn't work."

"It'll work," Rose said confidently.

The three of them waited there on the couch, staring at the telephone across the room. Several times, Rose tried to draw them into conversation. Matthew and Ray might offer one statement apiece. Then silence would fall again. Matthew was hoping with every bone in his body. He had his fists clenched on his knees. Ray could just see that his first and second fingers were crossed.

The telephone rang suddenly into the silence. Matthew sprang up and ran across to answer it. Ray trembled with anticipation. He watched the boy's intense face as he grabbed the receiver out of the cradle.

"Hello?" Matthew said. All of his taut muscles went slack, and his shoulders drooped. "No, I'm sorry. Mom can't come to the phone right now. I'll take a message." He felt around in the drawer of the telephone table and came up with a yellow crayon. He scribbled a message on the corner of a much-used paper blotter. "I got it. Good-bye."

"Hmmph!" Rose said brightly. "Just a false alarm. I told you it would take time."

Ray became more nervous as they waited. Fifteen minutes crept by. Twenty. Matthew's clenched knuckles turned white and stayed that way. Rose broke the silence again.

"Well, we can't just stare at the wall. Do you play Crazy Eights, Matthew?"

Matthew leaped up as if someone had lit a fire under his tail.

"Yes, ma'am!" he shouted. After all, he was just an eight-year-old boy.

"Don't *yell*! Can you find us a deck of cards?" she asked.

Matthew searched through the telephone table, then went through the drawers of a highboy and a wooden sideboard. He turned up a number of interesting oddments that he put in his pocket, but no cards.

"I think I have a deck of cards in my room," he said, with an apologetic glance. "I'll get them."

He started out of the room, when the phone rang again. The boy windmilled in a circle and scrambled back to it.

"Hello?" he shouted into the receiver. Ray tensed down in

his seat on the couch. His fingers were crossed now. But this time the boy's face lit up. "Hi, Dad!" Matthew said. "No, Mom's not home . . ."

Ray and Rose waited. Ray clenched his fist on his knee. Rose took his hand in both of hers and squeezed it hard.

"This is it," she whispered.

". . . You *are*? I mean"—Matthew lifted amazed eyes to the fairy godparents on the couch—"*how*? You said this afternoon . . . oh, they did? That's terrific! . . . Yeah, of *course* I want you to be there. Don't be stupid . . . I'm sorry. Yeah! Oh, wow, Dad!" He hung up the phone and turned a beaming face to Ray. "You did it! He's coming home! His boss wants one of the other sales reps to handle the negotiations. He says Dad has to handle a more important client up here! He's leaving for the airport in fifteen minutes! Wheeee-hooo!" Matthew danced around in a circle.

Ray, relieved and delighted, couldn't sit still a second longer. He joined the joyful war dance. He caught the boy up under the arms and threw him into the air. Matthew laughed, and pounded Ray on the shoulders.

"He said he wanted to come. He felt really bad!" Matthew said, kicking loose from Ray's grip to run over to Rose.

"I'm certain he did," Rose said, giving the boy a hug. "Happy birthday, Matthew. Now we *know* it will be happy."

"Oh, thank you," the boy said. He gave her a light hug, then went back to Ray. He stopped a pace away, looking up with a kind of awe on his face.

"You're really great," he said. "You did perfect. I can't believe this is the first time you ever made a wish come true!"

Ray held out his hands helplessly. He couldn't even tell the boy about the goodness and the way the magic gathered within him, and how now he shared the joy Matthew felt.

"It was," he said simply.

"It all worked out so well," Rose said. "But now, you know, we really have to go."

"Oh," Matthew said, the sunshine in his eyes dimming a little. He gazed woefully at Ray. "You won't forget me, will you?"

"Nope," Ray said, patting him on the shoulder. "You are my first fairy godchild, and you'll always be important." He drew an X on his chest with his wand. "Cross my heart and hope to die."

Matthew grinned at him. "Come back sometime," he said. "I want you to meet my folks. They're really great, even if they are busy. I'm gonna have a birthday party!" he yelled. He was dancing around in a happy circle as Ray and Rose slipped away through the wall.

"That was very good for your first try!" Rose took Ray's hand and beamed up at him as they emerged into the warm, damp air of the night. "I agree with Matthew. It's hard to believe you haven't been granting wishes for years."

"It was hard *and* easy," Ray said, unsuccessfully attempting to find the right words to describe the sensation. His hand was still tingling with residual magic. "But it wasn't as fancy as what you did for Clarice. Just one whisk of the wand, and a phone call."

"It didn't have to be," Rose said. "The Cinderella coach-and-four is not necessary in most cases, nor appropriate. Doing too much magic can take away a person's choices, their free will. You won't always be there with them, so they have to be able to straighten out their lives on their own. You're there to maybe reverse a downward spiral, to turn around a young person who was otherwise on his or her way down. In this case, Matthew was losing trust in his father, who really wanted to do the right thing. You just made fate whisper in his boss's ear. Nothing more."

"I thought flashy was good," Ray said.

"You play too many arcade games, young man. Every miracle is as different as the child it's for. We bestow transformation, transportation, intervention, incredible and unlooked-for healing, and so on, but not all on the same client. It has to be the very best thing, the one that your heart tells you is the necessary one. You saw. What else would have been right for Matthew?"

Ray felt in his pockets for a scrap of paper to write down

the list, and came up with a wrinkled receipt about two inches square. "Transformation, transportation ... what were the others?" he asked. He searched in vain for a pencil or pen.

"It's all in the manual," Rose said. "Read it, and we can go over any questions you have next time. Then, you can ask me anything. In the meantime, come on. The night is still young!"

Chapter 6

Ray was content to let Rose take over again after that. He wanted time to think, let what he had done sink in. Besides, he told her, he wanted to observe a pro a few more times before he tried it on his own again.

They found a fairly secluded niche between two buildings where Rose could do her detecting act without passersby seeing it. Ray wasn't that surprised to find that his attitude had changed from worrying people would think the two of them were crazy, to protecting her from prying eyes. He was finding a lot of respect for this energetic lady.

The narrow corridor of concrete was illuminated only by the star on the top of Rose's wand. She held the wand at chest level and turned around in a slow circle with her eyes closed.

"There aren't too many traces tonight," she said. "Quiet. Good for teaching without running too much. Oops, I spoke too soon. That way," she said, opening her eyes and pointing west. She led Ray out onto the sidewalk and strode energetically toward the next corner.

"Don't your feet ever get tired?" Raymond asked, trailing after her.

"All the time," Rose said over her shoulder. It seemed it didn't make her slow down.

"Well, my feet are on fire," Raymond said, hurrying to catch up alongside. "I want to sit down a minute. These are my good shoes. I don't use them for walking much."

"Don't worry," Rose assured him. "This call is very close by."

Just on the other side of the street at a tall frame house, Rose halted so quickly that Ray overran the destination by a dozen paces. He came back to see what she was looking at.

Above them, on the main level, the curtains of the sitting room window were wide-open. Inside, Ray saw a young boy with curly brown hair sitting on a sofa and just staring straight ahead of him. The boy's light hazel eyes shifted slightly in their direction, proving he noticed them, but he was too preoccupied with his own troubles to react further.

Rose smiled up at the child. The boy's eyebrows rose briefly in an expression of puzzlement as he wondered if he knew her, then drooped back over a sad frown.

"This kid needs *mucho ayuda*," Ray said, feeling through his wand the misery pouring out of the house.

"Well, we'll see," Rose said. She walked up the stairs and right through the closed door. One of her arms reappeared and beckoned to Ray to hurry. He trotted up the steps after her.

By the time they had introduced themselves, the boy Peter was already blurting out the story of the Little League game he had played just that day.

"We were tied, see?" he said, looking from Ray to Rose and back again to Ray. While Rose seemed to him to be more sympathetic, as a man Ray seemed more likely to understand the mechanics of a close game. "I was out in the field, because . . ." He stopped, a little embarrassed.

"Because everybody can't be the pitcher," Rose said. "I have grandchildren. Go on."

"Okay," Peter said, resuming his fielding stance. "The bases were loaded. The other team is full of big kids. We all think they're overage, but nobody listens to us," Peter added with a grimace. "They're winning, and that's all anybody cares about."

"Not me," Ray said emphatically. He'd never been terrific at sports, either, so winning *couldn't* be the reason he played. "Come on. So what happened?"

"Anyhow, this big kid—he must have been your height! Maybe bigger!—marches out, and wham! The ball is coming out my way. I'm running and running. I had it right here!" He hammered his fist into his open hand. "It was *right* there, and then Rudy, Rudolfo, ran into me from right field. I couldn't close my hand on the ball. I missed it. It hopped out of my glove and rolled away. We lost," Peter said, staring at the middle distance between their feet. "And everybody blamed me." He looked up at them. The whole thing lay so vividly in his mind Ray could almost watch the game in those clear green eyes. "I wish I could go back and catch that ball. I had it! It would've been a triple play! We'd have won the game."

Rose took a deep breath and let it out in a gusty sigh. "Time travel's not on our beat, honey. I wish I could help every child who has had a disappointment, who has been shamed in front of his friends and family, but you know it was just an accident. Missing a catch isn't life threatening. It won't scar you forever."

"It does! We would have *won* if I caught that ball," Peter insisted. He appealed to Ray. "We were tied! I could've caught them all out—a triple play. *Please*. We need that game to make it to the city series."

"It's only July," Ray pointed out.

"Yeah, but we stink!" Peter said. "And I stink the worst." Tears filled his eyes. "That's what I'd wish for. Take me back and let me catch the ball."

"You know what's wrong with regrets?" Rose asked, reaching out a forefinger to tip up the boy's chin. "You can't look back and forward at the same time. You have to let it go. All you can do is promise yourself to try harder next time." Peter looked unconvinced. "Come on," Rose said, slapping her thighs and getting to her feet. "I need an ice cream, and so do you."

She marched to the front door, wand held up like a majorette's baton. Ray followed, but the boy hung back. They turned to wait for him. Peter stood in the middle of the sitting room rug with his hands hanging down by his sides, looking shamefaced.

"I'm not supposed to go anywhere with strangers," he said.

"All right," Rose said, with a motherly smile. "That's a good rule. Then we won't go together. There's a carryout on the corner two blocks up. Meet us there." She took another step toward the door.

Peter giggled. "That's dumb. Okay. I'll come with you." He walked over to join them.

"Good," Rose said. With a wink over the boy's head to Ray, she took Peter's hand, and swept him straight through the door.

"Whhooooaaa-eeeee!" the boy howled, first in surprise, then delight as the solid wood swallowed him up. Ray followed, more slowly, but smiling. When he emerged on the stoop, Peter was beaming.

"That was great!" he cried, reaching back to touch the door panel. It was solid. "Wow! Can we do that again?"

"Not until we bring you home," Rose said. "Come on. I want a double-dip cone."

Peter jogged alongside Ray and Rose on the way up the street, babbling and laughing. Ray thought Rose was right. The boy just needed somebody to talk to, not a big magical wonder. Once he'd been able to share his woes with somebody, the ice was broken, and he was a normal, happy little boy once more. Peter ate a gigantic sundae at the ice-cream stand, and raced Ray back to the house, almost winning until Ray opened up his long stride and outpaced him in the last few yards. When they reached the house the lights were on inside on the upper floor.

"My folks are home from the movies," Peter said, looking up at the windows.

"Are you gonna get in trouble?" Ray asked.

Peter looked up at Ray sidelong, with a wicked glint in his eyes. "Naw. I'm allowed to go out by myself. I can tell 'em that I went out with my fairy godparents."

"If you like, you can tell them all about it," Rose said briskly, taking all the joy out of revealing forbidden information. Peter looked crestfallen. Rose bent down to look him straight in the eye. "Peter, are you feeling better now?"

The boy thought seriously for a moment. "Yeah, I guess so," he said.

"Good," Rose said. "You may need your miracle later on. I could see just by looking at you that this was not it." Handing her wand to Ray, she opened her purse and dug through the contents until she found a square of white pasteboard. "Here. This is my card. Keep it. One day you'll call me."

"Okay," Peter said dubiously, taking the small white square. "Uh, thanks. I had a good time with you guys." Rose beamed and patted the boy's cheek.

"Well, what's a fairy godmother for?"

The boy started to go up the stairs, then turned, his eyes appealing and puppylike.

"Hey, can we go through the door one more time?" Rose shrugged, but not at all reluctantly.

"Why not?" She and Ray each took one of Peter's hands. Together, they whisked him up in the air and carried him through the solid panel. Peter's round eyes were almost popping out of his head when they got into the hallway. He let out the big breath he'd been holding, and whispered, "Thanks!"

"Don't mention it," Rose said, with a swift glance up the inner staircase to see if anyone was coming down. She nodded to Ray, and led him into the front room. Once there, she stepped out through the window.

Uncertainly, Ray took his own wand out of his pocket and followed her. The first step was the hardest. Wall-walking he'd done, but window-walking felt different. The intersection of the glass with his body had a sharper feel than wood, and the panes *sang* as his body passed through. Rose waited for him, standing on the air six feet above the ground. Ray hoped the little training wand had the necessary *pfft* to keep him from plummeting six feet into the grassy square full of broken glass and cigarette butts. He stepped out after her, bracing himself. The air, though spongy, held his weight, and the magic slowly lowered them to the pavement. Ray let his shoulders sag with relief. He looked up toward the window when Rose did to wave good-bye. Peter was glued to the glass, his mouth gaping open.

"Was an exit like that necessary?" Raymond asked, turning on Rose as they walked away toward the main street. "You scared me half to death!"

"It's so he'll call me," Rose said confidently. "If I didn't do something like that, what do you think will happen tomorrow morning when he thinks about what happened? He'll think he dreamed it. He'll throw the card in the wastebasket."

"Oh," Ray said.

"What's the matter?" Rose asked, tucking a hand into his crooked elbow. "You look disappointed."

"I thought being a fairy godmother meant doing magic all the time, like we did before," Ray said, waving behind him. "All we did was walk through walls and buy ice cream."

Rose tapped him on the wrist. "You're right, but this was not a flashy case either. It's *bupkis*, nothing, to everyone except that little boy. We got him over the disappointment of losing the ball game. Now, he'll think hard about whether he needs us for real, but he'll be able to pick himself up from the little losses." Rose searched his face in the lamplight glimmer. "We gave him a tool for handling the rest of his life. The world is cold out there. Every so often a child needs to see that other people do care." Rose shook her head. "I blame the parents. They should have taken him out for an ice cream themselves after the game, not gone scooting off to the movies by themselves. I bet they're some of the parents who only care about winning. Did you hear what Peter told us?"

"Yeah," Ray said, remembering.

Together, Ray and Rose made three rapid stops, helping another boy and two more girls. Their wishes were easy ones, not requiring a Ph.D. in psychology, just a little good judgment in not going too far with the magic. The last was the fanciest of the three, where Rose wished an ugly birthmark off a girl's face, leaving her still kind of ordinary-looking, but unmarked. The radiant smile she gave them when they left made Ray feel all warm inside, but he kept thinking back to Matthew and Clarice. He liked the tricky calls best.

"That's about all for tonight, then," Rose said briskly. "It's after ten. Most of the children are going to be in bed or too sleepy to tell us what they really want."

She led Ray out of the last girl's home, through the alley, and onto the main street, where they emerged into the light of a streetlamp. Ray looked around him with surprise. He realized that they had started out right here on this spot only a few hours ago. In that short time, his whole life had changed. He was going to be a fairy godfather, *and* like it. He felt for the wand and the little book, and gave them both an affectionate pat.

Rose turned abruptly, so he had to jump back to keep from bumping into her. "You believe now, don't you?"

Ray hesitated. Rose seemed to know that he'd changed his mind, but at least she didn't throw it back at him.

"I guess," he said, not willing to commit himself out loud just like that. He had some pride. Rose was pleased all the same.

"If you do like what we're doing, and you can think of someone who'd be good at it, tell us. Or tell him. The meetings are open to anyone who's serious. You know what I mean." She nodded knowingly.

"Yeah, I guess so," Raymond said, thinking hard. Nobody sprang to mind, exactly. He'd have liked to tell his sister, but if he did, she would want to be right in the heart of it, wanting to go grant wishes right alongside him and Rose. Ray couldn't help but think that if Grandma Eustatia had wanted that, she'd have sent Chanel along. Maybe the child was too young. Well, what about Hakeem Barton, his best friend? Ray almost opened his mouth to mention him, then reconsidered. Hakeem used to shoplift candy from the corner store in their neighborhood. He really didn't boost stuff anymore, but what about past sins?

"They don't have to be moral *giants*," Rose said, reading his mind again in that maddening fashion of hers. "You know somebody who's reformed who'd make a good fairy godmother, that's okay. It's the ones who sell drugs to children who wouldn't fit in. The ones who steal from their bosses. The ones who beat animals. You know."

Ray knew. "Let me think about it," he said.

"We can't save the world," Rose said. "We don't even try with the hero stuff. That's for the people who like to make headlines. But we can make things a little better for one child at a time. Think it over. We work together well, Ray. I liked having you come out with me. I like the way you truly care about the children. We're going to make a good team, you and I. This is a partnership here, fifty-fifty. I'm teaching you, but you're teaching me, too." When Ray didn't say anything, Rose tucked her hand in his arm. "Come on, honey. It's late. Walk me home."

Raymond had so many questions he didn't even know which one to blurt out first. Just in one evening, a few hours' time, he'd seen so much, had so much to absorb. That they were doing a good and worthy thing for children he had no doubt. That he enjoyed doing it was dawning ever so grudgingly on him. Grandma Eustatia had been right to send him. But was it right for him to keep it up? He had to think how he felt about having magical powers. He glanced up at the sky, unable to see any stars because of the city lights. Did God think it was all right to do magic, even in a good cause?

"Rose?" he asked. "Where does the magic come from?"

She looked up toward the sky, too. "I think at its source it comes from God. When I first joined the Fairy Godmothers I worried that doing magic might take me farther away from God, in spite of the name, but I think it's brought me closer instead. I did a little experimentation. I thought that if magic was an evil thing, you couldn't do it in a church or a synagogue, or saying the holy name. So I said prayers while I was granting wishes." She smiled a little sheepishly. "I did a few good deeds while I was in churches and synagogues. Lightning didn't smite me down, so I have to guess it's all right with Whoever up there. In my personal opinion, what we do is a *mitzvah*, a good deed. How the Union channels the magic to our wands is from a vow made hundreds of years ago to help every child. A miracle is vouchsafed to each and every youngster at some time in his or her life. Where the miracle doesn't happen on its own, we give things a little push. It's all in your manual. You should read it."

"I will," Raymond promised.

"Here we are," Rose said, turning off the walk toward a yellow brick three-flat on the side street. "This is home!" Ray looked at the building, the glass door flanked by plantings of tulips and evergreens and little trees with their roots buried in colored pebbles, three long skinny mailboxes with the names and doorbells set above. It was a nice place, in a pretty nice street, but not special. There was nothing at all to tell that a fairy godmother lived here. And he was surprised to note how close it was to the neighborhood where he lived.

Rose turned to him. "Well, thank you for bringing me home, Raymond. Do you want to come in? I think I have some pop in the fridge."

"Uh, no, thanks," Ray said. "I've got to go."

"Fine, then. I'll see you again on, say, Thursday, all right?"

"Yeah, okay, Thursday," Raymond said. "No, wait a minute." Once he might let her run things, but not twice. He didn't know what he was thinking of. Didn't he just promise himself he'd be in charge of his own life? Did he want to devote hours on several nights a week to unpaid volunteer work, however unique and uncanny? He had college expenses to think of. When would he see his girlfriend? His friends? And yet, he thought of the faces of those kids when he and Rose helped them. And doing magic—it had been cooler than dry ice to walk through a wall and stand on thin air. Nobody in the history of the world had ever had so many incredible things happen to him in one evening. "Friday. I'd rather go out Friday," he heard himself saying.

"All right," Rose said, at once, without any complaint. "Friday is fine with me."

"Yeah," Raymond said, then stopped. Had she given in too easily? Was the matter not sufficiently important to start a dominance battle, or did she mean it when she said he could make some of the decisions? Was she telling the truth about making this a partnership instead of just a plain student/teacher relationship? That'd be too much to expect. "I guess. Uh, Mrs.—Rose, what are you gonna tell my grandma?"

"I'll tell her what a fine young man her grandson is," Rose said, with a smile on her face. She took a key out of the door and stuck it in the lock. "See you Friday, Ray."

" 'Night, Rose," Raymond said, turning away. He wondered again just for a moment if she was humoring him, letting him have his way. He'd have to see on Friday. Yeah, Friday. In the meantime, he had a lot to think about.

Chapter 7

Walking hunched over with his hands in his pockets, he didn't see Hakeem and Zeon as they fell into step beside him. He was so preoccupied he didn't even smell the smoke of their cigarettes until Zeon leaned over and blew a plume of it into his face. *I wasn't paying attention*, he thought, coughing and batting at the air to the others' great amusement. *That can get me killed.*

"Hey, Ray," Hakeem said, giving him a full-cheeked grin.

"Hey, man," Ray said, putting up a hand for a friendly salute. He and Hakeem had been best friends since they were babies. They had gone all the way through school together. Hakeem was exactly one inch taller and five pounds heavier than Ray. His cheeks had always been prominent and round, even though he grew out of the last of his baby fat years ago. Aunts and grandmothers couldn't help but reach up for a pinch. Hakeem stood it like a gentleman, but he cursed about it in private with Raymond. They had big dreams as kids, vowing to go to medical school or law school or invent something fabulous and become rich, important men. Things being what they were in the neighborhood, neither of them had put their whole hearts into making the straight A's necessary for any of the showcase programs. Their teachers were openly disappointed in them. Ray had kept plugging at his school-work, urged by his family to go to college and make the best he could of himself anyhow. Hakeem had given up and was falling back. As much as Ray tried to pull him along, he began to think he was losing him to the street. Hanging out sure was easier than trying and failing, but it went nowhere. Ray thought his smarter best friend would know that in his heart, if not his head.

Zeon was somebody Hakeem had started hanging out with a few months before. Hakeem thought he was all right, but Zeon gave Ray the creeps. He was a member of the Riverside Jackals. Ray was afraid he was going to try and recruit them into the gang whether they wanted to join or not. Ray's parents worried about the gangs, and for good reason. People who turned them down sometimes ended up dead in the alley. Ray had managed to stay out of their clutches in a friendly way so far, but it looked like Hakeem was drifting in. Every time Ray tried to discuss it with Hakeem, Zeon would appear out of nowhere and get in the way. He was dangerous, six or seven inches taller than Ray, and built across the shoulders like a professional football player and with hands like huge, black spiders. He had long eyelashes that would look effeminate on a smaller guy, but instead made him look more sinister. So far he hadn't used any real threats or violence on Ray, but Ray was always wary that that would come next if he kept saying no or prevented the Jackals from getting Hakeem.

"Saw you walking around with the old white lady," Zeon said. "What you doing with her?"

"Nothing," Ray said.

"Running *errands* for her?" Hakeem nudged the other, grinning lasciviously. "She want a little special company? Likes 'em young, does she? I saw Antoinette tonight. Should I tell her you've got somebody else and she should start dating other guys?"

"Chill it, *Darrell*," Ray blurted out. Hakeem made a face. That was his birth name. Hakeem had changed it when they went to junior high to sound more cool, and tried to persuade Raymond to change his. Ray had pointed out he was named for Ray Charles, and who could be cooler than that? Besides, Raymond meant "king of the world." "You don't know what you're talking about. Mrs. Feinstein's a friend of my grandmother's. You dissing *her* now?"

Hakeem, like the other boys on the block, had a healthy respect for Grandma Eustatia Green. He held up his hands in surrender.

"No, no, of course not, Ray. So how come you're spending time with the old lady and not with us? You dissing us? You disrespecting your own 'hood?"

"No," Raymond said, weary of the argument and of the television slang that had come into their way of talking. The gate of his house was about fifty yards ahead. He could make a quick escape if things started to get hairy. There was a light in Grandma's room upstairs, but none in his folks' room. Were they downstairs watching TV, or out? The front door would be locked at this hour. Grandma didn't like strangers in the house after dark. Could he get inside without having to ask the other two in? He tried to push past, and the two of them blocked his way. "Come on, man, I'm tired. I need to sleep."

"Old lady wear you out?" Zeon asked, a fierce and dirty grin on his face.

With difficulty, Raymond held his temper. "That's not it. My grandma made me join this group, see? A charity group." Hakeem and Zeon both groaned in sympathy. "The old lady's in the group, too. I was just walking her home. Streets aren't safe, or haven't you heard?"

The guys just thought that was hilarious. They laughed and slapped each other on the backs. "Yeah, we heard something like that," Zeon said. "Well, don't you try and avoid us. Don't you try, or we might have to take steps, you know?" He snapped his fingers under Ray's nose.

"Yeah, man, I know," Raymond said, feeling the tightness in his stomach. It took all his courage not to flinch or back away.

"You coming out later, Ray?" Hakeem asked, hopefully. He didn't look at Zeon.

"No, I can't," Ray said, trying not to look at the gangbanger either. "I'll see you tomorrow, okay?"

"Yeah, okay," Hakeem said, then hesitated, turning to look fully into his friend's eyes. "Hey, Ray?" Raymond saw that the pupils had dilated hugely. He recognized that his friend was strung out, and felt horribly uncomfortable. "You got any money? I need . . . something."

Ray backed away involuntarily, and saw the hurt look on Hakeem's face. "No, man, I don't have any."

"You could get some from your mama," Zeon said, urgently. He also showed dangerous signs of drug withdrawal.

"No. I can't." He said that with as much finality as he dared, and Zeon stood back, hugging himself under his athletic jacket. Hakeem grabbed his arm.

"Okay," he said, "but you get me some next time, you hear me? I need it."

"That junk messes you up, Hakeem," Raymond said, seeing a ghost look out of his friend's eyes. It terrified him, knowing that someone he'd been babies with could die so young. "It's poison. You know that?"

"Yeah, I know, man. Stop nagging me. Everyone is nagging on me. You sound like my mama."

At last they let him go inside. As quietly as he could he locked the dead bolt, but the faint snick gave him away. He walked upstairs listening to the derisive, too-brittle laughter of the youths in the street.

It was painful to see Hakeem turning into a street punk. Gangs had taken almost every one of their friends. He and Hakeem had been the last holdouts, and now he was alone. It had seemed like forever since the last time the two of them had sat around talking about the relative merits of their favorite sports figures, or just hanging around and having a good time. Now all of a sudden, there was the complication of drugs, maybe weapons, maybe turf wars. All of it was undesirable and dangerous.

Raymond had promised his family to keep out of the gangs. He did his best to avoid entanglements, but the neighborhood was changing. It got harder and harder every day to go around and mind your business. He wished it was still like the community it had been while he was growing up, but there seemed to be knives and guns and drugs everywhere he turned. The family couldn't afford to move. His mother and grandmother prayed he would get a scholarship to an out-of-state college, but his grades, while good, were unspectacular. Financial aid was the only way for him to attend a good four-year college one day. His dream, medical school, was right out of the question. In the meantime, he was scheduled to attend Roosevelt College that fall, right there in the city. Roosevelt was cheap enough for his wallet but close, too close to the gangs. The bangers didn't like a man to get an education. They wanted everybody to be equal but lower than the leaders.

If only the Crandalls could have found a way to pay for a four-year college. If Ray got a top-rated education, he could get a really good job, and the faster he could earn the money to move the family to somewhere better. But there was never enough money for fancy extras. Plenty of people were worse off, he knew. He saw them on the streets, on TV, and in the newspapers. Their church was a link in the Public Action to Deliver Shelter network that hosted the local homeless one night a week, and he'd done his part in helping to make beds and meals for people who had nothing.

"I'm grateful, God, you know I am," Ray said a silent prayer. "I just wish we were a little richer."

His parents both had good jobs, but everything a big family needed cost so much sometimes Raymond felt as if his family was just holding on. They didn't take fancy vacations. Mama kept her three kids down to one name brand, designer item a year, like a pair of Sports Figure sneakers. If only he'd stuck to his studies, or been a super brain, like Hakeem had been before he'd started hanging around with the Jackals. Ray carried a part-time job with the Chicago park district (which was full-time now that it was summer and he had graduated) and took on other odd jobs to buy clothes and records. He kicked in the rest to help out the household kitty. Ray wished he hadn't blown any of his share on clothes and saved every penny. He could have used it as part of his tuition to Howard University. Antoinette was going there. The two of them sighed that they'd be separated in September, but there was nothing he could do about it this year.

He wondered if the FGU could help him find money so he could transfer in his sophomore year. Maybe that benefit plan they talked about could stretch to give him a good start in life. They wanted to do good for kids, and he was pretty certain he hadn't had *his* miracle yet. He would swear to work off the loan in granted wishes in Washington, D.C., if they gave him a referral to the local chapter.

It would be terrible to leave Hakeem behind, but it looked as if Hakeem was already gone. Ray felt a deep, aching sense of loss. Could he use the magic to stop his friend craving drugs and pull him away from Zeon and the Jackals? But, no: Rose talked about impinging on free will by doing too much by magic. He didn't want to interfere with Hakeem, take over any of his personal liberty. It was frustrating to have the ability to do something special without it applying to the people around him who needed extra. To make a wish that Hakeem stop taking drugs might result in him being arrested and put on a rehab program. In any case, he'd hate Raymond forever, exactly the opposite of what Ray wanted.

The sound of soft breathing from the other bedrooms told him that Chanel and Bobby were safely asleep. That was good. He didn't want to have to answer their questions about his evening out yet. He didn't know what he'd tell them. Quietly, he crept into his room and eased the door almost shut. It creaked on its hinge, and Ray winced. A little sigh came from Chanel's tiny room. Ray listened with his ear to the door, wondering if the sharp noise had woken her up. No. He heard the rustling as she turned over and settled down into deeper sleep. Whew!

Raymond took the little wand out of his pocket and put it on his desk. He looked at it while he changed from his good clothes to the T-shirt and gym shorts he wore to sleep in. Such a funny, ordinary-looking thing, no more than a stick painted blue with a cookie-cutter star the size of a quarter on top, but just touching it gave him that fabulous feeling of goodness. He almost forgave the wand for looking like a thirty-nine-cent pencil. In a way he was sorry it would be almost a week before he'd be using it again. In the meantime, where would be a safe place to put it?

Ray looked around his small room. There were few places that he considered safe for anything private. His little sister, Chanel, had a typical eleven-year-old's views about property. If she thought he had something she needed, she rooted through his desk and dresser with a perfectly clear conscience. His parents seemed to think her taking his possessions and leaving his room a disaster was cute. He thought it was a menace. Who knew what kind of havoc she could wreak with a magic wand? His desk was unsafe, since it didn't lock. Same for his dresser. If he put the wand under his pillow, it might roll out during the night or, unthinkably, get put into the wash when his mother stripped the beds. No, he decided the only good place to keep the wand was where he'd had it all evening. He put it back into the jacket pocket and zipped it closed. There, it was secure. The funny thing was he could still sort of feel the goodness even though he was no longer in physical contact.

He slid into bed and folded his arms under his pillow, cradling his head and staring up at the ceiling. In his mind's eye he kept seeing the faces of Rose and those children over and over again. So much had happened in one day. Ray felt absolutely exhausted. He closed his eyes only to have them pop open again with excitement. If only Zeon hadn't been there when Hakeem dropped by. He would've had to swear Hakeem to secrecy, but it would have felt good to share his experience with his best friend. Or should he call Antoinette? No, she'd be in bed, too. He sat up, folded the pillow in half, turned over on his side, and tried again to settle down. In his mind he saw those pink-and-purple skates and heard Clarice's wondering voice say, "Are they really for me?"

There was a soft tap at the door. Ray sat up straight in bed.

"Come in," he called.

"Hello, child," his grandmother said, swinging the door open a few inches. "I could feel clear across the house that you wanted to tell someone something."

Ray replied with alacrity. "I sure do, Grandma."

* * *

"Hey, I thought you said he was flush," Zeon complained to Hakeem as they strolled away from the Crandall house. "He got nothing. Or he *say* he got nothing."

"If he says it he means it," Hakeem said, crossly. "Don't you call him a liar. He's my brother, Zeon."

"Yeah, but he don't act it." Zeon rubbed his nose with the back of his hand. "He ought to be giving you what he's got. We better score something quick. I'm starting to feel bad, you know?"

Hakeem still felt the pleasant light-headedness of the drugs in his system, but Zeon was bigger, so probably his dose had worn off too soon. "We'll find something," he said, but he didn't feel at all certain.

"I know a man who could give us a score, just like that," Zeon snapped his fingers, "but he want cash in hand. You sure you got no money?"

"I'm sure, Zee," Hakeem said, quickly, worrying whether Zeon would decide to disbelieve him. He'd seen the bigger youth casually beat the guts out of somebody he thought was lying to him. "I've got nothing but my bus pass."

The streetlamps burned too brightly in his eyes, and the air was hot and sticky. Hakeem felt all his senses were too intense. Four more brilliant white lights glared into his face, and he covered his eyes with his forearm. Out of the blazing whiteness, a man's deep voice spoke.

"Hey, kids, you need money?" The lights dimmed until Hakeem could tell they were only car headlamps. A silhouetted figure, its outline blurred, stepped up in front of them. "Do you two need some money?" The voice, when Hakeem heard it again, sounded melodious and educated, not quite a white voice, but something more exotic.

Zeon, his eyes bleary, turned toward the man. "Who wants to know?" he asked belligerently.

The figure paused significantly. "Somebody who could per- haps grant your wish. Somebody who could make sure you get what you need. Interested?"

"Maybe," Zeon said, weaving a little. "Yeah. Maybe."

"This way, then." The man tilted his head toward a flashy car. Zeon followed, almost as if in a trance. The door nearest him swung open, and Zeon slid inside.

"C'mon, Hakeem."

Hakeem held back for a moment, then the shadowed man moved a hand. The strong white light grew more intense, and suddenly, Hakeem felt . . . *receptive* to the stranger's offer.

With a final look of regret toward Raymond's house, he trailed along behind Zeon.

Chapter 8

*R*ose looked up and down the street in front of the Assembly Hall, and checked her watch again. Seven o'clock, already, and beginning to get dark. Where was Raymond? She'd been so certain he had decided to join the Union. And after Eustatia Green had called her with such a glad report on the child's first day, Rose was ecstatic, certain the two of them were right, that Ray was a willing and viable apprentice. Had he changed his mind in the past six days? Rose was disappointed. She drummed her fingers on the side of her purse and tried not to be impatient. If he came, he came. If he didn't, well, maybe he forgot. No, Mrs. Green said he never shirked appointments, and he was usually on time. Maybe he got hit by a car. The way people drove around here. Poor child!

"Hey, Rose," Raymond's voice said. Rose spun to greet him gladly, and felt her mouth drop open with surprise. "What's the matter?" he asked.

"Will you look at you?" Rose asked, before she could help herself. Ray looked down at himself and tilted his head up to meet her eyes with confusion. "What *are* you wearing?"

Well, it wasn't as if she couldn't see for herself what he was wearing, but why? The big pants and the enormous maroon T-shirt hanging out over it made him look like a fat man who had gone on a sudden, catastrophic diet. The bronze brocade vest he had on over the shirt was greasy, and his tennis shoes were only laced to the second grommet. He could fall out of them any step. At least he had spared her the backward-facing baseball cap.

"Something wrong with my clothes, grandma?" Ray asked, defensively.

"I should say so!" Rose said, thinking of things to say, then swallowing them. With the tact born of many years of dealing with children and grandchildren, she calmed down and began again. "I know the two of us come from very different generations, Raymond, and maybe I'm just not used to the fashions, but . . . but you were dressed so nicely the other night."

"Oh, yeah," Ray said, rolling his eyes up. "Those were my Sunday clothes. I wear that stuff to church and days when my mom says to dress up. But since we're going around the neighborhood, I thought it'd be okay if I went comfortable." His brows lowered. "You want me to go home and change." It wasn't a question; it was a challenge.

"How about a compromise?" Rose asked quickly, not willing to alienate him. "Let me explain why it's important in your position as a fairy godfather to look, well, professional, and you'll make the decision for yourself, all right?" He made no reply but a surly nod, so Rose pressed on. "All right. You're trying to engender respect and confidence in children. You're supposed to set an example. You can't do it if they can't distinguish you from the kids they see every day on the street."

"Isn't the fact I'm walking in through walls good for anything?" Ray asked, with raised eyebrows. "I'd believe in a man who came in through *my* wall."

"But sometimes we do use the door," Rose persevered. "And sometimes we're already in the room when a client enters. How will they know you're the one they can trust?"

"Even perverts can wear nice clothes," Ray retorted, but Rose thought she was breaking through to his natural good humor.

"Yes, because they're trying to gain the trust of someone who doesn't know them," Rose said reasonably. "It's the right behavior for the wrong reason. You need to do the right thing for the *right* reason."

"Aw . . . well, what about some special mark I could wear instead? You all need to lighten up. Everybody in that room the other night was dressed so *drab*." Ray considered for a moment. "Except maybe the Blue Fairy."

"The Blue Fairy?" Rose asked, amused.

Ray pulled an embarrassed face. "Uh, the chairwoman. Uh, what's her right name?"

"Alexandra Sennett."

"Yeah. Sorry. Well, I don't want to look like an office dweeb," Raymond said stubbornly. "I'm me, so I want to look like me."

"Raymond, you will never look like anybody but you," Rose said patiently, "but you know, you would have to dress up to go to work, to show that you have some appreciation of the importance of what you're doing, so why not treat this like a job?"

"Because I'm not being paid for this, which I would if it were a job," Ray said sullenly, stuffing his hands into the pockets of his capacious trousers.

"You do get paid, sort of," Rose said tentatively. "It's not money, but it's worth something."

"More intangibles? Like those good memories?" Ray asked, recalling their first conversation. He turned away from her into the shadow under the Assembly Hall marquee so she couldn't see his face, but she could guess his thoughts. There were a few special memories he was cherishing in that head of his, still too private to share.

"Very much like that," Rose said, with a smile. She grabbed his arm and pulled him out onto the sidewalk and started walking north, toward a minor need string she had sensed. They could talk while they walked. In the meantime, there were children waiting for help. "For one thing, you get to live happily ever after." In answer to a derisive snort from Raymond, she added, "Don't knock it. Listen," she said, stopping to face him. "There's something else. You do get another kind of reward for fairy-godparenting. We call them brownie points. You get them when you grant wishes, a point per child you've helped, plus fractions for other things, obedience, willingness, good judgment, good deeds." Rose tried to describe the effect with her hands, and threw them away from her impatiently. "Anyway, it adds up."

Raymond looked interested at last. "So I have some brownie points right now?"

"At least one," Rose assured him. If appealing to civic responsibility and self-respect didn't work, always go for the self-interest, she thought. "You did grant Matthew's wish. You did a fine job, too."

"Yeah?" Raymond asked, thinking hard. "So what do I have in brownie points?"

Rose shrugged eloquently. "*I* don't know. Not too many. You're the only one who'll know that for sure. You can figure it out by concentrating on the place where you'll keep them, a kind of mental bank account. They accumulate slowly. Don't try to build the Sistine Chapel in one day, Raymond."

"Concentrate?" Ray asked suspiciously. "They're not real?"

"Oh, they're *real*," Rose said. "As real as anything we did for those children the other day. Brownie points are *magic*. It's part of the process of fairy-godparenting. Magic has a certain rebound, like karma. Good people who do good things get good magic in return. You can use a brownie point any way you want. Of course, good people tend to use them in good ways. Which gets you fractional interest in brownie points on top of your original balance, just like that credit card, what's it called?" Rose waved her hands, trying to think of the name. She could see the logo in her mind's eye, but her mind's eye wasn't wearing its glasses. She squinted.

"How do I get them?" Ray asked, having patiently waited out the stream of consciousness narration. "Does somebody count up my visits and give them to me?"

"No. You just get them. They're available to you right away, like . . . like an electronic transfer," Rose said, finally finding a simile she liked. "Ah. This computer age, it's like ma—"

"Can you use brownies to hit the lottery?" Ray interrupted, spreading out his hands to collect his imaginary winnings. "Whoa! A million dollars! I would love to take my folks to Europe and Africa, maybe on one of those big cruise ships

to the Caribbean. Yeah! What I could do with a million bucks."
He stretched out his arms and grinned up at the streetlamps.

"That wouldn't be ethical," Rose said firmly, rapping him
on the wrist with her wand. He clutched his hand, and gave
her a hurt look. "That defrauds someone else out of real
money. If you entered a contest and used magic to sway the
judge, wouldn't that be as bad as somebody who bribed him?
Worse, because he wouldn't know you did it, or how."

Ray seemed to wilt, disappointed. "There are a lot of rules
in this game," he said, shaking his head.

"There certainly are," Rose said, but more gently. He was
so young, he didn't understand it in his head yet, but she
could see that he did in his heart. "And for good reasons.
Power corrupts, you know. It does. The rules protect you.
They protect your soul."

Ray kicked a fragment of concrete into the gutter. "If you
can't win money or influence people, what *can* you do with
brownie points?" he asked.

"*I* use them mostly for my grandchildren," Rose said, happy
to move onto one of her favorite topics. "Last Chanukah I
found one of those TV dolls, whatever they're called, when
everybody else had absolutely *stripped* the toy store. I found
a red one in a corner that somebody had returned, and the
box was only a little torn on one edge. I don't know if I really
needed to use a whole point for that, but my little Sharon,
you should have seen her face light up!" She sketched a
sunrise with her hands, and Ray grinned, diverted in spite of
himself.

"So you use them like little wishes," Ray said, mining the
small kernel of meaning out of her speech.

"Exactly," Rose replied, relieved that he seemed to understand at last. It would be nice to do something for Ray. He
had worked so hard the other day, without knowing any of
these things. A little reward was in order.

"Here, hold out your hand." She thought hard. It felt like
there were about eight and a half brownie points left hanging
around her. Mentally, she captured one like a firefly in a glass
jar, and let it blink at her while she thought about something

nice for Raymond. What was it kids always had hanging out of their ears these days? CDs? She was pretty sure he didn't have one. All right, then, she thought, directing the brownie point. To the best of your ability, give him a personal device that plays CDs with perfect fidelity so only he can hear them. She cupped her free hand, put it over his, and tapped both of them with the wand. She took her hand away. *"Voilà!"*

Ray looked down at the silver object on his palm. It had a round base about four inches across and a tapering spindle in the center, and weighed about the same as a pocket calculator. "What is it? It looks like a giant thumbtack."

"It's a personal CD player," Rose said, a little uncertainly. "For you." True, it didn't look like the ones in the magazine ads. But the magic never lied to her. It would do what she had wished it to do.

"Thanks," Ray said, just as uncertainly. He turned it over a few times. Rose shook her head impatiently and closed her eyes again. The request had actually used up two brownie points, but she felt the value of the demonstration was worth it. She captured a few of the fractional, minor sparks dancing around in her "bank account," and wished for a disk from home to test the device.

She opened her hand and directed a red-pink flash into her palm. A flat square lay there.

"Tony Bennett?" Ray said incredulously, picking up the box. "Cool. Thank you. You're not as antiquated as I thought."

Rose smiled. "I listen to the radio," she said. As she watched, Ray flipped open the Tony Bennett CD and popped the glistening ring onto the spindle. A second later, he flattened his hand over one ear, then the other. He turned a wondering stare on Rose.

"That's incredible!" he said, holding up the thumbtack CD player for closer scrutiny. "I'm hearing music. Nothing's moving, but I can hear the music absolutely perfectly. It doesn't even have moving parts! How's it work?"

"Magic," Rose said, with self-evident calm, but inwardly she was rejoicing. She had forgotten to mention headphones, but the magic took care of that, anyway. She had specified what function she wanted it to achieve, and it worked. He liked it, and no one around him could hear a peep. "It does good things for you, a reward for being a good fairy god-parent."

Ray laughed. "Yeah, but I've seen how it costs you. You're still out about ten bucks from last Saturday night, between the ice cream and the five bucks you gave Clarice to go skating."

Rose started to shoot back a friendly riposte, but something else caught her eye amid the bits of discarded newspapers and cigarette packs. She scooted to the edge of the sidewalk, and picked up a twenty-dollar bill. She showed to to Ray, then folded it up for her wallet.

"Sometimes yes, sometimes no," she said, watching his eyes widen. "One of the other side effects is you get a little bit more good luck than you normally would. But for sure there's the brownie points."

"Okay," Ray said, taking the CD off the spindle and putting both of them in the pocket of his huge trousers. "I believe. I believe! Let me take the first call. Otherwise, I won't learn anything, or earn any brownie points." He patted his pocket where the CD player and disc reposed. "And I've *got* to learn how you do that."

"All right," Rose said, grabbing his arm and shaking her forefinger in his face. "But only if you promise me next time you'll dress up."

"Okay," said Ray. He grinned at her charmingly and took his training wand out of his pocket. "You're the man."

Ray let the need string reel him in like a fish. They hadn't gone more than a couple of blocks when he felt the tug come down a cross street and take hold of him. He turned, almost unwillingly, toward the south, following the longing. Some child was hurting on the other end of this line, frightened to his marrow. Ray began to regret his insistence that he be in charge of this call. There was deep desperation in the vibration of the need string. He found himself hurrying along the street, far outdistancing Rose for a change. Traffic and pedestrians cleared the way around him, letting him dash through crowded intersections. Neon lights flickering in the windows disappeared as he rounded the corner into a dark residential street. Ray could see less of what was around him, so he could feel even more keenly the agony coming down the need string. The child at the other end had to be suffering torture or excruciating pain, or be dangling from the edge of a building by his fingernails.

"I'm coming, kid," he panted. "Hang on."

The reality, when he saw it, was a total disappointment. In a glass-walled room hot even in comparison to a Chicago summer night, in the midst of a hundred tropical plants hanging from hooks and stands, a small boy with big dark eyes and shiny black hair stood staring at a huge mess on the floor.

"I killed it," the little boy said woefully. "My mama is gonna murder me."

"It's just a plant," Ray said, looking down at the mess of broken china, shoots, and dirt. A huge pink blossom poked pathetic petals out from the black soil near the bottom of the heap. Something like a small, tan potato stuck out flag-shaped green shoots. The whole thing was liberally sprinkled with sandy white and red particles.

"It's my mama's prize Laeliocattleya orchid." The boy recited the difficult name with the expertise of a child born into a specialist's home. His lower lip quivered, showing he was not so grown-up as he was trying to sound. "She told me not to play in the hot room, but I didn't listen." He looked up at Ray with tear-filled eyes. "Tomorrow she was supposed to take it downtown for the flower show. The vase was my grandmama's from Mexico."

"It's an antique," Rose said, still out of breath from having to run and catch up with Ray. She knelt to pick up some of the pieces and turned them over in her fingers. "Very beautiful, too. Jorgito, you ought to have known better."

"I know," the child said, hanging his head. The tears overflowed and dripped off his long, dark lashes and down his face. Ray hunkered down beside him. A broken pot and a plant should be no problem at all.

"Hey, stop crying. We can help you," he said, putting a hand on the boy's shoulder. Jorge sniffed loudly and looked from Ray to Rose.

"You sure?" he asked. He pulled the hem of his T-shirt up and wiped his nose with it.

"Sure, I'm sure," Ray said, waving a hand to get the boy's attention away from Rose. "No problem. See? This is a magic wand." He showed the boy his training wand. Jorgito looked impressed. Rose pursed her lips in amusement. "Okay, stand back now. We're gonna do some magic."

Rose took the boy's hand and helped him back out of the way, leaving Ray a clear field. Jorge hung on to Rose, but his eyes were fixed on the young black man, following his every move.

Ray felt nervous. It was still only his second time in the driver's seat. This wasn't going to be like for Matthew, where anyone could tell it meant real happiness or despair. On the outside this didn't look like an important case to anybody but Jorge. Every child, every wish was different, Rose said. He could see the truth of that in just the few calls he'd accompanied her on so far. Not a flashy wish, so it should be easy, right?

The vase at his feet was a disaster. It lay in a million pieces. Reconstructing that had to be an integral part of the wish. It was up to him to lay out the phrase correctly, the way Rose told him to. He had to concentrate on wording things just right. First, bring the plant together with the dirt around its roots. Then, mold the pot in one piece around the dirt. What were all those white granules that looked like kitty litter? And where did the red pieces go in the pot? Well, anyway, Ray told himself, the magic will know what to do. He repeated his instructions to himself.

"Okay," he said, holding his hands out, palms down, with the wand extended. He arranged himself several times, like a batter taking his stance at the plate. Closing his eyes, he counted to himself, thinking of getting everything back in the right order from top to bottom. The plant, the dirt, the pot. *One, two, three!*

"*Ay de mi!*" Jorge cried. Ray opened his eyes. Surrounded by a haze of blue light, the bits of pottery were gathering themselves together, but the plant was hanging half out of the top with roots sticking up next to the blossoms, which were twisting weirdly as if in pain. The dirt was still everywhere, except where it was shooting out of the pot from a dozen directions. He dodged a chunk of red pottery that squirted out from the clay and white particles. It clattered to the floor behind him. Ray threw up his hands to protect his face.

"What did you wish?" Rose demanded, gawking at him and the fountaining debris.

"I wished it all back in the right order," Ray said, ducking more dirt. "What happened?"

"Plants don't have an order," Rose said. "A potted plant is an artificial arrangement. We impose that on nature." She swept her wand out and around. The cascade of dirt stopped, and the pot disintegrated back into a million pieces on the floor. She made a gathering gesture with both hands. The particles of soil and crockery started to creep toward the middle as if ashamed of themselves. "Let's try again, all right? It's okay, Ray." She turned to the boy, who was standing beside her, grinding his hands together nervously. "We need some help, Jorgito. Does your mother have any pictures of her orchids? We don't know very much about tropical flowers."

Jorge ran out of the room, and Ray heard his feet pattering on the stairs. Ray stared at Rose resentfully.

"I thought it would all go back together right," Ray said, thrusting his chin up. He was embarrassed to have made a mistake in front of the boy. His pride was in as many pieces as the pot.

"Magic is formless," Rose said, matter-of-factly. "I told you that before. You have to make it right in your own mind before you even start the process."

"I don't know nothing about fancy flowers," Ray shouted,

then lowered his voice quickly. "I only work for the Park District. I didn't say I was a horticulturist with a Ph.D.!"

"Neither am I. That's why we're getting a visual aid," Rose said. Jorge came running back with a heavy coffee table book hugged to his thin chest.

"This is Mama's best book," he panted.

Rose sat down on a chair with the book in her lap. Ray hung over her shoulder, looking at the illustrations as she turned the shiny pages. "My, my, aren't these complicated setups?" she said, thumbing past pictures of home greenhouses with internal spraying systems. She stopped on the series of illustrations of a woman's hands repotting a tiny white orchid. "Aha! Do you see this? I think that's how we have to arrange it. Surround the roots in the white granules—that's osmundine, it says here—because they keep the *pseudobulb* hydrated, then the dirt, with the broken crock on the bottom, and the pot all around. Simple!" she said, snapping the book shut with a smile.

"Yeah, right," Ray said, unwilling to share her optimism. But he took his place again next to the heap of petals and shards.

"Hurry, please," Jorge said. "My mama said she would be back by eight."

Ray glanced at the clock on the wall. It was a quarter to. "Okay." Keeping the picture of a correctly potted orchid in his mind, he waved the wand. The blue haze of light, so unlike the clear veil Rose and the senior fairy godparents got, spread out uncertainly around the broken orchid. Gently, it gathered up the flower, whose petals were drooping alarmingly in every direction. Ray glanced at Jorge, who looked more unhappy than ever. The plant had been in better shape before Ray's first try. He was sorry, but what could he do about it now?

The white grains came together around the odd-looking rootstock. Ray let out a tiny part of the breath he was holding as the green stems rose, the hot pink blossoms flying pennantlike at the tips. The rich, black soil, smelling fresh and cool, came next, followed by the sections of red crockery. They grouped at the bottom while the colorful chunks of pottery formed around the whole mass. Ray felt the rightness of layer after layer, congealing into the way each was before. It was like the picture, but like itself, too. The plant was happy to be back in its pot, alive and unbroken. Jorge's face, beyond the circle of power, was bright with wonder and joy. And then something began to go wrong.

Like a car running out of gas, Ray felt the small hum of power flag, and suddenly the air around his fingers went cold. The magical blueness began to fade, and the fragile construct of the vase shivered and fell apart in slow motion. His wand was failing. Ray reached deep inside himself, pushed at nothingness. He felt exhaustion, desperation, failure. He reached out to catch the pieces of broken china in his hands before they plummeted to the floor.

Suddenly, the faint blue light turned lilac, then warmed to red. Rose's wand was out, her magic supporting the vase. Spicules of root tucked themselves back into the soil, and the tuber nestled down among the grains of osmundine. Ray withdrew. He watched, half-relieved, half-resentful, as Rose finished the job. The little wand felt hot, as if it had blown itself out. Ray tossed it from hand to hand.

"What happened?" he asked Rose, angrily.

"Later," she said. As the magic light faded, she took the vase out of the air and handed it to Jorge, who took it gingerly, as if it might fall again, as it had twice already. "All done, honey. Now, remember," she admonished him with her star under his nose, "no more playing around the orchids."

"I promise," Jorge said. He put the pot gently on a chair and threw his arms around Rose's middle. "Thank you. I knew you were a real fairy godmother." He turned his head toward Ray. "And thank you, too, Ray. You are kind."

Ray, realizing with some resentment that the child had automatically transferred authority in the case to Rose, started to reply.

"Hush!" Rose said, raising a finger. "Listen!" They all heard the unmistakable sound of a key turning in a lock.

"That's Mama!" Jorge said, running out of the room. "Bye, bye!" he called over his shoulder.

"We'd better go," Rose said.

"But he . . ." Ray sputtered, pointing after Jorge.

"We've got to go," Rose said, pulling him hastily through the wall. "Come on, we'll talk outside."

Chapter 9

As soon as they were clear of the wall of the house, Ray exploded at Rose.

"Don't you just shut me up like that!" he said, pointing back inside. "I have to know what just happened!"

"I don't know myself," Rose said. She looked up at the windows of the house, and hustled him out onto the sidewalk where they couldn't be heard. "And we didn't need to have the discussion right there. That child was scared, Ray. He was depending on us to be the calm, adult authority figures."

"He was counting on *you*, you mean," Ray spat. "Because when the clutch came, this stupid *toy* you gave me broke down! I couldn't be the authority because everything fell apart on me."

He all but flung the wand down in front of Rose. At the last second he found he couldn't bear to mistreat it, so he just waved his hand angrily in front of her face. "Well, I can't *do* anything with this. I want a stronger wand. Give me one like yours."

"It's not time for you to have one like this," Rose said. "Yours is fine. I don't understand what happened just then. The spell should have held together. Here, give me that." She plucked the pencil-wand neatly from his fingers and held it for a moment with her eyes shut. Ray glared at her even though she couldn't see him. "What was the gain doing that far down?" she asked out loud. She tweaked something invisible.

"You and those others are trying to hold me back," Ray

said, all the resentment he felt spilling over. "Giving me doodads that don't work. You and my grandma just keeping me off the streets, or am I supposed to *do* something significant? Make the homeboy a laughingstock? Is that it?"

"No, of course it's not," Rose clucked. "The adjustment was a mistake. Forgive me. I should have checked it myself. I had no idea that it would poop out on a delicate wish like that. It's supposed to be strong enough to focus your desire and hold all the parts of the wish together. I can't understand. There may be some magical interference in this area." Shaking her head, she handed the wand back.

Ray took it. The goodness calmed him down a lot, as did her apologies, but he continued to voice his grievances.

"But Jorge didn't even look at me. He only looked at you."

"It didn't have anything to do with specific performance," Rose said, emphatically. "It was appearance. I have the appearance of authority, because I am wearing a dress."

"Oh, so you want me to wear a dress?" Ray turned up the glare to volcano laser destruct level. He was still sore, but half kidding at the same time.

"Certainly, if you want to," Rose said sweetly, refusing to take the bait. She tilted her head sideways and looked him up and down. "You'd look very nice in maybe cream, or I think a really nice sage green would look good with your skin and your eyes. No—rust red. Yes. Rust for daytime, and flame red for evenings." Ray snorted. "But seriously, sweetheart, he was willing to trust anybody who could help him, but even when you seemed effective he kept looking at me. I noticed that; did you? It was nothing I could help, but you can. Can you please show up looking nicer next time?"

"What do you call nice?" Raymond asked, offended. "These clothes are good. There's no rips in these. My *mother* let me go out in these."

"Did your grandmother?" Rose asked, pressing the advantage. "I love Shannon, but she's not a fairy godmother."

"Grandma didn't see me," Ray said. "She was out when I left."

"There, now. You're a teacher and a benefactor to these

children," Rose said. "You're going to teach them something about themselves they didn't know before. Think about what Jorge saw, not whether the wand pooped out."

"Does it have to be the usual *uniform*? You know, we could have a club badge or something," Ray suggested, his eagerness regaining momentum. "Something so we can all know each other, too. My cousin's an artist. She could do us up a really different design, something"—he hammered his fists together, trying to find the right word—"something fine, something *inspiring*. We could all wear it, and then it wouldn't matter how we dress!"

"And be shot at for wearing something that looks like a gang symbol?" Rose asked, outraged. "No, thank you! Besides, we don't need a sign to know one other. You'll see. One day, you'll run into somebody, and you'll be able to tell right away if they're in the FGU or an affiliated organization. You'll *know*. You don't need an outward badge. Besides, there are people you don't want to inform that you're a wand-carrying fairy godparent. There are predators out there. You're afraid of the gangs. You should be afraid of other things, too. What you do need to do is dress nice, if you want respect."

"All right, maybe we'll compromise on the clothing," Ray said. He pointed a finger at her. "I don't always say I'll listen to what you tell me, but we'll see."

"That's fine, Ray," Rose said. "You're a new generation. That's what I keep telling you. We're going to make compromises. I'm going to learn from you just as much as you learn from me. Just like these kids."

When Ray didn't offer a return argument, Rose decided the matter was closed at last. She leveled her wand at chin height and began to feel the air for leads. Not too many cases around tonight. Most of them were still simmering, so to speak. She didn't find any on the boil. But wait—off toward the east there was one tiny sensation of unhappiness. Rose tested the need string. Yes, this would be a good mission for Ray. She beckoned him along and started to walk toward it. He loped alongside her, his hands in his pockets, looking disgruntled.

"All right," she asked, after a block of silence. "So what's the matter?"

"How come we are stuck in this neighborhood?" Ray asked. "Is this the whole area of influence? We've covered the same ten or so square blocks both nights, now. Is this it? Can't we get out of this part of town, or is it just because I don't have front office appearance."

"Oh, this isn't our whole beat," Rose said. "Don't be silly, Raymond. This in particular has nothing to do with your clothes. I was staying in a familiar area for *you*, so you could learn the ropes."

"Thanks a lot," Raymond said, kicking a stone across the street. It skittered to a halt on the asphalt and a car ran over it. "It's so I can run into the people whose wishes I screw up." He pretended to wave to someone. "Hey, Ray, how you doing? Yeah, the plant's still blooming upside down, but that's okay. So long as you showed up, bro.' " Rose tut-tutted, which made Ray even more angry. "And by the way, I thought fairy godmothers could fly. I'm tired of walking everywhere." Rose turned to gaze obviously at his half-tied shoes. He seemed to be waiting for one of her comments, but she just met his eyes and answered his question.

"Well, we *can* fly, but only when it's necessary. You've only been on the job two days, Raymond," Rose said. "You've hardly had time to see a representative sample of the kinds of calls a fairy godparent goes on."

"Maybe not," Ray said, hearing reason come through, but he wasn't quite prepared to listen yet. "But how come we've got to stroll in everywhere? I thought we'd be able to like, you know, pop in and out, like in the movies."

"Because, one, we can only do what magic is necessary for the job," Rose said, counting off the reasons on her finger-tips with the star of her wand. "And two, I like walking around. I like to say hello to people. You're just being impatient because you want to do the magic. Fair enough! It's new to you, and it's very exciting. But there's a reason we don't just hop around. If you went from client to client to client, bing bing bing, the way that you're talking about, you wouldn't be able to distinguish one child from another in your mind when you got home that night, and each of them should be as special to you as you are to each of them. You ought to be able to remember them by name, and what the problem was, and how you solved it, and of course"—she ended by tapping her forefinger in the center of his chest once for every syllable—"how you felt about it."

Ray was silent for a long time. "I guess I didn't think about it that way."

"You have to give yourself a rest in between," Rose said. "Being clever and creative takes a lot out of you."

In a few blocks, Ray had managed to calm down a lot. He did like what he was doing, even if he didn't exactly understand the whys and wherefores. He'd had plenty of time to wonder over the course of five days' worth of pruning City of Chicago rhododendrons.

"Hey, Rose? Can anybody tell when we're doing magic? Does it show up on the radar screens or anything?"

"My, we are busy with the questions today," Rose said, with a little smile.

"Shouldn't I be asking?" Ray asked.

"Oh, no, no, no," Rose said. "Of course you should ask me things you want to know. It's good that you're relaxing enough to ask me questions. Keep going! You can ask me anything. I'll tell you anything you want to know. If it's none of your business I'll say so, but I'll always tell you the truth as far as I know it."

"Oh, yeah?" Ray grinned suddenly. "How's your sex life?"

Rose didn't turn a hair. "Mr. Feinstein died five years ago, sonny. It's been a little slow since then."

Ray was ashamed of himself. He dropped a few paces behind her and pulled his ego up out of his shoes, where it had suddenly fallen. "I'm really sorry. I just felt like I made a fool of myself in front of Jorgito, and I'm sore."

"Thank you, Ray," Rose said, stopping and patting him on the arm. "I'm sorry, too. I know how it feels when what you try to do falls apart. In this case, literally. But it won't happen again. You'll see."

"Okay." They walked for a half a block more. Wasn't Rose going to answer his question? "So, can they?"

"Can they what?" She had forgotten what he had asked.

"Can anybody detect us doing magic?" he said very patiently.

"In a way," Rose said. "You can sometimes sense when magic is going on around you, and with care, I'm sure you could work out who was doing it. You can definitely feel whether it's being used for good or bad purposes, though. Bad magic stinks. It smells like"—she wrinkled her nose—"ozone, or burning oil. A sharp stench."

Ray was fascinated. "What's good magic smell like?"

"You tell me," Rose said, with another shrug. "I've become so accustomed to doing things over the years, who knows?"

Ray tried to think if he had been aware of anything while the magic was going on.

"Air freshener," he said at last. "But not perfumey. The way the sky smells after a rainstorm."

"Hmm," Rose said. "That sounds nice. We should ask some of the others about their experiences."

"How many fairy godmothers are there? I mean, if it's like the motto says, 'every child deserves one miracle,' there must be thousands of FGU members in Chicago alone."

She seemed delighted and relieved he still wanted to talk. "Oh, there are thousands *worldwide*. There's more than a hundred of us in the Chicago chapter, but we're stretched pretty thin, which is why we're recruiting vigorous young people like you. The union needs to expand."

"Well, how come there aren't more? How come you aren't out there, running a membership drive."

"We're working on it, honey," Rose said. "You see why it takes so long to bring on an apprentice? We spend all our time talking when we should be doing." She whisked her wand in an arc, making sure that lead was still there. "Come on. Your next client is waiting."

"Up there?" Ray asked, staring up the height of the Scott Arms Apartment Tower.

"Up there. Thirty-seventh floor. You wanted to fly, didn't you?" Rose asked.

"Yeah! How?"

"You tell the magic you've just got to." Rose pulled him to the glass wall beside the door under the green-and-white awning. She pointed to the uniformed security man sitting at the high desk just inside. Further in, next to three bronze elevator doors, another man was visible.

"You see? It's so much trouble," Rose said in a singsong voice, shaking her head. "There are security cameras everywhere. Tch! And a doorman, too. It's more trouble than it's worth to do this. I guess we'll just have to find another way *in*."

As she spoke, Ray watched the glow around her star. The light increased a little bit at a time, but wearily, as if it had heard the excuse before and was just tolerating it.

"You know, I'm training Ray," Rose continued. "And he really needs to come with me, because maybe *he's* the fairy godparent for this child, and I'm not." Ray's small blue star lit up, but more brightly, as if eager to try out this new adventure. Ray felt himself being lifted from the shoulder blades. He snapped his head around to look at his back. By the time he glanced back at the ground, he was already two stories up.

"Whoa!" he cried. Rose floated in the air beside him, grinning.

"You see? So it's bending the rules a little. But it worked, didn't it?"

"Yeah!" Ray said. He flapped his arms, and found the movement spun him around in a circle. "This is great! Hey, how come you didn't sprout little frilly wings when the magic touched our backs?"

"Well, neither did you," Rose said. "I never do. Wings are not necessarily part of the tradition. In all the retellings about Cinderella's fairy godmother they don't once mention wings. She's always just described as a woman in a hood. That's because she wasn't a fairy. There's a difference. You'll see." They were fifteen stories up, and still climbing. The magic swept them closer to the building. Ray could peek through the curtains of flat after flat. Pigeons, nesting on the top of ornamental brickwork, squawked with surprise as they passed. "Now, you see," Rose continued, "that was traditional wear for the times. You don't have to wear a hood, but neither do you have to wear the clown pants."

"Rose?" Ray said, crawling up the white brick wall like a fly.

"Yes, honey?"

"I *got* the message."

Chapter 10

"What do you want, O my mother?" chorused from seven junior djins' throats as they flashed into being in puffs of smoke in the Enlightenment showroom early the following evening. Froister and the other senior members gestured them over to join the growing crowd of young men who stood staring straight ahead of them with folded arms aloft, waiting for their first instruction.

"I wish they'd always stay like that," DeNovo said, glancing at the silent throng. He reached for the next lamp and rubbed the brass surface. A black-clad youth appeared almost on top of him. DeNovo had to stumble out of the way. "Hey!"

"What wouldst thou, O my mother?" the boy asked.

"Oh, this one's had an education! Stand over there while I deliberate my will," DeNovo said. "Maybe you'll be the lucky kid who helps me out of my troubles with the IRS. How about it, Al?"

"This is the last," Froister said. He palmed the final lamp, a hand-painted china base with a silk shade, one of the best in the store. When the apple-cheeked young black man appeared, he pointed to the others. The youth strode, blank-eyed, to join them.

"Forty-three," Carson said. "Do you think that will be enough?"

"No, of course not. I think our young friends here will need to help continue the recruiting movement," Froister said. "It'll be enough to start with, though, if we can get everyone involved in granting wishes and bringing in prospects. Every time one of them does a deed, we accrue another morsel of power into the master kitty. That way, even if the merger between our organization and the FGU fails, we will still be building to release ourselves."

"And bolstering our position, so we will take control at the end," Timbulo said. "First, Chicago, then . . ."

"Tomorrow the Midwest," Bannion said sourly. "These kids will be running rampant in the meanwhile. We need to control them more. Did you hear about the rash of liquor store raids? I think that one there"—he pointed at a Riverside Jackal named Vaughan Matthews—"has stolen nearly the city's entire supply of tequila."

Gurgin smiled nastily. "Eating the worms is the only way he's ever going to see God now," he said.

Froister dismissed their argument with a wave of his hand. "I see our friends here not only as a source of those precious morsels that will someday set us free of our vows, but as a necessary diversion to the transfer of absolute authority. When we are our own masters, it won't take long before we're everyone else's, too," he said. The others grinned. He did not overestimate their rapaciousness. The assumption that one day there would be seven sharing absolute power kept his associates in line, too. "Something will be needed to keep the people who are currently in power busy while they are being tossed out of office. Everyone!" He clapped his hands, and the teenaged statues came to life.

"Hey, what happened?" asked Louis Fry, a huge, pale, and pimply youth who called himself Razorback, probably to coordinate with his scalloped, almost certainly self-inflicted haircut.

"It's time for our meeting, gentlemen," Froister said, smiling pleasantly. "I told you you'd all be called. We called you."

"Hey, I was on a date," Speed Guthrie protested. Nervously, he straightened out his jacket collar and yanked the waistband of his baggy trousers up to his rib cage.

"She'll still be there when you get back," Froister said,

tapping his watch. "It's seven o'clock, so everybody is on time. Admirably punctual."

"We didn't come here. You called us!" asked the chief Backyard Wolf, who was called Federico Morales. He pushed forward through the crowd. "You summoned us up by magic, man?"

"You didn't *walk*, did you?" Froister returned. "Isn't that a more efficient way to assemble? No one knows where you went, or how you got here. Being able to vanish without a trace adds to your mystique." He waited while the gang members discussed it among themselves. They decided that it was pretty cool after all, though some were still upset that the transfer hadn't been their idea at the time. The independent recruits just stared in silence.

"Hey, I don't like you messing me around like that," Razorback spoke up, the first of the gangbangers to challenge the new status quo. He clenched his big hands into fists, stepping close enough to Froister to threaten him. The guild chairman wasn't impressed. One spotty youth could not possibly match his long experience, nor his ruthlessness. It was time these hoodlums learned that, if they had any aptitude at all for survival. The others watched, tension showing in their stance. The old members waited, their mouths twisted in amusement. None of them rushed to help Froister. None of them needed to. He'd rubbed this young rascal's lamp himself.

Razorback closed in. Up close, the young man's face was a study in acne and neglected dental work. He probably used his appearance on the street to add to his fearsomeness. As he loomed over the guild chairman and drew back his fist, Froister nonchalantly waved a hand. *How dull*, he thought. Every one of them did this, *once*.

"You swear to obey the mother of the lamp?" he asked, almost casually.

At the sound of the words of the oath, the young man stopped short and straightened up. His eyes glazed over, and he folded his arms across his chest. The others gasped. "I swear to obey."

Froister pursed his lips, looking over Razorback's shoulder at the others. "Then, my lad, dance on the ceiling."

"What?" Morales demanded, lowering his brows. Razorback was one of his men. "Don't listen to him." The big youth paid no attention. Instead, he jumped straight up into the air, did a half flip upside down, and landed on his toes, fifteen feet up. He glanced up at the ceiling, then down at Froister and the others, his mind astounded at what his body had done.

"Now, dance!"

His cheeks glowing with embarrassment, Razorback lurched into a clumsy version of a cowboy line dance. He promenaded, slid, and tush-pushed silently around the chains of the hanging chandeliers. Not one of the other teens made a sound.

"Juggle!" Froister ordered. He took three light bulbs out of a fixture and tossed them up in a bunch to his captive performer. They stayed together and arrowed toward Razorback in a triangle pattern. The bulbs rather than the boy seemed to control the action as his hands tossed, caught, tossed, caught, all defiant of the force of gravity. "And keep dancing! Now, do a back spin!" Razorback's body obligingly lay down on the ceiling and did a break dance whirl, his hands still juggling the three light bulbs. "Flatten out. Now, kiss your toes."

Though Razorback's eyes begged for mercy, he was helpless to disobey even the most impossible-sounding order. He bent over, trying to reach his toes with his lips. The light bulbs continued to whirl over his head in their braided dance, without his hands touching them. One at a time, he grabbed each foot to bring it to his mouth, but he was not flexible enough. He groaned in pain. Then, suddenly, strangely, his body elongated until his torso had stretched enough to bring his face level with his feet. Face contorted with hatred, he kissed the toes of his unspeakably dirty sneakers one by one. At once, his body snapped back to normal. The others stared up at him, stupefied.

"That's what happens if you don't cooperate with us,"

Froister told them in a terrible voice cultivated for moments such as this. "You retain your free will so long as you don't presume to question our orders." He pointed up at Razorback. "And that happened because you have forced us to show you who is in charge here. Out on the street you may have other chains of command, but in here I, the guildmaster, am the sole authority. Do you understand?"

"Yeah, I understand," Morales said. "I understand you just fine." He cast around, searching the display floor for something. Froister watched him, a little smile on his lips. The gang leader went from one floor lamp to another, casting a measuring eye back at the warehouse owner. He grabbed one and rubbed it. Nothing happened. He pushed it aside and seized the next one.

"Are you looking for mine?" Froister asked, and had the satisfaction of seeing Morales jump and twitch. The gang leader tried to ignore the smooth voice behind his back, and went to the next floor lamp. This time one of the Jackals pushed him away. Morales slid away to face Froister, angry because he had been thwarted. "I'm not stupid. You won't find it because it's not here anymore. Do you think I'd risk one of you rubbing *my* lamp? And don't bother to try and attack me physically. I'll just vanish." He snapped his fingers. "Gentlemen, my associates and I are old hands at this business. You wouldn't believe how old. Cooperate, and you will share infinite power with us. Screw around, and you'll never stop paying. The lesson isn't over yet."

He looked up at Razorback, still whirling in dizzy circles. "Come down here."

Razorback kicked loose from the ceiling. With another half flip, the big youth stood on the floor with his arms folded on his chest. The three light bulbs stopped their spinning and floated lazily to the floor, their part in the demonstration done. Froister pointed a forefinger at the youth's nose.

"The first wish: go get the files the IRS has on Mr. DeNovo's business."

"The mother commands, and it shall be done," Razorback

said. He put his wrists together and vanished in a cloud of
black smoke.

No one spoke during the twelve minutes that Razorback
was gone. Morales retreated to the side of the showroom with
the rest of the Backyard Wolves, watching Froister and the
other old members suspiciously. The Jackals were on the other
side, similarly wary. They all knew now that the seven men
at the front of the room indisputably held the upper hand.
They might have been plotting revenge against Froister and
the others, but they were also scared to pieces that a fate
similar to Razorback's public humiliation might befall one of
them. Froister knew at that moment that he and the others
had nothing more to fear. He might just chance bringing their
lamps back, but why risk it? They were safe in their hiding
place.

A roar like an approaching freight train filled the room.
With a clap of thunder and another burst of smoke, Razorback
appeared in the same spot from which he had vanished. His
arms were full of papers and computer disks. Floating above
the physical impedimenta were numbers and words that
seemed to be printed in white on the air. Froister guessed
that Razorback had also taken all the data that was currently
running through the computers at IRS headquarters. The youth
was admirably thorough.

At a signal from Froister, Razorback laid his armload at
DeNovo's feet. When he set it down, the containment spell
around it vanished, and the papers scattered in every direction.
Razorback dived for a handful, but they swirled out of his
reach. The floating numbers whirled away and popped like
soap bubbles.

"Smooth move, kid," the businessman snarled.

"Hey, up yours, mmm-mother," the young genie strained
out in a monotone. His face was sweating, and hate burned
at the back of his eyes though his expression stayed blank.
He stood erect. With his arms folded, he nodded his chin, and
the papers gathered themselves together in neat heaps.

"Very nice," Froister said, approvingly. The loose data was

gone for good, but if DeNovo didn't have it, neither did the IRS.

Razorback seemed to shake himself all over like a dog, and his eyes returned to normal. Morales came over to peer at him. He judged that his soldier was unharmed, if confused, and turned back to Froister, his posture a study in nonchalance.

"Okay, so what? We're your robot messenger boys now whether we like it or not. What's in this deal for us?"

Froister had to admire his gumption in asking, after witnessing such a demonstration of power over will. You just couldn't faze today's young. He blamed television for taking all the awe out of life.

"Power, just as I promised," Froister said. "I didn't say you wouldn't like being djinni. Not at all. There's plenty of scope for your creativity. I'll show you more." He turned to Razorback, pointed the finger again. "The second wish." Razorback straightened up and folded his arms. "Revenge against the IRS employee who came after Mr. DeNovo. Bring him here. You shall be the agent of that revenge."

"It will be as the mother commands," Razorback said. Undoubtedly he still felt embarrassment about providing an upside-down floor show, but the order to be the instrument of vengeance seemed to appeal to his slow-working brain. His eyes slitted like a feral hunting cat's.

"You know, the command doesn't specifically require Razorback to leave the room," Bannion said, standing holding up a display rack with his shoulder. "It's an opportunity for the others to see the workings of a really powerful wish firsthand. Don't you go, son. Make him come here." Bannion pointed to the floor.

"Oh, okay." Eyes showed signs of enlightenment, when shown even the simplest alternative. The youth straightened up, flexed his shoulders, and squeezed his eyes hard closed. There was a lightninglike flash, followed by the sound of a heavy weight hitting the floor. When everyone's eyes had recovered, they saw a man kneeling in front of Razorback with his arm outstretched, shoving a videotape forward. He wore an open-necked sport shirt and a pair of beige twill

trousers, crisply pressed. His rimless spectacles hung over
one ear, as if they had been blown off during the magical
tornado.

"That's him," DeNovo said, walking over. He took the tape
out of the dazed man's fingers. "Look at that: *Bambi*. I bet
you like the part where his mother gets killed, right?"

"Where am I?" the man asked, blinking up at the crowd
of men. He recognized DeNovo, and scrambled to get to his
feet. Froister nodded to Razorback, who appeared next to the
man and pushed him back to his knees. "Mr. DeNovo, what
is this?"

"Judgment day," the businessman crowed. He bent and
grabbed a handful of the agent's shirtfront. "You creep, you
kept me waiting in your office for six hours, then you turned
my whole life inside out just because of a lousy two-line error
on my tax return. You made me crawl back to beg for time,
when you sat on my files. You made me waste months finding
every damned little receipt I ever got, and then you still
disallowed all of my deductions. Confess that you did it out
of spite."

"What?" the man said, straightening up on his knees.
Razorback pushed him down again with a single fingertip.
"But, Mr. DeNovo, you claimed twenty thousand dollars on
advertising expenses, and you're a government contractor!"

"It was advertising, all right," DeNovo said. "I spent plenty
on greasing palms so they'd look at my contracts at all, you
bum."

"But that's not an allowable deduction," the man argued.
He pushed his glasses up on his nose, and started to explain.
"Under section 47.002b. of the Uniform Tax Code . . ."

DeNovo clapped his hands over his ears. "Don't start spout-
ing regulations at me again," he shouted. "I've had it up to
here with tax codes." He turned to Razorback and tilted his
head back at the hapless agent. "Toss 'im."

"Wait a minute!" the agent cried, holding up his hands to
protect himself. "I'm only doing my job!"

"Yeah, so you said," DeNovo growled. He shot out a hand.

"Okay. Don't kill him. I just want him to feel humiliated, the way I did when he went after my family."

"With pleasure, mother," the young genie said, showing his teeth. He thought for a moment, then starting whirling in place. Smoke seeped from beneath his feet in a gray-green haze that thickened, turning the air murky. It swallowed up the struggling agent, whose voice faded into silence when the smoke rose above his head.

"Hey, what is this?" the agent cried. "Why are you doing this . . .?"

Men, cloud, and all disappeared with a loud bang! When it cleared, the young genie was standing alone with his arms folded.

"Where is he?" Froister asked.

"I threw him into next Tuesday, my mother," Razorback said, then his face returned to its normal expression, a fierce, vacant grin. "I didn't know you could see the days like that. Way cool. I also took his suit. He's stark buck naked."

"Well done," DeNovo said, stepping up to shake the youth's hand. "Good job. I can see you're really one of us." Razorback glanced at the man's hand warily, then clasped it with pleasure.

Froister turned to the rest of the crowd. "You see, you can enjoy doing service *to* others." He made certain they heard the emphasis. Most of them found the cruelty appealing. They would serve more willingly if they were allowed to exercise their bent.

"For those of you who were not with us for our first meeting, let me explain our aim. The membership of the DDEG unionized four hundred years ago because we were getting a raw deal. Rub, three wishes, spend the next years in a small enclosed space because your former master couldn't get anything else out of you but he doesn't want anyone else to get the power. He dies, and your lamp gets passed on to the next owner. Rub, three wishes, etcetera, etcetera. Or the lamp gets tossed on a trash heap, sold to a shop, or thrown in the river as a useless old bit of junk." The young djinni looked worried at the prospect of spending hundreds of years on a shelf. "Our aim is to break the thrall of the lamp, but keep the power it gives us."

Morales got so angry parts of him dissolved into smoke. He stuck an angry forefinger up under Froister's chin. "You mean you initiated us so we're stuck sitting in lamps forever like you, without telling us?"

"I told you the benefits. You accepted freely. You can live nearly forever. You have access to tremendous power. All you have to do is trust one another to make use of it. You're already employing the peripheral benefits." Some of the young members looked puzzled at his words, so he translated. "I've heard about all the robberies. You're already having a good time."

"There's safes we can't get into, man," one youth said. "I bounced off the one in Tiffany's a hundred times already."

"That's under the Guardian Angels' protection," Gurgin growled. "Damned nuisances."

Froister waved everyone quiet. "To answer your question, Mr. Morales, we are now all in the same boat together. We have to break out, and we need to use magic to do it. The slow way is to accrue morsels of loose power which the guild gets every time one of you grants a series of wishes. You ought to start right away. We need all the help we can get. You're going to supply the strong arms, we the experience. In exchange for your aid, we offer you your own absolute power in the future. You'll be granting wishes for yourself, anywhere, anytime. But, I'll be honest: it will take years."

There was a chorus of protest.

"That's too long," Morales said. "What's the fast way?"

"There are two fast ways," Froister said. "There are groups in this city that have the firepower to free us from the lamps, at the same time allowing us to retain the magical ability."

Every face in the room turned greedy. "How? Who?"

Froister held up a hand. "Ah, but first we need to learn cooperation. These people are not helpless. They're good."

"How good?" Razorback asked. "I can take anybody."

"No, dear boy, good in the sense of pure. Honest. Genuine. Truthful. Helpful. And all of those other tedious virtues." The others groaned in disgust. "I'm asking you to cooperate with me in blatant self-interest. I can see to it that you work together, whether you want to or not, threateningly, but you'll be that much more effective if you are doing it of your own free will."

"We got the power, but we can't use it right now unless someone wishes on us," Speed said.

"Right."

"These other dudes can separate one from the other."

"Just like an egg," Froister said.

"Then let us at 'em. Who are they?"

"Fairy godmothers." The name took a moment to register, then the entire group burst into hysterical laughter.

"You crazy," said Razorback.

"Not at all. Would you have believed a week ago that there were genies living in the city of Chicago? Would you have believed that you would become one?"

The laughter died away, as each of the boys looked at each other and at the bracelets on their wrists.

"I guess not," said Speed.

"You wouldn't have," Froister said absolutely. "They are an organization just like this one. A legitimate merger is proposed between our parent groups, the DDEG and the FGU, or Fairy Godmothers Union. They have so far balked at accepting our proposal, for reasons I can't imagine," he said, pitching his voice over the snickers from the crowd of young djinni, "since I intend to exploit them for our mutual benefit."

"Right! So they're supposed to grant our wish to get out of the lamps?" Morales asked.

"No," Gurgin said, speaking up in his ponderous way. "They can't do that, unless she—or he, there are male fairy godparents—is there to grant your specific wish. They have rules, too."

"So where do they keep the extra magic?" asked the tequila drinker.

Froister nodded to Timbulo, who stepped forward and cleared his throat. "Each one has a certain measure of extra credit, so to speak. They call them 'brownie points.'" There was more derisive laughter. The secretary snarled at them, and they quieted down. "Just like ours, the union accumulates a certain pool of this loose power. As an affiliate organization, after a merger, we would have access to it. But they are so far unwilling to agree to the merger. They cannot be forced to give the power points up to us, so we have to convince them that we ought to have them, or trick it out of them. That's method two."

"Well, we can do that!" Morales said. "Let's just wish 'em here, and start working on 'em. We'll convince 'em."

"Can't do that," Gurgin said, lowering his brows ponderously.

"Sure we can," said the chief of the Riverside Jackals, Mario Lewis. He was a tall, lean man with very dark skin. A pale streak down his cheek from his left eye to his jaw showed the track of a knife scar. His short hair was hidden under a colorful pillbox hat. He pointed at Razorback. "That dude brought the IRS man so easy. Let me do it. Come on. These folks can't be so tough." The others started to clamor agreement.

Froister sighed. "I suppose you'll never believe me until you try it. Go ahead." He turned to his associates. "Who had Mr. Lewis?"

Bannion stepped forward. "I did. The first wish: bring us a fairy godmother working in the city of Chicago."

"Piece of cake," Mario said, as his arms snapped up into the crossed position on his chest. He blinked his eyes hard.

Everyone in the room felt the outgoing rush of energy, but it all boiled back on him in an instant. Mario's narrow body seemed to be even thinner as it compressed in the middle of a seiche, until he was fifteen feet tall and only a couple of inches around. Every piece of metal, including the beams and conduit in the walls, let out a dissonant BOOOOIII-INNNNGGGG! Dozens of lamps fell to the floor and smashed. The membership ducked for cover to avoid shards of flying glass.

The magic receded. Mario sprang back into shape in the center of an area cleared of anything else solid. The gang leader stood there with his arms still raised, vibrating like a metronome. He shook his head to clear it.

"Do you see now why it won't be so easy?" Froister said, patiently. "Our magics are basically incompatible. They're on the other side. You'll have to bring them here physically, one at a time, in person. We need to get a list of the members. That is why I need a volunteer to act as our delegate to the Fairy Godmothers Union. We are trying to start a legitimate merger, you know. We're entitled to send an observer. Only someone with a good memory," he cautioned.

A few of the youths nudged one another until Speed stepped forward.

"I'll do it," he said, nervously wiping his nose on his jacket sleeve.

"Good. They meet at the Assembly Hall on Glenwood every other Saturday. Your job is to attend their meetings, memorize as many faces as possible at the meeting, and get a membership list." He turned to Bannion. "By the way, I'd like my shop back the way I had it."

"Naturally. The second wish: clear up this mess!" the red-headed man said in his soft, lilting voice. Mario gave a sigh, took a deep breath, and crossed his arms. Thick gray smoke swept out from around his feet and filled the room. Froister heard the reassuring tinkling sounds of glass reconstructing itself into bulbs and lampshades and bases. *Thank the powers that be for the magic*, he said to himself. *Otherwise my insurance rates would be sky-high.*

The smoke cleared and the lamps were back together. Each of the young genies rushed to his particular standard to make certain it was all right.

"The rest of you," Froister called, "look out for more apprentices. The more we have, the more of our own accrual magic we have, and the faster we will be able to look on a lamp as a piece of useful bric-a-brac and not as a second home."

"Aren't we going to do no wishes for ourselves?" an independent young genie asked, clearly disappointed. "We want some of those rewards now!"

Froister's gesture made them free of the whole room. "If you can work out how to trust one another, go ahead and make wishes! Experiment with one another. One day you'll be in charge of your own fates, and you should know what you can do with your abilities. Think of it! You could have a new car. You could give your girlfriends nose jobs. You could have your own chain of pizza restaurants, if only you could bring yourselves to cooperate."

All the gang members looked around for a lamp to rub. The potential rubbees sprang to protect theirs. At first the group separated into the gangs and the independents, but then it divided further as they found their lamps were not all on the same side of the room. Mario Lewis vaporized to try and make a wish on one of the Backyard Wolves, who turned into a fume and hung over the body of the lamp, repelling the intruder. Lewis rebounded, turning solid on the way. He staggered backward, almost hitting one of his own men, who was under siege from a couple of independents who had designs on his chair-mounted reading lamp. There was a scuffle, during which knives and razors were drawn. Someone yelped as another jumped at him with a homemade shank. He made his midsection into a gas cloud just in time to keep from being skewered. Another youth saw him do that, and tried it himself, vaporizing an arm to duck through another's guard and punch him in the face. Soon they learned to solidify parts of their bodies and leave the rest in gaseous form.

Froister and the others watched the byplay with interest.

"They're deadly fighters," Gurgin said, folding his massive arms over his chest. "What an army they'd make."

"Too unruly," McClaherty said. He had been a sergeant in the Marine Corps. "You'd have them falling out of rank all over the place."

"But there's a specific style to it," Froister said, pointing. "See how they all react the same way to a knife thrust toward the face: jerk back, duck under, *lunge*. Most interesting." The senior members enjoyed the scuffle until someone pulled a gun.

"Too bad. I hoped it wouldn't come to that." Froister vanished and appeared in the midst of the fray so quickly no one saw how he got there. He rubbed the nearest lamp.

"That's enough! Bring me every designated weapon in this room!" With a crash, a boom, and a roiling puff of smoke that left them all coughing, the djin complied.

"Very dirty," Froister admonished the young djin, a thin-faced white boy named Sid Mayer. "You'd better quit smoking."

"Shut up. You sound like my mama," the boy said, backing into the crowd. Froister surveyed the surprising mountain of hardware on the floor at his feet.

"It's a wonder you can all walk," he said. "You don't need these things to use your power. You need to learn to cooperate. I've said it before, and I'll keep saying it! Cooperate!"

Everyone eyed the person next to him, and the outcry was universal. "With them?"

"All the more devastating," Froister assured them. "Besides, we have a common cause. We want the free magic that exists. Be here one week from tonight when Speed has the information we need for our *legitimate* approach to the FGU. The rest of you should be refining your technique if we need to go for the second means. For now, good night. Meeting adjourned, gentlemen. You're free to go back to whatever pursuit you left."

The boys left, reluctantly, making sure no one touched a lamp. By means of threats and glares, they achieved a standoff. Each djin held his hands ostentatiously out from his sides as he vanished. One Backyard Wolf leaned toward the lamp belonging to a Riverside Jackal as if to brush against it, and hooted hysterically when the Jackal jumped for him. He disappeared, leaving his derisive laughter behind on the air.

One by one, the young genies turned into puffs of smoke, and the room emptied of everything but lighting fixtures. Timbulo and a couple of the others went from lamp to lamp to make certain none of the boys remained behind, hidden from view. The secretary nodded to Froister. He let out a deep sigh, and rubbed his eyes.

"Do you think they bought it?" Gurgin asked.

"Oh, yes," Froister said. "They're dying to get out and grant wishes for themselves. Since they won't trust one another, they'll do anything to hasten that day. They have no idea how many brownie points and extras it takes to wish one of us free."

"And it'll be us, first," Gurgin said, with a complacent nod. He looked at the others, who were glancing furtively at one another. "It was agreed. Al first, then me, then each of you in turn."

"I don't like it," said DeNovo.

Froister shook his head. "At least you don't have to worry about an audit anymore."

"Not until next Tuesday, anyhow," the businessman said, suddenly looking worried. Froister threw back his head and laughed until the glass shades around him rang.

"Do you think your little adversary will be in the office on Tuesday?" he asked. "First he'll have to find his clothes! And then . . . if you were a desk jockey in a tight-lipped government bureaucracy, would you tell anyone you were kidnapped by a roomful of genies?"

A slow smile crept across DeNovo's thin lips.

"I guess not," he said.

"These are bad mothers," Zeon said, as the two of them left the lamp warehouse and materialized sitting on the curb about a block away. "Whew! I love that. When I get the power, I know a lot of people I'm gonna make beg on their knees in front of me. Not that it'll do them no good. How 'bout you?"

"I dunno," Hakeem said thoughtfully. He was more than a little shocked at what he had just witnessed. More than the anguish of the IRS agent, he was haunted by the trapped expression in Mario's and Razorback's eyes. If he'd opened his mouth, it could have been him. "I . . . can't think of anybody just now. I'm sure there's lots, though," he added, glancing up at Zeon. He need not have bothered to try and sound tough. The bigger youth was far away in his own fantasies of domination.

"We supposed to recruit some more people for Froister to make genies, to get us all free power faster," Zeon said, snapping back to the present. "How about your friend Ray? Mario been wanting him in the Jackals for a long time. This way, he gets into two good organizations, maybe three."

"No way, man!" Hakeem protested, and then had to soften his voice as the other regarded him suspiciously. "I mean, he's a wimp. Boneless breast of chicken, man. Look how he jumps when his granny says go work for charity. That's why I'm not hanging around with him anymore." Mentally, he begged forgiveness of his best friend for maligning him, and hoped word never got back to Ray about what he'd said.

"I dunno," Zeon said. "I think the man only wants warm bodies. I don't think he cares if they'd be any good at genieing."

Chapter 11

*T*he door of the Assembly Hall flew open with more than usual force, and the small woman wrapped in turquoise silk draperies burst out into the hot night air.

"I cannot work with this man," Mrs. Durja said, turning to point at Mr. Garner, who strode out after her, ready to continue the argument. "Two weeks we have had the same fights, over and over again. I cannot communicate with him on committee. In person, you are a very nice man, but when you want to be unreasonable, you are very unreasonable."

"Me? I'm the nicest guy in the world," Mr. Garner said, holding open the door of the Assembly Hall to let out the people behind him. The chairwoman, Alexandra Sennett, followed, amid the rush of fairy godmothers and godfathers eager to be about their rounds, on their way home, or out on such a nice Saturday evening. Rose and Ray were close behind her. Mrs. Durja appealed to the Blue Fairy.

"Alexandra, it is a failure," she said. "We *cannot* agree. This man will not stop talking, even when you say 'meeting adjourned.' You will have to gather the recommendations for the central committee in some other way. I am resigning from the discussion group."

"And I'm tired of listening to the two of you carry on," Mr. Lincoln said, bustling out to join the growing circle under the awning. "We're supposed to consider changes to the proposed charter, not yammer on whether we're going to go through with the merger or not. Isn't that a separate vote?"

"That's right," Alexandra said, turning a placating smile to all of the feuding parties. "The central office would ideally like to have our full recommendations by the time of our next meeting. Which of you wants to continue in the committee?"

"I do, but without him," Mrs. Durja said, pointing at Mr. Garner, who spread his hands.

"I can get along with anyone," he said.

"That's not the whole truth," Mr. Lincoln said, shaking his head. "You get along with anyone who goes with your ideas. I'll stay."

"I'm just showing everyone the holes in the proposal," Mr. Garner said. "We've got to make certain we know what it is we're supposed to be signing—whether or not I think we should be."

"All right, but please, by next meeting?" the Blue Fairy asked, tapping her palm with her wand. "At that time, I'd like to take at least a preliminary vote on whether we would approve the merger based on these changes."

"Well, I cannot help anymore," Mrs. Durja said. "I have offered my suggestions, but this man"—she pointed at Garner—"has shot all of them down at once. I have nothing more to say."

"Let's try and work something out," the chairwoman said. "Are you coming to the bar?"

"Yes, thank you very much. I certainly need a cold drink," Mrs. Durja said.

"Let's discuss it when we're all more comfortable," Alexandra said, nodding. She glanced around. "Mr. Guthrie, we're all going for a drink. Do you care to . . . where did he go? My goodness, I didn't even see him leave. What about the rest of you?" she asked. The others shook their heads.

"I think he went . . . " Mr. Lincoln folded his arms and blinked.

"Of course he did," Alexandra said. "It's too bad. I wanted to ask him more about DDEG procedures. I admit I know very little, but he didn't seem to, either. I hope he's not an accurate sample of their membership. He was almost preverbal."

"I know they are all not like him," Mrs. Durja said. "My cousin is a most learned man."

"Isn't it just like a bureaucracy?" Mr. Garner asked. "To go and represent them in another venue, they send their youngest and most unseasoned member, who has so little experience he doesn't even know how to get out of being volunteered. It'd be like us sending you to audit their meetings, Mr. Crandall."

"Uh, Ray," Ray said.

"Pleased to meet you," Mr. Garner said, putting out a hand to shake. "Call me Morry."

"I couldn't go to meetings," Ray said. "I don't have the extra time."

"Smart boy," Morry Garner said, clapping him on the back. "Don't volunteer. Make them drag you kicking and screaming."

"I just wish Mr. Guthrie had stayed," Alexandra said with a sigh. "He must have gone away with the impression that we don't want to go ahead with the merger with the DDEG."

"That's what the majority of the membership feels," Garner said.

"We do not!" Mr. Lincoln exclaimed. "Darn it, Morry, did you even ask anyone?"

"Sure I did," Garner insisted. "I've asked more than thirty-five people. Eighty percent have said no to the merger. The WGA is a pipe dream."

"That isn't official yet," Alexandra said.

"I wish he had stayed, too," said the plump man Ray had sat next to his first day. His name was Chris Popp. "I wanted to talk to him in a very kind and general way about deodorants. Did you notice his B.O.? Whew!"

"No, I wasn't ever very close to him except at coffee time," the chairwoman said, "and then I don't notice anything but whether I'm pouring myself caf or decaf."

"Well, he did," Chris insisted. Ray nodded silently, remembering the faint, acrid smell of the visitor from the Djinni, Demons, and Efreets Guild.

"I thought it was gasoline," Ray said. "He was dressed for biking."

"That must be it," Alexandra said. "I think he had a bad cold, too."

Ray felt guilty on the strange young man's behalf, but felt he had to speak up. "I think it's drugs," he said. "He's a sniffer."

A few of the older members looked shocked, but Mr. Garner looked philosophical.

"If one of us gets him as a client, we could help him lose the addiction," he said. "Trouble is, it's still his choice. He could start again."

Rose looked sad. "This is when I would like to cure all the ills of the world, and then I feel overwhelmed all over again. It's so much easier to look at our mission one child at a time."

"Talking of that," Chris Popp said, his face brightening, "let me tell you about the stop I had just last Wednesday. There were twin boys in this house . . . "

"Save it for the bar," Alexandra said, holding up her hands. "Who's coming for a drink?"

Mr. Garner, Mrs. Durja, Mr. Lincoln, the secretary George, Rose, Ray, and Chris Popp all nodded in the affirmative. Alexandra smiled, and shepherded them deftly up the street.

They walked up the street a block from the Assembly Hall. Mr. Garner hurried to step in front of them all, and pulled open a glass door that Ray had never noticed in all the years he'd been walking down Glenwood Street.

"Ladies?" A rush of cold air blew out over them as Garner stood by, ushering them in. "Whew, the air-conditioning's on high!"

"Brr!" said Mrs. Durja. "I wish I had a sweater."

"You'll get used to it in just a moment, Ganya," Rose said. "Or somebody will spark you a warmth charm." A patrol car rolled by on the quiet street. Ray, keenly aware of being under age, started to pull back from entering a bar in front of a police officer, but Rose caught his arm. Completely unself-conscious, she brought him inside with her. *See*, he told the policeman silently, *it wasn't my idea.* "Come on, Ray. This is our little hangout, where we come for the required bull session after meetings."

"The complaints aren't required," said Alexandra, as she ducked in behind them under Morry Garner's arm.

"I've never noticed this place before," Ray said, looking around curiously. "I didn't know there was a bar on this street, and I have lived in this neighborhood all my life."

A couple of the senior members exchanged glances. "Well, we want it easy to ignore," Alexandra said. "It's a safe haven for us and the other affiliate organizations. A place we can let our hair down."

"Speak for yourself," Garner said, running a hand over a balding scalp. Rose smiled at him.

"Some heads don't look good bare," she said encouragingly. "But yours does."

"Flatterer," he said. "You should have heard what one kid called me this week. 'Chrome dome'!"

"Save it until I've got something to drink," Alexandra said, avidly, heading toward a line of tables that had been pushed together along one side of the room. "Mmmh! I get so dry, talking and *talking!*"

Ray let his eyes get used to the amber light of the room. To the unobservant eye, it looked like any corner lounge, one that could have been on any street corner in Chicago, or probably any other city in America, maybe even the world. Ray heard the clack of balls hitting one another and peered up. In the far back of the room, he glimpsed a pool table under a wall-mounted cue rack. Two men leaned over the green felt top under a square high-intensity light. A pinball machine jangled tinny, electronic music beside the dark corridor that led to the toilets. In the center of the room was the real eye-catcher: a rectangular bar made of maplewood, copper, and leather. Hanging racks made of black metal dangled hundreds of sparkling clean glasses of every shape. The crystal picked up light from the dozens of small sconces on the walls and scattered tiny golden stars everywhere. Leather-topped stools surrounded the rail.

Away from the center island, low tables of the same warm, toffee-colored wood seated dozens of people talking to one another in low voices. The difference was that on top of the usual scents of beer and coffee and furniture cleaner, Ray picked up on that special cool fragrance of good magic working.

"You see, we don't so much strong-arm nonunion people out of here," Rose said, guiding him forward, "as strangers never really feel like coming in. Maybe you felt something when we came in?"

Ray remembered a sensation, as if he was passing through a hanging curtain of silk threads. "Yeah. You put a . . . a charm on the door?" he asked.

"Yes, of a sort. We call them wards. They're permeable to anyone who is deeply in need of our services. A month ago a little child, a toddler came right in, in front of everybody." Rose chuckled. "You should have seen everybody make a fuss over her. But normally, it's just us. You get all kinds of affiliates in here."

The first few tables near the door were empty. Ray ran his finger idly along the smooth wood of one of the chairs, and sensed the same kind of goodness he felt in his wand. In the nearest corner was a round table full of men and women. On chairs and under the table legs were odd, white objects with handles. Ray caught a few words from one of the men when he raised his voice to make a point.

". . . Should be concerned with preventing tooth decay!" He picked up one of the weird objects, flung it down on the table, and clicked it open to distribute papers to the others. The object turned out to be a briefcase made to look like a giant molar. "Now, if you'll look at my figures . . . "

"Dentists?" Ray whispered to Rose as soon as they were past.

"Tooth fairies," Rose said, out of the corner of her mouth.

Ray turned to stare. One of the men noticed him, and smiled at him over the top of his own briefcase. Ray recognized him as the Indian shopkeeper who had a magazine stand on the corner of the street where Ray lived.

"He's a tooth fairy?" Ray asked. "My dad buys the Sunday paper from him!"

"So do I," Rose said. "Everyone's got to make a living, Ray."

"But I know him!"

Rose smiled. "You'll be surprised to find out how many people you know are connected with work like ours."

Ray loped behind Rose and the others toward a big table. Some of the FGU already assembled there waved to come and join them. Rose paused to exchange greetings with the bartender, a big, sandy-haired man in his fifties, with a fine mustache that curled at the ends.

"Ray, this is Edwin," Rose said, motioning him forward so he could shake hands. "He runs a clean establishment. I don't have to tell him that you're under age, so no booze."

"Rose!" Ray protested. His *mom* would have said something like that to embarrass him in front of the aunties. He shouldn't have to put up with it in the company of adults.

"Oh, never mind," Rose said, smiling a little. "I'm sure you'd tell him yourself. And I'm sure you don't drink anyway, right?"

Ray sighed. There was no point in trying to put on a sophisticated face in a room full of mind readers. "Right."

Edwin winked across the bar at him. "I'm used to the goody-two-shoes around here. What'll it be, ladies and sir?" he asked.

The Blue Fairy ordered a couple of pitchers of soda for their table, a half dozen bottles of mineral water, and one pitcher of beer. Ray heard a disdainful "humph!" from not far away in the dim room. He glanced over casually, then backpedaled and grabbed Rose by the arm.

"What's the matter, honey?" she asked.

Ray pointed, unable to make his lips and tongue say what his eyes could see. Some distance away from him, a woman in a pink summer dress sat at the bar with a shot glass of whiskey in front of her. She had seemed perfectly ordinary until Ray watched her reach for the glass. She had to lift it in both hands and steady it at her lips as if she was drinking out of a bucket. If she had been standing up, she could have been no more than fifteen inches high. On her back were tiny, lacy wings, the very sort he'd been teasing Rose about just the other day. Her hair was styled into fantastic loops and braids, and her skin had delicate roseate tints on the cheeks and lips, like a model on an Art Nouveau poster. The little lady was seated on a stool about the size of a hamburger bun but with very long legs so she was at elbow level to the bar rail. Beyond were four more like her, wearing different-colored dresses and with different hairstyles and color, but all with the same disgruntled expressions on their faces.

"Oh. *Fairy* fairy godmothers," Rose said in a low tone. "Ethnic. Some of them mix with us humans, some don't. But this is a safe hangout for them, just as it is for us."

"I don't believe it," Ray whispered, awed. The pink fairy tilted an eye toward him and winked. He gave her a weak smile, and dumbly accepted the trayful of glasses Edwin handed him.

"Say, she likes you," Rose said, surprised. "That's a point in your favor. Some of the rest of us they don't deign to notice. The union was started by the real thing. A few hundred years ago they started letting mortals join. They still control most of the leadership positions. Some of the real fairies think that the FGU has gotten too big. They want to throw us all out and go back to the old days when the union was much smaller, and all fairies. I think the realists among them know that those days are over. The population of children who need a wish granted is too big, and there's just too few of them."

"How many are there?"

"How many angels can dance on the head of a pin? C'mon."

With occasional glances over his shoulder to reassure his brain he had really seen what he thought he saw, Ray maneuvered his burden through the crowd standing around in the aisle.

At the table were some fairy godparents Ray recognized from his two meetings, and some who were strangers. They paused in the middle of spirited stories about granting wishes long enough to greet the newcomers and take beverages, but swept right back into the midst of their conversation. Ray wiggled into a seat, trying not to drown out the voices with the groan of his chair shifting on the wooden floor.

". . . And so, the child said she wanted a pony," said the man who looked like a used car salesman. Clad in a sharp summer suit, he was big, red-faced, muscular, and talked with his hands. They were sketching out the dimensions of a horse. "I mean, she really, *really* wanted a pony. Talk about your heart's desire. I know when I'm listening to the be all and end all of existence. All she could talk was 'horse, horse, horse.' So," he shrugged massive shoulders, "I put in the fix. Last thing I know," he slapped the table, "I hear from the girl. Her daddy's been transferred to Montana!"

"Promotion, I hope?" asked an Oriental woman in a nurse's uniform.

"Sounds like it," said the used car salesman, cheerfully saluting her with his glass. "So, watch out what you ask for; you might get it."

His tablemates chuckled. "So true," said a man in an expensive-looking sport coat. "*So* true."

George, the recording secretary, leaned forward in a confidential manner. "Speaking of getting what you ask for, did you see that boy from the suburbs on the news?"

"I blame the fairy godparent," Alexandra said. "What poor judgment she or he must have used. He couldn't have gotten that car any other way but by magic, but it had to look like grand larceny. The whole situation just put his poor father into the midst of so much trouble."

Ray, not knowing who or what they were talking about and unable to pick up enough from context, lost interest. Rose, Mr. Garner, Chris Popp, and Mrs. Durja were having a quiet conversation at the far end of the table. He abandoned the animated conversation to his left and waited for the three of them to pause and acknowledge him.

"So what's the problem with genies?" Ray wanted to know. "That guy in the back of the Assembly Hall didn't seem so bad."

"Mr. Guthrie didn't pay attention well," Mrs. Durja said, her nostrils flaring. "He did not behave in a respectful manner. I do not think that this local guildhall is good, if this is the person they send to us as a liaison."

"You see what I mean, Ganya?" Morry Garner asked. "Your cousin Raj might be the exception. I don't like the way they're pressuring us to merge, when we know so little about them."

"Don't start with that," Rose warned. "Not when we've all made friends again. The problem is they don't *seem* to be very nice people, Ray, and not just because of this one fellow's appearance."

"Or smell," Chris Popp put in.

"He seemed to be friendly," George put in, from Mrs. Durja's other side. "He wanted to know everyone's name."

"Hmmph! So do salesmen," Morry said, with a snort.

"This three wishes stuff," Rose continued, waving the peripherals away. "It's good in principle, but it's basically an all-over control issue. It sounds to me like this is one of the fundamental sticking points in the paper the committee has been discussing: the lack of free will to act on one's own behalf."

"That's exactly it," Morry Garner said, putting his forefinger down hard on the tabletop. "It makes you look too hard at the bottom line, and not at the welfare of the people you're helping."

"Right," Rose said. "One wish, they have to focus all their desires in one single phrase, however complicated it might be."

"Yeah, like the way you talk," Ray said, raising his eyebrows at her.

"That makes me a natural, honey," Rose said, unperturbed. The others chuckled. "But with three wishes, you're all over the place. They don't have to concentrate on what's really bothering them, which is what I see as one of the aims of our federation: to help them get back on the road of life. Your client just gets greedier and greedier, and in the end, all they have are *things*, not a solution."

Ray thought that he could easily do with some *things*, and

get back on the path to happiness afterward. Rose easily guessed what was going through his head.

"With a merger like this, as I understand, you wouldn't have the opportunity to have a fairy godmother, too," she said. She turned to Morry Garner and Ganya Durja for confirmation. "It sounds like they want it to be an all-or-nothing proposition."

"That's why I don't like it," Garner said. "It blurs our purpose too much. The children fall between the cracks, and I would never hand three unlimited wishes to a child."

"That, too. Besides, the terms of membership in the DDEG amount to virtual indentured servitude. A lot of fairy godparents would rather not join up with them. They're out for different things. And yet, it might cover some other gaps in service, for example the children whose wishes get bungled, like that incident in the western suburbs with the car." Rose shrugged toward the group at Ray's other elbow. "I don't know. I'm trying to figure out what I think. I've heard the same rumors about how unscrupulous they are." Mrs. Durja started to protest. Rose held up a hand. "It may be like Ganya says, that it's a problem with the local chapter, but I don't know. That's why we welcome a liaison from the DDEG, to answer our questions."

"But this one knew nothing," Mrs. Durja said. "Can we perhaps request a different delegate?"

"That's a good idea," Garner said. "Let's get one who can talk."

Rose looked around at the surrounding tables, then raised her voice to get Alexandra's attention. "Has anybody seen Mary Hodge or Paul Sanders?" she asked.

The Blue Fairy glanced around, too. "No, not since the last meeting," she said. "I think she might be on vacation this week."

"Rose, I'm sorry," George said, pushing up his little eyeglasses with one hand. "She phoned me this afternoon. They're having company tonight. She'll be around after the next meeting. I don't know where Paul is. I thought he'd be here, too. It's after eight already."

"I wanted to talk to him," Rose said, flicking her fingers through a bead of water on the table. "It's not important."

The door slammed open and Ray turned around to see. A party of large, hearty men and women walked in, talking loudly among themselves. They wore white berets with a small round badge depicting a pair of wings and a halo, crisp short-sleeved shirts, knife-edged trousers, and brand new cross-trainers. Otherwise, the individuals had little in the way of common characteristics. Black, white, Asian, Hispanic, male, or female, they all walked with a confident swagger, a manner that made you want to back out of their path—but in a nice way. Ray looked a question at Rose.

"It's the Guardian Angel Society," she said, with a shrug.

"Yes," George put in, sourly. "Read the initials: G.A.S. Don't confuse these folks with those brave people who ride the El at night."

"Now, George, the GAS does good work," Mr. Lincoln said, catching the last part of the conversation.

"The real ones do. These are effete snobs," George sniffed. "There are plenty of Guardian Angels who do their job, but that's the difference: they just do it. They don't talk about it endlessly, bragging about the one good save they made a year ago. You don't see the *real* ones in the bars so much." He lowered his voice as one of the men ordered beer for the table in a booming voice that could be heard clear to the pool table in the back of the room. One of the players glanced up, then went back to his game, shaking his head. "For one thing, their morals don't let them drink much, or idle around. Idle hands are the other fellow's province, you know."

"I've heard," Ray said, amused. These Guardian Angels sure seemed to be having a good time, or at least, they wanted everyone in the room to think they were having a good time. He had a sudden vision of the "cool" kids in his school cafeteria, who talked loudly to attract the attention of the others, whom they'd never consider letting sit down or hang out with them. Yeah, he understood what George meant. "Do we ever see the real ones, not the wannabes?"

"Oh, sometimes," Mr. Lincoln said. "Mostly when you least expect them."

"Wannabes," George said, liking the word. He glanced over at the white-capped group, hiding his sudden smile. "Yes. These people don't like to get their hands dirty. Look at those fancy quasi-uniforms. Those outfits would cost me a week's pay."

"What's the harm, if they want to look nice?" Morry Garner asked, dismissing them with a disdainful snap of his fingers. "The paint job doesn't improve the performance a hair, and everyone knows the difference."

George rose to his feet and picked up his briefcase. "The air has suddenly become too rarefied for me," he said. He reached into his pocket for his wallet and flattened out a couple of bills, which he weighted down under an empty glass. "I'll see everyone next time. Good night."

"Good night, George," Alexandra said. The rest of the table offered good wishes, and the secretary made his serious way out into the night.

"See you, George," Edwin called from behind the bar. George turned to wave a brief farewell as the door closed behind him.

"What's with him?" Ray asked Rose in a low voice.

Rose's eyes snapped back to meet his. She'd been watching George leave. "Oh, it's personal. He had to pick up the pieces when one of the 'wannabes' tried to be a hero on the El last year. Nasty."

"That's too bad," Ray said, sincerely.

"It certainly is," Rose said. "Sometimes I think he chose the wrong organization. He could have whipped those big blowhards into shape."

"Ssst!" Speed Guthrie said, motioning to the other djin clustered behind him in the alley. "I told you they all went into one of those places and magicked the door away. That's why we can't find them."

"Who's that one?" Mario asked, crowding him until Speed

elbowed him in the ribs. He turned the lower part of his body into smoke and hovered over the other.

Speed squinted through the gloom. Mr. Froister would be pleased. The meeting had been long and boring, but at least it gave him a lot of time to study faces. He was certain he could identify almost anyone from the FGU group on sight. The short man who appeared almost out of nowhere stumped along, scowling at the pavement a few paces ahead of him. They caught a glimpse of eyeglass lenses that reflected glints from the sole streetlamp and passing car lights.

"That's George," he whispered. "They call him the recording secretary."

"Don't look like no secretary," Razorback chuckled weightily from farther back in the dark passage.

Speed waved frantically for silence as the man passed in front of them almost close enough to reach out and touch. "Shh! He's the one who took attendance. He has the list Froister wants."

"Perfect," Mario said, his voice triumphant. "He's all alone."

When the secretary was several yards farther up the street, the three apprentice djin strolled casually out of the alley. There was no hurry. An old man like that couldn't outrun them, no matter how many magic wands he had up his sleeve.

George made his way toward the El stop. He looked up in alarm as a train screeched its way along the old tracks, then nodded to himself when it turned out to be going the wrong way. He smiled. He never missed one going the right way. A fairy godparent had that little extra bit of good luck going for him.

His wife would be waiting at home, probably watching television. Too bad he could never interest her in joining the union, but she disliked being outside so much, whereas he liked to get his exercise.

The sound of footsteps made him glance back over his shoulder and reach in his pocket for his bunch of keys. A body couldn't be too careful in this day and age, and he wasn't getting any younger. There was only one person on the street, about twenty feet behind him: a thin white boy with a red nose, clad in a black leather jacket. He was too far away in the dark for George to get any better look, but he could mean trouble. George reached the violent yellow light of the El station and reached out for the banister of the stairs up to the tracks. There should be an emergency call button at the top he could push for assistance, if need be.

Somehow, the skinny boy closed the distance between him in an instant. Two more youths, one white and one black, came out of nowhere and grabbed George's arms. The skinny boy reached into his coat and took his wand out. George cried out a wordless protest.

"Don't want you busting out through any walls, grandpa," the skinny one said. George took in a deep breath to call for help. A hand with a sleek metal band around the wrist clamped down over his mouth before he could make a sound. He jerked his arms free, and struck out defensively with his briefcase, connecting with soft flesh. He had the satisfaction of hearing his assailants cry out in pain before everything went dark.

Chapter 12

"What on earth did you do?" Albert Froister asked, peering through the warehouse window. The dark-haired, stocky, bespectacled man with the briefcase sat on a box, looking around with a look of distaste. Froister recognized him with dismay as George Aldeanueva, the recording secretary of the FGU.

"You wanted fairy godparents," Speed said, wiping his nose. The others shuffled their feet on the tile floor. They looked hurt. Clearly, they had expected their initiative to be rewarded.

"I wanted their *power*," Froister said, exasperated. "You've changed us from a legitimate organization to one of kidnappers."

Speed was undaunted. "You want his power, ask him. He's got some brownie points. He's got access to the rest, right? You said it's a pool. And they're going to say no. I heard them say so in the meeting."

Froister sighed, straightened his tie. "I suppose it's worth a try. *You* stay here." He pushed through the door and strode up to meet his unwilling and unexpected guest. "Mr. Aldeanueva, how very nice to see you."

Froister pushed back through the door, his ears still ringing from the tirade to which George Aldeanueva had treated him. Speed, who had been seated on the floor next to the door with the other gang members, stood up.

"Nothing doing," Froister said, to answer their unasked question. "You've torn it now. We can't let him go, or he'll tell the rest of the membership what we're up to. We'll have to keep him here until after the vote is taken."

"Sorry I jumped too fast," Speed said. "But hey, that's why they call me Speed."

Morons, Froister thought, rolling his eyes to the ceiling. "Well, in that case, *Speed*, you take care of him. From now until we let him go, you're in charge of feeding and caring for him, and preventing him from going anywhere or making contact with anyone else. He stays in that part of the warehouse, away from everything, until I say so."

"Man, I got better things to do," Speed protested.

"Do you want me to make it a wish?" Froister demanded, and had the satisfaction of seeing the big youth quail. "I thought not." *Lie down with dogs, rise up with fleas*, he thought unhappily. He took George's wand back to his office and locked it in his safe.

The conversation at Ray's left elbow shifted to new apprentices, and Ray suddenly found himself the center of attention.

"So how are you doing, Ray?" the Blue Fairy asked. "Are you enjoying your work?"

"I like it. I guess I'm doing fine," Ray said, with a glance at Rose, who nodded emphatically and reached over to pat his hand.

"He's a prodigy," Rose said, proudly. "He's very caring, and creative—you wouldn't believe some of the clever solutions he's come up with. I wish he was my grandson so I could kvell properly, but I'm doing the best I can. It's nice to have a fine, new mind at work on the same old wishes."

Alexandra smiled. "Really, I'd expect nothing less from a member of your family," she said to Ray. "We've heard all about you since you were all born."

Ray shook his head. "I never knew any of you even existed. Grandma has never talked about the FGU at all."

"Oh, well, it's easier that way sometimes. People do get jealous of one's involvement, just like any other activity. If you exist in a trusting environment, where you can be absent without question for hours at a time, that's best."

"This is," Ray started to say, then felt silly voicing his thought. Rose leaned toward him encouragingly. "This is almost too good to be true, with the brownie points, and everybody being nice."

Everyone at the table looked puzzled. "Of course! You don't get to be a fairy godmother by snapping people's heads off." Rose asked, breaking the embarrassed silence that followed, "By the way, I'm curious. What have you done with the brownie points? You were absolutely on fire to try them out last week. What did you do?"

"Well, nothing," Ray admitted at last. "I couldn't work up my nerve to try one out, and then when I did, I couldn't decide on what I wanted to do with it."

"Oh, go ahead," Chris Popp said encouragingly. "Indulge yourself a little. There's plenty more where those came from."

Ray did think about it again, more seriously. He tried to picture the brownie points, as Rose had told him. There were four, plus a scatter of tiny sparks. They rushed toward him, all willing to become good wishes. What should he do with them? They bobbed up and down eagerly in his imagination, all wanting to be first.

"No!" Ray said. "I can't. I've got to think about it some more."

Alexandra searched his face carefully. "You're not doing it just for the brownie points, Ray. I see you aren't. There's a lot of hard work involved, a lot of thought and caring. You have to do it for the love of it."

"No, ma'am," Ray said. "It makes me feel good to help kids. I thought I might like to be a pediatrician when I graduated, but there's no way I can get into medical school. I guess I'll try something else, but in the meantime, I can do this."

"He's community-minded," Rose said. "I admire that."

"It's too bad it doesn't pay," Chris Popp said, leaning back heavily in his chair. "I'd be happy to give up my job. I hate it, but I've developed this addiction to eating, and darn it, try as I may, I can't seem to give it up." He patted his round stomach.

"He's not doing it just for the brownie points," Rose said, just to make certain everyone understood.

"I sure wouldn't be if it was all like last Friday," Ray said, remembering, and his cheeks got hot. Luckily it was too dim in the room for anyone to see clearly. At Rose's prompting, he told the others about his misadventure with the orchid, and how Rose was forced to come in at the last minute because the wand was no good.

"The gain was on too low," Rose added, when he paused for breath. "It's been all right all this week. I told him it's okay."

"Maybe," Ray said, feeling as if he was betraying a confidence, "but I don't *trust* it now."

The others looked very concerned. Alexandra held out her hand and Ray gave her the training wand. She peered at it closely as if she was not only looking at it but *listening* to it.

"It seems all right," she said.

Ray leaned forward earnestly. "Yeah, but this little stick doesn't do the job," he said, giving her his most serious and persuasive look, hoping that she might give in and promote him to a real wand. "If you want me to really learn, I need a good one."

"Hey, sonny, you know better than that!" The used car salesman distracted everyone by giving him a big wink and nudging his neighbor with his elbow. "It's not the size of the wand, it's how you use it." He laughed uproariously, and the other men joined in. It seemed to be an old joke.

Ray, who honestly hadn't thought of the comparison between wands and other things yet, and wondered why not, sat up and grinned like a jack-o'-lantern. Rose looked prim.

"I wouldn't say a thing like that," she insisted.

"Oh, you were born an old fuddy-duddy," Garner said, scowling. "The doctor smacked your rump, and said, 'this one's going to be a drag.'"

"You should know. You were there for comparison," Rose retorted.

Ray looked around at all of them, realized he didn't have a clue as to how old they were. Did you maybe live hundreds of years being a fairy godmother? Live longer, anyway? Even the oldsters seemed healthier and happier than usual folks.

"Where's your grandmother, Ray?" Mrs. Durja asked.

"She's at choir practice," Ray said. "It's always on Wednesday and Saturday nights."

Garner snapped his fingers. "I should have remembered. Are we ever going to change the day, Alexandra? Saturday is damned inconvenient for anybody with a social life."

"I can't win," the chairwoman said, throwing up her hands. "If we meet on a weekday, everyone with a day job gripes. If we meet on a weekend, everybody else gripes. Saturday still seems to be the best compromise, even if everyone who wants to go out of town misses a meeting now and again. If you want to change the *time* to a rotating schedule during the day so we can pick up those members who keep missing because of evening commitments, I'll raise the issue. What's everyone think?"

She looked at each person in turn, seeking his or her opinion. She turned to Ray, and when he demurred, tilting his head so she would go on to the next godparent, she continued to wait, smiling. The other adults waited, too. They really did care what he thought, even though he was the youngest member of the group. They thought of him as a part of this community.

"I'd like to be able to go out on Saturday nights once in a while. My girlfriend . . . " His sentence ground to a halt, but he saw that she understood anyhow.

"Of course," Alexandra said, gently, and went on to the next person. "All right, that's settled. I'll bring it up next time as new business."

He gave Rose a look of joy, which she met with confusion, since it was all out of proportion to having his Saturday evenings freed up. He liked being accepted like that. There was a real interest, a real involvement with him and what he said. They chuckled over his retelling of his escapades, and sympathized when he was upset at having failed. This was a kind of family, where they squabbled and resolved differences, but didn't let it interfere with their mission.

"I'll check with the others who have training wands," Alexandra promised. "No one else has complained, Rose, but from what he said about that client, you might be letting Ray take more advanced cases than the others. I'll check. I'm so sorry, Ray. I should have checked each wand personally." She got up to order another round of drinks for the table.

Ray glanced over sheepishly at Rose.

"You're not holding me back, you're pushing me?" Ray asked. Rose made a modest little face, and raised her hands to the level of her shoulders.

"Is that worse?" Rose asked.

"No! That's good," Ray said, feeling a warm glow in the middle of his chest, almost as nice as the wand's goodness. "I guess that means you think I can take it."

"Absolutely," Rose said.

"Then I want to do more," Ray said, stretching out his arms. "I'll take any assignment. Let me try *everything*."

"Hold on, hold on!" boomed the big salesman at the end of the table. "Don't put the punkin carriage before the mice, kid."

"I won't," Ray said. "Rose won't let me." It was daring, to make the others laugh at one of their own, but they did laugh, and no one seemed to mind. He was allowed to banter, like one of the old-timers. He felt happy.

Rose looked at her watch. "Well, it's too late for our rounds tonight. I think I'd better get on home."

Ray rose at once when she did, but more reluctantly. "Me, too," he said.

Everyone wished them a good night and promptly went back to their discussions. Within moments, Mrs. Durja and Mr. Garner were at it again over the same old argument, speaking in staccato phrases and waving their arms heatedly. Chris Popp and Mr. Lincoln moved in at once to try and separate them.

Ray returned Edwin's parting salute. The fairy fairy godmothers were long gone from their tiny barstools. More people, some of them with fancy berets and some without, had joined the throng of Guardian Angels, who had pushed more tables and chairs into a rough circle just in front of the bar. Ray and Rose had to squeeze behind them to get out.

As they left the bar, Ray felt that secure feeling of the wards slip out from around him, and shivered, even though the night was still very warm. Rose's shadowy figure turned to him.

"Always remember, if you're ever afraid or in trouble, get to the bar. It's the best safe haven we have. You'll be protected there."

"I'll remember," he said. He turned his head to peer in the windows. Already, the cosy lounge felt like a second home. He had family there.

Traffic was light on the side street. By this hour of the night, anyone who was going out was out, and anyone who was staying home had found a parking place. They saw only a few pedestrians, walking in ones and twos, their shoes loud on the empty pavements. They didn't know that there were magic people only a few paces away, and a magic bar just behind the innocuous-looking window to their left. Ray found it hard to keep his voice down in his enthusiasm.

"So can we go out again tomorrow?" he asked.

"Sorry, honey. Normally, Sunday is all right, but my daughter's coming for dinner," Rose said, her brows wrinkling upward apologetically. "She's bringing the grandkids. I don't know when they'll leave." When he looked dejected, she took his arm. "You can come, too, if you like. You'd be very welcome."

"No, thanks," he said, pulling away. "I've got family stuff of my own, I guess. How about Monday?" Rose shook her head. "Tuesday?"

"I'll be knackered on Tuesday evening. I do my volunteer day at the local grade school every Tuesday." She tapped him on the chest. "That's where I met your grandmother, you know."

"Grandma doesn't do volunteer days there," Ray said, with a quizzical look.

"Oh, no," Rose's eyes twinkled in the streetlamp light. "We met when we used to go to parent-teacher meetings, back when we both had children there."

"My mama and Uncle Bradley and Aunt Selena?" Ray asked, astonished. "That was a long time ago!"

"Yes, indeed," Rose said, wryly. "Back at the dawn of time. My sons and daughters used to play with your mother and aunt and uncle. 'Creative' is the term the teachers used then, to describe the kind of hijinks all of them got up to. Since then, everybody's moved away except your mother." Rose sighed, reminiscing. "Your uncle was a sweet little boy. You look a lot like him. Mrs. Green was very proud when he was put on the honor roll for a whole year, back when he was in seventh grade."

"About when it happened to me the first time," Ray said thoughtfully. "How come you know my grandmother more than forty years and you still don't call her by her first name? Plenty of her friends do."

Rose shrugged. "She never asked me to. In my generation, you didn't push for the instant intimacy you see all the time now. I guess it's a hard habit to get over. But a little formality didn't hurt anyone."

"Grandma can be pretty formal," Ray admitted. Rose smiled at him.

"You two are very special to each other," she said. "When she started taking care of you when you were just a little baby, she was happy. Your parents were sorry to burden her with their child, but she didn't mind at all. She enjoyed raising another one, especially one as interesting as you. I think you have a special bond with her."

"Yeah, I guess we do." His parents had been very young when they got married, and it was only a short time before Ray was born. Finances prevented either one from being able to stay at home with their new child. It had seemed a natural thing for his widowed grandmother to come and live with them, and take care of baby Raymond. She had virtually primary care of him until he had started school. Their relationship was different than Ray's with his parents. She understood him when no one else did, not all that surprising for the woman who had witnessed his first steps, heard his first word, and read him, at two a night, more than 3,650 bedtime stories.

After Ray, the surprise, his parents had delayed having further children. By the time the other kids came along, the parents had more time to spend with them. Ray was a little jealous of the interest they took in their two younger offspring, even as he acknowledged how unfair it was to blame his parents for their youth and poverty when he was born. For their part, Bobby and Chanel were a little jealous of his closeness to Grandma Eustatia. She took his part sometimes when his parents didn't see things his way. Not that Grandma ever showed favor to one grandchild over another, but he and she had a familiarity between them that was impossible to duplicate. Her influence became diluted as the family's fortunes improved to the point where her daughter could be at home more, and her son-in-law was able to take time away from his schedule.

"Was she fairy-godmothering when I was little?" he asked.

"Oh, most certainly. She's been in the union for more than forty years," Rose said.

Ray was struck by a thought that made his eyes widen. "Did she ever take me on visits? I don't remember any, but that doesn't mean she didn't."

"That's true," Rose said. "Why don't you ask her?"

Ray nodded sharply. "I guess I will. Um, should I walk you home? It's not too far."

"Thank you, young man," Rose said, tucking her hand through his arm. "That would be very nice. Whew!" she said, fanning herself with her little clutch purse. "Isn't it humid tonight?"

"Sure is," Ray said, trotting alongside her. "So, Wednesday?"

"Wednesday is fine," Rose said. "Wednesday for certain."

"Why do we have to wait so long to go out again?" he asked, knowing he was whining.

Rose tilted her head to look up at him sidelong. "Sonny, when you graduate from the mentoring program and get promoted to full membership you can go out every night of the week from then on. In the meantime you have to put up with the physical restrictions of having a partner of a certain age."

"But I want to be out and doing things," Ray insisted. "For other people, I mean. Good things."

Rose made a sound like "tchah!" "You don't need magic for that. Clean your room. Wash the dishes. Mow the lawn. Mow the neighbor's lawn. Feed the hungry." Ray dug his hands into his pockets and stalked along beside her, sulking. "Look! I'm giving you the intensive course right now. I can't really do any more than I am. I've got responsibilities. What about you? How about your job?"

"What, clipping hedges and planting marigolds? I can do it in my sleep," Ray said, frustrated.

"But you shouldn't," she said. "You could hurt yourself."

"I don't need another mama, Rose. I want to get *out there.*"

"I know, I know. But it's not all fun and games, you know. We haven't had any of the real heartbreakers, yet."

"I can handle it," Ray said confidently.

They turned the corner onto the main street. Ahead of them, the silhouette of a tall, slender girl with her hair in a topknot bun was walking their way with an easy, athletic gait. As they passed under the next streetlamp, she quickened her pace and strode toward them. Ray felt his heart quicken. The leggy shape was his girlfriend, Antoinette. Her long, narrow face lit up.

"Ray? I thought that was you. Where've you been, boyfriend?" she asked, leaning back and putting a provocative hand on her hip. "You haven't been around much the last couple of weeks."

"I'm sorry," Ray said abjectly, realizing he hadn't been as available as he might have been, so involved was he in learning the ins and outs of wish-granting. "Grandma Eustatia got me involved in some charity work," Ray said hastily, glancing over Antoinette's shoulder at Rose and hoping she'd take his cue.

"Well, I guess I'll forgive you," Antoinette said, smiling so her almond-shaped eyes crinkled. She moved closer. Ray wrapped his arms around her and kissed her hello. "What kind of charity work?" she asked, as soon as her lips were free.

"Helping kids," Ray said shortly. A full explanation would take hours, and he wasn't certain he could explain it well, yet, but the short form seemed to satisfy her for the moment. "Uh, sometimes we give them clothes. Whatever they need."

"Really?" Antoinette beamed, swinging loose so she could see Rose, too. Ray clamped his arm around her waist instead. "That's so nice. *I'm* doing some special volunteering, too, but not only with kids. My uncle got me into it, you see. Helping people who need help." She appealed to both of them. " 'Looking out for the little guy,' he calls it. Good thing I take karate. Some of those little guys aren't so little, or so glad to see me." Ray remembered his manners after a surreptitious jab in the ribs from Rose.

"I'm sorry, Toni: this is Mrs. Feinstein. She's a friend of my grandmother," Ray said, gesturing from one to the other. "This is Miss Antoinette Smithfield. Her uncle is the Reverend Barnes, the pastor at my grandma's church."

"I'm very pleased to meet you," Rose said, taking Antoinette's outstretched hand. The girl shook hands with brisk cordiality. "Call me Rose, won't you? My goodness, no wonder Ray went on and on about you. You're even more beautiful than he described."

Antoinette dimpled prettily. "Thanks," she said shyly. "Where are you going now?" she asked Ray.

"He was just walking me home," Rose said, before Ray could answer. "The streets can be so unsafe at night."

"Tell me about it," Antoinette said, with a long-suffering sigh. "That's why I take karate classes."

"She got her black belt sooner than anyone in her age group," Ray said proudly.

"Congratulations!" Rose grabbed their hands, put them together, and patted them. "Well, you two haven't seen each other, so I'll just go on by myself. I'll be fine."

"Uh, no, I should go with you," Ray said, torn between his responsibility as her escort and the attraction of his girlfriend.

"No," Antoinette said, smoothly taking the trouble out of his hands. "We'll *both* walk you home. I'd feel better about it. Okay, Ray? There's no reason that just because I ran into you, you should change your plans."

"All right," Ray said dreamily. That was just like her, so considerate. And so beautiful. She had grace. The way she held herself, the way she walked, she looked like a queen next to short, chunky Rose. He'd been against the karate lessons when she first started, thinking that it would make her more macho than he was, but it had only given her confidence. Where she used to be awkward, she was now proud of those long, pretty legs. It was his ego that got in the way. She had had the wisdom to know that, and the patience to wait out the tantrum. Antoinette caught him looking at her, and gave him her special smile. His heart pounded wildly in his chest. She was wonderful.

At her door, Rose turned to face the young couple. They had trailed behind her, hand in hand, for the last five blocks. She remembered what first love had been like. The delicious memory stayed with one for a lifetime, even if the person didn't. In Rose's case, she felt she'd been lucky: he had. With a bittersweet pang in her heart, she smiled down at Ray and Antoinette from her doorstep.

"Thank you very much for escorting me home," she told them. They seemed to snap out of their little pink cloud when she spoke. The girl, embarrassed to have been caught in such a vulnerable state of mind as love, ducked her head and looked up at Rose through her long eyelashes.

"It was our pleasure," Antoinette said. "Really."

"You're very gracious," Rose told her. "I do appreciate your coming all this way out of your way for a stranger." Although they had just met, Rose felt unexpectedly warmly toward the teenage girl. Examining her reaction, she identified the reason with some amusement. "And thank you, Ray. You know, she's a very special girl. *Very* special," she added significantly.

"I know," Ray said, with a blissful smile that told her he had no notion what she was talking about. Well, the girl would tell him, or she wouldn't. Ray leaned in to whisper, and Antoinette withdrew tactfully to a few steps away. "See you Wednesday evening? There ought to be lots of kids around then."

"Absolutely," Rose said, also in a low voice. "Come for dinner. We'll go out while it's still light for a change."

"Thanks," Ray whispered.

"Wednesday!" she called to them as the couple went away. She took a last, quick check around with her hand on the wand in her purse to make certain there were no emergencies nearby. *What sweet kids*, she thought, as she opened her postbox for the mail. Ray didn't know what a treasure he had there.

The first apartment Zeon tried was empty. He hugged himself because the pangs of withdrawal felt like fire eating his ribs. Nothing here to spend or sell. Better try another, his dazed brain told him.

He turned into a puff of smoke and let himself float upward through the floor. Yeah, this one was inhabited! And they had lots of stuff. A VCR, new model—maybe not; ah, but who cared, so long as it worked? He started to undo the cables, when he felt that he was being stared at. A black kid, maybe ten or twelve years old.

"You came right through the floor!" the youngster said, his eyes wide.

"Yeah," Zeon said. He felt in his pocket for his shank, then remembered Froister had taken them all away. He had to get another one. Unarmed, he felt naked. "You be quiet now. Don't you shout."

"I won't," the child said, staring at him with admiration instead of fear. Zeon thought he was weird, but as long as he didn't get in the way, he wouldn't have to hurt him.

So Clarice wasn't lying after all, Colton thought. Weeks

ago, his stepsister had told the family all about her adventures with the white woman and the brother in the zipper jacket who had given her magic skates and five dollars to go out. He had scoffed along with the rest of them, assuming she had saved up her allowance for the bad duds and skates, and made up a story to make her life sound more cool than it was. Clarice was dreary. The only part of her story that had sounded true was that he couldn't fit in her skates. God knew he'd tried. But now it looked as if it was all true. This guy wore a zip-up leather jacket. He guessed it was the white lady's day off.

"Are you *my* fairy godfather?" Colton asked. The brother, his eyes slightly unfocused, turned to him with a grin that didn't look at all nice.

"Oh, yeah, man. I'm your fairy godfather all right. Sure! Hey, your folks home?"

"No," Colton said, uneasily.

"Great! Show me around, man. Let's see the place. Your old fairy godfather's got to know the lay of the land." Unwillingly Colton did. The stranger started to put things in his pockets, which seemed to have an infinite capacity. Colton felt more and more uneasy as the VCR, his sister's boom box, and a couple of knickknacks off his mother's special shelf all vanished into the leather jacket.

He spun, daringly, to confront the man at last. "Ain't you gonna grant my wish?"

"Maybe later," the magic man said. "I gotta score first. See you later!" Patting his pockets, he folded his arms and turned into a puff of smoke. Numbly, Colton stared at the place where the magic man had stood, realizing he'd been robbed. He didn't know what to do first. And what would he tell the folks?

Chapter 13

*T*hree whole days without a single wish to grant! It was only Sunday, Ray thought impatiently when he woke up. No magic to look forward to, no happy kids. He'd probably go mad with inactivity by the time Wednesday came along. At least on Monday, he'd have to go to work, but he saw the long, empty stretch of Sunday lying before him, a Sahara without oases. Even the sunlight peeking in through his bedroom window and the sweet warmth of the air failed to cheer him up.

All morning long he loafed around the house, feeling a little sorry for himself. There were plenty of little tasks he could be doing to help out, but he couldn't concentrate on any of them. He thought about trying to go out and find some of his friends for a game, but he lost interest in doing it even before he had put his shoes on. All he wanted to think about was fairy-godparenting, a subject which would only brand him as weird among his peers. To him, it was so new and so wonderful that he was utterly frustrated that he couldn't go out and *do* some of it. He'd been more than half counting on Rose to be available to go out with him. How dare she have other commitments before he was fully fledged and ready to go out on his own? Television, books, and computer games in turn all failed as diversions. He kicked discontentedly around the kitchen and living room with his hands deep in his pockets.

His parents manifested that maddening, parental long-sufference families got when they had a moody teenager in the house, so he took himself upstairs and out of their sight. He swung the door closed, careful not to slam it, and flopped down on his bed to stare at the ceiling. It took only two minutes before the fidgets set in again. Maybe some tunes would change his mood. He reached for the thumbtack thing Rose had magicked up for him, and Tony Bennett. Rose's invention was like something out of "Star Trek." Put disc on spindle, and listen. No moving parts, no batteries, and no headset. He marveled at the fidelity of the stereo sound, playing right inside his head. Amazing.

The album was full of old ballads such as his grandmother loved, jazzed up with modern rhythms and backup. It was as if someone had designed music around his life. He lay down and let the music ramble through his head, smoothing away the twitches.

At hand, on his bedside table, was the thick manual he'd been given by the FGU on the same day he'd received his wand. Out of desperation, he picked it up and thumbed through it, and found himself becoming interested. The little brown-covered book was printed in a tiny typeface that, while clear and easy to read, reminded him of nineteenth century literature books he'd read for school assignments.

The first section dealt with the history of the FGU. Various intriguing facts caught his attention, but he turned resolutely to the beginning and began to read. As Rose had said, most of the activity had started out in southern Europe, and spread from there in every direction. It gave Cinderella's real name, Ella von Schlampickenwald—what a mouthful!—and the name of her fairy godmother, Blomhilde Franchmuller. The girl's situation was even more dire than in the bedtime story, and he found himself sitting up on the edge of his bed, worrying about her before the part when Frau Franchmuller came to her rescue. Whew!

That story was followed by more celebrated case histories, but Ray preferred to save them for another day. One intense story was enough for a while.

The second section of the book dealt with the structure and

function of the union. There sure were a lot of rules governing union activity, he thought, as he went from chapter to chapter: *hundreds* of prohibitions, restrictions, bans, and other no-nos. It was worse than being back in school. Just reading them made him feel repressed. He found, to his surprise, that he already knew a good number of the regulations by heart. Rose had taught him the right way to do things, made him stick by the regs without shoving them down his throat. He thought she was clever. That way he'd see the point of the rules before he protested them. Rose must have guided a lot of other baby wishmakers before him. There were also suggestions and wisdom contributed by other fairy godparents starting from hundreds of years ago. The one that provoked the deepest reflection in Ray was "Sometimes to grant a wish, one must start the process to fulfillment, and not give the item itself, as being impossible." *Maybe that's what should have happened with that car out west*, he thought.

Raymond turned back to the beginning of the second section, and read the first and most important rule of conduct over and over. "Magic shall be used for good and never for evil." That seemed so obvious to him he wondered why it was in the book at all. Then he thought of people like Zeon, who wouldn't hesitate to make a crippled five-year-old dance on a hot griddle if he could get a laugh out of it. Was there any way to stop a Zeon from using fairy godmother magic, if he got hold of a wand? He flipped through the pages, but found no specific entry under "Evil persons, magic, usurpation by." Well, that must be a big reason there was a group like the Fairy Godmothers Union in the first place, to keep power out of the hands of wrong-headed types, or more precisely, wrong-*hearted* ones.

Not that Raymond thought of himself as particularly virtuous. It embarrassed him every time Rose referred to him as a Sir Galahad, or one of those other classical saints. He was just a kid, but he knew his folks had raised him right. There was nothing special about what he did, except most of the kids he knew weren't doing it. It could be lonely walking the righteous path, even downright dangerous sometimes.

Maybe there was a shutoff on the wand somewhere. What if he could rig it so it locked out any other user, like a computer password? He fished the wand out of his jacket pocket and looked at it closely.

He knew every stripe and dot in the pattern of the staff, every whorl and angle of the star, but maybe he'd missed something. Nope. Even under the most painstaking scrutiny, it was still a painted piece of wood. He flopped down on his back, holding the wand in the air, concentrating, to see if his inner eye knew about a shutoff valve.

"Oooh, look at that!" Chanel's voice squealed. Ray felt the wand being snatched out of his fingers. His eyes flew open, and he sat up to glare at his little sister. Because of the music playing, she had managed to creep into his room without him hearing a sound. Who knew what else she had planned to snitch?

"Give it back, Chanel. It's mine."

His little sister, already at the door, looked back at him and pouted. She was a pretty eleven-year-old, and already knew the power her charm had over other people.

"Oh, come on, Raymond!" she said, in her best wheedling voice. She cocked her head, waggling the puffy braids of hair tied up with ribbons and beads. "It's pretty. I want it."

"I know, little sis, but it's mine," Ray said. He realized with anguish that insisting on his claim to it would only make her want it more. "I mean, I can't give it away."

"Why not?" she asked, ignoring him and turning the wand over in her fingers. "It's so nice."

"Because I can't," Ray said. Chanel took another half step out of the door, the precious wand in her grasp. If he leaped up and made a grab for the wand, she'd tear down the stairs to their parents and whimper he was bullying her. Then they'd surely let her keep it. He couldn't let that happen, because the only way to get it back would be to tell the whole story about being a fairy godfather. He could hear his father's guffaw in his mind, and cringed. "Come on, Chanel. Give it back."

"Was it a present? From a *girl*?" Chanel teased, grinning

at him. She scented blackmail, possibly resulting in extortion. "You have a new girlfriend, Raymond? What happened to Antoinette? I'm gonna tell her you're seeing another girl. She'll kick your chops in."

"No, it's not that," he said, trying to appear casual.

"Then, who?" Chanel resumed her playful examination of the wand. "It's like one of those pretty pencils they sell, only without a point. I'll just take it downstairs and sharpen it."

"No, don't!" Ray said.

His grandmother came up the stairs at that moment, huffing at the effort. She braced herself on the banister at the top. The stairs were steep for a heavy, elderly woman. "Let him be, Chanel. Don't you have homework?"

"Grandma!" Chanel said, halfway between whining and exasperation, "it's *June*."

"Oh, I know that, honey." Grandma Eustatia smiled blandly. "You leave your brother alone. He's busy."

Chanel look surprised. It was rare that anyone supported Ray's wishes over hers. As the youngest of the Crandall children and the only girl, the folks found it hard to deny her anything. She was beautiful, smart as a whip, and so talented it was hard not to think in light of his new knowledge that three fairy godmothers hadn't said a blessing over her cradle. Like Grandma Eustatia, she had an incredible voice that had matured in advance of her body. She sang like an angel. He felt protective of her, but tried not to seem too soft about it. The eight years between their ages meant they'd never been in the same school together. His brother Bobby had started kindergarten when Ray was in fourth grade, so they'd been together three years, but Chanel was a mystery to him. Her giggly little friends hung around the house, playing dolls and dress-up, then mooning away over TV stars and rock idols, while he and his friends tried to find some peace and quiet away from them. In the perverse way of little girls, they'd tailed Ray and his friends, staying underfoot where they were least wanted. His parents had insisted that he tolerate them, since they weren't doing any real harm. Ray's protests of privacy had done no good. Chanel just had to look pathetic and cute, and she got her way. As a result, she had become a little spoiled.

Ray put out his hand for the wand. Chanel held on to it for a while longer, giving him a big, hopeful-eyed gaze. When he didn't change his mind or his expression, she gave in and handed the wand over.

"Thanks, little sis," Ray said. With a histrionic show of reluctance, she bowed her head as if his cruelty was too much to take. Ray pursed his lips, trying not to laugh. He put the wand in his jacket pocket and zipped it securely. "Don't be upset. I'll do something else nice for you." Chanel's face brightened at once.

"Take me downtown?" she begged, jumping up and down. No setback was too severe that it interfered with her permanent agenda of personal indulgence. "Can we go to the Art Institute? Can we go shopping? Water Tower Place?"

"It's Sunday, honey," her grandmother said. "Most things are closed. Why don't you wait until after school lets out next week. Then I'm sure Ray will be happy to take you to the Art Institute on a weekday when the crowds aren't too bad."

"I work weekdays, Grandma," Ray said, almost apologetically. He was grateful to her for bailing him out with Chanel, but he couldn't take a day off work just to bribe his little sister.

"Some Saturday, then," Grandma said. "All right?"

"You'll take me then?" Chanel asked Ray.

"Yes," Ray said. "I promise. Uh, next week." All the stores closed before he'd be going out with Rose, so that seemed like a safe offer. Chanel was overjoyed.

"All right! I'm going to call Mikala. She can come with us. I know you won't mind taking *two* of us," Chanel said, her eyes bright with plans. "And Sophia. She won't go anywhere unless Mikala's going, too. I wonder if her sister Rachel wants to come, too." She shot away down the stairs two at a time. "I'd better call them and make sure they don't have to do anything else that day!"

"Hey!" Ray said, starting after her. He hadn't meant to

make it a shopping party, but Chanel could blow even the smallest favor into a major production.

"Let her go, child," Grandma Eustatia said, in her soft voice. "I'll talk to her later." She skimmed rather than walked, a surprisingly graceful mode of locomotion for such a short, heavy woman. It had made men turn and look at her again when they'd mentally dismissed her for being too old to be interesting. Ray had seen the phenomenon at church, and in stores, when the two of them went shopping together. Her eyes were the same light brown as her skin. As her hair had grayed, she had tinted it that color, too, giving her the look of the bronze statue of a wisewoman. "Do you have a little time? I want to hear how everything's going for you."

"Sure, Grandma," Ray said. "There's nothing going on today." He glanced back at his room to make certain his fairy godmother manual was out of sight. Yes, there was a fold of blanket hiding it from direct view.

"Good," Grandma said, taking his arm so he could help her down the narrow staircase. "You can help me make Sunday dinner. If it looks like work, no one will disturb us."

Grandma's powerful laughter pealed throughout the kitchen, causing the glass in the windows and the pans on the shelf to ring. Ray took a quick peek through the living room door to make sure no one heard it and wanted to know what was so funny. Nope. Dad was bent halfway over the television, watching the baseball game, trying to hear the audio over the jazz horns blaring out of Mom's stereo. Bobby was nowhere in sight. The day was too nice for him to be inside. Ray thought that he was probably up the street at his friend James's. The bunch of them were trying to start a garage band. Grandma slapped the table.

"And the whole thing came apart, and it was shooting dirt all over the room? Honey, that's the funniest thing I've ever heard!" Grandma said, her round eyes gleaming merrily.

"It wasn't funny when it happened," Ray said darkly, his brows compressed over his nose. He started to think about it, and realized the absurdity of the situation now that he was a couple of weeks removed from it. He sputtered, remembering the dirt flying and Rose goggling popeyed at him. "But I guess it is now."

"Darling, every one of us has an orchid story," Grandma said kindly, handing him a bag of potatoes. "I'm sure anyone will tell you if you ask. Please peel five pounds. We're making salad. It's too hot to eat hot potatoes."

The small kitchen already smelled delicious. In the refrigerator Ray had seen the pork roast marinating in a bowl of Grandma's secret herb mixture. The only ingredient he knew for sure was black pepper, because the gray granules were impossible to disguise. Everything else was shrouded in long-standing mystery. The mixture made meat—any meat, even cheap cuts—taste wonderful. Friends at pot luck suppers had tried to surprise the secret out of her, even watched her shop, but they never figured it out. The grill on the back porch stood ready to light. Grandma put a bowl in one side of the double sink and filled it with cold water. She handed Ray the peeler and directed him to the other side.

"Everyone's been really kind to me," Ray said, glancing over his shoulder as he skinned potatoes and dropped them into the bowl.

"Mmm-hmm," Grandma said, busy slicing a big loaf of Italian bread on a battered cutting board over their wobbly Formica-topped table. "Now that you've been doing it a few weeks, do you still enjoy it? Is it something you'll stick with?"

Ray rubbed his thumb over the smooth, pale flesh of a potato. "I think so. It feels so good doing something that helps people. And it's so easy."

That brought Grandma's head snapping up, and she gave him *that look*. Ray quailed, turning his head back to potato and peeler. "It's *not* easy, child," she said to his back. "Don't you think that. It's a tremendous responsibility. You've got the best teacher, and you've got the aptitude, so it's coming easy now, but it won't always be so."

"Do you still go out granting wishes, Grandma?" Ray asked, much more meekly.

"Great heavens, yes, child," Grandma Eustatia said, her

voice warm. "I've been doing it so long I wouldn't know how to get along without it."

"Did you ever take me with you?" Ray asked. There was silence in the kitchen. He peeked back at her. For the first time in his life, he saw his very self-possessed grandmother looking a little embarrassed. He went back to his potatoes and skinned faster.

"I didn't think you'd remember," she said, at last. "You were the tiniest little baby."

"I didn't," Ray assured her. "I just wondered. Is that why you sent me to join the FGU?"

She appeared at his elbow and put her arms around him. Ray dropped his work into the sink, and hugged her.

"I sent you partly for that, and partly because I've been worried about you, sweetheart," Grandma said. "I saw the streets coming too close, threatening to swallow up my golden child. I never had to worry about your mother, or your aunt and uncle. The temptations weren't so close or easy when they were small. Oh, they committed their share of small sins, the kind that pass and do no harm. But, you! You're vulnerable. You need to belong somewhere."

"What about Hakeem?" Ray interrupted. "He's my best friend. We belong together."

"He hasn't been around much lately, has he, honey?" Grandma asked, softly. "I saw him the other day, driving around in a fancy new car."

"Maybe he got that job he was hoping for," Ray said sulkily. In the old days, even a year ago, Hakeem would have been on his doorstep to show off something as terrific as a new car even if it was midnight. "I think he's been busy," he added loyally. Maybe there was a good reason Hakeem hadn't been over to share his good fortune yet.

"Maybe so," Grandma said. "Anyhow, you need a support group that's bigger than the neighborhood. These are good people, who don't care what color you are, or how much money you make, or who your daddy is. You know, you'll always find your best friends among the people with whom you have the most in common. I've always wanted you to set your sights on the highest things you can attain. These people will help you if they can. In the meantime, you're involved in a worthy cause."

Ray listened with growing respect. That was the longest speech outside of a bedtime story he'd ever heard her give.

"Besides," she said, going for the record, with a twinkle in her eye, "I like the idea of keeping up the tradition of magic in the family. Our ancestors used magic in their everyday life. Why shouldn't we?"

Ray grinned. She gave him a short, hard hug before releasing him, then picked up the peeler and handed it to him.

"Come on. Half the day's wasted," she said. Ray went back to his task, and Grandma bustled around behind him, opening and closing cupboards. She started humming an old song, then broke into the words in her strong soprano voice.

". . . Seems to be all I see reminds me of you. Song birds sing, church bells ring . . ."

"And I think of you . . ." Ray joined in, his light baritone less certain, but on key. Joyfully, Grandma's voice took fire and soared up, ringing in the light fixture on the ceiling. Ray dunked another potato. Definitely, he was *definitely* going to use up some brownie points today, saving a very special one for Grandma.

He found Chanel sitting on the stoop after Grandma let him go.

"You still sore?" he asked, dropping down to one step below her so their faces were on the same level. He propped his elbows on his knees.

"No, not really," she admitted, after an unsuccessful attempt to make a woeful face. "I'm waiting for Mikala. We're going to the park. Ray, I like that little pencil. A lot. Could you find out where your girlfriend"—she corrected herself when she saw his eyebrows lower—"I mean, where your friend got yours? It was really nice, not like the ones in the corner store."

She had sensed the goodness in it, Ray thought. Well, she had some hereditary fairy godmother in her, too. "I'll see," he promised. "Meantime, isn't there anything else you wish you had?"

Chanel laughed at how serious he seemed. "Oh, lots of things! Patterned stockings, a dog, a new bicycle, the new Brandy album ... a hundred things! How come you're asking?"

Ray shrugged, and realized he'd caught the mannerism from Rose. "Well, what if you had to break it down to one thing, out of the whole list?"

Chanel narrowed an eye at him. "Why?"

"Oh, I don't know," Ray said, turning his palms up casually. In his imagination, the sparks that represented brownie points were jumping impatiently up and down, wanting to be out and doing. Mentally, he told them to be quiet. "Some of the other guys and I were talking about what we'd get if we could have one thing we really liked."

Chanel frowned, and stared out at the street. "That's a hard one. Sometimes my friends talk about the same thing. I didn't know boys thought the same way as girls. Why?" she asked, grinning. "You granting wishes today?"

Ray jumped involuntarily at her choice of words. It was just a coincidence, he told himself. She'd seen the wand, and it probably set her subconscious imagination going.

"No! But, maybe I had a little left over from my paycheck this week, and I thought *maybe* I'd be nice to my little sister and brother."

"Really?" Chanel cried. She threw her arms around him and gave him a big hug. "Oh, you're the *finest* brother. Do I have to decide now? Can I wait until we go shopping next week?"

Ray raised his eyebrows. "Sure. That's a good idea." The brownie points sat down and put their chins on their fists in dejection.

"What's my money limit?"

"Be reasonable, that's all," Ray said. Chanel stuck out her lower lip.

"You're making me be the grown-up," she complained. "It's no fun if I can't tease you."

"That's so I can enjoy the shopping trip, too," Ray said. She gave him another big hug, then jumped up from the steps.

"Hey!" she shouted. Her friend Mikala, still halfway down the block, looked up, waved her whole arm and shouted back. "Tell Mom I'll be home by dinner," Chanel said, and dashed away.

"Okay," Ray said, to her back. Something attracted his eye, another face watching Chanel. It was a nice day. A lot of people were out, but he was trying to find an uncomfortable gaze. He surveyed the street, checking out all the faces of the people passing, until he saw a Hispanic-looking man whose expression felt wrong to him. Ray stared hard. The other started and glanced around. He turned to Ray with guilty, narrowed eyes, as if upset to be caught looking at a girl. Ray met his gaze steadily, silently warning him off his sister. The man turned away hastily and slunk off.

Ray got up to go in the house as soon as he was gone. He locked the door behind him, and spent a minute standing in the hall, just breathing deeply. His nerves had just taken a wild roller-coaster ride. The stranger might not have meant anything by his admiring glance: Chanel was pretty and young and happy and full of life. Anybody might enjoy watching her. At the same time, the guy could have been a pervert with a gun or a knife in his pocket. Ray had risked a lot going eyeball-to-eyeball with him.

He was going to have to watch over Chanel for a while.

Chapter 14

"Are you serious about that nice girl?" Rose asked, early Wednesday evening. Ray, bless him, looked very spiffy in a button-down short-sleeved shirt and a pair of nice trousers. He resembled a very young substitute math teacher, but he wouldn't thank her for telling him that, so she just smiled her approval. It was a lovely evening, so bright and warm, with only a suggestion of clouds in the west. As the days grew longer, they'd be able to do more of their work in sunlight, which was a pleasant change from most of the year. Rose looked forward to enjoying their walk. "Have you considered whether one day you'll make it permanent?"

"Do you mean, do I have honorable intentions toward her?" Ray said, strolling along beside her. "Sure, someday. I mean, we're steady. I can't think about marriage for a long time. Neither can she. She wants to be a veterinarian, and that'll take years more of school. I mean, I'd support her once I got a good job. She really loves to work with animals."

"And what do *you* want to do after college?" Rose asked. "I know you were a good student. Your grandmother used to kvell about you." When he looked blank, she added, "It's a special kind of bragging reserved for elder relatives."

"Oh." Ray was silent for a little while. "I was okay. I wanted to be a doctor so bad I dreamed of it all the time. Every time I saw a doctor on a TV show, I thought: that'll be me. And when they started to show African-American doctors, I practically ate the TV guide. But I blew it. I goofed off a little, and my grade point average fell. You know, you have to decide you want to be a doctor in *grade school,* and stick to it forever, or it just can't happen."

"I know," Rose said, sympathetically. "The system doesn't let you be a child when you're a child. The competition is so fierce! Well, what else? You're good with plants—the ones you've learned about," she said, when Ray grinned with embarrassment. "Have you thought of botany?"

"Yeah, I have," Ray said, brightening a little. "I like plants, and if I can't go to medical school, I want a science career of some kind working with them. Botany, marine plant biology, genetics. If I flunk every course at college, I could still become a horticulturalist. It's a growing field, too." Rose chuckled at his joke.

"So what, after all the thinking and worrying, did you finally do with the brownie points this weekend?" Rose asked. Ray grimaced. Something clicked when she mentioned brownie points. "You have something on your mind. Want to talk about it?"

"Yeah," Ray said, his shoulders relaxing. He'd been waiting to unload on her. He told her about the man he'd caught watching Chanel. Rose understood his concern for his little sister. Not that stalking and abduction had been unheard of when she was raising young daughters, but it was far more common now, and far more deadly.

". . . And it's worse now, because I feel like I should be able to do more, now that I'm toting magic, but I couldn't think of a thing!" he finished breathlessly. Rose was sympathetic. She paused while a flock of youngsters milled past them, talking to one another in unnecessarily loud voices and throwing softballs back and forth.

"You're right," she said, when she'd had a moment to think. "We're not guardian angels. That isn't what our magic is for. But I think you're wise to worry. It may be nothing, but it's always better to err on the side of caution, as my mother always told me. How old is Chanel?"

"Eleven," Ray said moodily. "I don't think I really noticed before, but she's . . ." He stopped, embarrassed.

"Maturing?" Rose prompted. "Becoming a young lady?" He nodded. "Ah. And you don't think she's taking proper care on the street?"

"No!" Ray shouted, then lowered his voice as a dozen people walking nearby glanced toward them in surprise. "She doesn't even notice anything's different about the way people look at her. I didn't either, until yesterday. It's still a game to her. I know she and her friends are putting on makeup when they get to school, trying to be cool. She washes it off before she comes home, but I saw her once around lunchtime. I don't think Mom knows."

"Believe me," Rose said, with a heavy sigh born of long experience, "they're not fooling anyone. Your mother will know."

"I've got to do *something*," Ray said, scrubbing his fingers in his short hair. Rose was concerned about him. He was really upset. There were puffy bags under his eyes as if he hadn't slept for days. He was almost exhausted with worry, not at all normal for gentle, happy Ray. "Rose, I want to protect her. When I look at her, not as a big brother, but as . . . as a man, I see she's really kind of cute. People are going to start hitting on her, and she won't know what to do. What can *I* do? Could I use brownie points to make sure no one ever messes with Chanel?"

Rose was sympathetic. "That sounds like too much for one poor little brownie point to do, sweetheart," she said. "It even sounds like it would have to be her miracle."

"Well, then, give it to her!"

"Me?" Rose asked. "Well, all right, I'll try. Since you're the one asking." She took her wand out of her purse, and felt the air with it. There were need strings that required attention, but none that resonated with Ray's or Eustatia Green's family aura. She concentrated, following Ray's thoughts back to his sister. The girl was happy, wherever she was. She didn't need a fairy godmother now. Someday, she would.

"It's *not* her miracle," Rose said finally, propping the wand over her elbow like a long-stemmed bouquet. "Her miracle's still in the future. I can't take that away from her."

Ray kicked the pavement with the toe of his shoe. "I have to do something!"

"You're willing to spend brownie points on it?" Rose asked, watching him act out moodily. "I have an idea. I'm sure it would work. Ray? Will you listen?" He stopped. His eyes focused on her. This time he was really paying attention.

"Yeah?"

Rose gripped his hand tightly, willing him, guiding him. "Think of this in your mind: what if no one could ever look at her with evil intentions? That way, bad people who are thinking bad thoughts about innocent young girls *won't even see her*. Their eyes will turn elsewhere. Ricochet like a bullet. Hmm?" She looked at him with raised brows, waiting for his opinion. Ray frowned.

"But those perverts will just go after some other girl," he said, raising his shoulders helplessly.

Rose sighed. "It'll take a long time before we could protect them all, Ray. You'd do nothing else all day long, and you can never get a step ahead of all the bad ones out there. *You* can help *your sister*. Now, make the magic, just like a wish for a child. Every detail, remember. It's a good idea. It should work."

Rose waited while Ray worked on formulating the thought. He stood there with his eyes squeezed closed, concentrating until the tendons stood out in his neck. She certainly understood the frustration he felt. It would be wonderful if everyone could be enclosed in a magical shell that kept evil away. But, she reasoned, if you raise someone in a basket, they never learn what the floor feels like under their feet. Experience was good protection, too. Rose acknowledged that in this day and age it might not be enough.

With a strangled gasp, Ray said, "I got it." He opened his eyes. The image in his mind was so clear he was sure it was printed on his eyes for everyone to see. He envisioned Chanel in a translucent silver capsule that would stay around her wherever she went, forever. *Good* people could see her. *Bad* people would look away.

"Did you picture it?" Rose asked, encouragingly. "How much would it take?"

"About two points," Ray said, as the sparks in his mind's eye fought for the honor of granting the wish. The two victors bobbed with joy. "Hey, I'd have three points left!"

"If it's ready, then do it!"

"I will," Ray said. He reached into his shirt pocket for the wand, and pictured the silver shield again. Inside it, Chanel was happy and innocent and normal. He waved the wand across in a violent sweep that almost knocked a man into the gutter. The man gave the two fairy godparents a dirty look as he ducked out of their way, and crossed the main street at the light.

"Did it work?" Rose asked.

His smile of relief was as beautiful as the sunset. "Sure did," Ray said. "I *know* it did. I feel it. Those two points took off like rockets, zing! Right out of my head."

"They like their work," Rose said, smiling back at him. "So do I. Well! You ready to help other people's sisters and brothers?"

"I could climb a skyscraper in my bare feet," Ray said joyfully, making figure eights and spirals in the air with the star of his wand.

Rose sketched a theatrical flourish. "Then, Dr. Plant Scientist and Concerned Big Brother, find us a need string."

Ray went from cage to cage in the city pound with the small Hispanic girl clinging to his hand. With the magic's aid, they had arrived through the wall just in time to see the attendants going off for a dinner break. He figured they would have half an hour undisturbed, but he prayed the job wouldn't take that long. The dogs were leaping up in their wire cages, each barking for attention. The smell was incredible, and so was the din. Rose stood at one end of the long room with her hands pressed over her ears. She looked as woeful as he felt. Death Row for dogs, Ray thought. The steel cages were so small. The animals had food and water but no comfort. This was the end of the line. Unwanted, unloved, they had only a few day's grace before . . . The thought wrenched his insides so much he could hardly look at the frantic animals clamoring at him.

"I can't stand this too long," Ray said to the little girl. "Do you see Bianca anywhere?"

"I don't know," Mariana said, looking around her with her brow furrowed. About six, she resembled one of those expensive china dolls with shiny black hair and big, round, black eyes. Tears were leaking down her cheeks. Ray knew exactly how she felt. He was trying not to think of the fate of the poor animals here who didn't have owners dedicatedly looking for them.

"How come your folks wouldn't take you down here to look?" Ray asked.

"*Que?*"

Ray hunkered down in front of her. "*Porqúe*, ah, nuts, *sus padres no buscán en aqúi*?" he asked, wishing he remembered more Spanish from language class.

"*No sé,*" Mariana said. "*Ellos no quieran mi perrita.*" She started to cry in earnest, and Ray felt in his pocket for some tissues. Nothing. She'd used all of his up crying when she had told Ray and Rose her story at home. He glanced up at Rose, who nodded at him significantly. He clutched his wand. *Okay, magic*, he thought to himself, *this is for a child in need who asked for my help. Got any Kleenex?*

Suddenly, his shirt pocket sagged. He felt in it, and came up with a handful of white tissues. *Thanks*, he said silently, handing a bundle to Mariana. She buried her whole face in the tissues, sobbing. Ray stroked her hair and waited for her to surface. Her eyes were rimmed with red. Ray's heart went out to her. He was almost ready to cry, too.

"Come on," he said, standing up and taking her hand. "*Las policias* will be back. We've got to look."

The girl looked alarmed. "*Las policias!*" She cast around, terrified.

"Nothing to worry about," Ray said. "They're not here. Come on."

He didn't know how Mariana distinguished one bark from

another, but she must have. As they started into the last row, the girl's eyes widened, and she actually smiled.

"Bianca!" she shrilled, her voice carrying over the solid wall of barking. "*És* Bianca!"

At the end of the row, three cages away from a stained door, one bark turned to frenzied yapping. Bianca, a small white mutt, started throwing herself violently at the cage front. Mariana let go of Ray, and flew down the aisle. She plastered herself against the wire cage, as the dog jumped up and down, licking her small mistress's face over and over. Ray looked to his left. All the cages next to Bianca's were empty. They had saved the pooch just in time.

"Whew!" Ray said, his shoulders sagging. "Now, let's get the hell out of here!"

Another brownie point popped up bright and clear in his mind's eye when they dropped the jubilant child and her wiggling dog off at the small house on the west side of the city. Ray mentally shoved it to one side, refusing to take any joy out of a trip to a house of horror like the pound. He couldn't even work up enthusiasm for getting to fly all the way to Mariana's neighborhood, into the city for the dog, and out again, instead of staying in his home turf, as he'd once complained to Rose. Sure, he knew that animals were thrown out of their homes to starve. Sure, he knew people who refused to be responsible for spaying their pets, or couldn't afford the operation. It depressed him to have the situation shoved in his face.

Rose held out her wand to feel for need strings.

"Aha! I found one that's almost all the way home. Very convenient. I don't want to walk all the way, and I'm sure you don't." She looked at Ray, and let the wand drop to her side.

"Honey, talk to me. You're sulking."

"I'm *not* sulking," Ray shouted. "I'm just not talking. That was a heavy situation."

"I know. It happens. I hate to see it myself. It's hard to take comfort in one little doggie going home when the others . . . well, you know."

"Yeah." Ray looked around for a stone to kick. There were none on the pavement anywhere close. He saw a cigarette butt in the grass, and kicked that, instead. Two steps later, his feet were above the ground and rising. The magic swept them swiftly over rows of apartment houses, knots of expressways full of honking cars, and more houses. To his right he saw the skyscrapers of the Loop. They were traveling almost at eye level with the antennae on top of the Hancock Building and the Sears Tower. They flew over Wrigley Field, a cup of light in the middle of the surrounding neighborhood, just in time to see the graphics on the electronic scoreboard explode into stars and patterns for a home run. He could hear the cheers. Ray watched it all rush past him without a word. Part of his mind was appalled at him for being unable to enjoy it.

"Come on," Rose said, as they arrived back on Glenwood Avenue, not far from the Assembly Hall. But she didn't look all that enthusiastic about hurrying to another appointment. For a change she didn't go striding off.

"You need a little break," she said kindly. "So do I. You can come with me while I run an errand."

"Errands," Ray grumbled. He loped along behind her. His nice pants weren't as good for slouching as his baggies. He couldn't walk hunched over with his fists in his pockets without cutting off the circulation to his legs. Rose walked briskly. Eventually, he had to straighten up and hustle to keep up with her. She turned a corner.

"Where are we going?" Ray asked. This time he didn't even have a need string to help him guess their destination.

"My kitchen light finally gave up," Rose said. "I want something new and bright. I've promised myself one of those combination fixtures with the fan underneath. Ah, here we go."

Ray hated to guess the electric bill the owners of Enlightenment must pay every year. Or what it cost them to replace panes of glass. If he'd been a different kind of person, those huge, immaculately clean, plate windows would have been irresistible targets. Inside, thousands of lights of every kind glowed golden and white. The customers and staff were only dark blobs of shadow. Ray jumped forward to pull open the door for Rose.

"Thank you, sweetheart. It's nice to have gentlemen around one, isn't it?"

Rose sailed past him into the shop. A motion detector in the door announced their presence with an electronic tweetle. The place smelled heavily of dust, polish, hot metal, and chemicals. At once, a beautifully groomed man in a perfect charcoal gray suit became visible between all those lamps, and swooped down on them.

"Good evening, madam and sir!" he said. He smiled at Rose, up at Ray, and went back at Rose. Ray thought defensive, antiracist thoughts at him for a moment, then realized of the two the older woman was more likely to be buying light fixtures than the teenaged boy, and this man knew it. "How may I serve you this evening?"

"I'd like to see a combination light and fan for my kitchen," Rose told him. The man ushered them both toward one side of the store. As the man talked, Ray began to distinguish departments in what looked like a single mass of lights. Formal living room lights, casual lamps, illuminated sculpture, and glowing fountains were all grouped artistically together so a customer didn't have to charge all over to compare items. He liked best a hanging lamp probably intended for a family room. It was a long rectangular box made of patinaed bronze and green glass shades. Then something about the design made him think it was too sophisticated for a family room, but he really liked it.

"How much is this?" he asked, when the man paused for breath.

"Two hundred forty dollars," the owner answered, turning his full attention to the young man.

"Oh, well," Ray said, with a sigh. "Maybe someday."

The man gave him a chummy smile, one that said "you and I know something everyone else doesn't." "Do you like it?"

Ray glanced up at the hanging lamp, and admired the way

the colors in the metal picked up the tone of the glass. "Yes, I do. It's . . . subtle."

"You're very perceptive," the man said. "Few people your age would even notice it. I hope someday you can buy it." He swung back to Rose and resumed his description of a fancy white-enameled fixture. Ray let him babble on for a while, then wandered the store. A girl behind the counter gave him a wary smile in return for his friendly one. She glanced up to the right toward the ceiling. Ray guessed that security cameras were watching them both. He kept his hands hooked in plain sight on the edge of his pockets.

"Raymond?" Rose called to him. He hurried back to her, carefully squeezing between the display of standing floor lamps. As he got closer, that chemical smell that had been bothering him became stronger. He wondered if the man was wearing too much of a new kind of yuppie cologne. In any case, it offended his nose.

Rose looked a little uncomfortable. She moved alongside Ray and tucked her arm into his. "What do you think of this one?" she asked, nodding up at a beechwood-stained wooden fan with five lights pointing in five directions.

"Nice, I guess," he said.

"Good. I'll take it," she told the proprietor. Ray tried to shake loose, but Rose held on tight. He was surprised to see fear in her eyes.

The man rang up the sale and agreed to have the box delivered.

"My neighbor will take in the box if I'm not home," Rose said. "That's fine. Thank you. Come on, Raymond. We'd better go."

"Thank you, ma'am, sir," the man called, as they hurried out of the shop, weaving an intricate dance between the lamps to take the shortest path to the exit. Rose practically towed Ray out the door. The electric eye tweetled at them again. "Come again!"

She led him out across the street, almost under the wheels of a van that screeched to a halt. The driver rolled down his window and shouted at them over the roar of his air-conditioning system. Ray glanced back, giving an apologetic shrug, but the man had already closed his window, muttering to himself under his breath.

Once they were a safe distance from the shop, Rose stopped and took a couple of deep breaths, bracing herself against a light pole.

"Are you okay?" Ray asked, concerned. "I've never seen you run away from anything before." If she was going to have a heart attack, his CPR was a little rusty. He leaned close to get a good look at her in the poor light. Her color was all right, and so were her pupils. The red blotches on her cheeks were from exertion out in the hot night air, not circulatory distress.

"Whew!" she said, fanning herself with her hand. "It was whatever was in that shop. I was all right for a while, but then I just had to *get out* of there. I felt like someone was chasing me."

"I don't know about that, but did you notice the smell? I don't know what he used to clean those lamps, but it R-E-E-K-S." Ray looked at Rose. Her lips were pressed together.

"That was evil," she said at last. "You wanted to know what bad magic smells like? That's it. I didn't like that man, either. He was too smooth. Ecch."

Ray reviewed the proprietor's looks. He had tried too hard to be friendly and suave, but most salespeople didn't know when to back off. There was something oily about him. Ray thought again about the expensive, fashionable suit, then concluded he wouldn't like to touch it, not after that man had had it on. And the guy kept shooting his cuffs, like he was hiding illicit aces up his sleeve.

"Yeah, he was creepy. You mean he's practicing bad magic?"

Rose tilted her head, and gave a wry grin. She was recovering. "Maybe not. Remember, I told you there were natural magicians around? He might be one of them, not even know he's giving off the signs. Nice place, though. I was glad to find what I wanted so close to home. Very good selection."

"Yeah," Ray said, thinking of the art lamp with affection. *Maybe someday I'll get you out of there, pretty thing.*

"Ah!" Rose said, stretching out her arms. "I feel better. How about you? Did the break do you some good?"

Ray thought about it for a moment. The horror inherent in rescuing Mariana's dog had lessened already. He could think of the circumstances with distaste and regret, but it no longer crippled him. He felt much, much better. His natural humor was recovering.

"I'm okay," he said. "I guess a change was good. Hey," he said slyly, to break the tension, "I just thought of a movie the two of us can be in together."

Rose's lips twisted in a maternal half smile. "And what's that?"

"Driving Miss Tinkerbell."

Rose laughed. "As long as we're talking movie magic, I prefer *Top Wand*," she said, and Ray groaned, but playfully. "You see," she continued, drawing the picture for Ray with her hands as they walked down the street, "the Fairy Godparent Squadron, in order to win their lacy little wings . . ."

Chapter 15

With bounce restored to his step, Ray walked Rose back to her apartment. The night was fine and so clear he could actually see a few stars out toward the lake in spite of the overpowering light pollution of the city. Kids were chasing each other across the front of the yards and in between parked cars. Boys and girls his own age hung out near the street, gabbing about something in loud voices. A couple of young mothers sat on a concrete stoop, pushing their baby carriages gently with one hand to soothe the sleeping infants inside as they chatted softly. A male tooth fairy, hurrying purposefully up the street, carrying one of the oddly shaped white briefcases, gave them a quick salute as he passed.

"It feels good out tonight," Ray said, getting a faint echo of agreement from his wand, now nestled safely in his shirt pocket. "Peaceful. This is the best of summer. It's times like this when I really love the city."

"Me, too," Rose said, smiling around. One of the mothers glanced up as they passed and waved to Rose. She waved back. "You have the leisure to observe and react at your own pace, meet your neighbors, take care of little things, without the cold wind hammering at you. In summer people don't get so mean about parking spaces, either. Tell me how things work out with Chanel, won't you?"

Ray jumped. He'd forgotten all about having come crying to Rose that afternoon, and for three days it had been the most important thing on his mind.

"Don't beat yourself up," Rose said, watching his face. "I'm glad you feel you can ask me for help. You know, Ray, you can call me anytime if you need to. I'd be happy to help you work through any problems, anything at all. You have one of my cards, don't you?" Ray shook his head. Rose looked shocked. "You don't? How remiss of me." She pushed through the debris in her purse until she found her little card case. She tucked one of the pasteboard squares in his hand and clasped his fingers with hers. "You're not too old to need a fairy godmother yourself, honey."

"I'd rather do it for other kids," Ray said. "You know, I read the manual over the weekend."

"You did!" Rose exclaimed, pleased beyond words. "There are people who've been in this organization fifty years who haven't cracked the spine! My goodness, you're dedicated."

"Well, I like to be prepared for situations," Ray said, then he remembered something else, and was suddenly slapped by a wave of guilt. "Uh, what happened to the need string that got us back to the neighborhood?" he asked, feeling a little ashamed of himself for dragging them off the scent of a child in need.

"It's okay," Rose said. "We're not the only FGs working this patch. Someone else took care of it. There'll be more for us next time."

"Tomorrow?" Ray asked hopefully, although he knew it was unlikely he'd get two days of magic-making in a row.

"Better make it Friday," Rose said. "Is that all right? You've got two more days of work this week. Or are you going out with that lovely young lady Friday?"

Ray grinned. "I'm going to see her tonight, and almost every night. Stay well, Rose."

She grabbed his hand and gave it a squeeze. "Bless you, honey. Don't lose that compassionate heart."

Ray went home to change for his date. His good shirt still looked nice, but he felt that it was full of the smell of intense emotions and bad magic. He stripped it off and hung it over the back of his desk chair. On top of his bureau was a stack of clean T-shirts. Most of them were adorned with slogans or team logos. Was that too casual a note to strike? Antoinette always looked nice for him, no matter if they went out for dinner or just a walk around the neighborhood. He glanced at his watch. It was just about ten. They could be together for almost two hours before he had to go to sleep. He grumbled to himself about his job, but if he didn't have it, he wouldn't have any money to spend on Antoinette at all.

A raised voice and a burst of laughter outside on the street caught Ray's attention. He glanced out of his bedroom window. Under the lamp down on the corner, a group of neighborhood guys in black jackets were hanging out, smoking and showing off. Hakeem was among them. He must have been hoping to spot Ray, because as soon as Ray moved into view, Hakeem started waving wildly, gesturing for him to come down.

Ray counted sixteen people. They were all Riverside Jackals or their hangers-on. The latter were either drug customers, or the unfortunate kids who hadn't been allowed in as full members of the gang yet, because they hadn't passed the dire initiation ritual. Kids had died fulfilling the requirements. Either way, they were risking their lives.

He put on a Rockers group T-shirt, then slipped out of the house. His wand had allowed him to hide it down the side of his sneaker for confidence. It radiated comforting vibes up one half of his body and down the other. Too bad it couldn't provide him with a solid steel shell.

"Hey, Ray!" Hakeem shouted, as soon as he appeared. Hakeem looked calmer and happier than when Ray had seen him last. In fact, he seemed excited.

"Hi, man, long time," Ray shouted back. Hakeem grinned, his round cheeks bowing out and his white teeth gleaming. Things were better with him. Ray didn't know whether to cheer up or worry more if his best friend was enjoying being with the Jackals.

"Hey, Ray!" Zeon called, motioning him over. The big youth put a heavy arm on his shoulder and drew him into the circle. "Tonight is decision time, man."

Ray looked around at the gang, which closed around him like the claws of a wild beast. He became aware of an acrid smell, worse than sweat, worse than decaying garbage. Evil magic! No, he thought to himself. It couldn't be.

"Decision?" he asked numbly.

"Yeah." The big, bearded man who stepped up to face Ray was Mario Lewis himself, the high, almighty, great Howler. "See these?" Mario held up his wrists so Ray could see what was on them.

Gleaming steel blue in the lamplight were a pair of smooth bands like the cuffs of gauntlets. Ray examined them closely, but he couldn't see how they went on. There were no seams or clasps. It was as if they had been welded to the skin around his wrists. He knew Mario was tough, but Ray doubted the head Jackal would have stood still for hot-fitting.

"Go on, you can touch 'em," Mario said. Ray did. They were cool and smooth and undoubtedly metal. There was no way that they could have gone on except . . . by magic? He glanced around, and all the others stuck out their arms to show him they were wearing a pair of wristlets just like Mario's.

"Where'd they come from?" Ray asked.

"From a ba-ad club we joined," Zeon said, his long-lashed eyes looking more satyrlike than usual. He was high again. Mario jerked a hand, and Zeon stepped back into line like a whipped puppy.

"We are looking to expand membership," Mario said, carefully. "You're a smart guy. You would be a good addition to the gang—I mean, *group*. Because of the way their initiation is structured, we would be willing to waive the Jackal ritual, and make you a member of both *organizations* at once." He said "organization" with a hoity-toity inflection, suggesting he heard the word recently from someone else.

"What other group?" Ray asked. He was trapped. If he said no, he'd probably get the hell beaten out of him, right here. No one in the house knew where he had gone. He couldn't hope for rescue.

"The Djinni, Demons, and Efreets Guild," Mario announced,

carefully enunciating each syllable with pride. "This is the most incredible association you have ever heard of in your life, young brother—with the exception of the Riverside Jackals, of course." He nodded his head around at the others, who all agreed loudly. "They offer you power, man!"

"Power? What kind of power?" Ray asked.

Mario grinned. "The best kind, man, and all you have to do is become a member. Watch this!"

It happened in an instant. Where the man had been standing, there was a cloud of black and brown haze about the same size. Ray felt his jaw drop. They *did* have magic.

"Ain't that the baddest?" Zeon asked, and he turned into a puff of smoke, too. One by one, the physical bodies of each of the gang members around him burst from solid to gaseous. They swirled in a ring around him, weaving a complicated pattern, almost like a dance. All of a sudden, they were back in the same places they'd left, crossed arms held out stiffly before them. They broke the pose a moment later, and high-fived one another gleefully. Hakeem grinned at Ray.

"What do you think, bro?" he asked. "You going to come in? You'll love it."

Ray was astounded. None of the FGU had ever told him the Djin Guild had such abilities. He was really impressed, and wished he could turn into a puff of smoke, too. The Fairy Godmothers had so far displayed only wimpy powers that they could use for themselves—except for flying, of course. That was great. But he couldn't give up and join the DDEG. He had a calling, to help the kids.

"What's the purpose of the Djin Guild?" Ray asked.

"Purpose?" Zeon looked blank. Mario was more cagey.

"What purpose do you need, dude? You sign the paper, and you can flick in and out of existence for fun!" He jerked a thumb at one of his captains. "Baron, get the man a carton of smokes."

"To hear is to obey, mother," Baron said gleefully, and crossed his arms. Ray gulped at the insult the gang leader had spouted off before he vanished, but Mario dismissed it without a single twitch. Baron reappeared holding a couple of cartons of cigarettes, and presented them to Mario with an elaborate flourish. Mario extended one to Ray.

"Go on. Take it as an initiation present," he said.

Ray looked around him. How could he keep from getting conscripted? If he took the carton, certainly stolen from the tooth fairy on the corner, he was in. If he didn't take it, he was dead meat. At that moment Raymond felt grateful that he had let Rose prevail on the issue of clothing versus identification badges. The Jackals didn't know he was a member of the FGU.

Mario was losing patience. "Go on!"

Ray hesitated. Certainly his friends at the Magic Bar would think less of him if he went over to a guild in which they had no faith. It was doubtful he could be in both societies at once, and he didn't want to give up granting wishes for kids. Most of all he had no intention of joining the Riverside Jackals, no matter what fringe benefits came with it. But how could he escape without suffering grievous bodily harm?

"That's serious magic," Ray said, shaking his head, holding his palms upright so Mario couldn't put anything into them. "It's a big responsibility, accepting power like that. I don't know if I can handle it."

Before the sentence was completely out of his mouth, Ray felt rough hands strike him in the middle of the back, sending him sprawling on the street. Ray picked himself up to his hands and knees. A foot slammed down on his back, holding him in place. He turned his head to see Zeon glowering down at him. One of the other Jackals walked up, and drew back a toe and kicked him hard in the stomach. Ray gasped with pain. A thick ribbon of steam that turned into Mario appeared beside him and pushed the other gangbanger away.

"Not like that. He's got to decide of his own free will. The lamp won't take him if he doesn't recite the oath." Mario looked down at him, his eye sockets shadowed by the angle so they looked hollow and empty. Ray suppressed a shudder. "We've made you the offer you *can't* refuse, Crandall. Start thinking. Become a combination Genie and Jackal, or maybe they find you in the river tomorrow."

"I . . . I can't decide right now," Ray whispered, hating himself for sounding like such a coward. His ribs hurt like hell. He felt a stitch in his side, and wondered if one of the bones was broken. Hakeem materialized beside the gang leader, his usually cheerful face stricken. He had accepted the magical gifts without thinking about the source or the cost, of course, and was hurt that Ray didn't want them, too. Ray felt his heart sink. His friend was lost to him. "Really. This is not for me."

"You asked for it, moron," Mario said, drawing back his own foot to kick him again.

"Ray?" Grandma Eustatia's powerful voice echoed down the street. He turned his head. In the gap left between two parked cars, he saw that she was leaning out the door of the house, the light throwing the shadow of her body down the stoop. "Where are you, honey?"

Ray twisted out from underneath the restraining foot and leaped up. "I've got to go, man," he said quickly. "That's my grandmother. If I don't turn up, she'll call the cops."

"She will, too," Hakeem spoke up. He was clearly disappointed in Ray, but still acted out of the friendship they had once shared.

"Mama's boy!" Zeon taunted him, giving him a hard shove. Ray staggered. Another man pushed Ray back the other way, and in no time, all the Jackals had joined in the fun.

"All right," Mario said, sweeping his hand across his throat in a 'cut' gesture. "You can have a little time to think about it, but your answer next time I ask had better be yes. Got that, Crandall?"

"I understand," Ray said, "but . . ."

But suddenly he was talking to no one. All of the gang members, including Hakeem, turned into smoke, and joined together, whirling faster and faster in a ring that narrowed, becoming a funnel cloud that lurched away down the street. As it passed under a power cable, it tore it loose from the utility pole, sending sparks flying everywhere. The cable end landed on the street and lay there, spraying out hot, blue arcs of electricity. It bounced, arching up like a jumping rat, and

struck the side of a parked car, which promptly burst into
flames. The windows blew outward, showering the street with
glass.

"Grandma! Call 911!" Ray shouted.

He heard the door slam behind him, and he stood, staring
at the hissing blue sparks as the cable flailed around like a
loose garden hose. He had to do something about it. What
could he do? He knew he shouldn't get anywhere near a
hazard like that. It would kill him as easily as it would anyone
else. The burning car threw up clouds of harsh, black smoke
against which the blue sparks looked like the effects from a
science fiction horror movie.

The sound of a car approached from behind him. Ray turned
and yelled, waving his arms to attract the driver's attention.
The car, unable to see him until it was almost on top of him
because of his dark clothes and skin, screeched to a halt only
yards away. Ray shouted and pointed at the smoking cable,
now snaking all over the intersection. The man at the wheel
leaned out and looked past him. His mouth dropped open.

"My God! Thanks, kid," he yelled to Ray.

He pulled back into his car, which shot into reverse, made
a hasty three-point turn in the alley, and hurtled off in the
opposite direction.

The car was now burning furiously, threatening to involve
other vehicles and a tree only a couple of yards away from
it. The cable was still leaping all over the place. Where was
the electric company? Ray clenched his hands, willing them
to hurry. Someone was going to get killed.

"Come on, you guys!" he enjoined the brownie points in
his head, "*you* do something! Tie a knot in it!" He envisioned
a big glowing rope twisting around the end of the cable,
folding into a bow and choking the sparks off dead. The
brownie points flew in all directions out of his mind's eye.
Nothing he could do now but wait.

Suddenly, people came running from all directions. Their
footsteps clattered on the pavement like the clap of giant
wings. Two big men, one black and one white, positioned
themselves at opposite sides of the intersection, turning back

traffic as Ray had just done. More of them started directing to a safe distance pedestrians and curious onlookers who had come out from the houses and apartment buildings.

A glowing ribbon coalesced out of thin air. It closed around the sputtering cable, which spat one more tremendous burst, then stopped sparking. The long black snake lay still. Ray's hastily sent wish had done its work. He started to move closer to see. A hand dropped on his shoulder and pulled him back.

"Just a minute, son," said a man's voice. "That's not safe."

Ray looked behind him at the Reverend Barnes. The minister was a couple inches shorter than he was, but broad and strong. Antoinette said he had been a halfback in semipro football just after college. From the strength the man still had in his hands, Ray could believe it.

"I just wanted to look," he said.

"I know, but it could jump again at any moment," the minister said. "You stay here with me."

The two of them waited while emergency vehicles rushed into the neighborhood from three different directions. Fire trucks and police cars blocked off the streets as crews in rubber suits ran up and down, shouting orders. Three men wrestled a hose over to the flaming car, and sprayed it with water. Another firefighter came in with a cylinder of thick white foam, coating the hulk. The big men who had been directing traffic withdrew to the far ends of the intersection, out of the way of the technicians. Water filled the pavement, running right up under the soles of Ray's shoes.

When it was all over, the police came by to ask questions.

"Did you see what happened? How'd that cable come loose?" asked one of the policemen, an African-American man in his fifties.

"A gust caught it, sir," Ray said. It wasn't a lie. He supposed you could classify a tornado as a kind of gust. "It just fell across the street and hit that car. I told my grandmother to call for help."

"You probably saved some lives, son," he said. "Good work."

Ray felt a sudden pinch, like a charge of static electricity.

He thought for a moment that the power had come back on unexpectedly, giving everyone a shock, but no one else seemed to be affected. The only clue to its source was the wand in his shoe, now radiating unusual warmth. He shifted, bending down to pretend to scratch his foot. The wand was okay, but its heat must mean something. Ray closed his eyes and thought hard, and was surprised to see that in his mental piggy bank, the brownie points were back, and they had come with reinforcements. There were two extra sparks he was sure hadn't been there before.

What's this? he wondered, then remembered what Rose had said about good people doing good things with magic. The extras were interest on his "investment." *Hey, thanks*, he thought. The brownie points danced a happy pattern behind his eyelids.

"Thank you, sir," Ray said. The policeman nodded and went on to the next witness.

When the cable had been reattached and the crews were getting back into their trucks, Reverend Barnes's heavy hand clapped down on Ray's back again.

"That's all there is to see, Raymond. You'd better get along back home, now, son. See you Sunday."

"Yessir," Ray said. He looked at his watch. One o'clock! They'd been out there for over two hours. He'd missed his date. Antoinette must be hopping mad. It was much too late to call. "Um, sir? Please say hi to Antoinette."

The minister smiled, but not at him; past him. "Say hi, yourself, son. Am I supposed to do your courting and make your apologies for you? Don't keep her out too late."

"Yes, sir. No, sir," Ray said. He turned to find Antoinette just a couple of steps behind him.

"Her mother worries," was Reverend Barnes's final word on the subject. He turned away and walked off into the night.

"Hi, there, boyfriend," Antoinette said, getting comfortably close and cosy. "That was better than a movie. Just want to get something to eat?"

"Yes," Ray said gratefully. "I feel like I could eat a taxi, tires and all."

"Looks like you could have a roasted Volkswagen if you want one," Antoinette said, glancing back at the burned-out car, now being hitched up to a tow truck by a city driver.

Arm in arm, they went up the street, away from the scene of the fire. Emergency crews and firemen were still clearing up the mess. A team of three firefighters in rubber suits hosed the white foam off the street and into the sewer. Ray's shoes sloshed as he walked.

"Heavens," Antoinette said, when they got close to a light. "What happened to your shirt? You're all covered with grease!"

"Nothing much," Ray said casually. "Let's not talk about that. Let's talk about something good, like you."

Antoinette let the subject pass, but the matter of his shirt, and how it got that way, stayed on the edge of Ray's mind all evening. Magic power in the hands of gang members! Nothing would be safe, forever, if the gangs could wreak magical havoc like that.

More than fear, he felt sorrow over Hakeem. Ray had lost his best friend to the Jackals. At last, they had made Hakeem a deal he didn't want to refuse. How long could Ray hold out by himself? He saved up his questions, to ask Rose later.

Chapter 16

"And it's a high fly ball!" the announcer shouted. The crowd stood up and went crazy as the baseball arced down toward the bleachers and smacked straight into the little girl's hands. As people crowded around to congratulate her on the catch, she looked up into the stands where Rose and Ray were sitting, well out of the way of the action. "Two runs batted in by Petone! Cubs advance by three."

"Yeah!" Ray cheered, standing up with everyone else and waving his arms over his head.

"It's about over, folks," the announcer continued, as the organ played the "charge!" music. "The score, at the bottom of the seventh, with two outs to go is Chicago Cubs, 7, New York Mets, 1. And it's a beautiful Friday night here at Wrigley Field. Next up . . ."

Rose nudged Ray in the ribs. "Come on," she said, nodding toward the wall. "Next up is you."

"Aw, no! I'm enjoying the game," Ray said, settling down onto the bench seat with his elbows on his knees. What a terrific opportunity this wish had been—for him. They'd picked up on the need string of Penny, probably the most serious Cubs fan in Chicago. They got to crash the game for magical reasons, and they had flown in, which Ray had enjoyed almost more than Penny had enjoyed catching that fly ball. What with work, fairy-godparenting, and seeing his friends, he hadn't been to a game all summer. The Cubs walkover looked like a sure thing. That was, alas, rare enough that he wanted to be there to see it happen.

The Cubs second baseman went up to bat. The player squared himself across the plate, squinting at the pitcher. Ray wiggled on his bench seat and wrung his hands together, choking up on an imaginary bat, waiting for the pitch.

Rose, with a heavy sigh, reached across and took Ray's wand out of his breast pocket. She tucked the wand into his folded hands.

Suddenly, Ray was overwhelmed by a sensation of absolute, horrifying desperation so deep it nearly bowled him off the bench. The game, the crowd, and the park all went right out of his mind. He sat straight up, clasping the wand, goggling at Rose.

"What is *that*?" he demanded. "I have never felt a string like that. It's . . . it's as big around as a tree trunk."

"Someone who needs you badly," Rose said. "Let's go."

They left the ballpark, going over the wall at a dark spot between two lighting standards. If some of the people sitting on the apartment house roofs across the street saw them, they made no outcry about it. Rose led him higher into the sky, then headed south.

The sensation of need grew so strong that Ray was continually tempted to put the wand down, so he couldn't feel it anymore, but he was afraid if he did he would fall out of the sky. He wasn't surprised when they started to descend toward a cluster of buildings surrounded by parking structures. Someone in that much trouble had to be in a hospital. But what was wrong?

The two fairy godparents descended through a roof, made of tar paper and gravel and steel beams, that felt scratchy like sand paper, etching off more layers of nerves. When he stood at last on a solid floor, Ray dropped the wand into his pocket to give himself a breather. Disconnecting from the emotion was such a relief he trembled. The wand still pulled him down the hallway. The child calling to him was somewhere below. He and Rose hailed an elevator. To the annoyance of a nurse who got on with them, he pushed all the buttons. At each stop, the fairy godparents "listened" for the signal to get off.

When the elevator reached four, there was no doubt that this was the floor. Ray stumbled over the threshold, following the irresistible force drawing him. He dodged nurses, carts full of equipment, and patients on foot, in wheelchairs, and on gurneys, walking faster and faster down the wide, white-painted corridor more and more urgently until he found himself running. The sensation stopped abruptly halfway down the hall past the nurses' station. Ray overshot the mark by a few feet, and was yanked back to the correct door as if on a tether.

Rose caught up with him as he was raising his hand to knock softly. He listened, but no one invited him in. All that was audible on the other side of the door was the burble, click, and hum of machinery. He looked at Rose.

"Go on," she said. Tentatively, Ray turned the handle and went in.

The large windows opposite the door were heavily curtained, dimming the room so that all Ray saw at first was a cluster of tall square machines. Each of them had blinking screens showing constantly updating charts in amber or green, and all sprouted strands of clear, thin tubes in every direction. Ray recognized one machine as a sophisticated IV dispenser. Another was a respirator, wheezing like an old man as its valves drew breath. The tubes all led to a small body, almost invisible in the large, white bed. It was a little girl, just about the same size as the one he had just left behind at the ballpark. Some kind of square frame held the coverlet up off her feet, and a padded brace cupping her neck from behind dented the big pillows under her shoulders and head. The small hands resting on the coverlet over her thin chest were swollen and puffy from the fluids that poured into her arms from four different tubes. A translucent, cuplike mask covered the lower half of the child's face and the tubes stuck into both her nose and mouth, but her eyes were open and clear. She turned them to gaze at Ray.

Ray took the wand out of his pocket. No doubt about it: this was his client. There was also no doubt about her wish.

"She wants to die," he said, shocked.

"Her quality of life is shot," Rose said sadly. She picked up the chart at the end of the bed and read it. "Not that she had much to begin with. She was born without kidneys, her spine is malformed, she's got a dozen diseases. She's been out of this hospital only six months of her life."

"That's horrible," Ray said. "I guess maybe dying is the best thing that could happen for her." He stopped short, frightened by what he had just said. He stared at Rose, appalled at himself. "But I can't let a child die."

"It's what she wishes," Rose said. "She's counting on you. Her parents love her too much. They refuse to see clearly the truth that she understands so well. She could be on life support, getting weaker and weaker, for another six months or sixty years. Who knows? Her pancreas began to fail today, which is why we heard from her now. But her parents and her doctor have a resuscitate order, right here. They're ordering more heroic measures. They won't help." She handed him the chart, and pointed to a few lines of code and a signature. The scrawls meant nothing to him. The thin little face underneath all the plastic life-support equipment watched him seriously. "It's her life, Ray. Her decision."

The child turned her eyes to appeal to Ray. She probably couldn't move anything else, but even so, he couldn't countenance a wish like that. He made his protest stronger, raising his voice. "I can't *make* a child die. That would be murder."

Rose studied him, and shook her head. "No. You don't have to take care of this," the fairy godmother said, gently putting her arm around him and guiding him to a chair. "We have experts to deal with intervention."

Rose went to the phone next to the bed and dialed four digits. Raymond sat in the chair, clutching his wand between his hands. Who was Rose calling? Was there a terrifying being with bony hands and a hooded cloak that made house calls to cover tough situations for fairy godmothers? Rose gave him a sweet, encouraging smile, then bent to talk to the little girl in the bed, patting her small hands, smoothing her hair. Ray felt like he wanted to burst into tears. He didn't even know the child, and already he was grieving for her. Her skin was pale, with blue veins showing through on her wrists and temples. She had never been able to play outside in the sun, never ridden a bicycle, never had a best friend. Was it too hard to wish to start over?

The door opened almost silently, and Ray jumped as a narrow shadow fell past his feet. Instead of the tall, skeletal figure he feared, in came a small, scrawny old black woman with sad, loving eyes. She had on a worn, faded cotton dress, and old, shabby, down-at-heel shoes. In spite of her appearance, she had the dignity of a queen. Ray rose to his feet as she approached, walking with a slightly arthritic gait. She touched his arm with her clawlike hand, and an inexpressibly soothing feeling passed between them, giving him comfort. He looked deep into her eyes, and saw nothing there but kindness. When she let go of him, he felt the same woe and aching sympathy he had before. Ray understood the respect Rose had for this old woman. She *knew* how much this hurt. She was hurting for the child, too.

Rose moved away from the head of the bed to make room for her successor and came to stand next to Ray. The old woman sat down beside the girl and raised a forefinger to touch the child's still hands. There was no burst of magic, no rumble of thunder. The child simply stirred and sat up to look at the old woman. Ray goggled. He didn't think the girl had the strength to move on her own. It was magic, but was this a good thing? The little girl studied the old woman, with the first expression Ray had seen on her face: curiosity. The old woman just smiled the warm, weary smile. The girl looked into her eyes with total trust on her face. She wore the kind of smile one had when summer vacation is only minutes away, when one is about to be given the treasure one wanted most of anything in the world. Ray felt his throat tighten. He ought to stop this, make the girl back away from that threshold. He could cure her! She had a miracle coming. Why not that?

The old woman leaned over and gathered up the cords of

the respirator, the kidney machine, and the monitors. She showed them to the child in the bed. The small hands reached out for them, closed around them so hard the swollen flesh turned pale. Ray cried out and reached for her hands to take the cords away. Rose took his arm firmly and held him back.

With a sudden burst of strength, the girl yanked hard. The plugs flew out of the wall and clattered on the floor. The chattering, burbling, wheezing machines fell silent. The girl's face became wreathed in a beatific smile, and she settled down on the bed, as limp as she had been before. Her narrow chest rose once, jerkily. It was much harder for her to breathe without help.

"People will come running when they see the monitors have stopped," Ray cried. His voice sounded as loud as a thunderclap in the room. The girl was dying now. Ray saw blue tinges begin to show around her mouth and fingernails. All he had to do was hurry up and plug in all those machines again, and she would be saved, just as her parents wanted her to be. But he remembered her overwhelming despair that had brought them here. The child drew another labored breath, not as deep as the first. Having seen the chart, and the girl's resolve not to go on, he didn't know whether or not he wanted the doctors to come. "They'll save her!"

"No, they won't," Rose said. "They'll be too busy."

Before she finished speaking, the lights started to go off all over the floor. Through the partly open door Raymond heard cries from other rooms, and saw the shapes of nurses rushing in every direction in the corridor.

"They won't get in here in time," the old woman said, speaking for the first time. "It's almost over." Her voice was the soft, dry, gentle whisper of autumn leaves. She smiled at Ray. "You'd better go now."

Her face blurred in his vision. Ray reached up to wipe the tears away, and she gave him that understanding smile. Her kindness was the last straw. A great, tearing sob burst up from his chest. Rose reached up to pull his head down against her shoulder, and he began to cry like a lost child.

Murmuring to him like a baby, Rose led him out of the

hospital room. The voices of the nurses and patients faded out of his hearing like the noises in a dream. He didn't know how long they walked, but when he finally opened his eyes and wiped his face, they were in front of a bench on the lakeshore. It was full night now. Behind them were the lights and noise of Lake Shore Drive. Before them was the light gray, heaving mass of Lake Michigan. Reaching far out to his right was a tiny, thin row of lights like a diamond necklace. He stared at the lights until they blurred into a wavy line. Rose tucked something into his fingers. He identified it by touch as a handkerchief. He blotted his face with it, still staring out over the lake.

"Sit down, honey," Rose said, her arm still around his shoulder. Obediently, he plopped down on the bench. She sat beside him, and waited quietly until he spoke.

"Why me?" he asked. "Why me, and not one of your kids? How come you have to train *me* to go out and save the world, when it's impossible anyway. I'm wasting my time!"

"Because my kids don't want to save the world," Rose said, patiently. "You do. Sometimes the hardest thing in the world is to accept the inevitable. I know it took me years. Ray, you have so many rare talents. You have a heart big enough to care for everybody on Earth, and that's a quality not to be wasted. I'm glad you want to work with us. What you are doing is worthwhile. Never think it's not." She had another handkerchief ready the moment the one he was holding became too soggy. He took it and blew his nose hard.

"I don't want to do it no more," he said.

"Anymore," Rose corrected him automatically. "You know better. You're an honor student, Raymond."

Ray turned on her furiously. "Why didn't you tell me things like that could happen? That *hurt*. That child was just a baby."

"But she made the decision for herself," Rose said. "I *did* tell you it wasn't always easy to do this job. She's not the first one I have met who knew the end was coming and wanted to make it as painless as possible for everyone. Children are almost always more clearheaded than adults are about the really important things. Adults have an overlay of their experi-

ence that blurs the truth. Children don't. She felt the pain
outweighed all possible benefits."

"You don't know that!" Ray said, turning on her accusingly.
"You're just guessing."

"I *know*," Rose said. "I felt it through the wand, and what's
more, I felt it in my heart. You would, too, if you let yourself.
That's why you're so angry. You know you couldn't have
changed anything."

"We could have cured her!"

"No." Rose looked out across the lake, and her voice
sounded very hoarse. "It isn't what she wanted."

"Well, no more children are gonna die on my beat," Ray
said, drawing himself up to make the vow. "Hear that, wand?"
he instructed the little stick. "We're going to *make* them better.
All of them."

"Remember about power corrupting," Rose warned him.
"Free will. That's where we differ from the autocrats. You
can't go against a child's choice, even if you think you know
better. You won't be living their life for them. Once you're
through that wall, pfft! You're gone, and what you did is what
they have to deal with. Remember you learn from your clients
as much as they learn from you. What that little girl just
taught you was a hard lesson in how to die with dignity. Her
faith told her that her time here was done, and there was
something better on the other side, if only peace and freedom
from pain."

"Don't you *know*?" Ray asked.

"No. Of course not. We have no special knowledge. All
we can do is hope and believe, just like them." Rose let her
hand flutter up toward heaven. Ray felt so angry he had to
look away.

"I have to feel I can do better for them than that," he said.
"Otherwise, I'll hand you this pencil and go home."

"Then we'll try," Rose said softly. She let the need strings
draw them back to the hospital.

Ray spotted a dark-skinned boy sitting in a wheelchair next
to a glass-walled office. The child was listening hard to what

was going on inside the room. A man and a woman were talking to a woman in a white lab coat. No, the man was shouting, and the woman was weeping. Rose gave Ray an encouraging nod. Steeling his new resolve, Ray walked over and knelt down next to him.

"Hey, man," he said. "What's going on with you?" He tilted his head toward the door.

"They think I have bone cancer," the child said. "It don't hurt or nothing, but they say I'll probably die." He stuck out a thin leg and pointed to a small patch of mottled flesh on his shin that just looked wrong to Ray. He palmed his small training wand and passed his hand above the place the boy pointed to. The spot radiated prickly cold that made Ray feel queasy. He drew his hand away as fast as he could. The boy watched his face carefully.

"You think so, too?" he asked, trying to look like he didn't care.

"What do you think?" Ray asked.

"Don't matter what I think," the boy sighed. "I just want to get out of here and go home." He looked into the room, where the man had plopped down on the couch against the wall, and the woman was staring out the window. The doctor sat at her desk with her head bent over her folded hands, talking in a low voice.

"What's your name, kiddo?" Rose asked.

"Victor," the boy said.

"Well, Victor, what if I told you I could grant a wish so that would go away?" Ray asked him in a soft voice, nodding toward the boy's leg.

"You think I'm crazy?" the boy asked, giving him a sharp look.

Ray showed him the small wand. "I'm your fairy godfather. I can fix it if you want. Let me help."

The boy jerked his head toward Rose. "Who's she?"

"I'm an apprentice. She's teaching me to do my stuff right." Obligingly, Rose drew her long wand out of her purse and showed it to the child. He seemed impressed by the sleight of hand but, when there was no magic instantly forthcoming, let his face go blank again.

"I don't want anybody practicing on me. If you do it, you do it right," the boy insisted. He still looked like he didn't believe in the conversation he was having, but no strand of hope was too thin to hang on to. Inside the office next to him, they were arguing about life and death. His life and death. He could only have been about ten years old.

"I will do it right," Ray promised. He knelt beside the leg, letting the wand in his hand pull toward the hidden tumor of its own accord. Whatever was in there was *big*, and it felt horrible. In the room behind him they were talking about biopsies, radiation therapy, and amputation. *Give this child health*, he thought, putting into the wish everything he had. He tapped the skinny shinbone with his wand, and felt goodness in the pale blue light that poured out. Somewhere in the middle of the wish the lump stopped feeling hostile and cold. Now it just felt like the rest of the leg. Ray stood up. He'd beaten this one. The child would live and be whole.

The boy looked at him. "That's all?" he asked. "No lightning bolts?"

"Certainly not," Rose said, pointing across the hallway to a sign that said "No Smoking—Oxygen In Use." Victor gave her a grin that showed one and a half adult front teeth.

"We'd better get him down and get a tissue sample," the doctor said, coming toward the door. The parents followed him. Ray met their eyes and gave them the small smile of a stranger. He casually patted the boy on the shoulder.

"Take it easy, man." He turned quickly away and strode off. Rose trotted along behind him.

"Who was that?" the mother demanded in a stage whisper as she wheeled her son down the hall.

"My fairy godfather," the boy said audibly. Ray glanced back over his shoulder, then went on to the next need string.

In the emergency room, a teenaged girl sat on a gurney bed clutching her baby. Both of them were crying. There was something wrong with the way the baby's left leg was hanging, but every time the emergency room nurse tried to take it to examine, the young mother jerked her child away. The police officer writing in his notebook gave Ray and Rose a warning look as they approached. The fairy godparents backed off enough to listen without being in the line of sight.

"Don't look at the baby," Rose whispered. "Look at the mother."

Ray concentrated, his fingers wrapped around the wand. Rose was right. The need string came from her.

"Look, Miss DuShen," said the harried-looking woman on the other side of the bed. "Child Welfare only wants to do what's best for your baby."

"You can't take him away!" the girl cried. She was besieged from both sides. "I didn't hurt him. He fell down the stairs. I told you. He just got past me. The baby gate is broken. He crawled around the mattress I had blocking the door."

"Put in the fix for her," Rose said, urgently. "She needs it."

"I want cases that will make a difference," Ray said, disappointed in what looked like a losing argument to him.

"This will," Rose promised him. "Go on. She just needs a chance."

The nurse had moved in, and with gentle purpose, removed the baby from the girl's arms. He felt the left leg with practiced fingers. The caseworker from Child Welfare shook her head and made notes on her clipboard. Full of doubt, Ray waved the little wand in the direction of the girl.

"Miss DuShen," the caseworker began, severely, raising her eyes from her documents. Her face suddenly changed. ". . . Miss DuShen, you really need to get another baby gate. This could have been a devastating accident."

"I'll be more careful," the girl said, turning pleading eyes from one authority figure to the other. "I swear."

"Nice job," Rose said, softly. Ray shrugged. He felt the need string shrink in diameter and vanish. He took a deep breath and sensed around for the next one. Jerking his head for Rose to follow him, he strode out of emergency, heading for the elevators.

Chapter 17

"This handwriting is worse than my daughter's," Rose said, reading a chart on the end of an incubator containing a baby girl named Leah. "Her heart is weak. She's not getting enough oxygen. Her condition is critical."

Ray could have told her that without checking the chart. The baby's hands and feet were enclosed in puffy pads to keep the circulation going, and a tube ran into her nose. "What's she need?"

"All kinds of things, but first, a transplant. Her doctor is a"—Rose put her nose close to the chart and squinted—"a Dr. Marsh. She needs help soon. There's a telephone number, an internal line. This Dr. Marsh must be a resident here."

"What can we do?" Ray asked. "I refuse to be responsible for the death of another kid so that another will get its heart."

"The magic copes, Ray," Rose said impatiently. "We can see where this child is in the list for transplants."

"Too busy," Rose said, looking over the appointment ledger on the desk outside the sanctum sanctorum that bore the nameplate "Dr. E. Marsh." She tapped the uppermost page, dated tomorrow. "There's not a single spot open on this for weeks. He's run off his feet. This person needs a fairy godmother himself. No, he needs a genetic scientist, to clone him. Ah. Leah's number two on this list. There's a heart coming in tonight, but it's slated for a boy called Raheed. Another couple of days could be too late for her."

A noise behind them alerted Ray to the approach of a nurse-receptionist. She smiled at them with the cool cordial air that said she would be nice, but not easy to mess with. Her mere aura drove Ray two steps back from the desk as she sat down.

"Can I help you?" she asked.

"We wanted to see if the doctor was in," Rose said, smiling back, but vaguely, like someone's grandmother meeting a grandchild's new friend.

The nurse glanced down at her book as if to remind herself, then shook her head a little wearily.

"I'm so sorry. He's gone home for the night. He's in the operating room in the morning." She gave them a smile set in concrete, and waited for them to go away.

"Well, thank you," Rose said. She pulled Ray down the hall a dozen feet and around into the next doorway. As the telephone on the nurse's desk rang, Rose peered back. The nurse picked up the phone and spoke into it, taking her arms off the ledger. "Do it," she whispered.

Ray pictured that tiny child in the incubator, then made his mind zoom in to her heart, concentrating on a healthy organ beating in its place. Maybe the magic would make her real heart better. "Okay, wand, do your stuff," he said.

Around the corner, the nurse finished her call, and straightened a few papers. The telephone rang again. She picked it up.

"Hello? Oh, I see. Um-hmm," she said. She reached into a leather-covered can for a pencil. Turning it upside down, she erased a name from the page uppermost, Raheed's name. "Um-hmm."

Ray was horrified. All his adrenaline poured out through his feet, followed by his blood. He swayed.

"What did I do?" he asked. "I killed a child! What did I do?" He leaned against the wall, feeling devastated. Rose shook him and held her finger to her lips.

"Shh. Nothing. Listen."

". . . We're very happy to hear that," the nurse receptionist said, nodding and smiling. She brushed a curl of hair back behind her ear. "Really. Doctor will be very glad to hear that.

Remarkable. Yes, of course. I'll send the records tomorrow. No. Not at all. Good-bye."

"See?" Rose asked. "You made a miracle for two children. The boy on the other end of the phone doesn't need the doctor. He's cured. The baby will get that open appointment, and that available heart, which, they will find, is of exactly the right tissue type."

Ray opened and closed his mouth. His hands shook, and he clutched the wand to keep from dropping it. "I thought I'd killed a child."

"Good magic can only result in good," Rose said. "Come on. It's late. We'd better go."

"But there are more cases! More kids need us," Ray protested, swinging the small wand across the corridor. It wasn't the texture of the air making his hand quiver, and he knew it. He was tired, but he had to go on. They hurt, and he cared. "There's another need string."

"*Enough* already," Rose said, drawing him along. "You've had it for today. Look at you. You're trembling." She put her arm through his, and locked her other arm across her wrist so he had to walk with her. Ray went along, like a bull led by the nose, but he still protested. Another need string manifested itself, and tried to draw Ray along it. He strained at Rose's grip, seeking to follow the plea.

"There's another! I've *got* to help them!"

"If you don't get some rest, you'll be of no help to anyone at all," Rose said. She took the wand out of his hand and tucked it back into his pocket. He started to take it out again, but she slapped his hand lightly. "Enough. You got the most urgent cases. I told you, there are other fairy godmothers around. The ones who need help the most will get it. Look what you've done already!"

Loud voices attracted Ray's attention as they turned into the corridor of offices once again. The man and woman, parents of Victor, the bone cancer patient, were standing with the doctor, all looking down at the boy with expressions of amazement.

". . . Never seen anything like it," the doctor was saying, shaking her head. "I saw that mass on X-ray *this morning*."

"I told you," Victor said, as if all three adults were stupid and deaf. "It was my fairy godfather. He fixed it. Hey, there he is!" The boy sat up in his wheelchair and waved furiously to Ray. "I'm okay! Thanks, man!"

"No charge, little brother," Ray said, giving the boy a thumbs-up. The adults stared at him, bewildered. They only saw the same stranger who had stopped before to talk to their son.

"He's just a man, sweetheart," the mother said, very patiently.

"No, he's not," the boy insisted. "He did magic for me. You saw. He's my fairy godfather."

The doctor just shook her head again.

"There! See what good you've done already?" Rose asked, as they walked toward the elevator. "So many people happy. You did right by them."

"I ought to be doing more," Ray said. He started to reach for the wand once again and caught Rose's warning eye on him. He let his hand drop. "I've got only so much time. I can't be wasting it."

"You're driving yourself," Rose said. "Don't go too far. Too much effort is worse than none at all. Look! You were a doctor tonight. Better than a doctor. How about that?" She punched the "down" button.

The smooth metal doors opened. Ray hesitated. There were more kids here who needed help. Didn't Rose understand that? But she continued to guide him toward the door.

"I ought to stay," he said.

"No," Rose said, very calmly but firmly. "We're leaving now."

When they were outside, the lower light level let his pupils dilate. For some reason, that slight physiological change made him feel all the exhaustion he had been staving off for hours. The warm night enveloped him like a down quilt, offering him ease. His shoulders slumped, and he shook his head.

"I've been a raving maniac all evening, haven't I?" he

asked, turning a sheepish eye toward Rose. "The avenging angel with the cure, huh?"

"Maybe you went off the deep end a little bit," Rose said. She was silent for a long time. While they walked, Ray's mind kept going back to each of the children he'd seen and helped. He even found himself smiling. People passing by gave him strange looks, but he didn't care.

"You would be wasted as a botanist," Rose said at last. "You would be a wonderful doctor." He glanced over at her. She was studying him, her dark brows drawn together in a concentrated V.

"A little too late for that now," Ray said. He looked away. He didn't want Rose to see what was in his eyes. He was a little afraid himself.

"Maybe," Rose said. "Maybe not. Ray, I want you to take a few days off."

"Why?" Ray stopped short, and Rose overshot a few steps. She backed up, and put her arm through his. He tried to shake her off, but she hung on like ivy.

"Because you're tired. You pushed yourself too hard. I watched you all evening, and I'm seeing you now. I know I told you I'd give you every opportunity I can, but we're not going out again until you regain some proportion in what you're supposed to be doing."

Ray was aghast. "I know what I'm doing! I'm helping children. That's what a fairy godmother does, right?"

"This is heavy stuff for a young person like you," Rose said. She stopped just before setting one foot off a curb, pulling Ray back out of the path of a taxi he hadn't even seen. "Not every wish is supposed to be about life and death. You aren't meant to be trying to save the world, much as I know you want to. If you always go looking for these cases, you'll burn out, and I will not let that happen. You're full of promise. I want you to have a long, happy career, and you won't if you turn yourself into a supernova on your first hard call!"

"I can handle it," Ray said sullenly. "I thought you were

pushing me, from what you said in the bar a couple of weeks ago."

Rose shook her head. "I *was* pushing you. Now *you're* pushing you, too much. You need a break. You're on furlough. This is an order."

"You can't stop me," Ray said.

Rose sighed. "Certainly I can, if I have to. I'm your mentor, remember? I could make it an order, but I'm hoping your natural common sense will kick in by itself as soon as you've had a good night's sleep. Take a couple of days off. I don't want you coming back until you can grant a child a lifetime supply of jelly beans or a gold-plated bicycle without considering the implications. No more miracle cures for a while."

This time Ray did yank his arm back. Rose didn't look surprised, and he hated her for her mind reading, and her know-it-all calm.

"Maybe I'm never coming back," Ray said, snatching the wand out of his pocket. He made to throw it down, but the little blue stick hung on to his hand like glue.

"That is your choice," Rose said. She stopped walking. Ray halted, too, puzzled as to why, until he realized they were standing under a bus route sign. "This is my stop for home. Yours, too. Can we at least travel together amiably? You don't have to talk to me."

Ray stuffed the wand back into his pocket. "All right, because I'm not."

Rose bowed her head, but didn't smile. That would have been the last straw of condescension. He stood beside her, not looking. He studied the tall buildings around him, and counted the cars. A couple of tired-looking nurses in white pantsuits gravitated toward the sign. They chatted in low voices. Ray glanced at them, wondering if any of them had taken care of his clients that evening. One looked up and smiled at him. It wasn't an expression of recognition, but one of flirtation. Ray grinned back. She was rather pretty.

The bus came. It was so crowded he would either have to sit with Rose or stand. What was the harm? he thought, swinging into the aisle seat beside her. She wasn't meeting his eyes.

She was leaving him alone with his own thoughts. As the bus progressed on its route northward, more and more people got off, leaving plenty of seats open, but he didn't move. When their section was empty around them, Rose spoke.

"Did you hear about all those mysterious break-ins?" she asked. "I want you to take care of yourself, Ray. I haven't yet taught you how to shield yourself. You need to know that."

"Next time," Ray said. He forced the words out, and they sounded half-strangled. The weariness was even affecting his throat.

"Next time," Rose wiggled out from the window seat as the bus lurched to a halt. She gave him a warm smile. "You watch out for yourself, sweetheart." She patted his knee and slipped out the door.

As the bus covered the last few blocks to his street Ray remembered that he had forgotten to tell her about the Riverside Jackals joining the DDEG. It'd have to wait until next time. Until he learned to back it off. But how could you stop caring? When did you walk away from the next child who needed you? How did you know? He slammed his hands on the rail of the seat in front of him, causing the last two remaining passengers on the bus to gaze at him with alarm. Ray put his hands in his lap and tried to look benign.

He had wanted to talk about the Jackal situation, but it never had seemed the right time that evening. He'd start to open his mouth, but Rose would go gassing on about her granddaughter's piano recital. What could she say, except too bad? Your friend fell in with a bad crowd, but you're with us? Small comfort. He supposed he could call her up, as she had invited him to do, but he was certain he couldn't make her understand about Hakeem unless he told her in person—and she had just told him to go away for a while. His pride hurt. He'd been doing his job well, and she made him stop.

But the very combination of the Jackals and the Djin bothered him. He wanted to know why the DDEG would let gangbangers join in the first place. Weren't they trying to appear as respectable as possible so they could merge with the FGU? Why take a chance on known criminals and drug dealers? Did the guild think they could reform them? The DDEG must have no judgment or common sense at all. Ray finally agreed with Morry Garner. Kids would get lost in the shuffle for good, and so would the Fairy Godmothers themselves. The whole thing would turn into a magical autocracy with Mario Lewis and his friends at the top of the pyramid. He didn't want this merger. The gangs would take over, snuffing out the best thing he'd ever seen in this city.

The bus nuzzled the curb, and the doors creaked open with a deafening hydraulic hiss. Ray swung up, unable to sit still any longer, and jumped down the three steps to the pavement. It was quiet on the main street. By now everything was closed but the bars. The big Friday night crowd from the suburbs had gone away, leaving only the locals and the hard-core partiers between the sodium vapor lights and the garbage. Ray stumped past the Jazz Club on the corner, hearing a blast of trombone music as if the man behind the horn was just warming up instead of cooling down. Ray jogged a few steps to the beat, until the sound faded away. Only a couple more blocks, then he could fall into bed. What a welcome concept *that* was.

The street took a long, angled curve before reaching the corner where he had to turn to get to his own street, which lay back to back with this one. Ray decided to take a short cut, and knock a good block and a half off his walk. He couldn't go through the yard that lay directly behind his house, because the neighbor there kept pit bulls. He suspected, as did every kid who lived in the neighborhood, that the man sponsored dogfights in his basement, but it was more a whispered rumor than known fact. The white dog with the black ring around his eye was fact, so Ray scooted between apartment buildings and leaped over a four-foot fence into the alley that ran between the backyards.

He heard the furtive pitter-pat of footsteps and stopped to listen. The footsteps halted, too. Ray knew suddenly the furtive sound meant that the other walkers were stalking him. He felt cold sweat run down his chest, and his palms went damp. He reached into his pocket for his wand. The goodness warmed his hand. Could the wand get him out of there before there was trouble?

"I've got to fly up," he said under his breath. "I have to help children. Right now! I've got to get onto a roof, wand!"

The wand didn't buy the excuse. It knew he was off duty. He was a mere, ground-bound mortal, with people who meant him no good following him. Was it the Jackals again? If so, he had the Conquistador's choice of the cross or the sword, or in this case, the lamp or a swim in Lake Michigan.

He hurried down the alley, looking around anxiously for the gangbangers.

It was no use trying to hide from genies. Clouds of color and shadow swept in on him from every direction, crowding him. They coalesced into eight gangbangers, all wearing the Jackal colors. Ray felt his heart sink when he saw that one of them was Zeon.

"Decision time," the big youth said, putting an arm around Ray's neck. Nonchalantly, Zeon admired the fingernails of the other hand. "What do you say to us, my brother? It's yes, right?" He glanced at Ray under the curtain of his long eyelashes. "You gonna say yes?"

Ray didn't answer for a moment. He was afraid of being roughed up, but there was no way he would give in to the gang. He'd had some setbacks in his life, some of which he was responsible for, like his grades, but he refused to throw the rest of his life down the toilet. These creeps were not going to make it easy for him to keep to his resolve.

Well, nothing was going to change.

"I can't, Zee," Ray said, hating himself for sounding whiny, but maybe if he made himself out as a world-class bummer, they wouldn't want him. "That stuff scares me, man."

Zeon held him tighter, now examining his own fingernails up close. Ray waited for the big youth to curl up his fist and punch him in the stomach. He knew it was coming. It also smelled like it had been years since Zeon took a bath. He almost gagged on the other's odor, and it distracted him from the moment that Zeon took that first punch.

Whoof! Ray doubled over, his arms over his belly. Another Jackal stepped right up and drove a fist into Ray's left ear. With his head ringing, Ray tried to dodge another blow, and ended up throwing himself into the arms of two more genie-Jackals. They dematerialized all but their hands, so that their bodies wouldn't obstruct the others who wanted to pound on Ray.

Ray threw his weight onto the arms holding him and kicked out with both feet. Some of the genies, unused to immaterial bodies, jumped backward. Ray yanked one of his arms away from one of his captors. With all of his strength, he tried to free the other arm. He didn't try to go on the offensive. That would be fatal. So would yelling for help. *Pure defense*, he thought, dodging another power punch from Zeon. *Pure defense.*

One of the genie-Jackals flicked out of existence. The next thing Ray knew, something struck him in the kidneys with crippling force. Pain exploded in his back. Groaning, Ray slumped to his knees. The other Jackals gathered around, kicking. Ray heard their taunts and jeers. He just curled up, trying to protect his face.

Suddenly, he heard another sound like clattering footsteps. A man's strong voice rang out through the alley.

"You boys better get out of here now! Let him be!" Ray recognized the voice as the Reverend Barnes's. He dared a peek up. The reverend stood a few feet away, poised on the balls of his feet as if ready to tackle the gang single-handed. "Go on!" he ordered, pointing a finger at Zeon. "Scat!"

"You don't scare me, old man," Zeon said, his eyes flashing. He started walking toward the Reverend Barnes, turning into smoke as he went. Instead of recoiling in fear or surprise, the minister just stood there. His body seemed to glow with a strong, glad light. Ray blinked. The light was still there. He wasn't imagining it.

The gas form that was Zeon surrounded the Reverend Barnes in a ring. It crunched down, then, to Ray's amazement,

bounced off, diffusing into insubstance all over the alley.
Zeon appeared about five feet off the ground and fell heavily,
shaking his head. The other genies dematerialized and tried
to attack, but the same thing happened, over and over.

"There," the Reverend Barnes said, shaking his head.
"Don't you boys feel silly? Go on home."

Zeon snarled at the clergyman. He went back to his one
sure target: Ray. He grabbed a fistful of Ray's shirt and hauled
him up. The Reverend Barnes reached out and put a hand on
Ray's shoulder. The glow surrounded them both, and Zeon
lost his grip. Ray staggered. The Reverend Barnes caught him
and helped him get back on his feet. The rest of the gang
grouped at a distance, with Zeon at their head, clenching his
fists as if he wanted to try it again. One of the others, staring
wide-eyed at Ray and the Reverend Barnes, grabbed him and
pulled him back.

"This youngster is under my protection," the Reverend
Barnes said. "Hear that? From now on, you leave him alone."

"He's not worth worrying over," Zeon said at last. Folding
his arms, he dissolved into a fume. The rest of the Jackals
followed suit, and the whole mass swept away like animate
fog. It seeped under a fence at the end of the alley, and
disappeared.

"Are you all right, son?" Barnes asked, letting Ray go. The
glowing light had faded, but Ray could still sense a magical
goodness, like his training wand's.

"What are you?" he asked. He'd known this man all his
life, and never suspected anything unusual about him. But
then, he'd never known his grandmother was a fairy godmother, either.

"I'm your guardian angel," Barnes said, smiling. "Up until
now you've been pretty good at staying out of trouble on
your own, but it looks like you're starting to need a little
special intervention. That's all right. After a while you'll be
able to take care of yourself again. Right now, you're a little
vulnerable."

Ray was reeling a little. That sound he'd heard just before
Barnes intervened had sounded like the clap of wings. He'd

heard it the night of the electrical cable fire. All those people were guardian angels, real ones, the kind that George Aldea-nueva said didn't hang around in the bars. Ray certainly hadn't recognized any of them from the jolly group in uniform.

"You know all about"—he felt his pocket to make sure the wand was still there, and patted it—"this stuff?"

"Sure do," Reverend Barnes said, smiling broadly. "For a long time, now. Why don't you go on home now? The crisis is all over and it's late."

"Yes, sir," Ray said fervently. "Thank you, sir."

"See you on Sunday, son," Barnes said. He waited where he was until Ray hopped the fence into his own backyard.

Chapter 18

*T*he events of the night before chased through Ray's mind all the next day while he was digging, weeding, and chopping at plants on behalf of the Chicago Park District and his paycheck. His supervisor, Steve Landis, had to yell at him more than once to pay attention to what he was doing. Ray's thoughts kept bouncing from one emotionally heavy moment to another. He wished he'd brought his CD player along to break the tension.

The Reverend Barnes was a big surprise. Ray certainly never expected to find out he had a guardian angel. And he never expected to have his be anyone he knew. In spite of sitting in the bar only tables away from a whole cluster of the GAS for months now, his mental picture of guardian angels was of big, shining men and women in gowns and armor, with flowing hair like flames, who carried burning swords. The Reverend Barnes in his sweatshirt or his jacket and dog collar was nothing like the wonderful picture in his mind, but Ray had to admit that he was a lot more comforting than a remote, terrifying being that probably didn't exist in the first place.

Ray was also worried about the obsession that had overtaken him in the hospital. The *magic* hadn't taken him over, as he had feared. Instead, he had lost control of his emotions. Rose hammered away at her lectures on proportion, and he hadn't paid any attention to them, until he came face-to-face with his own sense of helplessness. She wasn't upset about that. She felt it herself. Ray could see that in her eyes. And she truly cared about him. He was ashamed at how he had behaved toward her the night before. He hoped she would forgive him. Here he was, always protesting he wanted to be treated like an adult, and he couldn't handle a perfectly understandable setback that was his own fault. He was doing more growing up this summer than he had in all his eighteen years of life to date. That was good. He had to tell Rose about his revelation. *After* he apologized.

The sunlight revitalized him, and he wondered how he had let himself become so gloomy the night before. With giant electric clippers, he snipped stray shoots off the hedges around the perimeter of the park. Behind him, Doug Worster pushed the aardvarklike lawn vacuum to pick up trimmings and garbage together, leaving the ground tidy. Ray liked to see the parks looking nice. In the summer, people took advantage of the good weather to eat outside and catch a few rays over their lunch breaks. Three young women, having discarded their drugstore smocks, lay sunning themselves in swimsuits and sunglasses on towels in the middle of the grassy square. Ray and his coworkers took a moment now and again to admire them.

The park was also just a couple blocks from a few fancy apartment high-rises. Small children, accompanied by mothers, nannies, or very rarely, fathers, shrieked and raced with one another, chasing pigeons and being chased by lapdogs. Ray laughed at one two-year-old who stood on the edge of a bench, trying to get the pigeons to come up to him by holding out his zwieback cracker.

"What's funny?" shouted Doug over the roar of the lawn-vac.

Ray pointed to the tot, now flinging pieces of cracker at the birds in his frustration at failing to be another St. Francis of Assisi. The birds fluttered out of the way, then swooped down to eat the offerings. The child pouted and tried to take his donation back. Doug grinned and signaled a thumbs-up.

"Bag's full!" Doug shouted. "Be right back!" He shut off

the engine and wheeled the unit back to the curb where their truck was parked.

Ray went back to clipping shrubs. He was worried about the genie-Jackals. Their attempt to make him join by force was nothing new. If it didn't hurt, he could pass it off as routine. It was the availability of magic to immoral thugs. Rose had told him time and again that magic was neither good nor evil. It did what you told it to do. He was bothered by something else. Zeon's body odor had an unnatural quality to it. At the time Ray had been offended by it, but hadn't associated it with anything. Now that he thought of it again, he was reminded of someone. Who? Now he knew: it was the man in the lamp shop, and what Rose had said about him. That stink was the smell of evil. Zeon and the Jackals had perverted the power they got from the DDEG for evil. He'd have to say something about it at the next meeting of the Fairy Godmothers. The committee needed to report the connection to the federation office, to make sure the bad element got weeded out, or no merger. There must be some way to expel members who broke the rules. Not that he'd be too sorry to keep the merger from going through. If the DDEG was too stupid to know that gangbangers made lousy wish granters, then he wanted no part of them.

How do you like that? he thought. *A few weeks ago, I didn't believe in unions. Now I'm concerned about one's continuing operations.*

In his new incarnation as the protector of children, Ray kept a close eye on the kids who played in the parks he maintained during the day. He had the training wand buttoned up ready in his front pocket just in case he needed to grant an emergency wish. Landis was annoyed that he started to drop the task he was working on to mediate disputes between children. When one small boy almost fell off the water fountain as he tried to take a drink by himself, Ray practically made a sacrifice catch, sliding on his belly to save him. The mother, who had been digging in her purse and not paying attention to her offspring, came rushing up to thank him.

Landis glanced up as Ray came back to the hedges, feeling

a little sheepish and brushing at the stains on the front of his coverall.

"You don't have to kill yourself to save the city money on liability lawsuits, Crandall," he said gruffly.

"Sorry," Ray said. He went back to work. With the wand tingling its good vibes against his chest it was difficult not to be conscious of the children and their feelings. He watched a couple of little girls who were sitting very, very quietly on a park bench as their mother read. They radiated unhappiness. Ray purposely moved close enough to them to try and strike up a conversation, but it took a long time before they looked his way. He waved a friendly hello.

The mother became aware of his hovering, and watched him with alarm. Just then, the elder looked back and Ray smiled to catch her eye. That was too much for the mother, who gathered up her belongings, and hustled the children hastily out of the park. She thought he was some kind of pervert. Ray felt stupid. Maybe he was being too intense. He buckled down to work.

Only real need strings, right, wand? he thought at the little star.

That afternoon, Landis had them dig up a bed of pink petunias that were past their best, at one edge of the park, and replace them with golden summer marigolds. The petunias looked sad, their blossoms ragged and darkened. Their time was past. Ray gave them each a mental apology as he knelt along the bed, pulling up the dry shoots and tossing them into a basket. The marigolds, in wet, plastic flats, were just leaves and tight, yellow-green buds. In a week they'd be a sea of bright orange-yellow, gladdening the eye, just in time for Independence Day. Ray thought of college botany classes, and wondered if they went into genetic manipulation. He wanted to breed a hot yellow marigold that you could see a mile away, like natural fireworks.

The wand turned the air around him into a nest of fine threads with a single unhappy string in the middle of it. Ray glanced down at his chest, feeling for the little pencil shape in his breast pocket. There was a need string that required attention. It was even close by. He turned his head and glanced over his shoulder. There! He saw a small boy of five or six walking with his mother. The kid pouted as the woman hauled him along. They came over toward the flower bed to watch him. Ray saw an easy opportunity to grant a wish, freelance. He'd handle it all by himself. Rose would be proud. He got to his feet as the woman approached.

"Afternoon," he said.

"What are you doing?" she asked, pitching her voice in the way mothers did when they were trying to teach their kids something.

"I'm replacing spring flowers with summer flowers," Ray said. He knelt down next to the boy and showed him an infant plant. "This is a marigold. It'll have bright orange petals. It's a hardy flower, and ought to keep blooming all summer."

"I don't see any petals," the child said sullenly. He turned away, kicking at the basket full of dead petunias. The mother sighed.

"Thank you," she said. She took a firm hold of the boy's hand and pulled him away, hissing at him angrily.

"You were very rude to that man," she said. "He was telling you something interesting."

"I don't care about stupid flowers!" the boy shouted. The mother smacked his hand. They headed hastily toward the park exit. Ray settled back onto his knees, frustrated. There was no chance even to ask the kid what was eating him, let alone grant a wish. He glanced after the boy. Ray would never know now what it was the boy desired. He'd failed as the child's fairy godfather. He wondered if he should run after them and ask bluntly.

A nice woman in an expensive summer suit intercepted the mother and son just inside the park. They were too far away for Ray to hear what they were saying, but by the pantomime he guessed the nice woman was praising the child to the mother. The child pouted, but the mother smiled and preened herself. The nice woman dropped to her knee beside the boy and chatted a little bit. When the mother and the boy turned away to go, the woman opened her purse and drew out a wand, and whisked it a couple of times over the retreating form of the boy. Ray's jaw dropped open. No one else commented on the glistening wand with the peach-and-gold star because no one else could see it. But the nice woman was aware of him. She turned and smiled at him, recognizing another fairy godparent. Ray stared at her.

"Forget it, Crandall," Landis's voice growled from behind him. Ray jumped. "She's too old and too rich for you, kiddo. Dream on."

Ray started to dig furiously, pulling up plant after plant. Now he'd seen what Rose had been talking about. It was nice to know there were people to pick up cases he missed. He did not have to do the whole job all alone. There was a union out there to support him.

"Forget it. You keep saying we stink," Bobby said, as he scraped his dinner plate into the trash. At just fourteen, he was still skinny and small-boned, but their mother was always saying that one day Bobby would be taller than Ray's six feet. Bobby waited impatiently for that growth spurt. "I don't want you sitting in with us. You'll throw us off."

"I'm sure you stink less," Ray blithely told his younger brother, reaching over him for a dish towel. "I know your band's been practicing hard. Let me hear it. I'm willing to change my opinion."

"Don't patronize me," Bobby said warningly, holding up a forefinger. He opened the refrigerator for a can of soda, which he opened with very deliberate motions, watching Ray out of the corner of his eye. Ray could tell Bobby was dying to have him to hear them play, but he would rather have his fingernails pulled out with red-hot pincers than say so.

"Come on, Bobby," Ray wheedled. "I'll sit quiet. The only noise you'll hear me make is applause." He made it sound like his brother was granting him a special favor. Bobby relaxed. This was not a ploy by his elder brother to cut him down.

"You're honestly interested?" he asked.

"You bet," Ray said.

"Well, okay. Then you move the car out onto the street for me."

The Voice Dancers, as Bobby and his three friends called their embryo band, had been evicted from Kevin's house down the block, and the music practice room at school before that. After a lot of pleading, the Crandalls had agreed to give them temporary shelter in the detached garage on the alley. Since Bobby couldn't drive yet, he had to ask one of the four adults in the house to repark the family cars every time the Voice Dancers wanted to rehearse. So far, there had been no complaints about the noise from the neighbors. So far.

The instruments played by the Voice Dancers had all come from pawnshops and Salvation Army stores except for Kevin's keyboard, a Christmas gift from his grandparents in Georgia. Bobby's electric guitar looked great, but sounded terrible. Ray guessed that that was why it had ended up on the Unredeemed shelf in a pawnshop. The rhythm guitar was acoustic, imperfectly adapted to electronic use with a microphone leading to an amp. The percussion section was represented by a couple of snares and a pedal cymbal, played by Kevin's brother DeVon. On the whole, it was an impressive assembly for a group of boys in their freshman year of high school who got by on odd jobs. They had a set of ancient folding chairs, plus six silver globe lamps on adjustable tripods that had once been in a photography studio. These acted as backlighting, spotlights, or just lights to play by at night.

Bobby ordered Ray to sit on a folding chair as far away from the band as he could, to give them the most room possible to practice their moves. When the Voice Dancers struck up their first number, Ray thought that it was a good idea to give them all the distance he could. Put most tactfully, they were still very rough. Only Bobby had a sure sense of pitch. The others made from one to three tries to find a note, unless it was music they knew very well. There wasn't a lot of music they knew very well. They were also very nervous about having an audience. Ray kept smiling, and tapping his hand on his knee to the beat, when there was one to follow. One thing he could say about the Voice Dancers was that they were loud. Their music rang off the walls of the garage and echoed down the alley. The occasional motorist passing through had a pained look on his or her face.

After an hour and a half of torture, practice ground to a halt over an argument on how to play the musical bridge from "Soul Man." Bobby tried to play it as it had been done on the record made by Sam and Dave.

"I'm the leader of this band," he said, looming as pugnaciously as anyone could at eighty-five pounds, "and I say it ought to be just guitar and nothing else."

"It needs more keyboard," Kevin said, plunking out chords that were half a key too high. Ray winced. DeVon threw in a few percussive tricks.

"See? That sounds good, too," he said persuasively.

"No, guys, it's like this," Bobby said, playing Colonel Steve Cropper's riff over and over again. The sour notes almost brought Ray to tears, and he could see the frustration on Bobby's face.

"Come on, we have to put our own stamp on it," said Shawn, the bass guitarist.

All of them kept glancing at Ray. None of them were comfortable arguing in front of an interloper. In the end they couldn't agree on one way to play the piece.

"Nuts," Bobby said. "It's late. Let's hang it up for the day." He took a quick vote, which got unanimous ayes. The others hurried off to their respective houses, and Bobby cleared their chairs and lights to one side of the garage. Ray pulled his mother's car back in, and Bobby stood by to pull down the door.

"What do you think?" Bobby asked, as soon as Ray killed the engine and got out of the car. They headed back toward the house.

"You're getting there," Ray said encouragingly.

"We're going nowhere," Bobby said, in a burst of candor. "We still reek, big-time. Part of it is this ratty guitar. I'd bust it up, like Pete Townshend, but who knows when I'll have the money to buy another guitar? This took me almost two years to earn."

"I could help you, maybe," Ray said, studying the guitar. It did look nice. The body was cast in sparkly gold resin, and its neck was inlaid in wood the color of maple syrup. There were no moving parts in an electric guitar, so what was wrong with it had to be in the circuitry. Perhaps he could fix it by magic. He reached out a hand to examine the instrument. Bobby snatched it out of his reach and cradled it. No matter what he said, Bobby prized the guitar as if it was real gold. A lot of his pride was tied up in his musical aspirations.

"How come?" he asked suspiciously. "Why are you suddenly taking such an interest in the Voice Dancers? You haven't done much to date except make fun of us."

Ray was casual. He carefully kept his hands in plain sight, not making any sudden moves toward the instrument.

"I want to see my little brother succeed at something he really wants."

"This something like you did with Chanel?" Bobby asked, relaxing. "She told me you wanted to do a nice thing for her."

"Sort of," Ray admitted. And he had. Their little sister was now protected by a luminous shell, which was invisible unless he was holding the wand and concentrating on seeing it. Bobby shook his head.

"You took a whole bunch of those silly girls shopping. That wasn't just giving a money gift. Are you doing penance? You just learn you're terminal or something? Figuring how to divvy up your earthly possessions?"

Ray sighed. Chanel had been willing to accept presents as her due. Bobby was more inclined to turn a hairy eyeball on anything that looked as if it might have strings in the future.

"No, bro," Ray said, having provided himself with all the patience he had, and borrowing some against the future. "I just felt philanthropic."

"Yeah, but can you spell it?" Bobby said cynically. "Okay, man, if you're casting bread around, how about a new guitar? I need a studio quality machine if we're going to cut a demo recording."

"No offense, but you all need more practice before anyone will want to listen to it," Ray said.

"Hey, if I have a good guitar, I'll *practice*," Bobby said.

Ray calculated the wish for a really professional instrument against the four brownie points and change left in his head. The total left four and a *half* spots like black holes with bright coronas, like the sun in eclipse. It was just out of his range, magically. "I can fix this one, though," he said.

Bobby scoffed. "What do you know about guitars?" he asked.

"More than you think," Ray said. He had enough *pfft* for a custom job on an existing model. Three brownie points stood up to be counted. "Let me have it, and I'll fix it tonight."

Bobby started to hold it out to him, then again jerked it back before his brother's hands touched the neck. "This is part of a plot by Mom and Dad to get rid of my guitar. They hate our band."

"No. I swear," Ray said. "I swear by . . . everything."

"Okay," Bobby said. "I'll let you have it in exchange for hostages. I want your key to Dad's car."

"What for?" Ray demanded. "You can't drive!"

"Yeah, and neither can you if you ruin my guitar," Bobby said.

People are so untrusting, Ray thought, trailing behind as his brother marched up to his room and set the guitar down lovingly on Ray's desk like a sacrifice on an altar. Bobby gave him a suspicious, searching look, then left. As soon as Bobby had shut the door of his own room, Ray went to work on the guitar.

"Okay, wand," he said. "Fix what's wrong. Make it sound pretty, for Bobby."

The next morning, he left the instrument in plain sight, with a pair of wire cutters and a screwdriver beside it, to add weight to his story of repairing it by hand. He didn't see Bobby before he left for work.

"Ray? Is that you?" Bobby's voice shouted, as Ray pushed open the door that evening. Ray followed his voice into the kitchen. Their mother and grandmother were there, looking at Bobby and his guitar with trepidation. Bobby turned the volume on his amplifier up to five. Ray, seeing the worried expression on his mother's face, strode over and turned the amp down to three. Bobby was too happy to notice.

"Listen, man, listen!" He started to play "Stairway to Heaven." His mother clapped her hands over her ears, but let them drop in astonishment when the tune sprang forth sweet and pure from the speaker, instead of rough and tinny.

"Beautiful, baby!" she said, wonderingly. She gave him a kiss. "You've really been practicing. I'm proud of you."

"No," Bobby explained, running his fingers down the neck to try out successive chords. "Ray fixed my guitar. It sounds fabulous now."

"It certainly does," Grandma Eustatia said. "Almost like magic." She gave Ray a conspiratorial smile.

"About that," Ray said, grinning back.

"I guess I don't stink as much as I thought," Bobby said. "Thanks, brother."

"No charge," Ray said. He was surprised at how much pleasure he got out of a simple gesture like rearranging a couple of electronic circuits. And yet, this was magic, too. It wasn't life and death, but he'd granted a wish. There was nothing life-threatening here. He remembered at last how it had felt to grant that first wish for Matthew, the first time the goodness had taken over. That was fun, and so was this.

As usual, Rose had been right. The other night in the hospital had been an aberration. He'd let himself get worked up into an obsession. Fairy-godfathering wasn't supposed to be onerous and depressing. He was doing a service for children. Sometimes there would be sad moments, but there were just as many times to laugh. Ray promised himself he would keep things in proportion from that moment on. He would never shy away from the hard cases, when kids really needed him, but he'd also look out for the joyful moments like this one.

Bobby strummed another chord or two, enjoying the sweet sound. Then he let his fingers climb over the strings, reaching for more difficult chordings. He tweaked one string and choked a wowing tone out of it, as he thrust out the guitar like Jimi Hendrix. He closed his eyes, and a blissful smile spread over his face. He must be seeing himself on a huge stage, surrounded by screaming fans. Ray knew that in a second he'd start to play the national anthem. His mother must have had the same idea pop into her head.

"Not in the house," their mother said warningly. That broke the spell. She started to reach for the amplifier cord, and Bobby leaped to protect his equipment. He pulled the plug himself. "Use the garage. Ray can move my car for you."

"Go practice some more, honey," Grandma said. "I'll come and listen to you later."

"Yeah!" Bobby said, beaming, as he coiled up his cables like a practiced roadie. "That'd be great. You come, too, Ray."

"I will," Ray promised. "I've got to do something first."

"Hello, Rose?" Ray asked, clutching the phone tightly. His fingers were sweating. Why was he nervous? She'd told him to call her whenever he wanted. It was because he'd been a little snot to her the other night, and he knew it.

"Good evening, Ray! How are you?" Her voice sounded surprised but pleased. He guessed she'd forgiven him.

"I'm great," he said, and realized it was true. "Uh, I'm sorry about the other night."

"Forget it," Rose said. "It happens to everybody."

"Well, uh, thank you. I just wanted to let you know you can bring on the kid with the jelly bean jones. I'm ready for him. I think I've got things back in proportion, and I'm itching to boogie." And, he added casually, "How about it?"

"Absolutely!" Rose sounded delighted, and Ray almost collapsed with relief. "Well, tomorrow evening's a meeting, so we can go out before that, or on Sunday."

"Both," Ray said at once, keeping his fingers crossed. Rose laughed, but she didn't say no.

"We'll see. You have a resilient mind, Ray. Everyone is so pleased with you."

"Yeah. And I'm pleased with me, too," he said. He hung up the phone, looked at himself in the oval mirror hung over the hall table. "Yeah. I am."

Chapter 19

"...*E*very child deserves one miracle!"

Ray stood proudly with the rest of the members and belted out the union song with plenty of vigor. He didn't have to look at the words, because they appeared in the fairy godmothers manual, which he had finished reading cover to cover. He'd already committed some of the most important parts to memory. A song that rhymed was a piece of cake. Chris Popp, in the seat next to him, gave him a lopsided grin of approval. Ray sat down with his hands behind his head.

The Blue Fairy waved her wand over them, spreading silver light around the room. Ray fancied that he could feel the light touch of the magic as it settled on his upturned face. Rose, on his other side, chuckled low under her breath.

"You're amazing, you have so much energy left," she said. "My feet are killing me."

"I'm terrific," Ray said, tapping a lively rhythm with his toes on the floor. Rose reached over and smacked his leg in a playfully nagging way.

"Stop that. It's distracting. Listen to the chairwoman."

Ray stopped tapping, but he continued to drum an inaudible pattern on his knee with his fingertips. He was in a good mood. Three quickie stops in the afternoon, two of them wishes he'd granted all by himself. Rose had applauded his ingenuity, too. Later there would be a chance to schmooze with the other eff-gee-yews in the bar.

At the rostrum, Alexandra peered around the room. "George

still isn't here yet. Does anyone know if he's going to be here? Did anyone hear from him?" The audience murmured "no." "Oh, well, maybe he is going to be late. We'll get started, and he can take up his duties when he arrives. Mrs. Sayyid, perhaps as treasurer you'll act as secretary for now."

"Certainly," said the small woman in the sari, rising from her place in the third row. Alexandra handed her a pocket tape recorder and a notebook.

"Thank you," she said. "For the moment we'll waive the reading of the minutes from the last meeting, mostly because George has them with him. We'll begin." She gestured toward the back of the room. Ray turned his head and saw the black-jacketed punk who had been there at the last meeting. He sat with his feet propped up on the back of the chair in front of him. When Alexandra named him, he glanced up from a bored examination of his fingernails.

"We'd like to welcome back Mr. Guthrie, our observer from the DDEG, of course, and we'd like to extend a special welcome to visitors from Local 36, out in the western and far western suburbs." Four people stood up, an old man who looked like a school principal, a young black girl in very expensive duds and short, beaded dreadlocks, a matronly woman with olive skin, and a young white man with a heroic profile, dark red hair, and light green eyes.

"My, isn't he *handsome*," Rose whispered. Ray nodded, wondering if he had seen the young man on television somewhere, or if he just happened to have that kind of movie star looks naturally.

"I hope you will get to know them when we break for coffee," Alexandra continued. "They've expressed a wish to accompany some of you on your rounds. If you have the time, it would be a courtesy."

Rose and Ray exchanged a glance. Ray thought he knew what she was thinking. Rose wanted to ask the handsome young man. Ray didn't mind. It would be nice to get to know fairy godparents from another place, and the stranger looked like a nice guy.

Mrs. Sayyid came forward and stood beside the podium. "Is there any old business?"

"Progress on the WGA merger agreement?" Alexandra asked.

"We have a full draft of our suggested changes," Morry Garner said, standing up. "They won't like it over there, but in order to preserve our unique quality of service, we have to have some concessions from this proposal."

"For example?"

"Darn it, we need to keep our specific function areas separate!"

"Mr. Garner! Please stay within the boundaries of parliamentary language."

"Sorry," he said, although he didn't look contrite. "I don't care if both the memberships answer ultimately to a single central entity that oversees ethical control, but the training and function of fairy godparents must remain intact. Otherwise, we lose our identity, and the goodwill built up over centuries." He turned to glare at the DDEG representative, who returned his look with bland nonchalance. "If they don't like that idea, then I think it would be better to scrap the whole thing."

"Hear, hear!" cried most of the members. Ray added his voice to the hurrah. Mrs. Durja sat with her hands clenched in her lap, holding her tongue. She took the matter personally.

"I'll have copies of the draft made for everyone," Alexandra said. "Then, at the next meeting we can take a final vote on the proposal, with our recommendation for or against." The wand tapped a demand for silence as everyone murmured to his or her neighbor.

Mr. Guthrie sat up and scrutinized each naysayer in turn. Maybe he was thinking of approaching each one in hopes of turning their vote toward the merger. Ray thought it deserved to be a lost cause.

"Any new business?"

"Yes, I have some." Morry Garner stood up again. "I want to bring to the attention of the chair this bad press we've been getting lately." He took a clipping and his glasses out of his pocket. Putting the latter on his nose, he read aloud from the former. " ' . . . A man claiming to be a fairy godfather robbed a northside apartment building. Police are baffled as to how the burglar got into the building, which had a functioning security system that was not tripped at the time of the incident.' What's going on here? People are starting to talk about us as if we're nothing but crooks and con artists. I want to make an official complaint. Our reputation is suffering!"

Alexandra stepped forward again. "I saw that, too, Mr. Garner. I called the reporter from the *Chicago Tribune* to ask why we weren't approached for a statement. She said she based her story on an eyewitness, a young boy who was fooled by the first reported perpetrator. She has promised to print a retraction, and send us a copy of the corrected article."

"Not that that'll do any good by the time it appears!" Garner protested. There was a general outburst of agreement.

"It happened right here in this neighborhood," Mr. Lincoln said, standing up. "Children who know about the incident are acting afraid of us when we make our calls. And it's still going on! Kids think that one of these illicit invasions is a visit from a tooth fairy or one of us, and their house gets robbed right under their noses."

"Who *are* these people?" Mrs. Lonescu asked.

Ray stopped tapping on his leg. He had a sinking feeling he knew who was behind the rash of burglaries. It had to be the genie-Jackals, taking advantage of a situation that practically fell into their laps. It was too easy. Kids were so trusting that they'd probably lead the hoods to the family silver if they thought the visitor was a legitimate fairy godmother. The only thing he was worried about was if he might get Hakeem into trouble by telling, but he was sure Hakeem would never lie to little kids, or rob houses. He turned to Rose to tell her, but she shushed him.

"Later," she said. He rolled his eyes to the ceiling, and resumed his nervous drumming. He'd wait until the coffee break.

"Well, I need a break," Alexandra said, after a long report on the trends of wishes asked and granted, presented by Mrs.

Lonescu. "George still isn't here. How very odd. Let's call a halt for now, shall we?"

"Seconded!" Morry Garner said, bobbing up like a jack-in-the-box. The chairwoman's wand tapped down, and the membership scattered. Ray followed Rose toward the coffee urns. He was dry. He also felt like a cigarette, but he didn't have any, and fairy godparents tended not to smoke. Even he had dropped from his previous total to about one a day. Maybe today would be when he quit altogether. On that cheerful thought, he poured himself a cup of coffee and dumped plenty of sugar into it.

George's absence was discussed over the mugs, along with the outbreak of burglaries and other magically enhanced crimes. The police were baffled, of course, on how the perps got in and out without signs of entry. A few of the FGs wanted to offer their services, but Ray thought they'd be laughed out of the station house. Most police had enough trouble with ridicule when they tried working with psychics. Fairy god-mothers would be the ultimate last straw.

"I tell you, children jump when they see us," Mr. Lincoln said. Mrs. Durja nodded vigorously in agreement. "As if they're being haunted by apparitions. We've got to put an end to it somehow."

"But who's behind it?" the others asked.

Ray turned to tell Rose what he'd been thinking, but she had abandoned him to go to talk to the newcomers, probably to invite one of them to join their rounds. Ray hoped it would be Sunday. He was on a roll of good magic, and wanted to keep the streak running. He started over to find Alexandra and tell her about the gang connection.

"Hey, dude, c'm'ere." The white man in the black leather jacket gestured to him from the archway at the side of the room that led to the washrooms. Ray glanced around him, but saw no one else. Mr. Guthrie was looking at him. "Yeah, bright boy, I mean you. C'mon."

"Can I help you?" he asked, very politely. Here it came, the request for unity, a bid to help the DDEG join up with the FGU. Fat chance, he thought. He gave Guthrie a quick once-over, taking in greasy hair, black jeans, new Sports Figure high-top sneakers, a greasy T-shirt, and the jacket. He wasn't going out of his way toward sartorial splendor for the sake of the FGU, but he also wasn't wearing any insignia or colors. So he might not necessarily be a gangbanger. It just seemed as if the DDEG admitted grungy types. "Would you like a cup of coffee?"

"No, man, I wanted to talk to you in private." Guthrie glanced over Ray's shoulder to make certain no one was approaching them. "Look," he asked, "what are you doing in a group like this?"

"What am I doing?" Ray echoed. "I'm helping kids. I like it. What are *you* doing with the Djin?"

"You don't look feebleminded, man," Guthrie said, shaking his head. "A young guy like you should be more on the ball."

This discourse was beginning to border on insult and didn't seem to be going in the direction Ray had predicted. He folded his arms and loomed over the visitor.

"What exactly are you getting at?" he asked, suspiciously.

Guthrie wiped his nose with the back of his hand and leaned closer in a conspiratorial manner. Ray leaned back. Chris Popp had been right about the guy's BO.

"Hey, bro, you've got to get out of this organization. They're *using* you. Word is that you're just a milk cow to them. You know about these brownie points? Uh-huh," he said, as Ray nodded slowly. "Well, you look out. You get a lot of these brownie points, and slurp! they're gone."

"Oh, come on," Ray said, glancing at the other members. Some of them looked their way curiously over their coffee cups, wondering what the observer was saying. Ray wanted to shout out that the guy was telling him lies and trying to subvert his loyalty. "They told me my brownie points were mine, for use as I saw fit. Nobody's going to take them away."

"No, I mean it. This is the *word*," Guthrie said, in a low, intense voice. "Everywhere but here, that is. You're getting led by the nose. In no time, you'll be jumping when they call. These brownie points are in a pool, see, and some of the bigwigs are draining it dry at their end. Anything you earn is available to them, and when you're not looking, they'll sweep you clean."

Ray immediately checked his mental piggy bank. "They're still there, man," he said, scornfully. "You don't know what you're talking about."

"Yeah," the visitor grinned. "Maybe they're with you now, but they won't be later. Wait and see. It's happened in a bunch of other cities. Some of the bigwigs use everyone else as a 'personal pixie dust repository.' Think about it. I mean, that guy, George. Hasn't been around lately, right? I bet he had his fingers in the cash register. You ought to check. See if anyone else is missing a few, huh? He probably had access to thousands. Maybe he's on a South Sea island somewhere he bought." Cocking a finger like a gun, he fired an imaginary round at Ray, and walked off. "See you, bro."

"Boy, he is a jerk, isn't he?" the visiting fairy godfather from the western suburbs said, coming over. Ray shook his head disgustedly after Guthrie. The man had managed to shake his confidence by starting a niggle of doubt deep inside him, where he had never doubted before. It was a matter he'd have to consider in private. He turned apologetically to the visitor.

"Yeah," Ray said. "Not my favorite person, but he had some things to say." What bothered Ray was that the lies sounded plausible. Could he have been set up for eventual betrayal? Surely not by his own grandmother!

The visitor stuck out a hand. "Doyle," he said. "Jeff Doyle."

"Ray Crandall. Nice to meet you," Ray said.

"My God, you people look good here," Jeff said, casting a quick glance around at the members, who were circulating with coffee and complaints, and ended by smiling at Ray's tie. "I mean, you can't believe what crummy clothes some people show up in for meetings out in our neck of the woods. Or for missions, either. You'd think they were going to wash the car, not fulfill a little kid's fondest dream."

Ray scowled, trying to remember something he'd heard on his first visit to the Magic Bar. "You're from out west, right? You weren't the one who granted a car to a poor kid, were you?"

Jeff Doyle grimaced. "No. That was some babe-ette with mall hair who was admitted to the union because her *mother* had been in the union. A fine fairy godmother, too. Her daughter is a dip. She just went ahead and did what she thought that guy wanted, not what he asked for. Not really. It was a mess. We're all walking on tiptoe, now, trying to keep out of the papers until the scandal blows over."

"Too bad," Ray said, meaning it.

"Yeah, well," Jeff said dismissively. "Say, your partner was talking to me about coming out on patrol with the two of you, maybe tomorrow?" he asked, smiling his earnest smile. "I'd really like it, but she said it was up to you."

"Yes, sure," Ray said. He knew he sounded lukewarm, but Guthrie's words were playing over and over again in the back of his mind.

"If that's all right, then," Jeff said, sounding uncertain. "She told me to come here after dinner tomorrow evening."

"Yes!" Ray exclaimed, then lowered his voice. "Sorry. I've got a few things on my mind. That'd be fine with me."

"No problem," Jeff said, giving him a friendly slap on the back. "Hey, Ms. Sennett is calling us to order again. I wish our group had some structure. You people are lucky."

Ray wondered through the rest of the meeting whether it was possible that he had put his trust in the wrong people. Perhaps Grandma Eustatia had never been robbed of her brownie points. It would take a stronger mind than his to rip off that formidable woman. But he had never seen in anyone's eyes the kind of furtive look they got when they were ripping a person off. These people were so sincere they'd cheat themselves to help another. Look at the way Rose was always giving up a quarter here, a dollar there, to help put the finishing touches on a wish. His fears gradually tapered off, but did not disappear entirely. Was one gang just like another?

Speed waited until the meeting had started up again before he slipped away to the telephones.

"Yes, sir, it's me," he said, as soon as Froister picked up.

There was a pause and a click, as the djin-master on the other end waved to his cashier to hang up her extension.

"Well?" he said, in his slightly nasal voice.

"They're still not interested in doing this peaceable," Speed said. His voice echoed in the small hallway, and he lowered it. "I think that even if the main federation ratifies that paper, they may still refuse to go along."

"No!" Froister said. "I don't want to have to go to Milwaukee to connect. We will have to do this the hard way."

"Good," Speed said, hearing the call to action. "I'll get the guys."

"No. I will send them to you."

Speed heard footsteps in the hallway. "Someone's coming," he said. "I'd better go."

He hung up the phone, crossed his arms, and blinked himself out of the hall.

"Hello?" Chris Popp walked into the dark corridor. "Are you going to be on the telephone long? I need to make a call . . ." He squinted at the telephone. There was no one there. "Funny, I thought I heard a voice."

Chapter 20

*T*he magical thefts were the subject of conversation throughout the magical community. The Guardian Angels were
already in the Magic Bar by the time the meeting broke up.
Ray heard them bragging while he waited for Edwin the
bartender to pour pitchers of beer and soda.

"Yeah," said a big-shouldered black man loudly enough to
be heard halfway across the room, "we've taken care of a
dozen attempted robberies. There is some mighty bad magic
around here, but we'll keep it under control." The others
raised their glasses to one another, and they drank. Ray made
a face, and Edwin grinned at him.

"Pay no attention," he said.

"My protective wards at Tiffany's have shown no fewer
than a thousand attempts at penetration," said a female GA,
settling back in her chair and resting her elbows along the
top rail. "Those creeps ought to know that they can't get past
the power of good!"

There was a lot of hearty laughter as Ray shouldered the
tray of drinks and carried it back to the fairy godparents' usual
table.

Alexandra was talking about the same thing. ". . . I've
consulted the other affiliate groups around the area. Urbano
of the Tooth Fairies, Froister of the DDEG, Mrs. Washington
of the House Brownies, Lucarnoff of the Guardian Angels,
Pinkwater of the Sandmen. . . . No one knows a thing. Nor

do they know who's spreading the rumors that the group committing these crimes is the FGU."

"Huh! At least they're not doubting our magic," Rose said, accepting a glass of soda from Ray.

Garner cupped one hand over the side of his face, and glanced back at the Guardian Angels, who were still loudly congratulating one another on their heroics. "You know, if it was me, I'd just make something up, to keep those nitwits running around the city." He and Ray exchanged a conspiratorial grin.

"So how are you doing, son?" Mr. Lincoln asked, looking up as Ray gave him a glass of beer.

"He's a prodigy," Rose said proudly. "I've had some good pupils in my time, but this young man! This is a natural wonder. He creates, he has humility, he has empathy, and most important, he bounces back."

"Aw, Rose." Ray was embarrassed at her praise, but it meant a lot to him. He felt a warm glow inside, and the wand answered with its vibes of goodness. The others smiled at him.

"You have no idea how important resilience is," Alexandra told him seriously. "I've had fairy godparents turn in their wands when they could not cope with the job." Ray looked around. All the eyes were sympathetic and sincere.

"You all know about . . . that one child," he said. Everyone nodded, still watching him. "I'm okay now."

"It's rough, kid," Morry said, slapping him on the back. "But it's not all low spots, is it? And it's worth it. Don't you feel that?"

Suddenly, the doubt that Guthrie had engendered came back. Ray had to gulp half a glass of cola to swallow his concerns.

"I sure do," he said. "I wish I could get Hakeem into this. He's my best friend, and much smarter than I am."

"I don't believe *that*," Rose interrupted him.

"Well, he is," Ray said. "Boy, the two of us, we could cover half a city at night." The others chuckled, but Ray started to like the idea. Yeah, that might straighten Hakeem out, having

a really good cause to espouse. He already believed in the
magic. If Hakeem could be brought into a good gang, not an
evil one, then he could belong without destroying himself.
He might even get back to the way he used to be. Then Ray
remembered Speed's words, suggesting a pattern of hidden
exploitation. He took another sip of cola, and almost choked
when he felt his throat was closed. *Stop that*, he told himself.
Relax. You've got no reason to believe him. He's sowing
discord on purpose!

"How about that lovely girl of yours?" Rose asked, inter-
rupting his thoughts. "Wouldn't she make a wonderful fairy
godmother?" Ray hesitated. "Oh, come on. You were willing
to support her so she could finish veterinary school."

"It's like this," Ray said, very sheepishly. "I'm a modern
guy, right? But I'm still a guy. It's okay if we're not rivals,
but if we went head to head on the same job—she'd probably
be better at it than me, right away. I'm not sure how I could
take that."

"You need a shot of self-esteem, sonny," Morry Garner
said. "But if that's the way you feel, then you're right. But
after you're married and the kids start coming, you'll have
to tell her why you're going out nights, or there'll be hell to
pay."

"Oh, I'd *tell* her," Ray said unhappily. "Ah, damn, I guess
I've just got to learn to deal with it if she wants to join."

"There, you really are a modern man," Alexandra said
encouragingly. "I couldn't imagine my father saying anything
like that. My husband has *learned*, but it took time." The
others laughed.

"I don't think it's anything you'll have to worry about,"
Rose said confidently. "Besides, that girl loves you too much
to make you take a backseat, even if she was better at something than you."

"I've got to tell you something," Ray blurted out. "I know
who's behind the burglaries." And he told them about the
genie-Jackals, the stolen box of cigarettes, and the fire on his
street. "They haven't bragged about it when I've been around,
but I'll bet anything they're the ones who are responsible."

"I told you so," Morry Garner said, raising his eyebrows at Mrs. Durja.

"I tell you it is only the local chapter," Mrs. Durja said furiously.

"George would laugh," Morry said. "The Guardian Angels should have detected something like that, but it took one of our own to discover the truth."

"You were wise to tell us, Ray," Alexandra said brusquely. She was upset, though not at him. "Thank you. I'll take it up with Albert Froister, in person. Damn him for lying through his smooth, slimy teeth. He must have known all the time. I'm going to take this up with headquarters. The fairy fairies are going to want to gut Mr. Froister."

"Perhaps he could not control a fringe element of his membership, and was ashamed to tell you," Mrs. Durja said.

"That's impossible," Alexandra said. "You know the terms of Djin membership. The guildmaster's authority is absolute."

"That puts an end to any silly blather about a merger," Morry Garner said with satisfaction. Mrs. Durja shot him an angry look. "Well, you can't expect us to condone criminal activity. This has to be straightened out in the DDEG headquarters."

"I'm still worried about George," she said. "It is not like him to miss meetings. He's the most responsible person I know."

"He's never missed a meeting," Mr. Lincoln said. "Not in forty years."

"Maybe he's sick," Mrs. Durja suggested, looking worried. "I will call him at home. His wife, Estrellita, will tell me how he is."

"Oh, well. He'll have to conduct the next meeting," Alexandra said. "I won't be here. He's known that for weeks. My family and I are going up to Door County for a week. We leave next Friday at noon. If we drive like the wind, we'll get there in time for the fireworks. I'd better get going, now."

"Enjoy!" everyone chorused. "It's lovely up there," Rose added.

"That little bit of luck'll get you there on time," Mr. Lincoln said, with a wink.

"I hope so." Alexandra pushed away from the table and picking up her purse. "I'd better get home now. I have a genie to beard in the morning."

"There's one of them now," Speed said. It was uncanny how the people just kind of popped into existence on an empty street full of vacant stores. He peered at her. "Hey, we've hit the jackpot. That's the chairwoman. Cool. We're starting at the top." He signaled over his shoulder at the alley full of shadows.

"Let me go!" Alexandra screamed. "Let go, you . . . !"

Her words were left behind on the street with her purse and one of her shoes as she was surrounded by a gang of ill-dressed teenagers. She managed to get a wrist free, and tried to turn and run, but she was no longer on the street. Alexandra was enveloped by a stinking black cloud, then suddenly she was surrounded by brown cardboard cartons printed with codes in black, block letters. She put out her hands to feel them. They were real. She had been kidnaped by magic. But by whom? And where was she?

"Are you all right?" a familiar voice asked. Alexandra spun on her bare foot.

"George!" There he was, little round eyeglasses and all. She limped to him, holding out her hands. His usually neat shirt and trousers were wrinkled, and his beard had grown out, scruffy and graying. He came to meet her, glaring defiance at the pair of juvenile guards who stood on the edge of the cleared space. His handclasp was reassuringly strong.

She looked around at the wall of boxes surrounding them. They were arranged to leave a large, empty square. To one side was a small cot and a tray table. A pair of shoes was neatly placed underneath the cot. Alexandra glanced down. George was in his stocking feet, and his toenails were beginning to show through the thin, knit fabric.

"How long have you been here?" Alexandra asked, astounded.

"Since the night of the last meeting," George said. "I couldn't fight them off. Too many of them. They wanted the membership list from my briefcase, but they got me along with it. Where did they get you?"

"I was kidnapped right outside the bar," Alexandra said. "They were waiting for me. I can't believe the Guardian Angels didn't sense a thing either time!"

"Well, Alexandra," George said, and she saw a glint of dark humor in his eyes. "I told you those damned gas-bags weren't any good."

"That's exactly what Morry Garner said you'd say," Alexandra said, reassured that his imprisonment hadn't done him any harm. "Who are these people?"

"The DDEG," George said, with a sigh. "Looks like Morry was right again."

"What? What is this place? What's in all those boxes?" Alexandra asked.

"Lamps," George laughed bitterly. "Appropriate, isn't it? Welcome to Enlightenment. Genie Central."

"What do they want with *us*?"

"They want brownie points," George said wearily.

"What?" Alexandra exclaimed. "They don't get brownie points for kidnapping."

"No, they want *ours*."

Alexandra put her hands on her hips. "What for? Their magic is intrinsically more powerful than ours. They grant three wishes at a throw ... Oh," she said, light dawning. "They want to wish themselves free of the lamp. Not in the ordinary way, but with all the fringies still attached."

"Exactly," Albert Froister said, appearing in a puff of smoke beside them. Alexandra coughed and batted a hand to clear the air. The guildmaster smelled terrible. It was the stench of evil. Young Ray Crandall had given the FGU an important piece of information, but too late to do her any good. "And the sooner you and your members turn yours over to me, the sooner you can leave."

"Oh, nonsense," Alexandra said, picturing an infinity of empty suns in her mind. There wasn't enough in the whole union pool to even start the process. "Do you know how many brownie points it would take to break the fundamental agreement between a genie and his lamp? Even *one* genie?"

"No," Froister said. "Tell me." He leaned closer, his eyes gleamed with a frightening light. Alexandra was terrified. The man had gone absolutely mad. Then her native obduracy took over, and she crossed her arms in defiance. She only looked like a fashion doll. She was not malleable by threat.

"I won't tell you," she said, her voice very calm. "That is not a legitimate question. And this is not a legitimate way to ask me. Mr. Froister, if I had to think of one way which would be nonconducive to getting my cooperation, this would be close to the top of the list."

Froister had evidently come to the same conclusion. He took her arm, led her to the cot and gestured for her to sit down. She frowned as he knelt beside her.

"Mrs. Sennett, as you have guessed, we need your union's pool of free magic to liberate our membership from our traditional bond," he said, sliding his cuffs down over his wristbands. "It has become onerous, and we crave relief. I am making a formal request for cooperation between two affiliated organizations."

Alexandra laughed. "That's impossible. Why, it would take—" She stopped short as Froister held up a warning hand.

"Just one moment, please," he said. He turned to the young apple-cheeked guard and taller, broader, rougher-looking guard standing close by. "Leave us now."

They vanished in puffs of smoke, wafting upward into the rafters of the high ceiling. "All the way!" Froister shouted. In the corner of the room, Alexandra saw the two small clouds start with surprise. She hadn't spotted them, but Froister must know all the tricks of his trade. The two youths vanished completely from the warehouse, and Froister returned his attention to his captives.

"Please go on," he said.

"Not a chance," Alexandra said, folding her arms. "Section

119 of the manual says that we cannot be coerced out of any benefit which may accrue naturally in the course of our duties, and RULE ONE says magic cannot be used for evil."

"What makes you think we'd use magic for evil?" Froister asked nervously.

"Because this place stinks of it," George put in. "As I have been telling you for a week. In fact, it's getting worse. If you were ever doing your job properly, you're not now. I bet you're behind all those robberies. And rumors!"

"He is," Alexandra said, as Froister pantomimed innocence. "I've had information from . . . a reliable source. Whether he is aware of it or not, he's accruing their form of brownie points, and they smell of evil!"

Froister was not inclined to implicate himself. He smiled nervously, and stood up. "Well, you'll stay here until you cooperate," he said. "I can't let you go now." He vanished in the characteristic roiling fume. Alexandra jumped up to look for him, but he had disappeared thoroughly. In his place, the two young guards rematerialized, and took up sentry posts at opposite corners of the square. Alexandra approached the younger of the two. He looked as if normally he was good-natured, and he seemed frightened.

"Young man, let me out of here."

"I can't, ma'am," he said apologetically. He stuck a hand out to her. She reached for it, but her hand bounced off an invisible barrier. Perhaps it was only at shoulder level. Alexandra tested the air at different heights, reaching up on her toes, but the invisible wall extended everywhere.

"He wished on me," the boy whispered, his face hollow under his round cheeks. "We can get in, but you can't get out."

"My poor child," Alexandra said. If anyone really needed a wish at that moment, it was this unwilling young guard. She'd have done it in a moment, but she was suffering from a double loss at that moment, her freedom and her wand. It wasn't this child's fault. She smiled kindly at him, and went back to the cot. George reached up and patted her hand.

"They took my wand," Alexandra said, feeling woebegone as a tot.

"They took mine, too. First thing," George said. "They don't want us communicating with the outside world at all. And I've tried, believe me. I'm sure my wife is frantic."

"My husband and children are going to go mad," Alexandra exclaimed. "And so am I! They can't keep us here indefinitely."

George sighed. "They can. They have."

"Will they at least feed us?" Alexandra asked.

"Oh, yes," George reassured her. "Food's pretty good, really. Three times a day. You have to make specific requests, though. Our young jailers," he nodded to the young men, "haven't got the slightest idea of what constitutes proper nutrition. Two mornings running, they brought me cupcakes and cola for breakfast."

"Yuck." Alexandra looked at the empty square. "We have to think of a way to get out of here!"

George lifted his hands helplessly. "If you have suggestions, I'll bring them to the committee," he said.

"Aarrgh!" Alexandra clenched her fists. She had an urge to rush at the barriers, testing them all until she found a little crack she could squeeze through. But she would be dashed if she would create a hysterical emotional display for Froister and his gang. Forcing herself into a calm state she only felt on the surface, she sat down on the floor beside the cot and rested her back against it. "Well, with all these lamps the least they could do is provide us with something to read. If he's waiting for us to capitulate, we could be here a long time."

Chapter 21

A carroty red light from a training wand joined the blue and deep pink glows as Ray and Rose, plus their visitor, searched among the Dumpsters and trash cans in the shadowy alley that led behind a row of apartment houses.

"I know I felt a string back here," Ray protested. He was running point for Rose and Jeff Doyle. The other two were testing the air behind him with their wands as if they were feeling their way along with canes. He stopped, sure he'd missed the source.

"It doesn't look like anyone lives back here," Jeff said, brushing his hands as he eyed the unsavory piles of garbage bags. "There's no room for a living body."

"You'd be surprised," Rose said sadly. "The homeless tuck themselves in wherever they can."

Ray felt for that trace again. It hadn't given him the impression that it was in the depths of despair, as so many of his homeless clients had. It felt more confused, more lonely, and very small.

"Wait," he said. "I'm on it."

He swept the blue wand around in a circle until he felt the string push up from the surface of the air. Beckoning to the others, he followed the trail toward a dirty, red-painted Dumpster. He peered into it. It was empty, except for a stench that made him gag. Angrily, he pushed it aside.

Cowering behind it was a minute figure with tousled blond hair and a flowered overall suit. She looked up at the three adults with fearful brown eyes, her little pink lips quivering as if she was about to cry.

"My God, she's a tiny one," Ray said, hunkering down. "I don't think she's much more than two years old. Hello, honey. Don't be afraid."

The child's eyes welled with tears at the kind tone of his voice. Jeff stooped down and picked her up.

"Hi, there," he said. "Do you believe in fairy godmothers?"

"No," said the tot positively.

"Then, we're just nice people who found you," he said, without missing a beat. "Are you lost?"

"Yes," the child said, and then she did start crying.

"Ohh, don't do that. Where do you live, sweetheart?" Rose asked, stepping close to dab the little girl's eyes with a handkerchief.

"I don't know!"

Rose turned to Ray. "She's too little to have come very far. Honey, go out on the street and flag down the first patrol car you see. This child doesn't need a wish, just some good common sense."

Ray wove his way swiftly between the Dumpsters and cans, until he emerged into the waning sunlight. Halfway down the block he spotted a police car coming his way. He waited until it was closer, then jumped up and down, waving his arms. As it pulled up, he recognized the driver. It was the policeman who had been on his street the night of the fire.

"Hey, hero, how's it going?" the sergeant asked.

"We've found a baby," he said. "A little white girl." He gestured back into the alley. "She's with my friends."

"You found her?" a woman's voice exclaimed. Ray bent down. There was a young woman in the backseat of the car. She scrambled out, and ran around the back of the car to grab Ray's arm. "Oh, show me! Where's my baby?"

Ray led the way. The police officer followed them back into the alley, where they found Rose and Jeff singing a nonsense song to the child. The toddler let out a giggle, which turned into a wail as soon as she saw her mother. She held out her arms. The young woman seized her daughter, and kissed everybody.

"Oh, thank you!" she exclaimed, over and over, as the police sergeant led her out of the alley.

"You're just doing good all over the place," the sergeant said to Ray. "But I'd like to know just what you were doing back here." He looked curiously at the three fairy godparents, evidently considering them to be an unlikely group.

"I was looking for something," Ray said with complete honesty. "My friends were helping me find it."

"You find it?"

"Yes," Ray said.

"Then you don't want to hang around back there, do you?" the sergeant asked, severely. Then his face softened. "See you around, hero."

"Yeah," Ray said, feeling another spark drop into his mental piggy bank. Oh, come on, he told the magic, that wasn't that special. He threw the police officer a polite salute. "Later, sir."

"Well, I am ready for a break," Rose said, dusting off the front of her dress. The pervasive stench they had picked up in the alley was fading, and she started to think about something to eat. "How about you? I think Ray deserves a sundae for finding that little girl."

"That wasn't half so interesting as the little flourish he threw in for that girl at the zoo," Jeff Doyle said with a grin.

"Yes, indeed," Rose said. "I felt like breaking into applause right there when the giraffe came over to eat out of her hand."

"That was nothing," Ray said, giving Rose a sour look.

"It was great!" Jeff exclaimed. "I can't wait to tell the folks back at our local. Granting the wish practically under her parents' noses. Very neat. All they thought was they were raising another Doctor Dolittle. And she was so happy."

Rose could tell that they were embarrassing Raymond, but she was truly proud of his progress. His confidence grew by the day. She was also enjoying their visitor. Young Jeff was not only remarkably good-looking, but friendly and enthusiastic. He and Ray were hitting it off splendidly. She hoped she was seeing the beginning of a long friendship.

"Well, the ice-cream stand is this way," Rose said, getting in between the boys and tucking her hands into their arms. "So, Jeff, how did you get into the Fairy Godmothers?"

"I caught my brother doing magic one day," Jeff explained. "I was absolutely fascinated. He's pretty good, really, but he keeps getting into jams because he's sort of on his own. He said this kind of talent runs in families, so I wanted to do some, too. My mother pushed me into this because she said it was more structured. The rules tend to protect you. I get to try out all sorts of things, all good for people, without any of the hazards my brother keeps falling over. Of course, I think he leaves himself open for them." Grinning, he shook his head at the memories.

"He's a natural magician?" Rose said, delighted. "That's rare."

"He's a good guy, for a brother," Jeff acknowledged.

"Things can happen to fairy godfathers, too," Ray pointed out.

"Well, I just take them as they come."

"You this cheerful all the time?" Ray asked, narrowing an eye.

"Well, you know," Jeff said, with a conspiratorial wink, "the optimism comes from the Irish side of my family."

"And which side is that?" Rose asked.

"Both!" Jeff laughed. "How about you, Ray? How'd you get involved?"

"My grandmother got me into the FGU," Ray said. "She used to take care of me when I was a baby, and I guess she took me on missions with her."

"Cool!"

"None of my children are interested, alas," Rose said. "I have to rely upon adopted grandchildren, like Ray. Ah, here we are."

Jeff sprang forward like a gentleman to pull open the door of the ice-cream shop. The cold air inside hit them all like a wall of snow falling on them. Ray held back a little, but Rose pulled him in with her. He had been trying so hard all day not to make any mistakes in front of their guest, and it was wearing him out. He was going to take a break if she had to sit on him. Jeff was new enough that he wouldn't notice anything wrong if Ray had made any errors, and was too polite to say something if he had, so there was really nothing to worry about.

Rose felt her skin break out in goose bumps as she scanned the menu over the cases. This place was a delightful oasis in the neighborhood. The bright yellow-painted walls always looked so cheerful, and the floors and glass-topped tables were remarkably spotless. She had long suspected that a house brownie had this store under its care, but she didn't quite know how to approach the owner to ask.

"Anything you want," she said expansively. "We all deserve something nice, and boys are always hungry." Ray and Jeff looked at each other with abashed smiles. She'd guessed they were looking at the big sundaes at the top end of the menu. "It's all right," she said. "Indulge yourselves. Once in a while is fine."

Each of them selected something large and gooey, with four scoops, fruit, sprinkles, and two or three kinds of sauce. Rose took something slightly smaller, but just as sinfully rich. The sauces here were always so good, and the hot fudge never tasted burned. The three of them watched avidly as one colorful scoop after another was dished into paper bowls.

"Well, well, what have we here?"

She turned to smile at Fred Lincoln as the swinging door slammed shut behind him. The big, dark-skinned man wore a neat, short-sleeved denim shirt wet around the collar with perspiration. He sighed with pleasure as the cool air enveloped him.

"We felt we could use a little treat," Rose explained. "I'm rewarding Ray for a clever bit of magic. Not that he needs a reward, but you know, I'm a grandmother."

"Yeah, I know," Mr. Lincoln said, with his wide, generous smile. "Well, I felt like spoiling myself, and to heck with the diet." He sucked in his stomach and patted it heartily with both hands. "I've had a few interesting calls today which I'll tell you about when you've got some time."

"Any time, dear," Rose said sympathetically. "Bad?"

"Not all bad," Fred Lincoln said. She eyed him to make sure that whatever was on his mind wasn't urgent. He gave his order to the young man behind the counter, and pulled up a chair to join them at the table. His posture was relaxed, so Rose stopped worrying. Fred reached out a hand to their visitor. "Nice to see you again, Mr. Doyle. We'd like to propose sending some of our people out to your neck of the woods."

"We'd be happy to have them, sir," Jeff said, shaking hands. "I've been having a great day with Rose and Ray. They're terrific."

"Yeah," Fred said, patting Ray on the back. "They're as good as we've got." Ray ducked his head modestly, and started spooning up ice cream faster. The counterman held up a big double-dip cone. "There's my treat," he said. "Be seeing you. Think it's gonna rain." He put up his collar with his free hand. Saluting them with his cone, he ducked out into the street.

"Oh, dear," Rose said, peering out the plate glass window at the growing gloom. It did seem to be getting dark too early for the middle of summer. A quick glance up told her that Fred was right. Clouds had scudded in while they were slurping strawberry syrup. Condensation was beginning to form on the inside of the windows, obscuring her view of the street. "We may be in for a real downpour."

Outside, the exhaust vents from air-conditioning units on the roofs of buildings spouted plumes of white steam. No one passing by with his head down against the first sharp droplets of rain noticed that some of the plumes solidified into human form. These slipped stealthily down the drainpipes and sank through solid brickwork to emerge at the street level in the narrow walkway between two stores. One of them, a white male in a black jacket, took the lead, directing his associates out of the rain.

A heavyset black man emerged from a brightly lit shop. He was taking licks from the bottom dip of a large double-dip cone where the ice cream met the edge of the cone. The young man signaled vigorously to his companions, and they sprang out of the alley to meet him.

Rose pushed open the door of the shop. It was raining pretty hard now, one of those unexpected summer showers. The few pedestrians left on the street had covered their heads against the sudden storm with anything they had in their hands: briefcases, newspapers, magazines.

"It's really coming down, now," Rose said. She felt in the bottom of her purse for the little plastic bonnet she always carried. It was getting shopworn, but she never left it out when she cleaned her purse because it might come in handy, as now. The others huddled close by her, staying under the eaves. "Should we call it a day?"

"No!" both young men chorused. The stars, rust and blue, appeared out of their pockets.

"We want to keep going," Ray said.

Rose, loving them for their eagerness, smiled through the droplets that settled on her cheeks and eyelashes. "All right, then. Where are we going?" She watched as Ray's face contorted with concentration.

"There's a really big string going that way," he said, pointing south.

Rose took her senior's wand out of her purse to check. "That is a tough one," she said. "But it feels too far away to walk. We'll get soaked!"

"I have my car here," Jeff said. "I'll drive us wherever we have to go."

"No. Parking is awful in the city on a weekend," Rose said.

"Not for fairy godparents," Jeff said, with an insouciant grin. "I've noticed that parking spaces just open up when I need them."

"Well, we'd be a little conspicuous in some neighborhoods," Rose said. "We're right near public transportation. It's better if we're on foot."

Ray took Rose's arm and leaned down to put his mouth

next to her ear. "I haven't got any money," he said in a low voice. "Payday's not until Tuesday."

"Not to worry," Rose said. "You've been reading the bylaws, right? 'Persons shall not hinder a fairy godparent in the pursuit of her duties, and should help whenever possible.' "

"And how does that apply?" Ray asked.

Rose turned them toward the El station, and took a boy by each arm. "Come on and see."

She stepped over a milky stream that poured into the gutter from the remains of a double-dip cone, kicked out of sight behind the door of the ice-cream parlor.

Ray was very wet, and wishing he had brought a jacket, any jacket, by the time they were under the wooden canopy. If he only had himself to consider, he'd be on his way home to a nice dry room, but that need string pulled at him.

A train was just arriving as they started up the steps. A man came down toward them. Ray pushed to one side of the narrow stairs to make room for him. As the man came level with him, he pushed something into Ray's hand.

"Here," he said. "It's still good. I'm going home."

"Hey, thanks," Ray said. A woman in a tight-fitting cerise business suit cut between him and his benefactor, who disappeared down and into the street traffic. As he got to the platform, Rose was behind him, panting and clutching a pass. Jeff had another transfer and an umbrella.

Ray looked at the papers in their hands. "They know, or were they just being nice?" he asked. He flipped his collar to get the water out of it, and Jeff held the umbrella over all of them.

The droplets of rain on Rose's rain hat twinkled in the station lights.

"Yours was just being nice," she said. "Mine knew. That was Sheila. She doesn't get to too many meetings, so I'm not surprised you don't know her. Jeff's was a good Samaritan, too. You see? You need, and our little bit of luck prompted two people, all unknowing, to give you what you needed. Thank heavens, and let's go!"

A train roared into the station, spraying them all with rainwater. Ray just wiped his face again and followed her into the train.

The invisible wall now contained more than fifty fairy godparents. Froister had stopped counting. He had too much else on his mind in coordinating their capture. The apprentice djinni were enjoying themselves almost too much. Armed with only a list of names, they were using resources they probably had not bothered with in all their lives, such as libraries, post offices, telephone books, to track down the membership of the FGU. Speed Guthrie would have been worth a fortune to any general as a reconnaissance man. When this was all over, Froister was going to recommend that he should go and hire himself out to mercenaries in South America, or someplace where they would be shooting at him.

"I didn't have an idea that there were this many fairy godmothers in all of the city," McClaherty said, standing next to Froister as the two of them peered into the warehouse from the showroom door.

"Nor did I," Froister admitted. "When I saw the list I was amazed. If I had realized, I might have let Gurgin enlist more of our young friends to help us."

"They're enough," McClaherty said grimly, his ruddy face set. "Why aren't you keeping them here in between assignments, Albert? They're trying to ruin the whole city."

"They are serving their purpose," Froister said. To tell himself the truth, that he was overwhelmed by the gang members, and wanted as little sustained contact with them as possible, would be to admit that he was failing at his dream of unrestrained power. If it hadn't been for the absolute control of the lamps, he'd have been unable to cope with their personalities. He was also having to keep a careful rota of which senior member had rubbed which lamp, so as not to run beyond three wishes per wisher. He couldn't afford a magical backlash on top of the buildup already occurring in his guest corral. The FGU was already enough of a headache. But it meant that all seven of the senior djin were having to stay around his shop day and night to put each apprentice under control as needed. That was making *them* short-tempered as well. He had had the young members blink up luxurious accommodations in the back of the warehouse area for the seven of them, but they were beginning to feel as much a captive force as the Fairy Godmothers Union.

Its members had so far shown no signs of capitulating. The young thugs wanted to use physical force on them to make them give up the precious brownie points. Froister could not do that. What was wrong with today's parents that they raised their young without scruples? he asked himself. Violence was abhorrent to him. Let psychological torture do the work. If this worked, he would be rid of the damned lamp, and the damned guild. Wasn't that all that mattered?

By the way that each new addition reacted to his request for brownie points, he had come to the conclusion that it would take more than the combined total of the Local 3–26 resources to break his oath. The chairwoman refused to acknowledge it, but each of them unwittingly confirmed it to him. Well, logic dictated that if one fairy godmother could "borrow" from another's spare magic, then one federation could borrow from another. All it would take for him to get what he wanted was one fairy godmother who was willing to act as a conduit. So far he had no takers. They were showing damnable solidarity. All he could do was raise the level of emotional tension, something the young thugs were doing already.

A couple of youths who belonged to the Backyard Wolves suddenly flew in through the walls. Between them, they were carrying an old woman. They came in twenty feet above the ground, running down a slope of air like a jet coming in for a landing, and dumped the crone into the arms of a few of the men and women already there. They helped to dust her off and calm her down. Shaking his head, Froister straight-armed the door and went after his apprentice djinni.

"Carmichael, Gallega!" he shouted, and pointed to the ground. The two, who had flown up into the rafters with the others to smoke and laugh, stiffened. They couldn't not obey, but they appeared before him wearing sullen expressions.

"I want them in a mood to cooperate," he hissed angrily, "not ready for a cardiac crash cart. Do you understand?" The youths raised their eyebrows, which maddened him, but he would not let the ire show. And yet, the woman was not hurt, and a few of the fairy godmothers huddled in the corners of the enclosure were looking more wary as the two apologized and floated back up to join their friends.

He turned to survey his unwilling guests. The apprentices had brought nearly all of the membership here within the space of only forty-eight hours. Some looked frightened; others, angry. None of them came forward to offer assistance. He wanted to get them out of his nice, clean warehouse. His watchman was on vacation, so he had a week before anyone else came through here, and he wanted the FGU gone before then. That was very little time. Since it was impossible to coerce them physically, he had to rely upon psychology.

The room was large and brightly lit, and spotlessly clean, as befitted a successful upscale establishment, as well as complying with the fire laws. He looked around for an apprentice djin.

"Barton!" he called. The chubby-cheeked youth dropped to the floor before him.

"Yes, sir?" he asked.

"The second wish: make this room less inviting for our guests, please. Use your imagination."

The youth folded his arms and blinked. Suddenly, the lights dimmed. All the men and women looked up as gigantic spiderwebs formed over the skylights and drifted down to brush their faces with dust. A chill, dank wind flowed through, swirling bits of paper. The very walls appeared to turn decrepit and unstable. The rattle of bones or chains echoed from corner to corner, and a mysterious laugh welled up from the very bowels of the earth. The membership of the FGU fell silent. They looked solemn and wide-eyed.

"How *impossibly* tacky!" announced a woman's voice. The youth making the spell looked disappointed.

Froister waved a hand angrily. "Take it away!" he commanded. The young man blinked, and the warehouse returned to normal. Froister was in a temper. Two wishes wasted!

"You're going to have to do better than that if you want to scare us," said George Aldeanueva.

"Then I will," Froister said. He turned to his magical facilitator and explained what it was he wanted. The boy nodded, and closed his eyes to concentrate. The power of the wish rose again. Instead of turning the room into a haunted slum, he made it even more austere. Suddenly the chamber appeared cold, remote, and barren.

That worked much better. Now women hugged themselves involuntarily, and men turned a wary eye on their juvenile guards. Hollywood stage props didn't impress them, but the uninviting walls of the prison did. He might get cooperation from them soon.

"Get the rest," Froister said. "Crowd them in together. The longer they're away from their families, the more inclined they will be to cooperate. When they see that they simply cannot escape, they will have to give in, or be here forever. It's that simple," he said, turning to his guests. "Give up the brownie points and leave. You can make more. Or keep them and stay. Your choice. You are your own jailers."

"You stink," said a tall black man who had just been brought in.

"So you have all been telling me," Froister said. He was keenly aware of the growing odor as his djinni committed sin after sin. He was hardly able to stand himself anymore. No amount of cologne seemed to cover the stink of inappropriate behavior. But it would be worth it if he could fulfill his dream to gain control of his own magic.

"You'll yield the brownie points to me, drawing on the national, and even the international federation to get enough for our purposes, to release even one of us," Froister said, trying to sound threatening. "That's the price of your freedom."

"You're through when we get out of here," George Aldeanueva said through clenched teeth.

"That's assuming you leave," Froister pointed out, as he turned to go. "I've spent two hundred years in a museum display case. I have more patience than anyone you'll ever meet."

Chapter 22

The rain stopped, but it hadn't been troublesome to a genie who could turn into smoke and slip between the raindrops. What was really bothering Hakeem was his conscience. Innocent people were being snatched off the street and stuffed into a warehouse in pursuit of something that sounded impossible. If it was possible to have the magic without bracelets, someone would have had it long before now. The novelty had long ago worn off for Hakeem. He'd tried dematerializing his wrists to leave the metal bands behind, but it was as if they were part of his skin. When he turned to air, they turned to air. When he made himself solid, they were solid. Nothing but magic would set him free.

He sailed over rooftops, heading for the street where Ray lived. He had to hurry before he was missed. He and Zeon had a job to do. Froister got really nasty if they took too long, or if they failed, but Hakeem just had to talk to Ray. He knew he'd been stupid to let himself get sucked into the gang by the tough talk and the drugs. He laughed, too, when the guys ripped booze or smokes out of stores right through the walls, but he didn't want to be involved with kidnapping, extortion, and assault! The guildmaster wanted them to go kidnap an innocent lady nurse. Hakeem had been naive. If he didn't get a prison sentence for these crimes, Froister would probably just shut him up in his lamp for all eternity.

He knew he would probably be leading a dangerous life if he joined the Jackals, but he was afraid not to say yes when they asked. For the longest time he thought Ray was stupid to keep saying no to the gangs, because they got violent with people who refused them. Hakeem never thought what would happen to him after he finally said yes. The peril and humiliation of gang life were multiplied a dozen times over with the djin. He had certainly never pictured eternal servitude to household appliances.

"I've got to talk to Ray," he kept saying over and over again to himself like a comforting mantra. "He's the smart one. We can figure a way out of this situation together." At the very least Ray could go into the lamp shop to rub his lamp and wish him free.

At first it had sounded like fun, being able to grant three wishes for anything, but it was much more hassle. The distrust the gangs felt for each other made it impossible for anyone to let anybody have any fun. He wasn't at liberty to do anything on his own anymore. It would be no trouble to leave the magic behind if he could just get out. He felt a pang at the thought of not being able to turn to vapor. Maybe he'd show Ray just once before Ray got him out, but oh, man, Ray had to help him!

He made his feet solidify as he dropped to the pavement in front of the Crandall house so he wouldn't sink straight through the ground. As the rest of him was still taking shape, his feet were running up the concrete steps. Keeping an eye out for Zeon and the other Jackals, he knocked on the door.

No one answered. Impatiently, he hammered with his fist. Throwing his scruples aside in his desperation, he smoked out and passed under the door and into the house. He ran up the stairs to Ray's room. It was empty. He checked all the other rooms, listening for voices. Sunday was family dinner day at the Crandalls'. Where was everyone?

He became aware of a discordant thread of rock music drifting up from the backyard. From the kitchen window he saw a stout, bronze-haired figure in a housedress sitting on a folding chair on the wet grass, tapping her fingers on her knee and nodding her head in time with the music. Grandma Eustatia was listening to Bobby's garage band wailing away.

The Voice Dancers sounded middling good; they must have been practicing a lot. Mostly the adjective that applied to them was *loud*. Hakeem let himself out through the back wall of the house, and went to talk to Grandma Eustatia.

She seemed to know Hakeem was behind her before she turned toward him. As he got closer, she pulled the cotton out of one ear and smiled at him.

"They're improving a ton, aren't they, honey?" she said. "Is there something I can help you with?"

"Uh, no, ma'am," Hakeem said respectfully. "Is Ray home?"

"No, honey, but he should be back soon for dinner. Why?" She stood up, approached him in that smooth gliding walk of hers, put a gentle hand on his, and squeezed. "You look worried. Are you in some kind of trouble, dearest?"

Hakeem took a deep breath to tell her, then felt all the blood in his body turn cold as something new and unexpected struck him.

"Um, no, ma'am," he said, shocked. "I've gotta go. I'd better go. Sorry!" He shook loose from her hand, backed away and ran out of the yard, even forgetting to turn into smoke. He had to get away from there before Zeon found him. She watched him go, with a puzzled look on her face.

Not Grandma Eustatia! Hakeem thought desperately, running down the street until he started to fly. He spread himself out on the air, heading as far away from the Crandall house as he could. He couldn't believe it, but the fresh air scent was unmistakable. Grandma Eustatia was a fairy godmother, just like all the other people he and the gang had been rounding up for two weeks. He was horrified. Here was a woman he had respected, and occasionally feared, all of his life, his own best friend's grandmother. Any minute he could be expected to kidnap her, too.

As a djin, he ought to report her location to Froister, but no matter what consequences he faced, he would not do that. Hakeem had seen the list of names the guildmaster had of all the members of the Fairy Godmothers Union, but no addresses. Thank heavens none of the other Jackals knew that

Ray's Grandma Eustatia was Mrs. E. Green. Even he hadn't associated the name with her when he had seen it, not until now. So no one else knew there was a fairy godmother in the neighborhood. He was going to make sure it stayed that way. He'd fallen pretty far from grace in the last weeks, but he wasn't going to go all the way down if he could help it. Loyalty ran deeper in him than fear. He must not let any of the Jackals know who she was.

Why stay in at all? Why couldn't he just quit the DDEG? If he had the guts, he would resign, bracelets and all, but would they let him? Oh, God, he thought, flying over the park where they used to hang out in more innocent days, where was Ray?

"Hey!" There was an explosion like a returning crack of thunder, and Zeon appeared next to him, lying on the air like Superman. "Hey, man, the Big Bulb wants you." That was the gangbangers' name for the guildmaster. "You shouldn't'a split. He's bummed."

"Sorry, man," Hakeem said. "I had to take care of a family thing."

"Well, you better come now," Zeon said, looking at him sidelong under his lashes, an expression that meant trouble. "We got things to do." He turned flat on the air toward the north, beckoning Hakeem to fall in behind him.

With a final, regretful look at the park, Hakeem followed.

"You don't have to try so hard," Rose said, following Ray out of a home in the neighborhood east of theirs. Jeff Doyle tactfully trailed several yards behind them. He waved happily to the child, now looking out the window at them. Ray scowled.

"I was doing what he wanted, wasn't I?" he demanded. "You don't have to nag me."

"I'm not nagging you," Rose said. "You were getting the job done, of course, but you can take your time. You'll get the same results, anyway, and," she added with a smile, "the same brownie points."

"Yeah, so you and the other bigwigs can rip me off one fine day, when you think I'm not looking?"

Rose looked stunned at the sudden outburst. "What?"

"Yeah," Ray said, all of his rage boiling out of him. "You old-timers make us young fools do all the work, and then you take our rewards. And there's nothing I can do to stop you, so why don't you just take them now?"

"Hold the phone!" Rose said, catching his arm. He tried to throw her off, but she held on. "Where on earth did that come from?"

"From Mr. Guthrie," Ray admitted at last. From the surprised expression on her face he wasn't so sure all of a sudden that his informant was right. "He said you'd just soften me up, let me think I was in control, then, one day, bam!"

She shook her head sadly. "You've been carrying that around with you for how long?"

"Since yesterday's meeting," Jeff said, coming up. "I saw Mr. Guthrie take him aside. That's what he was saying to you? Wow. He's an even bigger jerk than I thought."

Rose laid a hand against Ray's cheek. "Oh, my poor dear. Don't you have any more faith in us than that? Or if not us, how about your own judgment? Do you think, knowing what you do in here"—she tapped his heart—"that we could ever undermine your self-esteem like that? How long do you think we could exist as a benevolent organization if we were always ripping one another off?"

"Not long, I guess," Ray mumbled. "I'm sorry. I feel dumb."

"I suppose it's only natural," Rose said, including Jeff in the conversation. "My mother always said, if something seemed too good to be true, it probably was. But not always," she said. "We do have access. But we trust one another to keep hands off. Of course," she said, "there's always emergencies. In that case, feel free to draw on me."

"Or on me," Jeff said. "Distance is not a factor, as far as I can tell."

"Thanks," Ray said, staring at the ground between his feet. "Now I feel like I don't deserve it."

"Of course you do!" Rose said encouragingly. "Now come

on. It's getting late, and you've got to get home for Sunday dinner. One more stop, and then we'll go."

Rose looked down at the young Hispanic girl sitting on the concrete stoop and put her hands on her hips so that the gleaming star on a stick bobbed against her shoulder.

"You don't really need a fairy godmother to have a baby," Rose said, trying to sound reasonable. "There's the usual method, of course. But I'd absolutely forbid it for you. What are you, Honoria, eleven?"

"Ten," the child said, hunkering her shoulders down closer to her knobby knees and tilting her head to look at them. Her face was half in shadow and half painted yellow by the bulb from the enclosed porch. "You don't understand."

"All right," Rose said, sitting down beside her and putting her wand across her knees. Ray remained standing in front of them, watching warily for anyone coming out of the house. "Make me understand why you want to do something unnatural and unhealthy at your age."

"My sister's pregnant," Honoria burst out unhappily. "But she's not very strong. If she has this baby, it'll kill her. The doctor said so. But she wants it so bad, and it means everything to my brother-in-law. It's going to be a boy, and that's all Paulie wants in the world. A son," she said bitterly, and turned to appeal to each of them in turn. "You said I can have a miracle. Put the baby in me, so my sister won't die. She's my only sister."

Ray watched Rose's face change up and back among outrage, astonishment, and admiration. He felt taken aback, too. Of all the visions he'd had since the first night of granting wishes to kids, he'd never have dreamed up anything like this. He knew where Honoria got the idea. Surrogate maternity had made the news dozens of times.

"Yes, well," Rose said at last. "Honoria, this is not your miracle." The girl cried out wordlessly. "No, this'll be *his* miracle, your unnamed baby nephew." Rose raised her wand and felt around her as if she was testing the wind. "Here's my interpretation of your wish, that he is to be born alive

without harming his mother." Ray felt the backwash of good
feeling as the pale pink light poured out of the wand and
swept backward over their heads, going into the house. That
must be where the sister was.

Honoria watched the magic light with shining eyes. Rose
flicked the wand in a tight circle, and the veil faded.

"There," she said. "All done. Your sister will know better
after this, maybe have her tubes tied. Once they have a son—
who thought up this nonsense about primogeniture anyway?—they won't feel the need to have any more. They
can adopt. As for you"—she turned to the girl—"you're a
generous young woman. You have the right name, Honoria.
We'll have something really special happen for you one day.
I'll be watching for you. The day your wish is supposed to
come true, I'll be back with bells on." Rose stood up and
patted the girl on the shoulder.

"Me, too," Ray said hoarsely, too overwhelmed to come
up with anything snappy to say.

"I'll come whenever they call me," Jeff added.

"Yes," Rose said, enthusiastically. "We'll make it a real
princess's coming-out."

Honoria looked at all of them with her mouth open. "Why
would you do this for me?"

"Because you're so unselfish," Rose said. "I don't know
how many kids have begged me for a Teenage Morphin What-
zit Turtle doll, but not many want to do something really
heroic for someone else."

Honoria bounded to her feet, her eyes bright in the porch
light. "*Dios mio!* You are so kind. Maybe one day I'll be a
fairy godmother, too."

Rose tilted her head to look up at Ray and slowly closed
one eye in a wink. "Maybe you will, sweetheart."

"I could never have made a call like that in a million years,"
Ray said, as they walked down the path to the sidewalk.

"Me, either," Jeff said, behind him.

"Nonsense," Rose said, bringing up the rear. "All it takes
is experience."

"It's more than that," Ray said, stopping lightly on the pavement. "It's so natural with you. You've got the magic touch." The imp got into him as he remembered one of the old standards Grandma liked to sing. He struck a pose, spotlighting her.

"You-oo-oo've got—the Ma-aagic Touch."

And Jeff chimed in with "Oh-oooh."

"Oh, go on!" Rose said, blushing.

"—You ma-ake me ga-low so-oh much. You cast a spell, your magic's swell, the ma-gic tou-ouch!"

Rose laughed and applauded. "Bravo!" she cried. "You've got quite a musical talent, too."

"Naw," Ray said, falling into step next to her as she headed toward the bus stop. "My sister and Grandma Eustatia are the ones with talent."

Rose tucked her hand into his arm, and he held it close against his side. "You have absolutely unplumbed depths, honey. You're amazing." Ray just shook his head, enjoying walking in the warm summer night with good friends. If anyone came up at that moment to make fun of him or his companions, he'd punch them in the nose.

"Well, I've enjoyed myself," Jeff said, after they had walked back within a few hundred yards of the Assembly Hall. "I'd better get home. It's a long drive back. Come out our way soon, and I'll try and show you a good time. Ray, stay in touch, huh?"

"You bet," Ray said. He watched Jeff drive off, thinking he'd made a new friend. Rose waved good-bye until Jeff's car was out of sight.

"What a nice young man," she said, turning them around toward their part of the neighborhood.

"Yeah, he is. So, how about Monday?" Ray asked, starting the familiar banter, as he walked Rose home. He knew she'd say Wednesday, and he could start negotiating. He was feeling pretty good about things. The betrayal Guthrie had suggested had turned out to be just a ploy to divide him from his peer group, and they'd had a really good day.

"Tomorrow," Rose began with significant emphasis, and Ray felt his hopes soar, "my son and his family are coming over to spend a few days visiting the old lady." Ray felt his spirits plummet. "So I've got to do some fairy-*grand*mothering." She laughed. "And my son is going to install my new air conditioner. It's been so hot these last few days I hate to go home. It'll be nice to have it in for August. The *Farmer's Almanac* said it'll be the hottest month in ten years."

Ray felt bereft. "For how long?"

"Oh, a week. No longer than a week. They can't stand my little apartment for that long." Rose chuckled. "And I need my privacy. I never thought I'd say that after raising a houseful of children, but there you are. People change."

"What am *I* supposed to do?" Ray asked. The question came out a wail, and Rose looked sympathetic.

"I know! How about coming over on Tuesday for supper? It's the fourth. We can watch the fireworks together." Ray shook his head, too disappointed to accept a substitute for fairy-godmothering. A whole week! "No?" Rose asked, watching his face, and completely misinterpreting his unhappiness. "How about cookies and lemonade? My son would like to meet you. You're both so smart."

"Okay," Ray said, accepting a compromise. A snack wouldn't take up much time. He liked Rose, but he didn't want to spend hours talking to her kids, since they weren't interested in fairy-godparenting. He'd rather be out with her, granting wishes. "We can go out after that?"

Rose frowned. "Not really, sweetheart. Not with them there. But you don't need me. Go ahead and practice on your own. You're developing good judgment. Or you could always hook up with one of the other senior members for a day or so."

Ray kicked the pavement, and a pebble, invisible in the dark, bounced off into traffic. "I'd rather wait until you're free. I'm more comfortable with you."

"I like you, too, dear, but sometimes I have to do family things. I really cannot go out granting wishes while they're around."

Ray sulked. "You don't want your family to hang with me

because I'm a kid. Or because I'm black." He knew that was dishonest and untrue, but it escaped his lips before he could call it back. In the pale neon light of the next store front he saw that Rose looked very hurt.

"No, dear, dear Ray," she said, very gently. "For the same reason you don't want to haul your little sister with you everywhere you go, I don't want my son hanging over our shoulders. He complains about everything. He thinks magic is uncontrollable and unpredictable. And he would worry! 'Where are you going?' he would ask us. 'When will you be back? Mother, you can't go out walking at night! The streets are dangerous!'" Her mimicry had so many characteristic gestures it was obviously taken from life. "And it's too bad he's so skeptical about magic. I think he'd make a wonderful tooth fairy." Ray grinned in spite of himself.

"Okay, I'm overreacting. I'm sorry I said that. Really. I'm just tripping over my tongue today."

"Yes, you are overreacting, but I understand," Rose said, reaching up to pat him on the cheek. "Look, you don't need to hang around the old lady to have fun. The summer is so short, you'll be back in school before you know it. Go be with your friends. Enjoy."

"You're my friend," Ray said softly.

Rose squeezed his hand. "And you're my friend, too. But I meant the friends who are your age. We'll be together again very soon. You know that."

Ray wasn't completely satisfied. "What about clients who come up while you're 'doing family things'? Emergencies?"

Rose said briskly, "You can go out and take care of any cases you think you can handle on your own. You're very capable. I trust you."

Well, that did it. Ray wouldn't dare to take on a major wish-granting session on his own, particularly not emergencies. He'd sooner call in one of the bigwigs to do the job for him. "I'll take the week off," he mumbled, as they got to her door. "See you next week, I guess."

"Monday," she said, pulling open her purse. She put the wand inside, and extracted her house key. "That's a promise."

"Monday?" he asked, surprised. "Don't you have to grade papers or serve juice or something?"

"No school," Rose said. "Summer vacation. It's July. Remember?"

"Right," Ray said, shaking his head at his own obtuseness. "Great! See you soon." He glanced at the dial of his watch, and gulped. "I've got to roll. I've got to get home for dinner, or Grandma will skin me."

Ray threw her a quick wave and dashed away into the night. Rose felt sorry for him. He was such a good, eager pupil she hated to deprive him of any opportunity to practice, but there it was. She could not be in two places at the same time. Soon enough he'd be out on his own, and he wouldn't want her hanging around him while he worked. He was going to be a star, Rose thought, as she closed the door and locked it. What a terrific kid. She was very angry at that Guthrie person for filling his head with lies. Rose promised herself she would see to it that Alexandra evicted him from the next meeting.

She dropped her purse on the floor next to the telephone table and hit the button on her answering machine. Nothing special, except for the message from her son.

"Mother, we'll be coming by about three. I have reservations at Le Chat Noir for dinner. The kids are looking forward to seeing you."

"Me, too, sweetheart," she said fondly. The rest of the messages were trivial. As she was about to go to the kitchen and get herself a cold soda she heard the doorbell ring. It must be Ray. He probably forgot to ask her something about going out on his own. He'd like a soda, too. She opened the door.

The caller on the doorstep was about the same size and build, but it was not Ray.

"Can I help you?" she asked.

"Mrs. Feinstein?" the young man said. She nodded. "Uh, I'm a friend of Ray's. Can I talk to you for a second?"

Was this Hakeem? He didn't look like the picture Ray had in his wallet of the two of them.

"I don't know," she said uncertainly. "I'm a little busy. I'm waiting for my son to come back . . ." She smelled the burning ozone smell, saw the wristbands. It was the genie-Jackals Ray warned her about! She started to back away and close the door, but the grasping hands came right through the wood and grabbed her wrist. Rose fought madly, but she was outnumbered. More boys piled into the apartment, through the doors, the walls, even the floor, until she was surrounded. She kicked one of them in the shins, and two of them sank deeply enough to seize her legs. One of the brutes picked up her purse, and opened it.

"Hey, young man," she said indignantly, struggling with her captors, "that's personal!"

"The wand's in here," said the boy who had rung her doorbell, ignoring her. The other youths nodded. A black fume rose around them until it obscured the walls of her apartment. Rose heard the ceiling smoke detector howling as they all vanished together.

Chapter 23

*R*ay strode quickly down Madison Street, heading for Michigan Avenue. It was bright and very hot. Sweat ran down his body under his coveralls. He had just enough time to get to Roosevelt College and pick up his placement papers for the fall semester. His boss wanted him back in double time to keep working on getting Grant Park and the area around Buckingham Fountain in shape for the fireworks display on Tuesday night.

"Every minute counts," Landis said. If Ray had not wanted to go do something that was involved in furthering his education, Landis would have insisted he eat his sandwich and go back to work right away with the others, skipping the rest of his lunch hour. Thank heavens for small mercies. Ray put a new CD he'd bought at a used disc store onto the thumbtack player in his pocket, and timed his walk to the rhythm in his head. He was so intent on the music he hardly noticed when Hakeem fell into step beside him.

"Hi, brother," Ray said, surprised. He dislodged the disc with his thumb to turn off the music. "I haven't seen you around lately. Where have you been?"

"Around," Hakeem said casually, but Ray could feel tension in him. Hakeem walked scrunched over with his hands in his pockets, always a bad sign.

"Me, too," Ray said. They walked in silence for a moment. Hakeem seemed to want to say something, but he was having trouble getting it out.

"Uh, hey, you want to do something sometime?" he said at last.

"Yeah. I've missed seeing you," Ray said, hoping to elicit more details with a hopeful attitude.

"Me, too," Hakeem said. Suddenly, he wheeled to a stop twenty feet from the corner. Ray stopped, too, and let the lunchtime crowds part to walk around them. "Look, man . . ."

"Hey, Hakeem," Zeon said, appearing next to them from out of the ground. Ray guessed his entrance was intended to keep people from noticing the puff of smoke that seemed to accompany the entrances and exits of all genies. "When you're finished associating with the bottom-feeder, we've got more places to go."

"You don't have to go with this dude if you don't want to," Ray said, getting between his friend and the gangbanger.

Hakeem gave him a sad, pathetic look. "You just don't understand, man," he said, looking as if he desperately wished Ray could.

Worried, Ray asked in a low voice, "Are you in some kind of trouble, brother?"

"See you around, man, all right?" Hakeem asked, pushing past him to stand by Zeon. "I'm sorry what I said about your friend, the old lady." He held up his hand to catch Ray's in a clasp. Ray caught the glint of the djin bracelets and a matching glint in his friend's eyes. He started to ask again, when Zeon gave Ray a tremendous shove, catapulting him into a knot of businessmen in shirtsleeves. While he made distracted apologies, Hakeem and Zeon vanished in a cloud of choking black fumes.

Ray straightened up, too late to pull his friend back. He had to get Hakeem away from those genies. Maybe Rose had some advice on how to help.

From the college, he called Rose's house. The phone rang several times, but only the answering machine picked up. Ray hung up before her message finished. Rose was probably out buying presents for the grandchildren. He'd go there after work and ask her in person. He wondered how much it would cost him in brownie points to pull Hakeem away from the

DDEG. Too much. Would Rose lend him some? Discontented
and frustrated, he collected his documents and went back to
work.

"Damn you, let me out of this filthy jar!"

The shrill voice was beginning to eat away at Hakeem's
eardrums. He was having reality-check problems. All right,
so it wasn't all that normal to be flying through the air granting
wishes, or chasing fairy godmothers who waved wands, but
in a million years he would never have believed in the teeny
little woman he and Zeon had between them, trapped in a
pickle jar. Zeon carried the butterfly net proudly over his
shoulder like a hunter's gun.

It had been a piece of cake to capture the first fairy. They
caught a whiff of the air-freshener scent while looking for a
different prospect, and followed it until they saw the little
woman sailing along like a luna moth. She was as beautiful as
a dream, tiny, delicate, almost translucent, with her glistening,
jewel-colored dress. She dematerialized to go through the wall
of a house. The djinni were right behind her. As she was
identifying herself to the wondering child, they dropped
Zeon's jacket on her and brought her back.

The other thing he couldn't believe was how such cute
little creatures could have such dirty mouths. Each of them
had sworn a bright blue streak when they had laid hands on
her, and kept it up all the way back to the warehouse. As they
added the third fairy to the bird cage under the eaves of the
building, the other two spouted expletives deleted at them
until Hakeem felt his ears burning. Zeon only grinned.

"Look, I'm sorry," Hakeem whispered, as he shut the door
on their captive.

"If you deserved the soul you have, you'd let us go!" the
first fairy pleaded. She turned big blue eyes on him in desper-
ate appeal. His stomach tense with sympathy, Hakeem almost
released the latch, when Zeon's hand dropped down on his
arm.

"The Big Bulb says no," he said flatly.

"I'm sorry," he told the fairies. At that moment, if he had

in his power to quit the DDEG, he would have turned his back and never returned. They screamed obscenities at him as he and Zeon settled down to the floor of the warehouse.

The pretty chairwoman, or so Speed had identified her, was trying to calm everyone down. There were dozens of people trapped in the enclosure that he had made. The place was full of camp beds and chairs. In spite of the rough conditions, most of the fairy godparents were really nice people, who were polite and gracious to their captors. They made him feel even more ashamed of himself than he already was. As he passed a short, plump woman with graying dark hair seated in an overstuffed armchair, she smiled at him in a friendly way. She was one of the ones that had been brought in the night before. She looked familiar to him, but for a moment he couldn't place her. He'd seen her—where? On the street. Walking with Ray. Walking with *Ray*? Was he ... was his best friend one of these people? He had to get out of here, and ask him, warn him!

"Hakeem? Is that you?"

A stentorian female voice dragged his attention away from the first woman. He'd know it a million miles or a million years away.

"Grandma?"

Hakeem spun around and searched the crowd for the rounded, bronze figure. She beckoned to him from a deep, overstuffed armchair at the back of the open square. He was so shocked he didn't even feel his feet hit the floor as he walked to her.

"There you are, son!" she said. "What are you doing involved with these skunks and ruffians?"

"I ... I kind of fell into it, Grandma," Hakeem said, his head bowed. He was ashamed to have anyone he knew see him under these circumstances. The big djin who looked like a genie from the movies appeared next to him.

"Is this your grandmother?" Gurgin asked.

"No, she his friend's grandma," Zeon said, who followed Hakeem across the floor. "His friend the spineless piece of crap, right?" He nudged Hakeem in the ribs with his elbow.

Grandma Eustatia rose to her feet and sailed over to sla
Zeon across the face. Clutching his cheek, he gaped at her

"Don't you call my grandson names," she said, glidin
back to her chair. She seated herself like a queen. Zeon lunge
at her. Hakeem pulled him back and bent over her protectively
Zeon glared. Gurgin jerked a thumb over his shoulder, an
the Jackal went off to join the others on top of a heap o
cartons. Hakeem watched him, feeling his cheeks burn.

"I'd let you go if I could," he whispered. "I . . . I can't do
anything."

"I'll be all right, but you ought to go, Hakeem. You'r
above this nasty crowd," Mrs. Green said loudly.

"Please, Grandma, not in front of the others," he begge
her.

"What's the difference?" Grandma Eustatia said, raisin
her voice to concert pitch. It rang off the concrete ceiling an
dented his eardrums. "They should hear this, too! Shame o
them! Shame on you!"

It was impossible to ignore her. Every fairy godmother i
the room turned around to look at them. Even Mr. Froiste
emerged from his little office in the corner to see what al
the fuss was.

"If I could get out, I would," Hakeem whispered. Grandm
Eustatia gave him a tender look, as if he were six years ol
again.

"It's always your choice, honey." She patted his hand
Hakeem resolved that now would be the moment he woul
take charge of his own life.

He marched up to Froister, who was standing, arms folded
on the perimeter of the enclosure. The guildmaster looke
curiously at Hakeem, and raised a hand to permit him t
speak.

"I don't want to do this anymore, sir," Hakeem said. "
want out."

Froister's eyebrows rose toward his hairline. "This is a
inconvenient time for you to quit, young man."

"I'm sorry about that," Hakeem said. "I've got to go.
can't do this anymore. Please." He was begging now, but h

didn't care. If he didn't get it all out at once, he never would be able to again. He was already starting to feel his resolve ebbing. He glanced back at Grandma Eustatia, who nodded encouragement at him. "Let me leave. Please."

"He'll rat," Zeon shouted from the skidload of lamps.

"Zeon!" Hakeem exclaimed, staring up at him in horror. The rest of the fairy godmothers were still silent, watching.

"You can tell he's not really your friend," Grandma Eustatia said, from across the room.

"He's not steady, Mr. F.," Zeon complained. "He must have known about that old bitch, and he didn't say. He'll split if he can. He'll bring the cops."

"No he won't," Froister said assuredly. Hakeem hated him for his complacency. He'd sweep-kick the oily bastard off his feet, but the important thing was just to get out. If he could go get Ray, they could think of some way to free his grandmother, and get the others out, too.

"I should have refused in the first place," Hakeem said bitterly, "like Ray's been doing all along."

Froister's eyebrows went up again. "I'm sorry I don't know your friend. He sounds like a man of integrity."

"He is! I won't do this anymore," Hakeem said, squaring his shoulders. He held up his hands. "Please take these things off me. I quit!"

"No," Froister said with a half smile. "You can't quit. You swore an oath. You'll perform your tasks with dignity, or without. You have no choice. Go." Hakeem folded his arms and stood his ground. Froister sighed. "Pity. Well, I can't have you defying me to my face. Kneel."

Hakeem paused, just for a moment. He knew Froister had used up three wishes on him, so he thought that there was nothing else that could happen. Hakeem was bigger and stronger than the guildmaster. If no one got in the way, he'd be able to take the man down by himself.

Then Froister asked, very deliberately, "You swear to obey the mother of the lamp?"

Hakeem could no longer help himself. The magic took

over, weighing down his limbs and chest. He dropped to the floor on his hands and knees, gasping.

"That's better," Froister said, that maddening smile on his lips. "Into the lamp, young man. Think of your sins and promise to be a better djin in future." The guildmaster seemed to go all misty, but Hakeem knew it was his own eyes turning to smoke. The faces around him got larger and larger.

The magic hurt horribly as it sucked him in, but Hakeem bit his lips, refusing to give Froister or Zeon the satisfaction of a scream. The spell kept twisting him into a smaller and smaller package until he saw the milk-white walls of his prison around him. The squeezing stopped. Jumping up, he hammered on the sides of the lamp. He could hear voices outside. No one could hear him. He tried to dematerialize and solidify outside the lamp, but for some reason the spell wasn't working.

Ray Crandall and his grandmother were fairy godparents! Hakeem kept thinking over and over. At that moment he knew the most remarkable fact of his life, and he couldn't tell anybody except the people he didn't want to hear it.

Froister picked up the painted milk glass lamp and hefted it. A show of defiance, but he should have expected something of the kind. These young men didn't grow up in a vacuum. There was bound to be an overlap in membership of affiliated organizations. The only thing to do was to prevent any more fraternization in future. And with luck, this ordeal would be over very soon. By sequestering the troublemaker, he hoped to demoralize the fairy godparents still further.

"Keep getting them in here!" he ordered his gang of apprentices. "I want every fairy godmother in the Local 3–26 in this warehouse by nightfall. No exceptions!" He carried the lamp away to his office, and locked it in.

Ray leaned on the bell marked "Feinstein" at Rose's three-flat. Nobody answered the door. No Rose. Just when he really needed her advice, she wasn't around.

He sat down on the stoop to think. Her family had probably

taken her out to dinner, in which case it would be hours before she came back. Or maybe they had taken her off on vacation, in which case he would be waiting days to talk to her. No, she had offered him a meal on Tuesday, so she must still be around. He'd come back later, after dinner, and beg a few minutes alone to talk.

Ray headed for home. He wished he wasn't going to be inactive for a week. The wand told him there were need strings here and there, coming from houses, apartments, parks, and passing cars. He thought about getting involved, but none of them pulled him so hard as that little girl in the hospital had, so he made a judgment call that they weren't urgent enough for him to intervene. There'd be another fairy godparent along in a while, to take care of these. He would rather have had Rose overseeing his efforts than blowing a child's one miracle with overkill or underkill.

As he turned the corner into his block, he heard the hubbub of many voices. Warily, he craned his neck to see who was there. About halfway down the street was a bunch of neatly dressed men and women. Ray recognized them as guardian angels. Some of them had been here the night of the car fire, but some were the crease-trousered bunch from Edwin's bar. They were casting around as if looking for someone or something. One of them looked his way and pointed. As one, all the heads turned toward him. He felt nervous at the attention, but it must be okay: these were the good guys. Most likely they wanted to ask questions about the genie gangbangers.

The Reverend Barnes was at the head of the group. He spotted Ray, and, instead of beckoning, he threw a "go away" gesture toward him. Ray halted, puzzled, and the big man *flew* across the street to meet him.

"Don't go home!" Barnes shouted. "There's someone hunting fairy godmothers!" Half the group lifted up off the pavement to follow. Ray looked at them in bewilderment.

"What?" he demanded, as they all landed around him, talking at once. Finally, the broad-shouldered white man who had been directing traffic that night got them all quiet.

"There's someone with a list of your names," Reverend Barnes said. "They're grabbing the FGU off the streets in droves. You're the only one we've seen in the last hour."

"The last one?" Ray asked. "What about my grandmother?" He pointed toward his home.

"Should there be someone in that house?" the big white guy asked the Reverend Barnes.

"There certainly should be!" Barnes said. They followed Ray to his house. His mother came out on the steps at the noise.

"Oh, Ray! Thank heavens you're here," his mother said, giving a puzzled smile to the crowd of men and women at the bottom of her stoop. "Did you know if your grandmother was going out? She isn't home. I thought she'd at least leave a note."

"When did you last see her, Shannon?" the Reverend Barnes asked politely.

"Oh, I don't know," Ray's mother said. "I came back here for lunch. She said she was going to run some errands, that's all."

One of the women had broken away from the group and gone around the back of the Crandall house. She returned with a solemn expression on her face. Barnes looked a question at her, and she shook her head.

"Maybe she's at the church," Barnes said, with a smile for Ray's mother. "I'll check back, and if she's there, I'll give her a lift home."

"You're very kind. Are you coming in, Ray?"

"Not yet," he said. "I've got some things to do first." His mother nodded, bemused, and shut the door. "Now what?" he asked the guardian angels.

"The window of her room was open," the female GA reported, now that Ray's mother was out of earshot. "I smelled evil on the air."

"It's got to be the gangbangers," Ray said, frantic.

"We heard all about that," one of the yuppie-uniformed angels said. "We'll be on the lookout for her. Let us handle it."

"No, I've got to help you!" Ray said. "She's my grandmother."

"That does it," the Reverend Barnes said, and took Ray's arm. "You're not going anywhere you'll be in danger. We have to get you to somewhere safe, and start a real search."

Irresistible as a hurricane, the guardian angels swept him up off his feet and over the roofs of the houses. They landed on the pavement just in front of the Magic Bar, and all but stuffed him in the door, past the comfort of the wards.

"I wish I could say you'd be safe in the church, but these people don't respect its sanctity," Mr. Barnes said. "You'll be safe here with Edwin. And don't do any more magic yourself! That's how they'll find you."

The bar was a warm and comforting place most times, but it was creepy to be in there alone. Dust motes danced in the light from the glass door. Even the jukebox was silent.

"Sit down, Ray. We're going to be spending some time together." Edwin took down a glass and poured him a cola. "I hope they can find the rest of the FGU before whoever it is gets them."

Ray reached for the frosty glass, his mouth watering. He was thirsty and tired, and it would have been good to relax, but his hand stopped halfway. He was thinking of the doorbell that rang on an empty apartment. If the genie-Jackals had already gotten Grandma, had Rose been one of their earlier victims?

"I can't hide here," Ray said. "I've got to go—go find my friend."

"Ray, there are people out there hunting you," Edwin warned, the points of his mustache alarmed.

"I don't care!" he said, running out the door. "I've got to go find Rose!"

He felt the comforting wards slide away from him as he popped out onto the hot, sunlit sidewalk. He noticed now that the air did stink of evil, once he was out of the protected environment of the bar. The genie-Jackals had been everywhere. He only hoped he'd be in time to save Rose from them.

He pulled out all the brownie points he had, and told the little sparks he wanted point-to-point transportation to Rose's house.

A dog barked madly as Ray appeared in the middle of the lawn in front of Rose's three-flat. Questions in his head vied with one another for his attention. What was the DDEG doing collecting fairy godmothers? What about the merger?

This time when he leaned on the bell, someone buzzed him in. Thank heavens, maybe the genie-Jackals hadn't found Rose yet. He burst in the door and stood panting on the threshold.

Inside the apartment, there was a pretty woman of about forty with blond-streaked hair, two boys and a girl of assorted grade school ages, and a nice-looking man with dark hair and Rose's eyes and determined chin. But no Rose. Ray pulled himself together as they gave him bemused, questioning smiles.

"Mr. Feinstein?" he asked the man.

"Yes?"

"My name's Ray Crandall." Ray's voice was hoarse with tension. He cleared his throat. "I'm a friend of your mother's. Um, she asked me to come over ... today," he said, telling half a lie, "but she wasn't here when I came by earlier. May I speak to her? Is she home?"

"No, she's not." A furrow formed between the man's eyebrows. "That's strange, too. She said she'd wait home for us. We were going to take her to dinner. We have reservations."

"Who knows with her?" Ray asked automatically, then wondered if the family would take offense at his familiarity. Maybe Rose got a hot need string and had to go out. Reservations could be remade, but a kid only got one shot at a miracle. "I like her, Mr. Feinstein. She's a lively lady."

The man grinned shyly and shrugged, a copy of his mother's gestures. "I know. I can tell you're a good friend of hers. Well, Ray, I'll tell her you came by."

"Yeah. Thank you."

Ray left, his mind whirling. The genies had gotten her, too. Where could he look for them? There must be a hangout somewhere. Ray strode down the street, dodging people as he thought deeply.

Hakeem must have known something. That's why he had come looking for Ray that afternoon. They must have had Rose then! *That* was why he had said "sorry about your lady friend." But he wouldn't go along with something like *kidnapping*. Ray hoped he still had some morals left. So he had seen it happening. But where?

The GAS said he was the only fairy godparent still loose. That meant it was only a matter of time before the DDEG tracked him down. But it also meant that he had to be the one to rescue the others. The GAS were no good. They wanted him to hide while they did the rescuing. Forget it. The FGU was his society, his friends—and one of them was his grandmother. That made the stakes personal. The fairy godmothers believed in him. Ray couldn't let them down.

But he couldn't do it alone. He needed an army.

Chapter 24

"May I say something?" Rose said, getting up on a chair with Christopher Popp's assistance. The young guards standing in their corners glanced at her, but since she didn't seem to be trying to escape, they paid little attention to what she was doing. "I think that since we're all stuck here, we should have a meeting. It's not often that we have the entire membership handy."

"I second it," said Grandma Eustatia.

"Thank you, Mrs. Green," Rose said.

"A pleasure, Mrs. Feinstein."

"But we don't have ..." Alexandra said, looking around. Rose knew she was looking for Raymond. She held her finger to her lips. "... Don't have our *podium* here," Alexandra finished.

"Use a chair," George said, pulling one from the side of the room. Rose smiled as Alexandra took her place, and cleared her throat. George and Mrs. Durja flanked the chairwoman, looking as official as possible under the circumstances. The others moved their chairs or cots into rows, trying to make some order out of their enforced captivity.

"Well," Alexandra said, clearing her throat again, "I declare this to be an official meeting of the Fairy Godmothers Union, Local Federation 3–26." She moved her hand to tap on her improvised podium. "I feel almost as if I'm missing a hand, without my wand. We'll have to forego the usual wave." The thers murmured agreement. "Do we have the minutes of the last meeting?"

"Sorry," George said. "It was in my briefcase, too."

"Never mind," Alexandra said. Rose could tell she felt better, having something constructive to do. "Is there any old business?"

"Hey, you can't do this," one of the guards said.

"Certainly we can, young man," Alexandra said. "And you are out of order."

The guard blinked out of existence, and in a moment, he returned with the largest of the DDE guild officials.

"This is out of the question," Gurgin said, pushing through the barrier into the midst of the assembly. "Stop this at once."

"You dare not interfere with a legitimate meeting!" a shrill voice from above cried out. Rose looked up at the cage containing the ethnic fairy godmothers. "Let us out of here! We will take this up with the Grand Djin at the next board of directors meeting! They will disband your branch office!"

George breasted up to Gurgin, even though he only stood as high as the djin's middle shirt button.

"We are following correct rules of conduct according to our bylaws. It's all in the manuals, dating back hundreds of years. You have similar strictures. Don't you read your own regulations?"

Gurgin retreated, blasting out of the invisible cube in a puff of stinking cloud, and Alexandra tapped her hand on the back of the chair to regain order.

"I would like to thank our hosts for giving us nearly perfect attendance. Mrs. Feinstein is right. I haven't seen so many of the members in one place in years, if ever. No old business? Well, on to new business."

Rose bounced to her feet. "I propose that an official vote be taken right now on the question of whether to merge the FGU permanently with the DDEG to form the Wish Granters Association."

"What?" Froister burst into the room, with Gurgin behind him.

"So we all know where we stand," Rose concluded.

"Seconded," Eustatia Green said.

Waving his arms, Froister dashed in between the chair woman and the rest of the membership. "Stop this at once! he cried.

"Very well," Alexandra said, paying absolutely no attention She peered around him. "On the proposal to merge and form the WGA, all those in favor, say 'aye.'"

The room fell completely silent.

"Those opposed, say 'nay.'"

"NAY!" As one, the entire membership rose to its fee Even Mrs. Durja added her vote with vigor.

"That's it," Alexandra said. "The motion is defeated. W will not merge. Meeting is adjourned." She banged her han down on the chair back.

"In that case," Froister said, into the following silenc "you will stay here until the end of time."

"Then we will," Alexandra said, facing him with folde arms. "You can't attack our principles. That's what we stan for. We took a vote, and that's our response. If the internation federation insists that we join, we can't stop that, but we wi give them a complete report of our experiences."

"If they make you merge with us, we will have access your free magic anyhow."

"But we are in no position to receive an official mandate Alexandra said sweetly. "I'd have to believe that any directiv that came through you is spurious. And if you allow us contac we will tell them our side of the story, which will put an en to the official efforts altogether."

"This is outrageous! Give up the points, and you can g free now! All will be forgotten."

The chairwoman shook her head, and Rose was proud her. Froister looked ready to have apoplexy.

"Sorry. Those are personal and union property. You can have them without a court order."

Albert Froister slammed out of the room, wishing he never heard of unions or fairy godmothers.

* * *

"Well," Morry Garner said sourly. "We're standing on our principles right here in our nice little cellblock."

"Don't worry," Rose said with more optimism than she felt. "We're not beaten yet. Ray's still out there somewhere."

"And when he gets picked up by these goniffs?" Morry asked. "What then?"

"Trust to luck," Rose said. "Remember, we get just that little bit more than other people."

Ray hopped on one foot as he pulled on his most comfortable sneakers. He had cleaned up and changed clothes from the skin out. He didn't know how long he'd have to be on the streets, so he wanted at least to start out presentable and good-smelling. He didn't want to scare any of his conscripts. His first two were sitting side by side on his bed, looking absolutely skeptical.

"I don't understand all this stuff about fairy godmothers," Bobby said. "You're not gonna tell me you go around waving a wand on people."

"But he does!" Chanel said, her face lighting up. "That pencil in your jacket!" Ray took it out to show her. "That's really a magic wand?"

"Yes, it is," Ray said proudly. Chanel regarded it with awe. And avarice. Ray would have to deal with that later, in case she thought such things were transferable.

"Looks wimpy to me," Bobby said scornfully.

"Look, shrimp," Ray said, grabbing a handful of his brother's T-shirt and pulling him off the bed. "Grandma needs us. You going to help me, or not?"

"Yes—all right! Don't wrinkle the merchandise!" Bobby pulled away and brushed himself down.

"We're going to help Grandma?" Chanel asked.

"What's wrong with her?" Bobby asked.

"She's in trouble," Ray said. "I'll explain as we go. We have to get some more people together."

* * *

"You bet I'll help you," Clarice said, sitting down to lace on her skates when Ray asked for her help. "I move faster on wheels. Do you want me to get my boyfriends?"

Matthew jumped up as soon as Ray appeared at the door and hardly waited until Ray finished making his request before he went for his jacket.

Peter didn't say a word. He just went upstairs for his Little League bat, and fell in with the growing crowd of children.

Mariana went big-eyed and put her precious dog on a leash to follow them.

"I will tear apart enemies of Rose with my bare hands!" Honoria said bravely. "In the name of my little nephew who will be born, I swear it."

Victor, grinning at his astonished parents, dashed out the door of his home as soon as he saw Ray and the other children appear.

Ray had had no trouble remembering each child's name, location, and story. Victor was the only challenge, because Ray had met him in the hospital, not at home, but the brownie points knew how to locate him. Ray was glad Rose had made him take his time with every child, to make them all memorable, to make each individual wish right for them. When he explained what was going on, each and every one of them was willing to help. They were raring to go and take on the genies on behalf of the kindly woman who helped make their dreams come true.

"But where are we going?" Matthew asked practically, as they landed back in the neighborhood. Ray's brownie point piggy bank was empty—*below* empty, and he had no more ideas.

Ray sat down on the curb with his back against a parked car to think. Where *did* they start? There were no footprints to follow. Genies who could turn into plumes of smoke didn't leave trails. What about the fairy godmothers? Could he trail them in some way? There were the need strings. Did people stop having need strings when they got older? Ray took out is wand, to the awe of the crowd of children and the disdain of his brother, and started feeling the air with it.

The need strings were no more imperative than usual. If five dozen fairy godparents were in trouble, you'd think there would be some kind of psychic resonance, but he felt nothing. He tried concentrating particularly on adults. He could sense his mother, in the same way he had found Chanel by remote control the day he put the good spell on her. Mother would be frantic about Grandma, who was *her* mother. Could he sense her anxiety? No, not really. A clue! he begged the universe. Could he find Grandma the same way he found Chanel? He reached out through the goodness of the wand, but felt no trace. It was as if she had vanished from the face of the Earth.

Jorgito watched him with big, sympathetic eyes. He had been weeping for Rose ever since Ray had told him what happened. Now he let out a tremendous sniff, and rubbed his nose on his sleeve. With a sigh, Ray reached into his pocket for a tissue. Jorge honked his nose miserably.

"That's it!" Ray said, patting the astonished boy on the back. He jumped to his feet. Mr. Guthrie, the nose-wiper! Ray remembered how he stank of evil. That was his best, and truthfully, his only clue.

"We're looking for people who smell really bad," Ray said to the others. They looked puzzled, and he tried to explain. "A kind of a stink comes from them. They can't help it."

"My dad sometimes stink when he come home from work," Jorge said helpfully. "He does constructions."

"Not like normal smell," Ray said, then became frustrated trying to explain. "It's like . . . it's like that *man!*" He stood up, realizing the answer had been literally under his nose all the time.

"What man?" Bobby asked, looking around with disdain. "You're the only man here."

Ray made an impatient gesture. "You know the lamp shop down on the main street?" he asked. "Enlightenment? I think he's the one who's behind this whole thing. Maybe."

Logic said that a) evil magic smelled bad, b) that man

smelled bad, and so, it followed that c) he must be doing evi
magic. Ray had no specific reason to think the man wa
involved with the DDEG, but it was pretty far to go for
coincidence. And Enlightenment was a big building. Who'
notice a few extra people hanging around?

He explained his conclusion to the kids. Bobby was scornfu
of Ray's premises involving magic, but he couldn't fault th
syllogism. "It's worth a try," he said.

"If you're wrong," Clarice said encouragingly, "all we hav
to do is keep looking somewhere else."

Ray knew that he was right before they even stepped int
the door of Enlightenment. The smell was so strong the kid
started making faces when they were half a block away. Bobby
stopped issuing disparaging comments and started looking a
Ray with a trifle more respect. The stink was nauseating. Ray
gulped.

"We won't have much time. They're going to try and stop
us right away," he said, just before they went inside. "Star
looking for a place they could keep a lot of people."

The girl, looking a little queasy, stood up from behind her
cash register as Ray pushed open the door and led his little
army into the arena.

"Can I help you?" she asked. She watched the file of children enter, and her face went blank with shock. It only took
her a moment to recover, but she shouted, "Mr. Froister!"

Froister! Ray thought. That was the name of the DDE
guildmaster, according to the Blue Fairy. His guess, as if he
needed any more clue than the stink, had paid off.

The man in the dapper suit came rushing out of the back
room. He didn't look quite as dandy as he had the other day.
His air of crispness had wilted. He looked at the children,
too, and started making shooing motions.

"Please," he said, gesturing toward the door. "This store
really isn't for children."

"But we're customers," Ray said, sidestepping and getting
in his way. He signaled to the kids to scatter throughout the

displays. "You've got this great lamp I want to talk to you about. In fact, you know a *whole lot* about lamps, don't you?"

"It's my profession," Froister said uneasily. The man seemed to recognize him, and started to come closer for a better look. Ray held his breath, but he couldn't help it. He sucked in a deep lungful of air, and gagged.

"*And* your avocation?" Ray asked pointedly. "Aren't you a *genie*?"

By the shocked look on Froister's face he'd hit the target dead center.

"Please," the man said, with deep disdain, "the term is 'djin,' not 'genie.'" But Ray must have been exuding a recognizable odor, too, because Froister's expression changed from shock to amazement.

"*You*? You're a fairy godmother?" he exclaimed.

Ray pretended to look pained. "Please. We prefer the gender neutral term 'fairy godparent.' And my guess is you've got a whole crowd of them stashed here."

Froister pursed his lips in a crooked smile. "That's right. It's very nice of you to come here and complete my collection without having to chase you down."

"Forget it. You've got my grandmother here," Ray said, folding his arms. "I've come to get her and my other friends, and then we're all leaving."

"I think not. You'll all stay," Froister said, and shouted to the air. "Grab him!"

Genie-Jackals started to appear out of the air, and Ray recognized most of his street adversaries. They were all tough fighters, but at least they weren't carrying weapons. Ray drew his wand. It wouldn't be much protection, but what about good versus evil? Could he start some magical interference and blow their fuses? *I'm granting wishes for kids later*, he thought at the wand. *Don't let me down now!* The little blue star burst into brilliant light like a supernova, pumping out all of the goodness it could.

"Get them all!" Froister yelled.

"Lamps!" Ray shouted at the kids. "Start rubbing lamps!" The kids dived away from the attacking djinni and toward the lighting fixtures. Being so much smaller, they had no trouble ducking under the displays and around tables. Bobby made a grab for a tall floor lamp, but before he could touch it, a Hispanic man in a black leather jacket appeared out of nowhere and threw his arms around him. Bobby stamped on the man's foot, and flung himself away under a table. Out of the corner of his eye, Ray saw half of the man turn to insubstantial smoke to follow him. Bobby scrambled out of sight.

Mariana's tiny dog stood between her and a couple of big white kids. She leaped for a lamp. The gangbangers jumped right over the dog, but it hung on to one of them with its teeth in his leg, distracting them long enough for her to duck behind a cluster of statues. She stuck out a tiny hand and rubbed a lamp vigorously. One of the gangbangers suddenly changed sides, pushing his brothers away from her. They turned into smoke to try and counter him, but he spread out across their path like jelly on a piece of bread.

A handful of older men burst out of the back room, and fanned out through the showroom, following the children. These looked like they knew what they were doing. Better start getting some more of the djinni on his side. Ray reached for a lamp, and passed his palm over its surface. A gangbanger wearing a Jackal badge appeared next to him with glassy eyes and folded arms. Before Ray could open his mouth to make a wish, a clump of smoke turned into a wiry, dark-haired man, who rubbed the lamp right after him, undoing his control. The djin turned to the man, instead. Peter sneaked under the man's legs and rubbed the lamp again, preventing the man from making a bad wish. A redheaded man came in behind *him*, until the gangbanger looked dizzy, not knowing to whom he should answer.

Ray broke away and went for the next lamp he could reach. Peter tried to follow, but Redhead picked him up bodily and carried him toward the pair of big swinging doors at the back of the showroom, walking straight through the displays.

"Help!" Peter yelled.

Ray dodged around the tables, trying to get the boy back. Genie-Jackals and others were appearing and vanishing all over the place as the children and men fought over control of their lamps, getting in each other's way.

Peter swatted down at the man's back with his bat, hitting nothing but his own knees when his captor turned partly to smoke. As Ray ducked around the displays, trying to reach him, Peter got smart and smacked Redhead's arms. The djin couldn't dematerialize and hold a solid boy at the same time. Peter dropped to the floor and fled back toward the lamps.

Ray's helpers had the advantage of size, but if the djinni could walk through solid objects, it wouldn't help them for long. Ray worried that in his desperation he had led the children into deadly danger.

A couple of gangbangers grabbed Clarice by each arm, and flew with her, shrieking, toward the ceiling. She kicked out with her tiger-striped skates, sending sprays of crystal pendants flying off a nearby chandelier. The other children caught on, shoving lamps toward the floor. Over the crashing and shattering of glass Froister started screaming orders in a more hysterical voice. Ray had a chance to grin before someone else took a poke at him. Maybe being uncompromisingly solid had its advantages after all.

"Be careful of the displays!" Froister howled.

Chanel's high, concert hall–trained voice shrilled over all the noise. "I found Grandma! She's in the back room!"

"Good!" Ray shouted back, but his voice wasn't as mighty as his sister's. "Tell her we're coming!"

"There's a hundred people back there!"

"I know!"

"Him!" Froister shouted, standing on the cash register desk and pointing at Ray. "I want him! He's a fairy godfather. Take him!"

A big man, who looked like he had just stepped out of the Arabian nights and put on a business suit, waded through the displays. Ray backed away from him, but found himself trapped against the statue of a verdigris dolphin and shell. The big man picked Ray up effortlessly and pinned him against the wall by his arms.

Froister addressed him over the man's shoulders.

"Why are you fighting us, young man?" he asked in a reasonable, conversational tone as if there wasn't a mad chase going on all around them. Another glass shade exploded, and he winced. "We're allies, you and I. Our organizations are all set to merge."

"You're evil," Ray shouted at him. He kicked at his captor, but the man just made his midsection into steam. "Ugh!"

Froister regarded him with sympathy. "Young man, did you ever think of what you could do with *real* power, not the poor wave-the-wand type the fairy godmothers let you have, or whatever you can glean with a few spare brownie points? You could control a city! Hoard untold riches! All this could be yours, if you help us." His voice rang with triumph and conviction, but Ray knew a nut when he heard one. "Help us, and you'll have power! All you have to do is cooperate on one tiny thing. That's all I ask. And then vast power will be yours!"

Ray narrowed his eyes and twisted his lips to sneer, even though his shoulders felt like they were dislocating, and his back was pressed against something sharp.

"I've heard all this crap for years from these gangbangers," Ray spat. "Easy power. Easy influence, free, *if* you pay their price. I wouldn't fall for it from them, and *I am not going to listen to you, either*. I know you're evil. I won't serve evil. You want something? You can whistle for it." He felt another sharp stab in the spine as the big man shoved him harder against the wall.

"Integrity," Froister said unexpectedly. He nodded. "Too bad. Destroy him and his little friends!"

The big man yanked him away from the wall and threw him over his head and into a glass table which crashed under him into a million fragments. Ray lay on the ruins of it, stunned. Someone screamed. The sound cut into his consciousness.

His head spinning, Ray picked himself up. He was bleeding from hundreds of tiny cuts, but the real pain came from an eight-inch-long daggerlike shard of glass sticking into his thigh. Warm blood seeped down his pants leg and pooled on the floor. Ray just looked down at it, gasping. It was so deep it didn't hurt yet. He reached through his overdrawn mental piggy bank, pleading for help. *I know I don't have any more brownie points*, he thought, *but I'm going to bleed to death!*

Suddenly, his bank account was full of thousands of tiny, glittering suns. One of them hopped up eagerly and vanished from the picture. The rest of the FGU was helping him! He felt pressure in the gash as the glass popped out. The wand echoed the goodness of the magic that stopped the bleeding and mended his flesh.

He had no time to concentrate on the wonder, because he found himself in the middle of a whirlwind of black smoke. The wind blew his arms up like gravity flipping into reverse, leaving his midsection vulnerable to the fists that lashed out from the smoke, pummeling him. Ray immediately dragged his elbows down against his ribs, and jabbed out at his attackers. There were howls of delighted laughter in the dark cloud. His punches hit nothing substantial. A fist knocked him in the jaw, and he tripped backward against the frame of the glass table. Glass cut into his palms as he tried to save himself.

A heavy fist connected with the side of his head, and Ray gasped as stars danced in his eyes. He wiped blood onto his face when he clapped his hand to the side of his head. It was time to fight back! He started grabbing the hands that punched out at him, crushing knuckles and fingers with the strength built up over a summer of digging flower beds. There were cries of anguish in the circle of smoke. The hands disappeared, but not before he saw blood from the fragments of glass in his palms.

One arc of the circle suddenly vanished with an audible "Poof!" and Ray heard Matthew's voice cry out in triumph.

"I've got one!"

"Wish for him to protect us!" Ray shouted, cradling his hand. "All of us!"

The senior djinni immediately went after Matthew, but there was suddenly a wall of shimmering force between them and the boy. The circle of smoke around Ray dissipated when the genie-Jackals found their punches were no longer connecting

with their targets. Ray scrambled over the shattered displays
gathering up the children as he went, until they were pressed
against the inside of one of the sidewalls of the showroom.
A huge man with a scalloped crew cut stood facing the other
djinni with his arms folded, protecting them.

"Break through his spell!" Froister shouted. "He's only
one."

The big man gave Froister a strange look. Ray knew there
was some reason that they couldn't just wish through the
protective spell. The young djinni regrouped in three bunches.
Ray saw gang badges for not only the Riverside Jackals, but
the Backyard Wolves as well. Two gangs! The conspiracy of
evil had spread farther than he had dreamed. They had to be
stopped somehow before they really did take over the city.
The solution lay with the fairy godparents trapped in the back
room, if only he could get them out.

"Ray, you're hurt!" Matthew said, goggling at the broken
glass dusting his clothes. Ray brushed at himself, then decided
his condition wasn't important. They had to get them from
this spot to the warehouse, and it wasn't going to be easy.

"Now, what?" Bobby asked.

Ray turned to Matthew. "Tell your guy here to keep a
protective shell around us as we move. We're going in the
back." Matthew, wide-eyed, nodded, and passed on the
instructions.

Without turning his head, the burly djin said, "I hear and
obey."

"Okay. Everyone stick together." Ray gripped Chanel's and
Jorge's hands, and started moving toward the back room.

The other djinni hung outside the protective barrier like
piranha watching a side of beef being lowered into their tank.
Froister was still jumping up and down shouting orders.

Their protector shoved open the doors of the warehouse,
and Ray stood and stared, shocked.

Chapter 25

Beyond the first aisle of boxes, the warehouse looked like a Red Cross camp after a disaster. Rows of camp beds were set out along two edges of a big open square, with people in bedraggled clothes asleep or resting on them. In the middle, dozens of chairs of every description were huddled in little circles. The men in them were unshaven, and the women's hairstyles had flattened out. They all sprang out of their chairs as the doors flew open against the walls. Everyone rushed to the edge of the open square, but could come no farther.

"Ray!" Grandma Eustatia cried.

Ray saw his grandmother and tried to run to her, but he bounced off an invisible wall that extended all the way around the room. He got to his knees and felt his way along, but he sensed no gap in the spell. His bloodied hands left a streak on the solid air for a few seconds before fading. Froister had his prisoners securely locked up. Ray had to find a way to break the spell.

"I'll get you out," he said. He turned to Matthew to have him make another wish.

Suddenly, he felt a cold wind on the back of his neck, and spun around. The children huddled against him, terrified. Their protector was no longer standing beside them. He was back with the other gang members. All of them showed their teeth in fierce grins as they advanced, snarling like wild animals.

"The lamp!" Ray cried. "We forgot to protect the lamp!" He reached into his piggy bank for some brownie points to take up the slack. The evil magic in the room caused the tiny sparks to twist into abnormal shapes as he wished on them. He was afraid to trust them. Ray's group was stuck with what flesh and bone could do to defeat the djinni.

"Scatter!" Bobby shouted. The children broke back out into the showroom, dodging gangbangers and rubbing lamps as they went. The senior djinni followed in their wake, to keep the membership under their control, but they were outnumbered by Ray's miniature army. Ray faked to the left, and tried to run out into the showroom, but Zeon pounced on him and caught his head in a hammerlock. The big man had an insane look on his face.

"I'm gonna take you out," he whispered, his face close to Ray's, his eyes glinting ferally under the long eyelashes. "I'm gonna pull your guts out and tie them into knots around every light pole on this street. You gonna die in pain, sucker," he said, sneering. He caught Ray's flailing arm and twisted it up against his shoulder blades. Ray gasped. The rest of the Jackals crowded around, kicking and punching him.

Suddenly, outside the circle of fists and feet, Ray heard the voice, almost inside his head, "What wouldst thou, O my mother?"

"Do *something* to help me and the other kids," Chanel's voice stated, loud and clear. "Especially my brother!"

"Where is that voice coming from?" Froister asked. "Somebody, find that girl!"

Ray gasped. He fell to the ground, and got kicked hard in the ribs. He curled up in a ball to protect his face and belly. Blows kept impacting his back and rear. He was worried that they'd do permanent damage to his kidneys, when the blows started to become fewer. He dared a peek up under the angle of his elbow. One of the gangbangers, and not the largest one, either, was yanking djinni off him one by one and tossing them over his shoulder like handkerchiefs. He got to his feet. Chanel was standing next to one of the lamps, her magic shell glowing brightly enough he didn't need the wand to see it. She looked scared, but not one of the djinni even paused as they got close to her. They couldn't see her at all!

Clarice on wheels got to Ray first, but the others were close behind. They helped him to his feet. Ray grabbed Peter and planted him next to Chanel with his baseball bat. "Stay near this lamp. Don't let anyone else close," he said.

Froister was furious. "How dare you corrupt one of our membership! You asked for it!" he said. "Listen up!" He clapped his hands, and the djinni stood to attention. "The next wish: kill the intruders! Destroy them! Oh, my beautiful shop," he moaned, as the other adults echoed his orders.

The genie-Jackals and genie-Wolves dematerialized. The next thing the children knew was that they were in the hands of the enemy. Each of them was seized by one, two, or three gang-genies, and hauled inexorably toward the back room. They kicked, struggled, and screamed, but they were held tightly. Ray tried to go after them, making up wishes and discarding them, as the deformed stars danced in his head.

Something tripped him up and a heavy foot planted itself in the middle of his back. Once again, failing to pay attention to his physical surroundings, Ray had put himself at risk. He planted his sore palms on the glass-strewn floor and pushed up. The foot pressed down harder and he sprawled, barking his chin on a fragment of lamp frame. Chanel looked at him from her post near the lamp. She made as if to come to help him, but he waved her back. A voice over his head laughed, and Ray groaned.

"You're mine," Zeon whispered dangerously. "Your ass is history. I'm gonna take you apart. I'm gonna . . ."

His low voice was suddenly drowned out by a sound like flapping wings. Suddenly, the room was full of men and women. Ray didn't know whether the smell of evil had attracted them or Chanel's wish had brought them, but the cavalry had arrived in the person of the entire Guardian Angel Society. Ray heard a grunt as someone knocked Zeon off his back. He scrambled to his feet, brushing glass off his front, and stared.

"Hi, boyfriend," Antoinette said, as she delivered another hearty kick to Zeon's brisket. The big gangbanger turned his middle to smoke, but somehow the foot connected anyhow.

Zeon moaned and dropped to the floor. Antoinette gave Ray a brilliant smile, and waded into the fray against another genie-Jackal.

It didn't seem to matter if the djinni were solid or not. The guardian angels grabbed at any part of a djin they could reach, and held tightly. The gang-genies struggled furiously, but magic couldn't get them free. When they struck out physically, the guardian angels twisted arms, grabbed feet and lifted, or just engaged their opponents with fisticuffs or hearty hammer-locks. They were effective, efficient fighters.

Ray, panting, followed in Antoinette's wake as she warded off an attack with a two-handed karate block. "I didn't know you were a guardian angel."

"Your partner knew right away," she said, evading a kick from a black-clad djin and flipping him upside down into a standing lamp. Another djin ran to save the lamp, leaving his companion lying flat on the floor. "My uncle got me into the society. I told you I was helping him out, but you didn't ask me any details. I was there the night of the fire, and you never even saw me until the end."

"I'm sorry," Ray said, feeling more than a little stupid. "You knew about me?"

A glass fixture fell to the ground between them, shattering with a hearty *crash*!, but none of the particles struck either one of them.

"Sure did. My uncle is your guardian angel. He thought it was important that I know."

"I was going to tell you," Ray said sheepishly.

"I know," Antoinette said. Her eyes flashed adoring fire at him, and he felt a wonderful tingle in his belly. Her face changed suddenly to alarm. "Duck!" she cried.

A djin melted a whole brass lamp in his hand and hefted it straight at Ray. The Reverend Barnes caught it in his bare hands and put it on the floor, where it bubbled, setting the linoleum ablaze. A couple of the GAS jumped the fire-setting djin and sat on him.

"Organize!" the Reverend Barnes shouted. "I want them all in there!" He pointed to the warehouse doors. Matthew,

emporarily free of entanglement, jumped forward and started
o muster the other children.

"When you get genie lamps, carry them in after me!" he
cried.

The kids started polishing lamps furiously. Now that they
had protection, they could keep the genies who answered their
summons. Peter saw the fire-starting djin appear before him.
Peter pointed to the warehouse entrance. Obediently, the djin
vanished, and reappeared to stand with the others, glassy-
eyed, and the angels sat heavily on the floor.

"I knew you couldn't keep out of it," the Reverend Barnes
said to Ray over a gangbanger he was holding in a hammerlock. "You did good, son." The youth struggled, but even
when he turned into smoke, the guardian angel held him tight.
A moment later he vanished. His lamp must have been rubbed.

"Get them! Get them!" Froister called, shaking his fists
over everyone's head. "Obey the third wish! Destroy them
all!"

"Uh-oh," Ray said. He could feel a force building up around
them as the djinni strove to follow their guildmaster's instructions. Something incredibly evil was going to happen. The
whole building began to shake. Winds howled through the
broken windows, whipping what was left of the chandeliers
until they smacked into the ceiling. Desperately, Ray threw
all of the brownie points in his head out to protect him and
the children and the guardian angels and the FGU. He flung
himself to the floor as the two powers collided, overfilling
the building, and the roof blew off.

Ray gawked up at the daylit sky. It was full of pretty sparks
and flowers made of light. His dazed brain even enjoyed the
shower of little pieces of shingle and rafter as they pattered
harmlessly down around him.

Antoinette was next to him in a second, helping him to his
feet.

"What did you do?" she asked. "That was spectacular."

Ray stood up rather unsteadily. He looked around, but he
could see only guardian angels and children. "Where's Frois-

ter?" he asked, all of the last few minutes coming back to him in a rush. "I want a word with that man."

"Gone," Reverend Barnes said.

Ray threw his head back and howled at the sky. "Coward!"

"Now, calm down," the Reverend Barnes said severely. "That's not worthy behavior for a conquering champion." Ray was embarrassed.

"Sorry," he said. He heard another outcry, dozens of voices together.

"Get us out of here!"

Ray and the others ran through the swinging doors to the back room. Chanel threw herself at her grandmother and was rebounded several feet by the barrier. She tried again. When she couldn't batter through, she turned on Ray.

"Get her out!" she demanded, her face set. "Right this minute!"

"Hold on, Chanel." The Reverend Barnes shook his head. "It takes the genie who put it up to break it down. Who was that?"

Matthew was in a corner of the warehouse, imperiously ordering all of the other children to place lamps in rows. The djinni stood in rows, too, staring straight ahead with their arms folded. Reverend Barnes put the question to them.

A glassy-eyed Zeon was unable to lie. "It was Hakeem."

"Hakeem?" Bobby asked. "Ray's buddy made an *invisible wall*?" His whole concept of big brothers and their relative boringness had been dented forever today, if not entirely shattered.

"Hakeem's not here," Ray said, searching the crowd of gangbangers.

"All the lamps are accounted for," Matthew said. "We rubbed all the others left in the showroom twice to make sure."

"Then he's somewhere else in here," Ray said. He looked around for the shop's cashier, and found her hiding under the cash desk. He helped her to her feet. "Miss, excuse me, are there any more lamps in this store?"

She looked at him as if he was crazy. "The place is full of
em. In boxes. In the back."

"No, it'd have to be a used one," Ray said. "Like these
thers." She shrugged, looking dazed. Ray went back to Zeon.
Where'd it go?" he demanded, stifling the urge to grab the
ther by the collar and shake the information out of him.
eon must have thought worse was in store for him. His face
as covered with beads of sweat.

"I don't know. Froister, he took it with him the other day."

"Need string," Rose shouted, leaning on the barrier. "He's in
rouble. He'll be needy. I'm sure you can find him, Raymond.
ou're the only one with a wand."

Ray looked at her gratefully. He emptied a load of broken
lass out of his pocket, but the wand was there, too, safe and
vhole. As his family and friends watched with wonder, he
ested the air with the shining star.

The wand felt so marvelously good in his fingers after all
hat evil that he enjoyed it just for a moment before concentrat-
ng on the task. Off to one side was the bundle of need strings
elonging to the gangbangers, a pretty pathetic lot all told.
Ray tested the cube containing the FGU. No wonder he wasn't
ble to sense them from the street. This thing was a very
effective barrier. It was a miracle the brownie points had
gotten through to him.

But there was one hopeless string calling to him, apart from
all the others. He followed it, with Antoinette, the Reverend
Barnes, and all the kids trailing behind him, to a small office
in one of the near corners of the warehouse. Ray pushed
through the doors. The trace was coming from the desk, from
a pretty, dainty lamp made of milk glass with a painted scene
on the body. He gawked at it.

"Hakeem? That's his lamp?"

"Well, *I* like it," Antoinette said. "I'd hate to see what you
would choose. Maybe you have hidden artistic tendencies,
too."

Ray thought ruefully of the green art lamp, now smashed
to splinters. "I guess so." He brushed the side of the milk
glass pane. Hakeem appeared with folded arms.

"What wouldst thou, O my mother?" he said, in a flat voice. Then he blinked. "Ray? Thank heavens, brother. I've been stuck in there for ages!"

"It's all over," Antoinette said reassuringly. "Are you all right?"

"Where's Mr. Froister?" Hakeem asked, his eyes wide.

"Split," Ray said. "His buddies, too." Hakeem looked relieved.

"Son, destroy that magical barrier out there," the Reverend Barnes said, pointing out the door at the crowd of fairy godparents leaning as closely as they could to see. Hakeem looked at Ray for instructions.

"What he said," Ray told him.

"With pleasure!"

Hakeem blinked, and the crowd of fairy godparents swelled toward them as the barrier dropped, and the ones leaning on it stumbled over. Rose pushed her way through to come in and kiss Ray.

"Oh, I am *so* proud of you!" she said. Ray was so glad to see her alive and well and spunky that he couldn't say a word. He hugged her back.

Hakeem held up his wrists as if the bracelets were handcuffs. "Somebody, get me out of these things, please! Now!"

"Does it take anything special?" Ray asked the guardian angels.

"Not if he doesn't mind letting go of the power," Alexandra said, pushing her way through the crowd to stand at Ray's side. "Just wish him free."

"I don't mind at all, ma'am," Hakeem said, desperately. "Please!"

"I wish you to be free," Ray said, at once. The bands fell with a clang to the floor. They all looked at them. Hakeem stepped over them, breathing in great gulps as if air was a new and wonderful commodity.

"Never again," he said, beaming until his round cheeks bulged out. "No gangs, no drugs, no nothing. I swear it." Ray grinned at him, and they embraced.

The crowd surrounded them as they came out of the office,

apping Ray and the others on the back, and shouting congrat-
lations. His grandmother came to meet him, with Bobby and
hanel hanging on to each hand. Grandma Eustatia shook off
e two young ones and gave Ray a warm hug.

"I always knew you were special, sweetheart," she said.
he gave Hakeem a hug, too.

"Ray, you should have seen this child," Grandma said,
olding onto Hakeem's hand. "He told off that ridiculous
roister to his face. Real dignity. You'd have been proud."
lakeem looked ashamed of himself.

"I should never have gotten into this in the first place,"
lakeem admitted. "I wasn't so smart."

"Well, you got your second chance, child, and it didn't
ven cost you your miracle," Grandma Eustatia said.

Ray pulled Rose forward.

"Grandma," he said, "this is Mrs. Rose Feinstein. Rose,
his is my grandmother, Eustatia Green." They both looked
t him, puzzled. "You're two of my three favorite ladies in
he whole world. Why don't you two call each other by your
irst names?"

They looked at each other. Rose shrugged. "I didn't know
f you'd want it," Rose said. "You never asked me."

"I thought you just would if you wanted to," Grandma said,
uzzled. They laughed and embraced one another. Antoinette
ut her arm around Ray and squeezed his waist.

"What do we do with the rest of these boys?" George
Aldeanueva asked, surveying the rows of djinni. Alexandra
ocated their wands in a safe. It took a quick wish from one
of the static djinni to open it. She distributed them to the
membership, who received them with joy. The fairy fairy
godmothers received theirs and flitted away without so much
as a backward thank-you to anyone but Raymond Crandall.

"First, fix their wounds," Rose said, whisking her wand to
and fro. She enjoyed the feeling of being connected again. It
was time to do some more good in the world, as soon as
they'd cleared up in here, and she'd made some kind of
explanation to her son and his family. "Then, we'll have to

make these tykes forget what they saw. It's not a good id
to have them involved in magic too soon. They need to gro
up first."

"Awww!" the children chorused.

"Hey, we helped," Peter protested, coming up to put h
hand in Rose's. "Don't make us forget!"

"Oh, sweetheart," Rose said, trying to think of an explan
tion that would satisfy him. Eustatia came to the rescue.

"You can all remember it in your dreams," Grandma Eu
tatia said, and no one dared to sass in her face. Then Ros
George, and Alexandra went into a huddle to come up wi
exact wording that would free the genie-Jackals and geni
Wolves from the magic bonds.

"I wish you were a normal young man again, with
interest in gangs, drugs, guns, or mayhem," Rose said, starti
with the big youth Ray identified as Zeon. "I wish you
forget all you had to do with the DDEG and magic. A
finally, I wish you free."

The wristbands fell off with a clatter. "There," Rose sai
"He can start over again. I hope he'll do better."

"What am I doing here?" the big youth asked.

"How do you feel?" Rose countered, smiling at him.

Zeon gave Rose a suspicious look, then stepped over t
bands, and walked out of the ruin of the shop without looki
back. The others followed him one by one as their magic w
exhausted and their bonds were released.

With Speed Guthrie, there was a difference of opinion
to what to do.

"I want him to make some kind of reparation," Geor
said. "He kidnapped me. He misused his special knowledg
as the observer to the FGU. And he's the one responsible f
this nonsense, apart from Albert Froister, that is."

"Well, no revenge," Alexandra said. "You don't want
stink up your reputation."

"Please," George said, pained. "You only had to breathe
for a few days. I've been here two weeks. In that case, he

st going to have to grant a lot more wishes than the others
d. It'll take a lot out of him, but serve him right. First, let's
up this place. We can't leave it as a fire hazard for the
ighborhood."

"You heard him," Matthew ordered.

His face strained, Speed Guthrie waved his arms. A huge
oud of smoke rose around him, but Ray was relieved to see
at it was silver, not dark. Mr. Guthrie was doing a good
ed, so there was no evil smell.

"Second, we send all these children back home." Clarice,
ter, and the others pleaded to stay, but the magic surrounded
em. In a moment, there were no children left in the shop
it Matthew. Even Bobby and Chanel had been sent home.
e wondered what they were going to tell their mother.

"Wish number three," George said. "Make sure none of
e lamps in this building can ever be used to contain djinni
ain." Matthew, nodding, repeated the wish carefully to his
ptive djin.

"My turn," Rose said, taking the boy's hands off the lamp.
Matthew, thank you for everything," she said. "You'll always
special to Ray and me." She leaned over to kiss him. Ray
ook his hand.

"You mean you're sending me home?" Matthew asked,
sappointed.

"I'll visit," Ray said. "Promise. Remember, you're my first
dchild." Matthew was reluctant, but mature enough to know
at there was no arguing with the adults.

"At least I get to remember the adventure," he said, as
ose's first wish wrapped him into a golden cloud that dissi-
ated like a pinch of powder. His voice faded away like an
ho.

"My goodness, I can see why this would get to be
dictive," Rose said, amazed at the ease of using lamp magic.
Before anything else happens or any of us get tempted, I
ish you free, young man."

Speed Guthrie wiped his nose, looked at the collection of
sorted adults whose identities he no longer remembered,

and sauntered casually out of the store. The cashier came ov
very timidly from where she had been watching.

"Do you . . ." she began tentatively. "Are you looking f
members?"

Chapter 26

"There's only one more matter to deal with before we all go home to our families," Alexandra said, dusting her hands as the last of the young ex-djinni left the empty shop. "What shall we do about Ray?"

"Why?" Ray asked, hearing his name. "Did I do something wrong?" He hurried over to where the officers of the Fairy Godmothers Union were standing with Rose and his grandmother. He was no longer limping; the wish session had taken care of his cuts and bruises.

"No," Rose said, reaching out to squeeze his hand. "You did everything right. You were our last hope, you know, and you didn't let us down. I'm so proud of you."

"I wasn't sure for a while there," Morry Garner said. "Now I'm sorry I didn't believe in you."

"I knew he had it in him," Grandma Eustatia said positively.

Ray was embarrassed. "I'm just grateful everyone's okay."

"Well, we must do something for you," Alexandra said, limbering up her wrist. Ray looked into his mental piggy bank. The federation's store of brownie points had gone back to their proper owners, but there were a few new, bright stars that belonged just to him. "Did you know he hasn't had his miracle yet? Who's his fairy godparent?"

"I'll do it," Morry Garner said.

"No, I will," said Mrs. Durja. "He is such a good boy."

"He's one of mine," said the beautiful, green-eyed lady from TV. Ray turned to her with shining eyes. "I think, though,

I should cede the honor to Rose, because she knows you best. But I'll give you my own reward." She leaned over and gave him a kiss. Ray felt as if he had been sent on a quick trip to heaven. Antoinette nudged him in the ribs. When he opened his eyes, he saw Rose studying him intently.

"I know what you want," Rose said.

"A regular magic wand?" Ray guessed.

"Certainly not. That will come in time."

"That new car?"

"Nonsense," Rose said, waving away speculation. "I know your *real* heart's desire."

He felt a jolt in the midsection. "But I blew it!" Ray said. "Insufficient grade point average, lack of application, no money, right? It's impossible!"

"Pooh!" Rose said. "If it wasn't impossible, it wouldn't be a miracle. Trust me, right?"

"Right," Ray said, squaring his shoulders.

"Right." Rose raised the pink and gold wand and leveled it at him. Antoinette squeezed his hand tightly. Ray closed his eyes as the veil of pink light spread out over him.

The lamps jostled from one side of the cargo container to the other as the truck sped on its way. The seven men tried as best they could to make themselves comfortable in the dark crate on boxes and camp stools.

"Where did you say this thing was going?" Carson asked.

"California, for a ship to Yokohama," Froister said, pulling a box under him just as the truck hit another bump and toppled his lamp standard over on his head. Swearing, he set the lamp down on its side and held it there with his foot. "Part of the US trade agreement with Japan is that they've eased the imports on American-made goods. They won't be looking too closely at us."

"And when we're there, we can reformulate our plans," Gurgin's deep voice rumbled out of another corner of the container. "One day we'll go back."

"What good will that do?" Timbulo asked. "I bet the guild

revokes our charter, just like that." Froister heard his fingers click.

"And what of it?" McClaherty's ringing voice demanded. "We've still got our lamps. They can't take that away from us."

"They can," Bannion said. "But they gotta catch us first."

"Dammit, the IRS will probably seize all my assets in the meantime," DeNovo's voice said irritably.

"Don't worry," Froister said with supreme confidence that he didn't really feel. It was a good thing the others could not see him. "You'll get it all back one day." However many years it took, he thought.

The truck hit another bump.

"At least we're rid of the damned kids," DeNovo said.

Ray sat on the bus, heading north along Sheridan Road toward Evanston. He had to pick up his registration materials and get his orientation packet for pre-med. School started in less than six weeks. He had so much to do, and he and Hakeem were going to take in a ball game later on. He was going to miss Antoinette when she went away to Howard, but between school and going out to grant wishes with Rose, he was going to be too busy to blow his nose unless it was on the schedule.

The evening news had been full of the explosion at Enlightenment. People thought it was some kids, celebrating the Fourth of July a day early. Let them think that. Hakeem told him the way the slick guy, Froister, had talked about his dreams to take over the country. It'd be better if no one knew how grim the situation could have been. It was going to take time for the fairy godparents' reputation to return to normal. He and Rose were already doing their parts. Last night had been fun, dragging Hakeem along with them, to see if maybe he was interested, although it sounded from what he'd said in the bar later that perhaps a career with the tooth fairies was more his speed. He didn't want any more excitement, and Ray couldn't blame him. The guys who owned the lamp shop had vanished, but the FGU had complained officially to the DDEG main headquarters. The merger was off for now.

Things had been a lot quieter on the street the last few days Ray was content.

The wand in his breast pocket radiated its goodness at him, agreeing with his happy mood. The bus stopped. He glanced out at the line of people waiting to get on. A little boy got on with his mother and moved toward a seat farther back in the bus. As he passed, Ray felt the need spring into being on the surface of the air. He started to get up. The bus was only a couple of blocks away from where he had to get off. He wondered if he could handle the kid's wish in that time. Otherwise, he'd miss his stop. He took the little blue star halfway out of his pocket.

Someone touched him on the shoulder. He glanced around. The pretty lady in the cerise business suit was already on her feet behind him, red wand in her hand.

"I'll take this one," she whispered.

"Thanks," he said.

"No," she said, with a smile. "Thank *you*. See you at the next meeting."

"Yeah," he said, settling into his seat. He felt like bursting into the union song. Instead, he just hummed a few happy notes, and swung off the bus at the next stop.

Don't Myth, uh, *Miss* Out On These Hilarious High-Fantasy Adventures From Jody Lynn Nye!

HIGHER MYTHOLOGY
(0-446-36335-9, $4.99 U.S.) ($5.99 CAN.)

MYTHOLOGY 101
(0-445-21021-4, $4.95 U.S.) ($5.95 CAN.)

THE MAGIC TOUCH
(0-446-60210-8, $5.99 U.S.) ($6.99 CAN.)

"A great sense of humor."
—Piers Anthony

"A wonderfully whimsical new fantasy writer emerges in Jody Lynn Nye."
—Anne McCaffrey

Available wherever Warner Books are sold.